A Place for Us

A Place for Us

FATIMA FARHEEN MIRZA

HOGARTH

LONDON · NEW YORK

3 5 7 9 10 8 6 4 2

Hogarth, an imprint of Vintage,
20 Vauxhall Bridge Road,
London SW1V 2SA

Hogarth is part of the Penguin Random House group of companies
whose addresses can be found at global.penguinrandomhouse.com.

Penguin
Random House
UK

First published by Hogarth in 2018

penguin.co.uk/vintage

A CIP catalogue record for this book is available from the British Library

HB ISBN 9781781090695
TPB ISBN 9781781090701

Typeset in 12.75/15.25 pt Walbaum MT Pro by Jouve (UK), Milton Keynes
Printed and bound in India by Thomson Press India Ltd.

Penguin Random House is committed to a sustainable future for
our business, our readers and our planet. This book is made
from Forest Stewardship Council® certified paper.

In the name of God, the Compassionate, the Merciful

For my parents, Shereen & Mohammed,
who taught me that love is an ever-expanding force

And for my brothers, Mohsin, Ali-Moosa, Mahdi,
who call me home

I am not to speak to you, I am to think of you when I sit alone,
  or wake at night alone,
I am to wait, I do not doubt I am to meet you again,
I am to see to it that I do not lose you.

—WALT WHITMAN, "TO A STRANGER"

Part One

AS AMAR WATCHED THE HALL FILL WITH GUESTS
arriving for his sister's wedding, he promised himself he would
stay. It was his duty tonight to greet them. A simple task, one he
told himself he could do well, and he took pride in stepping forward to shake the hands of the men or hold his hand over his heart
to pay the women respect. He hadn't expected his smile to mirror
those who seemed happy to see him. Nor had he anticipated the
startling comfort in the familiarity of their faces. It had really been
three years. Had it not been for his sister's call, he might have
allowed even more years to pass before summoning the courage to
return.

He touched his tie to make sure it was centered. He smoothed
down his hair, as if a stray strand would be enough to call attention,
give him away. An old family friend called out his name and hugged
him. What would he tell them if they asked where he had been, and
how he was doing? The sounds of the *shenai* started up to signal the
commencement of Hadia's wedding and suddenly the hall was
brought to life. There, beneath the golden glow of the chandeliers
and surrounded by the bright colors of the women's dresses, Amar
thought maybe he had been right to come. He could convince them
all—the familiar faces, his mother who he sensed checking on him
as she moved about, his father who maintained his distance—he
could even convince himself, that he belonged here, that he could

wear the suit and play the part, be who he had been before, and assume his role tonight as brother of the bride.

✧

IT HAD BEEN Hadia's decision to invite him. She watched her sister Huda get ready and hoped it had not been a mistake. That morning Hadia had woken with her brother on her mind and all day she willed herself to think as other brides must—that she would be using the word *husband* when speaking of Tariq now, that after years of wondering if they would make it to this moment, they had arrived. What she had not even dared to believe possible for her was coming true: marrying a man she had chosen for herself.

Amar had come as she had hoped. But when she was shocked at the sight of him she realized she never actually believed he would. Three years had passed with no news from him. On the day she told her parents she would invite him she had not allowed herself to pray, *Please God, have him come,* but only, *Please God, let my father not deny me this.* She had practiced her words until her delivery was so steady and confident any onlooker would think she was a woman who effortlessly declared her wishes.

Huda finished applying her lipstick and was fastening the pin of her silver hijab. She looked beautiful, dressed in a navy sari stitched with silver beadwork, the same sari that a handful of Hadia's closest friends would be wearing. There was an excitement about her sister that Hadia could not muster for herself.

"Will you keep an eye on him tonight?" Hadia asked.

Huda held her arm up to slip rows of silver bangles over her wrist, each one falling with a click. She turned from the mirror to face Hadia.

"Why did you call him if you didn't want him to come?"

Hadia studied her hands, covered in dark henna. She pressed her fingernails into her arm.

"It's my wedding day."

An obvious statement, but it was true. It did not matter if she had not heard from her brother in years, she could not imagine this day without him. But relief at the sight of Amar brought with it that old shadow of worry for him.

"Will you call him here?" Hadia said. "And when he comes, will you give us a moment alone?"

She returned Huda's gaze then. And though Huda looked briefly hurt, she didn't ask Hadia to share what she was, and always had been, excluded from.

✧

AS SHE GLIDED between guests and stopped to hug women she had not yet greeted, it occurred to Layla that this was what she might have pictured her life to look like once, when her children were young and she knew who her family would contain but not what life would be like for them. She walked with a straight back and careful smile and felt this event was hers as much as it was her daughter's. And Amar was nearby. She looked to him between conversations, tracked his movement across the hall, checked his face for any displeasure.

The wedding was coming together wonderfully. People were arriving on time. There was a table for mango juice and pineapple juice and another for appetizers, replenished as soon as the items were lifted from the platter. White orchids spilled from tall glass vases on every table. Little golden pouches of gifts waited on each seat for guests to claim. Huda had helped Layla make them and they had stayed awake late into the night, singing a little as they filled each one with almonds and various chocolates. The hall was grand—she had chosen it with Hadia months ago—and as she walked beneath its arches into the main hall she was pleased with her decision. It had been dimmer when they first saw it, but now it looked like the set of a movie, high ceilings and every chandelier twinkling so bright they seemed to compete with one another to illuminate the room. Men looked sharp in their dark suits and *sherwanis,* women dressed so that every shade of color was represented, light reflecting off of their beadwork and threadwork. Layla wished her parents had been alive to see it. How proud they would be, how happy to attend the wedding of their first grandchild. But tonight even their absence could not dull all she had to be grateful for, and beneath her breath she continued to repeat, *God is Great. God is Great, and all thanks are to Him.*

Just an hour earlier she had helped Hadia into the heavy *kharra dupatta,* whispered prayers as she clasped safety pins in place. Hadia had not spoken as Layla moved about her, only thanked her once, quietly. She was nervous, as any bride would be, as Layla herself had been years ago. Layla adjusted the outfit's pleats, hooked a *teekah* into Hadia's hair, and stepped back to take in the sight of her daughter. All her intricate henna. Her jewelry catching light.

Now she searched the crowd for her son. It felt unfathomable that just days ago she still had trouble sleeping when the darkness called forth her unsettling fears. In the daylight she could reassure herself that it was enough to see her son's face in the photographs she saved, hear his voice in the family videos she watched—Amar on a field trip she had chaperoned, his excitement when the zoo-keeper lifted up a yellow python, how his hand was the first to shoot into the air, asking to touch it. It was enough so long as she knew he was still out there, heart beating, mind moving in the way she never understood.

But this morning she had woken to a home complete. Before her children could rise she took out *sadqa* money for them, extra because it was a momentous day, then more, to protect from any comment about her son's return in a tone that could threaten its undoing. She drove to a grocery store and stocked the fridge with food Amar enjoyed: green apples and cherries, pistachio ice cream with almonds, cookies with the white cream center. All the snacks she once scolded him for. Was she cruel to feel more happiness, greater relief, at his return, than for her daughter on the day he had come back for? Before Rafiq left to oversee arrangements in the hall— the tables brought in, golden bows tied to the chairs, the setting of the stage where Hadia and Tariq would sit—Layla climbed the stairs to their bedroom, where he was getting ready.

"*Suno*," she said, "will you listen? Can you not say anything that will anger or upset him?"

She always found ways to speak around her husband's name. First it was out of shyness and then it was out of custom and a deep respect for him, and now it would be unnatural; she felt obliged to avoid his name out of habit. He paused buttoning his shirt and looked at her. It was her right. She had not interfered with his decisions for so long. She pressed on. "Please, for me, can you stay away from him tonight? We can speak tomorrow, but let us have this day."

The previous night, when Amar first arrived, the two of them had been amicable. Rafiq had said *salaam* before Layla took over and guided Amar to his bedroom, heated him a plate of dinner.

For a moment, she wondered if she had hurt Rafiq. Carefully he clasped the button at each wrist.

"I will not go near him, Layla," he said finally, dropping his arms to his sides.

✦

WHEN HE MET his father's eyes from across the crowded hall, Amar understood that an agreement had been made between them: they knew who they were there for, and why they would not approach one another beyond the expected *salaam*. Amar looked away first. He still felt it. His anger, and the distance it caused. It was as if something had clenched in him and could not now be loosened.

Amar had played a game during the first few conversations when asked what he had been doing lately. A painter, he said to one guest, of sunsets and landscapes. The look on their faces amused him. To another uncle he said engineer but was annoyed by how it impressed him. Once he said he was pursuing an interest in ornithology. When the man blinked back at him he explained. Birds, I would like to study birds. Now he spoke without embellishment. He excused himself from conversations shortly after they began.

He stepped out beneath the arched doorway, past the children playing, past the elevators, until the *shenai* quieted. He had forgotten what it was like to move through a crowd feeling like a hypocrite among them, aware of the scrutinizing gaze of his father, expecting Amar to embarrass him, anticipating the lie he would tell before he even spoke. He walked until he found himself standing before the bar on the other side of the hotel. Of course, no one invited to Hadia's wedding would dare come here. The sound of the *shenai* was so far away he could catch it only if he strained to hear. He took a seat beside two strangers. Tonight, even that felt like a betrayal. But taking a seat was not the same as ordering a drink. He leaned forward until he could rest his elbows on the counter, lowered his face into his hands and sighed.

He could hardly believe that, just the night before, he had managed to walk up to the door of his childhood home and knock. What had surprised him was how little had changed—the same tint of paint at nighttime, the same screen missing from his old window on the second floor. There were no lights on. Wide windows, curtains drawn, nobody home. Nobody would know if he decided to step back into the street. It was a comforting thought—that he would not have to face his father or see how his absence had impacted his mother. The moon was almost full in the sky, and as he had when he was a child, he looked first for the face his schoolteacher had said he could find there, then for the name in Arabic his mother always pointed out proudly. Finding them both, he almost smiled.

He might have walked away were it not for a light turning on in Hadia's room. It glowed teal behind the curtain and the sight of it was enough to make his chest lurch. She was home. He had made his life one that did not allow him to see or speak to his sister, to even know she was getting married until she had called him a month earlier, asking him to attend. He had been so startled he didn't pick up. But he listened to her voicemail until he had memorized the details, felt sure some nights he would return and on other nights knew no good would come of it.

Her lit window and his own dark beside it. One summer they had pushed out their screens and connected their rooms by a string attached to Styrofoam cups at each end. Hadia assured him she knew what she was doing. She had made one in school. He wasn't sure if he could hear her voice humming along the string and filling the cup, or carried through the air, but he didn't tell her this. They pretended a war was coming to their neighborhood. This was Hadia's idea—she had always been brilliant at thinking up games. They were in an observation tower making sure nothing was amiss. Bluebird on branch, Amar said, looking out the window before crouching down again, over. Mailman driving down the street, Hadia said, lots of letters, over.

That night their father had been furious to find the screens discarded on the driveway, one of them bent from the fall. The three of them were made to stand in a line. Hadia, the eldest, then Huda, then Amar, the youngest, hiding a little behind them both.

"You instigated this?" his father said, looking only at him.

It was true. It had been his idea to push out the screens. Hadia stared at the floor. Huda nodded. Hadia glanced at her but said nothing.

His father said to his sisters, "I expected better from you two."

Amar had sulked to his bedroom, closed his open window, sunk onto his cold sheets. Nothing was expected of him. And though Hadia never pushed her screen out again, he had, every few years, until his father gave up on repairing it entirely.

"Have you changed your mind?" the bartender asked him.

Amar looked up and shook his head. It wouldn't have been so bad to say yes. It might have even been better for him and everyone else. A drink would calm his nerves, and maybe he could enjoy the colors and the appetizers and the sorrowful *shenai*. But he had come home for his mother's sake, his sister's sake, and this night was the only one asked of him.

His phone buzzed. It was Huda: *Hadia is asking for you, room 310.*

All day he had feared his sister might have only called him out of obligation, and suspected that maybe it was that same sense of duty that had brought him back. Now something swelled up in him, not quite excitement or happiness, but a kind of hope. He stood and stepped back toward the music. His sister, surrounded by close friends and family, was asking for him.

✧

ANY MINUTE NOW Amar would knock and the important thing was not to respond to him the way she had the night before, when she was so stunned she could not speak. She should have been kinder. Three years had changed her brother, lent seriousness to his features, shadows pressed beneath his eyes, a fresh scar on his chin to join the old ones by his lip and eyebrow. He seemed to slouch and she realized that his confidence had left him, as though confidence were a physical feature as much a part of him as his winning half-smile. But what pained her was how small his face had become, the pronounced bone of his shoulder and collarbone visible even through his T-shirt, and the fear that accompanied the sight: he was still trying to disappear. Tonight, she would keep her observations to herself and welcome him with a smile. Hadia sat still as she waited, not wanting to disturb her clothes. The slightest movement caused the pleats to shift and scrape against each other. The *ghoongat* draped over her head was surprisingly heavy, the *teekah* moved if she turned her head abruptly, the choker-like necklace pinched her neck. When she looked in the mirror she barely recognized herself.

A knock at the door. Even if she had not been waiting for him, she would have known it was Amar, always hesitant at first tap, a brief pause, and then two louder taps. Huda let him in and Hadia overheard Huda thank Amar in the reserved way she spoke to those she was unfamiliar with. Then the click of the door closing and Amar appeared and he had washed his face and combed his hair, dressed in a black suit and found a tie to match. She patted the space beside her but he stayed standing.

"How is it down there?" she asked.

"I might have told Samir Uncle I'm trying to paint professionally." He twisted his mouth and pushed his tongue against the inside of his cheek, the way he so often did when he was lying or was nervous, completely unaware of his habit, and this instantly endeared him to Hadia. It was him. Her brother. The expression was an exaggerated version of itself—his jaw had become defined, cheeks hollow, but it was his unmistakable, signature look.

She tried to say his name in a scolding tone but began laughing at the thought of Samir Uncle, the most gullible friend of their father's. The old Hadia would have told him to be careful—that everyone either would know he was lying right away or would soon find out. But she was not sure anymore what she could tease him about without causing offense. Again she tapped at the spot beside her.

"You look really beautiful," he said.

"Not too much?" She lifted her decorated arms that looked like they belonged to someone else, gestured to her jewelry. He shook his head.

"Mumma must be so happy. You finally accepted one," he said.

"It wasn't arranged."

He looked surprised for a moment. Then he smiled. "Now I'm not the only one who has disappointed them."

"No. But you did make it a little easier for me to."

Was their laughter born of ease or discomfort? Amar took a seat by her. A boyishness still lingered in the way he carried himself. You won't tell Baba, will you, he would ask her, each time he snuck out telling her to leave his window open, or anytime she caught him smoking. Always the same look on his face. Always the big brown eyes. All those nights she had spent waiting at the window for him, tracing the little etching he had carved on his windowsill, tensing each time there was a creak in the house that could be their parents waking to discover them. As the years passed he stopped waiting for her answer—he did not doubt her, he already knew, had always known, that she would never tell.

"I wanted to ask if you would do something for me," she said now.

"Anything."

He hadn't hesitated. His tone so sincere she felt sure she had been right to invite him. She explained to him that she would soon walk downstairs with her eyes downcast, with only Huda to guide her. Her closest friends would be holding a red net cloth above her as she walked through the crowd to the edge of the stage, where Baba would be waiting to lead her up the stairs to Tariq.

"Will you walk on the other side of me?" she asked.

Amar nodded.

"You don't have to."

"I know. I want to."

She reached over to put her hand over his. It did not matter if the old way between them was gone and a new way would have to be found; it was a comfort to sit next to him, the kind of comfort only possible between two people who had been in each other's earliest memories.

"I have something for you," Amar said, reaching into his suit pocket and pulling out a small, messily taped package. "But don't open it yet."

He placed it in her hand. She shook it a little, tried to guess what it could be. She tucked it in her purse and told him it would be the first gift she opened. He was solemn, looking down at his own lap. Then came the knock at the door. Amar helped her stand. When they opened the door, Mumma's eyes filled at the sight of her. Huda too had to touch beneath her eyes with her knuckle, and this surprised her, Huda being the one among them who was never emotional, and Hadia nudged her as if to say not you too.

"Are you ready?" Huda asked.

And everything Hadia had not been thinking of all day rushed toward her, and she told herself: Huda is asking you if you are ready to go downstairs and walk through the hall, and if you nod yes to this, then it means you want to be with Tariq, you are ready to be. To him and to that life, she nodded yes.

The photographer lifted his camera. Her mother touched Hadia's forehead with her index finger and traced *Ya Ali* in Arabic, the gesture done for her protection and luck before every first day of school, every big exam, any flight she had to catch. Something about the movement of her mother's finger on her forehead, the look of concentration on her face as she prayed, calmed and comforted Hadia.

Even if she could not bring herself to pray for grand things, she could trust her mother's faith, depend on her mother's belief. Mumma fixed her *ghoongat* so that half of Hadia's face was hidden for the entrance. Huda took the crook of her arm. Before taking a step Hadia turned to Amar and held her other arm out until he took it.

Her wedding was both a celebration of the life she was about to embark upon and a night to mark the departure from her old life at home. Her friends waited by the elevator and stretched their arms high to hold the red cloth like a canopy above her. The cloth filtered the light red and had little mirrors sewn into it that threw sparkles on the carpet. The drummer began to drum for her arrival and she felt the beating in her whole body. She stepped forward.

They entered the hall and on the periphery she could see the rows of tables, people seated in chairs whispering, taking photos that flashed. They stopped walking and her friends removed the red cloth and the light was suddenly golden and warm. Huda whispered in her ear, "You can look up now."

Baba was holding his hand out for her, a look of tenderness on his face she swore she had never seen before. Baba kissed her forehead softly so that the jewels of the *teekah* did not dig into her skin and Hadia was surprised by how deeply cared for it made her feel. He led her up the stairs to the stage. And there was Tariq, and the drummer stilled his beat, and she was struck by how handsome Tariq looked in the light, handsome in the cream-colored *sherwani* he wore, and she prayed, *Please God, let me remember this.* When their eyes met he grinned and she knew: I chose this. I chose him. This is my life. I did not think it would be possible for me. But it is. It will be.

❖

SOMEONE HAD SPILLED water on the front of her sari and it bloomed into a dark, embarrassing splotch. Layla excused herself to try and dry it as best as she could. She hoped this fabric was not the kind that stained after it got wet. There were pictures they needed to take. She wanted one good family photo to replace the one that hung in their living room. It was about time she took it down. She had not changed a single photo since Amar left. She glanced once more at her daughter seated on the stage next to Tariq, a modest gap between them until the *nikkah* was complete. The two of them were smiling and speaking discreetly. They looked like a king and queen of an ancient, magnificent time. She walked quickly with her head down and burned with pride when she overheard a table of women saying how luminous the bride looked.

Never had she looked at her daughter with as much awe as when Hadia stepped from the hotel room, looking both mature and ready for this step and also like that hesitant, wide-eyed girl she had dropped off on the first day of kindergarten. How long she and Rafiq had waited for this moment. It had come later than she might have wanted—her daughter would soon be twenty-seven, and with every year that passed her worry had grown, especially when attending the weddings of younger and younger girls, while Hadia insisted her priority was finishing her studies. But there was much to be thankful for. Tariq was respectful, an educated young man. Layla reminded herself that he was the kind of man they had wanted for her. Rafiq too had taken to him more than he liked to admit.

The air was cool in the bathroom, the light dim, and for the first time in hours Layla was alone. Her face relaxed. Her cheeks hurt from smiling. She dabbed at her sari with tissues but the stain remained. She would have to wait. She massaged her face in the mirror, starting with her cheeks, then moving to the back of her neck, where she always suffered a dull pain. She wanted to find Rafiq and see if he was happy, wanted to say, *Look what we have done together.*

Rafiq had been so quiet when he came home from the hall earlier, Layla could not read him. And the small progress she had made with Amar, walking in the garden together, showing him the suit he would wear—it was all undone when Rafiq came home and Amar fell silent. The only men she had left in this world to love and neither of them knew how to be with one another. Just before they left for the wedding hall, Layla laid out her prayer rug upstairs, then Rafiq's just a few steps in front of hers. It was the time of day she looked forward to most, and even though nothing passed between them there was still a sense of peace, a feeling of unity. She had been the one to teach her children how to pray. The girls had been easy, but Amar was different. He had copied her every movement, looked up at the way she cupped her hands to the sky and did the same, made whispering noises even though he had not memorized the *surahs*, and at the end she told him it was time to speak his wishes directly to God, and he asked for the lollipops that were green apple and dipped in caramel.

"That is all you want?" she asked him, and he nodded.

"But you can ask for anything," she said, half hoping he would. She disliked those lollipops the most because the caramel got stuck in his teeth.

"If I ask for only one thing, then it is more likely to come true," he said.

"God doesn't work like that."

"How do you know?"

She was amazed. She did not know. He was six or seven years old then and asking her a question she had not thought to ask all her life. Nor had Hadia or Huda ever questioned her. And Amar had been right without knowing it: the next day she went to the grocery store and bought the smallest bag she could find of those terrible lollipops, tucked them beneath his pillow. He had asked for something so easily granted, and she thought that maybe if she gave it to him at that impressionable age he would pray wholeheartedly. They were told not to question the way God worked, not to think too much into it. That it was a mystery. And she was happy to think of it as such. She pictured a dark sky with the fog in front of it, how her mother had once explained it to her: we don't have to see past the fog to know there are stars.

She studied her reflection now. Her sari had dried as best as it would. She adjusted her hijab to hide the remaining stain, and reapplied some lipstick. When she returned to the hall, the *hadith-e-kisa* was being recited and soon it would be her favorite verse: that

15

God had created the blue sky, and the changing landscapes, the bright moon and the burning sun, the rotating planets and flowing seas and the ships on them sailing—all out of love for the five beneath the blanket, the Prophet, his son-in-law Imam Ali, his daughter Bibi Fatima, and his grandsons, Hassan and Hussain.

She searched the crowd for Rafiq and found him at the other end of the hall, seated at a table, his head bowed in respect. He looked content. She would go to him once the recitation was complete. She would say: We did this. We created this. These children who are adults now. What is the use of all this living if we don't stop once in a while to notice what is actually happening—our daughter on-stage, our son safe, and all our friends and family, who have traveled miles to gather in this hall, just to celebrate with us?

✧

HE NEEDED TO feel the cool breeze on his face. To be away from anyone who might try to speak to him. Maybe a nice sky to look up at, if the haze of the streetlights didn't dim the stars too much. Amira Ali was there. They had not made eye contact but he was certain she had seen him. How could she not have? All around him, the people were indistinguishable from one another—shades of blue, green, yellow—and then that jolt at the sight of her. But while everyone else's face was turned to watch the bride enter, Amira had been facing the stage, looking, if he were to guess, at either his father or Tariq.

He had known there was a chance she would come, had told himself that he would get through the night with or without her possible presence. He drew a cigarette from his pocket and lit it. It had been the line of her neck, the curve of her cheek, her chin, the shock of her dark, dark hair. He had to remind himself to keep walking until they reached the stage, and then he had forced himself not to look back. Just waited until Hadia had taken her seat beside Tariq before slipping from the hall, looking only at the shine of his shoes.

When he was sitting with Hadia in her hotel room, it had

occurred to him he knew nothing of the man she was about to marry. It felt too late to be concerned, or worse, like he had lost the right to feel concerned. But Hadia had not only invited him, she had also asked him to participate, to stand by her and Huda. He knew she didn't have to do that. He had been so nervous when he went to her room, afraid she would ask a question he did not want to answer, but she had spared him any discomfort. The least he could do now was compose himself. He crushed the cigarette with his shoe and then lit another.

Earlier that morning, alone in his old room, he had locked the door behind him. He had opened his closet and parted his clothes—from what he could tell, all of them still there—and stepped into the recess. And there it was, behind extra comforters and unused suitcases, his black keepsake box, exactly as he had left it. For a moment he just touched the soft leather surface. He had always known he would come back one day, if only to reclaim it. He knew the combination of the lock by heart. The click of the lock unlatching. He sat and reacquainted himself with the mementos of his old life: journals, foolish poems he had written, poems he saved by others, photographs he stole from family albums, until he found in an envelope taped for extra security, the letters written in Amira's delicate handwriting and the photographs of her looking back at him, or lifting her hand to hide her face. He could tell he had taken them, not only because he remembered every movement toward her and every movement away, but because it would be apparent to anyone who saw them that they were taken by someone who looked at her with love. He knew if he read the letters, his determination to attend would leave him, and so he had put them back still folded, carefully closed the lid, and snapped the lock shut.

His head throbbed. He had not come this far for nothing. The *dua* that had been about to start when he left the hall would end soon. He closed his eyes and saw redness, the swarming insides of his eyelids when he pressed his eyes with his thumb and index finger, the color of his sister's *kharra dupatta*, the color that had risen to Amira's cheeks when he had opened the door to her, long before they had begun talking, and he had complimented her for the first time, something small like *I like your shoes* and, as he would later learn, because she was unable to conceal anything, her face had burned.

AT THE APPETIZER table he busied himself by filling his plate with samosas and small chunks of tandoori chicken. He wanted to mask the smell of alcohol on his breath, wanted to make sure he had something in his system to dull its effect. He felt calmer. But he should not have gone back to the bar. Less than one hour here and he had already made a mistake. The rest of the night he would abide by their rules. For his mother, for his sister. Her hello caught him by surprise. A jolt like the one before. He looked up to see Amira standing only a few feet away. She picked up a plate, slowly, as if still deliberating, and offered him a smile. He replied to her hello. He was afraid to meet her eyes for too long and focused instead on her wrists lined with red and golden bangles, how they slid on her arms as she moved her plate around. He felt far from his legs, so he tried to stand very still. He looked up at the chandelier, then at the colors that shifted around him. How deliberately and desperately he did not want to look at her. The trick was to appear as though he felt nothing.

Soon they were standing side by side. She set a single samosa at the center of her plate. When she opted for the mint sauce, he felt an unexpected sadness at having predicted it. She turned to face him. Her hair fell across her face and formed a curtain over her eye. He wanted to reach out and tuck it back into place behind her ear. But he could not touch her anymore. He signaled to his own forehead, and she, perhaps also remembering how often he would move her hair from her face, immediately mirrored him and swept it away. A light color rose to her cheeks. He had missed this. A heavier silence ensued, both now painfully aware they still shared a language they should have long since forgotten.

Part Two

Part Two

1

THEY ARE ALL WAITING ON THE DAMP LAWN
for the sky to light up, at a park near their home on the Fourth of
July. How they got there is a miracle. It is the first Fourth of July
Hadia remembers coming even close to celebrating, and this—
sitting and blinking at the empty sky—feels like a feat. Just an
hour earlier, when the sun slipped away, they began begging Baba
to take them to watch the fireworks, and he was reluctant, telling
them that people would be out drinking and they could watch just
fine on their television screen. But even Amar, too young to fully
understand what he was asking for, repeated please, please, please
like it was one long word until Baba said fine, let's go.

Hadia and Huda are holding hands and sitting cross-legged.
Indian-style, her friends call it, and she does not know what this
means or why it makes her feel a tiny bit strange. Just a tiny bit.
They have laid their jackets down like blankets, spread their sleeves
out like the points of stars. Baba is beside her. He scans the park, his
gaze rests on other families who have brought collapsible chairs
and thick, checkered blankets. Families that smell like popcorn and
hold red cups that look purple in the dark. Mumma is next to Huda
and Amar is next to Mumma, leaning on her with his thumb in his
mouth. Then there is a bang and a streak of light hisses up, and
when it is far past the tops of trees it explodes with a pop—and it is
a firework, the exact kind she has seen frozen in pictures. Huda lets

go of her hand and claps and shrieks. One after another they pop. Hisses and booms and all the while it feels like each sound is in her own body. That is how loud it is. Amar holds on to his ears but his eyes are wide with wonder, and not terror. Hadia notices that she can follow the tiny flare of light as it shoots into the sky before it explodes into a firework. She tries to watch with her mouth closed, because she is seven years old and not a baby anymore, but she can't, she keeps smiling until her cheeks hurt and sometimes she says "oh wow" without meaning to.

Each one is different. Some light the whole sky a bright green, as if it were a haunted time of day. And Hadia is grateful for their yellow sun, its rays a blinding white. Some of them die so soon and others fall softly, become specks that look like bigger stars. These are her favorite—the delicate golden ones that burst and stay, their twinkling tails slowly dissolving. Smoke lingers. Amar hasn't taken his cupped hands off of his ears but he giggles at the ones that sound like rockets, the ones that fizzle out in coils, and Mumma is holding him in her lap now, her arms wrapped around his body like she is hugging him, her chin resting on his head. It feels like the show has been going on for so long. Like it will go on forever. Each explosion makes her a little afraid: what if the tops of trees catch on fire, or what if the flame, which feels so close, lands on their jackets?

"How will we know when the finale comes?" Huda whispers into her ear. Her voice tickles Hadia's hair, her neck. At home they convinced Baba to come by telling him about it, how there were a bunch of little fireworks and in the end a big one, a finale—Hadia had offered the word—like in an orchestra.

"You'll just know," she says, but she has no idea when it will be, or if she will know the end when she sees it. She looks back at Baba, and even his mouth is open, and she can see his white teeth. His face flashes green. And he looks like he is also thinking that the sky looks beautiful. Also thinking, How can I look up without smiling? Then comes the sound of the rocket ones and Hadia can hear Amar's laughter and the tiny, twisty explosions, and Baba's face is red, then blue, then gold, and then dark again, just his teeth still bright.

✧

THE SUN IS relentless. Layla sits with her back straight against the balcony wall, practicing her posture. Her younger sister, Sara, is beside her. They are not touching one another. It is their rule for sitting on the balcony on a hot day: any contact between the two of them could make the heat unbearable. She is comforted by the sounds of her street. The man who tries to sell pomegranates and mangoes. A boy who shouts at his friend with words forbidden to her. The honking of the cars and the clacking of a hoofed animal that walks by their house and into the bustle.

"You have a secret?" Sara whispers. Speaking softly is the other rule of the balcony, they come here only when they want no one to overhear them.

Layla wants to be the one to tell her. She reaches up to tug at one of the magenta petals of the bougainvillea above Sara's head. This summer is the first time she has felt close to her sister. Before, Sara was just a little girl with whom she had the unfortunate fate of sharing a cramped bedroom. One she had to make sure wasn't listening with her ear pressed to their door when Layla's friends visited. Now she is the sister Layla whispers to late at night before they fall asleep. The one she goes to with her complaints about her strict teacher or if she wakes from her dreams alarmed. Sara is a light sleeper, a patient listener. She wakes as soon as Layla calls her name and is eager to be included, to be regarded by her as a young woman, as a friend.

"I might be getting married," Layla says. She twists the *orni* around her finger until it is tight.

Sara asks her when and there is hurt in her voice, and Layla wonders if it is because she hasn't told her until today, or if it is because it means she will be leaving soon. Later that night, the proposal would be coming with his uncle to speak with Mumma and Baba and to meet her.

"Mumma tells me it is a great proposal. That I have no reason to refuse it."

Sara leans her head on Layla's shoulder. Layla does not remind her of the balcony rule.

"Where does he live?" Sara asks.

"America."

"That's far."

"There are farther places."

"What does he do?"

"I'm not sure. Mumma says he has a good job. And that he works very hard—he's been an orphan for years. He moved there by himself, got a job, a place to live." She does not know why she sounds like she is trying to convince her sister.

"You said yes?"

The wind rises. It moves through the branches of the bougainvillea and all the leaves quiver like clapping hands, their rustle a round of applause. It is one of Layla's favorite sounds in the whole world.

"Not yet."

"But you will?"

The *orni* wrapped around her finger will not twist any tighter. She does not know what she will say. She has never had to make a decision so big before, so life-changing.

"Because there is no reason to say no?" Sara's voice sounds like she is a child again.

"Mumma thinks he is a good fit."

Mumma had been eager to share the proposal with her when it came. She told Layla he was from a good family, that his parents had been respectable people before their passing, and he was one of the lucky ones who had gone to America. But to move so far from her family? I want you to have a good life, her mother had said to her, an enriched one, a pious destiny. Layla felt a strong intuition that if she listened to her mother, if she trusted her, if she aimed to please her, it would be all right. The little fears she felt now would be resolved somehow. After all, her parents would not find someone for her who would be unkind, or someone who was lacking in values. God would be pleased with her if she pleased her parents, and she would be rewarded.

"You could be like those women in the movies, the ones who say, 'But, Babu-ji, I can't marry him! I love someone else! The one who is forbidden.'"

"Don't be silly."

"What about Raj?" Sara whispers, still smiling.

Layla tells her to shush. The joke is not funny anymore. But something about the mention of his name excites her, and as soon as it does she feels a soft sadness. Raj sells ice cream outside of her school. He always nods when she walks by. Layla has not noticed him doing this with anyone else. She orders a scoop every few days—even when she does not want one. And once in a while, he will shake his head when she offers up her coins, and she will walk home with her gift. They have begun to joke about him. Raj and her future with him, the flavors of ice cream they would serve at their wedding, the successful business he will start all over Hyderabad.

"What's his name?" Sara asks after a long time.

Layla opens her mouth to answer but realizes she has forgotten it.

THAT NIGHT LAYLA repeats his name in her mind: Rafiq. Will she go with him to America? What will the roads look like there, and the people in their houses? She cannot sleep. She tries to recall his visit, how he wore a light brown button-up shirt that did not suit his complexion. All evening she studied her own hands in her lap, the one knuckle redder than the rest, the unevenness of her fingernails. Mumma had advised her before he came: do not dare look up unless directly spoken to. But even then, Mumma said, do not look at him. She had stolen one glance just long enough to note the color of his shirt.

She calls Sara's name in the dark and Sara mumbles a reply, rubs her eyelids, stretches a bit, and when she speaks again her voice is thick from sleep.

"Do you remember anything about him?" Layla asks.

"About who?"

"You know who," she says, suddenly aware that she is too shy to speak his name.

"He was wearing an ugly shirt," Sara says.

Layla laughs. Sara begins listing what she remembers: he smiled at Baba's jokes but did not laugh, he did not eat the sweets Ma had made but did finish almost all of the almonds in the bowl of mixed nuts, he coughed into a folded cloth, he never started a conversation, just added to them, and he looked at Layla from time to time.

"Do you like him?" Sara asks.

Layla shrugs and in the dark Sara does not see it.

"This is how it is for everyone in the beginning," Sara says.

Layla nods and still Sara does not see it.

Sara continues, "Maybe he will know to close the curtains as soon as it is nighttime. And to wake as soon as the first alarm rings. Or he'll be able to tell when you want to be alone and when you act like you want to be alone but you actually want him to speak to you."

"You mean like you."

Layla asks if there was anything else she noticed.

"How you knew the whole time which voice was his."

✧

HADIA IS CONCENTRATING on curling the tail of the y when the phone in her classroom rings. She wants to make sure her handwriting is neat, just in case Baba is in a good mood that night and asks to see her schoolwork, so she steadies her hand and bites down on her bottom lip before remembering it is bruised. It pulses. Sometimes, Baba would tap at her papers and say to Amar, look, this is how you write properly. And Hadia's happiness would turn into guilt when she saw the pained look on Amar's face: having wanted Baba to notice, and wanting him to praise her still. Her teacher,

Mrs. Burson, drops the chalk into the silver tray, steps to answer the classroom phone, and Hadia presses her nails into the skin beneath her wrist as she thinks, *Please God, not again.*

Mrs. Burson hooks the phone back on the wall and turns to look directly at Hadia. She nods at her. Hadia knows what this means. Her classmates begin to whisper. They shift in their seats. She hates when anything draws extra attention to her. She already looks so different from them, being the only girl in the entire elementary school who wears hijab. Even when her teacher calls on her for an answer, she blushes. She puts away her notebook, scoots her chair into her desk, and avoids looking at all of them except her best friend, Danielle, who waves as she walks out the door.

It is likely that nothing is wrong. She takes her time walking down the empty corridor, annoyed at Amar for embarrassing her again, for pulling her from her lesson. Her footsteps echo and she tries to quiet them by walking on tiptoe. Sentences from classrooms drift from open doors. Grades older than fifth grade, where they are talking about spelling, math, stars, and stories. She pauses at every open door just to see what those lessons are like. But what if, this time, it is not nothing? She thinks of grazed knees and broken bones. She thinks of hearing Amar cry out after he has hurt himself, how she recognizes his cry even if she hears it when they are at mosque and separated by a divider. How she rushes down the stairs or through the hallways until she is at his side, how she has to go, even if her parents are around. She quickens her pace. By the time she reaches the corner she is running, and the reflection of the lightbulbs on the floor blur beneath her.

The school nurse looks up from her paperwork at Hadia, who arrives breathless, and she welcomes her in with a wave that tells her all is well. Bad news is always delivered in a hurry.

"He's in the sick room," she says, and gestures down the hall, though Hadia knows where it is.

"He's been calling for you," the nurse says.

Hadia knows this too. Amar is lying on the tan bed wearing red corduroy pants and a white T-shirt, the outfit of his that always reminds her of a little bear, and as he shifts the paper cover crunches beneath him. The room is cool and gray. He looks fine, suffering only from boredom, blowing the hair in his face so it lifts up and falls on his forehead again, but he stands when she enters and waves at her as if he's been waiting for her to join him at a tea party.

"What happened?" she asks. She tries to catch her breath.

"Nothing," he whispers in Urdu. He looks like a boy keeping a secret, excited to let her in on it.

"Then why are you here? Why did you call me?" she replies in Urdu as well, not wanting the nurse to overhear and confirm her suspicion that nothing is wrong. Her tone is harsh, like her mother's.

"I didn't want to be in class," he says, and she glares at him. "And I didn't want to be alone."

She had been taking notes for Social Studies when the call came. They were learning about the American Revolution. She had not finished copying the board, and now it would be erased. She turns to go back.

"It was a hard lesson, Hadia Baji. It made me feel sick."

He only called her *sister* when he needed something from her.

"Don't go."

Why do things always sound sadder in Urdu? Prettier too. She likes that they speak to each other in Urdu, how even speaking it feels like access to their secret world, a world where they feel like different people, capable of feelings she could not experience let alone speak of in English. She turns around and faces him. He looks worried and scratches his cheek. He is only six. First grade has just begun and he has had a hard time adjusting to the longer hours.

The year before Amar started kindergarten, there were three days when Mumma disappeared and Baba took them to a family friend's house. Amar was almost four and it was his first time being away from Mumma. Hadia remembers asking Baba where Mumma was as Baba packed a duffel bag of their clothes and toothbrushes, but Baba gave her a silent look that said, Don't you ask me again. They had never spent the night in anyone else's home before. It was not allowed. Then, as if Baba regretted his look, he told her Mumma was fine, everything would be fine. His face was serious like it always was but this time it was sad too, and when he dropped them off at Seema Aunty's house, even she looked so concerned when Baba passed her their duffel bag that Hadia felt even more alarmed. Hadia watched Huda and Amar follow Seema Aunty into her big house. Even the fact that it was so big frightened her: what if they got lost, and Baba could not find them when he came back? Baba placed a hand on her shoulder. He told her he would be back to check on them tomorrow evening after work.

"It's your job as the big sister to take care of them," he told Hadia. "You are like their mother when Mumma is not here."

Hadia held on to her arm and pinched her skin so tight she had no space to feel sad about what Baba was saying.

"I know you will do a good job, Hadia. I am certain," Baba said, then he leaned down to kiss her forehead.

She had the ugly thought that she would be okay not seeing Mumma for a day or two if it meant that Baba believed in her. But when Baba pulled his car from the driveway, Amar realized he was not coming back, and that Mumma was not coming that night either, and he latched onto Hadia fiercely and screamed if she tried to pry herself from him. But he did not ask for Mumma once, and Hadia wondered if he understood something that she did not.

The next day, Hadia couldn't go to school because Amar cried when she put her socks on, and screamed when she zipped up her backpack. He even threw things and Hadia was so embarrassed because now Seema Aunty would know about his misbehaving. Seema Aunty called Baba and Baba told her Hadia could stay at home with him. So everyone went to school—Huda and Seema Aunty's sons—but Hadia stayed back with Amar and Seema Aunty's baby girl, who was almost two and learning how to speak. If Amar watched TV, he looked at Hadia every few minutes, as if he were afraid she too would disappear if he looked away for too long. When she went to the bathroom, he waited outside in the hallway until she emerged again. Seema Aunty let Hadia play with her son's video games. Amar threw a little ball that squeaked at the baby girl and the baby girl laughed. Hadia liked to pick her up and point to things and name them, and the girl repeated the words back to her: light, fire, tree. Amar pointed to his nose and said his name, and the girl tried to say it, but said *mar* instead, and that was the first time Hadia and Amar laughed, knowing it was the Urdu word for hit, or hurt.

In the evening when Baba visited, Hadia watched him carefully for signs of what was going on, but he just looked tired, or like he was just pretending to be there with them. When Baba got ready to leave, he hugged Hadia and Huda and stood for a long time watching Amar sitting on a couch, his back to Baba. Hadia tried to look at Amar's back too, tried to see what Baba was looking at there, but saw nothing special.

"You should be so proud of Hadia," Seema Aunty said to Baba. "She helps so much it is like I hardly have to watch them at all."

Hadia waited for Baba to react, but instead he nodded and said he had to go. Hadia watched the headlights of the car pull away and all the terror she had felt the night before came rushing back, even though she knew that Seema Aunty was nice to them, that her baby was cute, that the food tasted like Mumma's, and the boys in the house shared their toys with them.

Those days were the first times she really felt like a sister. Like it was a job she had to do, and that she would do her best at it. And after, she never stopped feeling it. She took the job as seriously as listening in class or cleaning the kitchen counter when Mumma passed her a dishcloth. When Amar cried and shook his head if Seema Aunty tried to spoon rice into his bowl, Hadia sat up in her chair, took the spoon, and served him, remembering what Baba had told her. She did not let Huda tease Amar. She thought of games they could play together. She told them stories before they went to sleep. The one they liked about when the Prophet split the moon, or the one about the two children who get lost in the woods but find their way home by sticking together and by dropping breadcrumbs.

"You're good at telling stories," Seema Aunty's oldest son, who was Hadia's age, told her. He was nice, but Hadia kept forgetting his name.

"My Mumma tells good stories," she told him proudly, and that was the first time she missed Mumma, and she felt bad that it had taken her so long to miss her when Amar missed her every day.

By the third day, Amar was calmer. Maybe he knew that whoever else left, Hadia would not, or maybe he was bored with her and wanted to play with the toys that filled the big house. Hadia left his side and spent the whole day playing with Huda and Seema Aunty's three boys. She took breaks to check on Amar, and he was fine, helping Seema Aunty by carrying snacks to them outside, or playing with the baby girl when Seema Aunty was busy cooking. The baby girl followed Amar around the house. And when she reached across to scratch his face, leaving a long red line that raised instantly, Hadia was impressed that Amar, despite having not spent time with many toddlers, knew not to hurt her back, and he just laughed.

In the garden, the oldest boy asked Hadia where her parents were, digging in the dirt with the edge of a long stick, and she said she didn't know. *Inshallah*, God willing, they'll be back and all will be well, he said, and Hadia thought that it was weird that a boy her age was talking to her like the grown-ups and she told him so. He shrugged and said he was just trying to be nice. He had green eyes and in the sun she saw specks of gold and orange in them. That was before Hadia started to wear a scarf, and she played soccer with the boys in the backyard, their lawn that was as wide as a park. He was rough with his brothers but slowed as he approached her and passed her the ball gently. That night Baba came back and told her to get her things and Hadia knew that Mumma was home. She was surprised to find that she didn't want their visit to be over. Amar held her hand while they walked to the car and she turned around to wave at the boy whose name she had forgotten and he stood on his doorstep, waving back.

At home Mumma was sitting on the couch and Hadia stopped walking when she saw her, because Mumma looked so much smaller. She looked back at Baba to see if he thought she looked strange too, but Baba looked as he had for the past few days, like only his body was with them. She felt obligated to hug her mother. Once Amar climbed into her lap he did not leave it, and he refused to look at Hadia. She watched the two of them, the way Amar followed Mumma, the way Mumma did not put him down but carried him from room to room even though he had become too old for that. Hadia ran upstairs and wished her mother had not come back, then felt so awful for thinking it that she began to cry, and she said to God, *I am sorry, please forgive me.* In the weeks that followed, Amar hesitated before responding to her, as though her presence now reminded him of Mumma's absence. When Amar began first grade, and the school days grew longer, Amar would call Mumma to pick him up right after lunch, and he would go home early. But that made Baba too angry; he hit Amar once with the shoulder of a hanger and told him that he had to stop being a baby, that he had to stay in school for the full day like everyone else, and after that Amar had only called for Hadia.

In the nurse's room she takes a seat next to him. The tissue paper crumples beneath her weight. He thanks her, speaking in English again.

"Your lip looks funny," he says, twisting his mouth to one side.

She presses her tongue against the bruise.

"Is it from last night?" he asks.

Hadia does not say yes. Recently, Amar has begun sensing when Baba gets even a little irritated with her, or with Huda, and he acts out in a way that guarantees Baba will only get angry at him. If Huda complains about the dinner and Baba gives her a look, Amar will chime in, say he does not just dislike the dinner, he hates it, until Baba is only looking at Amar, willing only Amar to test his patience.

"It's just a small bruise," she says. The clock ticks. The nurse types in the other room, hitting the keys quickly and loudly.

"Once there was a boy who cried wolf," she tells him again. "The whole village rushed to his side. His sister too, who was afraid for him. But when they reached the clearing and there was no wolf, only a boy with a mischievous look on his face, people thought to themselves, Now we can't trust this boy's word. Next time when he calls wolf, wolf, wolf, we will look away. We will busy ourselves."

Amar blows at the hair on his forehead like he's not even listening to her.

"And eventually," she adds, trying to make her voice very serious, "even his sister convinces herself that she should not listen to the boy, that there is no wolf, and she should just keep taking notes in class instead."

"I don't believe it," he says.

"You don't have to *believe* it, it's the lesson part that's true."

"What is the lesson?" he asks.

"They stop going to help him. He gets eaten by the wolf because the whole time he said it was there when it wasn't, so they didn't believe him when the wolf actually did come."

Before she leaves, she will tell him that he has to stay in class, no matter how hard it is, and that he can't disturb her classes anymore.

"But you would not do that. You would still come," he says at last.

She gives up. She wonders how long she will have to stay until Amar is calm, until he is ready to go back to class. She rubs the marks her nails made on her arm with her thumb.

"Why do you always do that?" he asks her.

She pulls down the sleeve of her sweater until it covers the marks. She feels as though he has uncovered one of her secrets. She watches the hand on the clock move.

"Hadia?"

"Hm?"

"Don't tell Baba, please?"

"I won't."

They sit. There is nothing left to speak about. Even though he was lying about his tummy hurting, he holds two arms folded over it anyway. He really does look like a little teddy bear. His feet don't touch the floor and he swings them back and forth. He leans his head against her arm and she looks at the poster in the nurse's room, of the body and the food it needs to eat to be healthy, and she studies it, thinking that if she memorizes at least one fact, her time will not be wasted.

✧

EVERY WEEKEND THERE are countless functions and family-friend parties, and Amar hates almost everything about them. The ceaseless small talk. The constant gaze of his father following him, making sure he is treating elders with respect, that he is not fighting with or being vaguely rude to the other boys his age. Or disappearing with the few he is friends with and offending the host, sometimes to smoke a cigarette a few streets away, sitting on the curb and complaining with them about everyone else, mints at the ready in their pockets. Other times just to drive to the nearest 7-Eleven and get a soda, despite the endless supply of soda at the party, just for the thrill of that ride, for that momentary escape, for the pleasure derived from the click of the ring pull on the can that is his, purchased by him in secret. He detests, most of all, the importance placed on maintaining a sense of decorum that feels stifling, false. Always the same menus, the same combination of dishes. Even the segregation annoys him—males confined to one side of the house, females to another, sometimes divided by a wall or a cloth pinned between walls.

But still, he would go. Because Abbas would be there, as well as Amira's other brothers, and maybe one of them would bring her up in conversation. He would catch snippets, little clues that he could piece together. From them he learned how she loved peanut M&M's, because Abbas would purchase a packet for her every time he went to the 7-Eleven; and how she wanted to go to college on the East Coast in a few years, had already begun improving her grades and researching schools despite the resistance of her parents; how she hated the sports her brothers watched; how she did not shy from fighting with her middle brothers and that she demanded her parents treat her the same as them. And of course, he could not resist the pull of the possibility that she would be there, that he might catch the sound of laughter that was hers, note the shoe in the pile of shoes that was hers. If the timing was right, if all aligned, if he stood near the divider just as someone was passing with a tray of food or jug of water and they lifted the curtain, and if she happened to be standing behind it, maybe he would catch a quick glimpse of her, her delicate features, her slender body, always clothed in bright colors.

Today, at yet another function hosted by a family friend, he walks into the backyard and leans against the rough wall. Young women have found seats at the garden table. One glance informs him: Amira is sitting with them, in the center, dressed in a midnight blue *shalwar kameez*, sipping Coke from an orange-and-white-striped straw, her hair cut shorter than he recalls. She is one of the few young women who does not wear hijab, does not even pretend to during gatherings. The young women are all laughing, as if trying to get his attention in obvious ways. He sees only her. The girls whisper among themselves and she looks up at him. She blushes. Looks away. He turns to the thin telephone wires cutting across the sky, focuses on the little birds perched on them to avoid looking at her, and puts his headphones on and begins to play a song. His father had been engaged in a conversation with boring Samir Uncle—meaning he would be occupied for a while—but he still looks once to the sliding door to make sure no one is coming. Headphones alone are enough to ignite his father's anger, an anger that will fester during the party, escalate to a fight in the car, and become a disaster by the time they reach home. He attempts to appear as though he wishes he were anywhere but here. He knows it is a lie. This moment. That one glance. The color that rose to her cheeks, the way it suited her— it is the best thing that has happened to him this week.

When he thinks that his luck at being in her presence unnoticed is sure to run out soon, she stands. The folds of her clothes fall and straighten. She walks toward him. He tries not to look. Birds on a wire, one flapping its wings, rising into the sky. The girls she left, still seated at the table, have stopped giggling to watch her walk;

they meet each other's eyes, some turn to one another to whisper. Others would consider her steps indecent. He thinks her bold. Bold to stand, bold to leave the flock of women, bold to be beside him, at a gathering full of community members, all with a penchant for exaggerated, condemning gossip. Bolder, he thinks, than he could ever be.

He lowers the volume of his song with every step she takes, just in case she speaks when she reaches him. And when she does speak, when she asks a question so simple—what are you listening to?— he realizes that though he may not have known it until that very moment, he has been waiting his whole life for her to walk through the crowd of whisperers and speak to him. Amira with her laugh louder than the others beyond the partition, Amira running in a game of tag in the mosque parking lot, so fast that neither he nor the other children playing could ever catch her.

He removes a single earbud, keeping the other in, an attempt to appear nonchalant. He has been listening to a song he did not think anyone knew, had chosen it because it reminded him of her. He tells her its title. Her face lights up and she tells him that she knows it, her voice quickening. This must be how she is when she is excited, and sure enough she tells him she loves it, with such generosity of expression that it takes him by surprise, that someone could be capable of being moved, in that way, by something so small.

He almost smiles. She asks him if he wants to know her favorite line. At the realization that there could be nothing about her he would not want to know, he suddenly feels shy, a word he has never used to describe himself before. He raises an eyebrow and waits. Unbothered by his reticence, she shares the line. He looks at her then and says, Mine too.

It turns into a game. One question leads to another. Back and forth they try to find things that connect them. They have the same first initial, Amar offers this one—even the fact that his sisters shared the same initial had felt to him, as a child, like an exclusion. Do you like waking up before the rest of the world? Do you wake up in the middle of the night after a bad dream and find that you cannot remember it, but you can taste having had it? When you stand in prayer, with everyone, all in a line, does your mind wander? Do you try to break those thoughts, stop them, but can't, and everything you've ever wanted to think about comes spilling out? Do you feel, then, like you are pretending, like you are the weakest link in the chain of worshipers? When you were little and you caught sight of the moon from the car window, did you feel like it was following you? And what do you see when you stare at the moon? Do you see a face, or Imam Ali's name in Arabic? Does your father's voice shake the walls? Would you run away if it weren't for your siblings? Do you like to catch glimpses into strangers' living room windows? Wonder what their life is like? Do streetlights make you sad too?

At that she confesses, so unguardedly that he hopes he will remember it, "Sometimes I sit on my bed and focus on the closest streetlight when I don't want to cry, when the day has been long, when I feel the stillness, that feeling of being awake when no one else is."

In this new game they do not respond to their responses, so he moves on to the next question. "What is one thing you're afraid to lose?"

Her mother's sharp voice from the open sliding door startles them both before Amira can answer. Seema Aunty looks at the two of them and frowns. Amira rushes inside, aware that she has stayed too long. She does not dare turn back to look at him.

THAT NIGHT, HE stares out his window, at the quiet street and magnolia tree, at the streetlight a few houses down, and tries to picture her looking at one just like it. The moonlight illuminates the white-painted wood that frames his window. With the thin tip of a pushpin he carves out her initial, *A*, then realizes again that his is the same as he carves another beside it, and he feels as though he is committing his affection to the world, that a decision has just been made.

He hopes that tonight is not a night that she has sat up in her bed and focused on her streetlight, hopes that the look her mother gave them when she saw them talking hasn't led to trouble. And if she is awake, on the other side of the city, he hopes she can sense that he is awake too. He looks down at the initials, as if for the first time, as if he had not realized what he was doing until it was done, and he takes comfort in how thin the strokes are, how almost indistinguishable, how no one but he would ever notice them there, carved so close together that they appear not like two letters but an M with a line cutting through it, or two mountains with snow that has fallen on a straight line.

2

LAYLA OPENS HER EYES TO THE SOFTEST MORNING light and Rafiq's face, so close and half obscured by his arm. He will remain asleep until their alarm rings or she reaches out to touch his shoulder. All night she woke to the dark, then blue light and knew there was still time, turned around to try and fall asleep again. But the light that comes through their still curtainless windows now fills their whole room, washes out the shadows. White comforter and white pillowcases and Rafiq's dark hair and dark lashes and dark skin she often feels affection for—odd, to feel affection for the color of his skin, but it is true, there is something comforting about it. Layla feels nauseous. He is leaving in a few hours. His small suit-case is ready and waiting by the front door. Three days, two nights. The first time he has to fly to another branch, a city six hours away. It was a requirement of his promotion, from now on he would leave for days at a time, every other week almost, and Layla knows she should be proud of him and happy for what it has allowed them: purchasing a used car that would be hers, moving, just a few weeks prior, into their new home, an actual house, still oddly empty and quiet to her, as if it were a size too big, and Layla unsure if her life would ever expand enough to fill it. Soon, Layla will leave the warmth of their bed to pack Rafiq's lunch, and Hadia's and Huda's too, and Rafiq will sweep Hadia off to preschool and Huda to a day-care they are trying for her because she also wants to have somewhere to go with a backpack. Then Rafiq will drive himself to

39

the airport and she will continue unpacking in the empty house, attempting to create a home.

What will it be like for her to fall asleep tonight without him? She cannot remember the last time she slept alone; before Rafiq, her bed had been an arm's length away from Sara's. Tonight she will be the one to go from room to room, closing windows and locking doors, checking them twice, turning off all of the lights. She will have to become comfortable driving at night—she has only ever driven in the daytime, when he was not there. She never thought of him as responsible for doing these things until now. She moves closer to her husband, breathes in his scent. So familiar that she never notices it anymore, almost five years into their marriage, unless she seeks it out. His most beautiful face is his sleeping one, no stern expressions, just eyelids, lashes, defined nose, jawline. She pictures those cartoon cottages in shows her daughters watch, where a woman inside the cottage throws open the shutters and appears at the window singing. That is how it feels today to wake up and see his face, like a window in the room of her heart is being thrust open. Rafiq stirs. Layla shuts her eyes, not wanting him to see her looking at him. What is it about caring for another, feeling love, feeling affection, at times desire, that makes one shy? Even in front of her own husband she feels that hesitation of expression.

"Is it time?" he asks.

How he knows she is awake.

"Yes, I think so."

She rises to wake the girls. Her sight goes black for a moment, and she stands very still, presses her fingers to her eyelids until she feels steady. She must be stressed, which is natural, they are all growing accustomed to the new home and the new city, slowly getting to know the mosque community. Hadia has just started preschool, three days a week for only three hours, but still, the emptiness of her home is new to her. From their doorway she watches her little girls sleeping in their shared bedroom. Who am I without them, she wonders, having become so used to them—her husband's face in the morning, her daughters' steps throughout the day.

Her girls are easy to wake. She is a lucky mother. They do not resist or fuss, she only has to walk in and move the blanket off their bodies and they begin to blink, rub their eyes.

"Wake up, wake up," she sings, and leans in to kiss Hadia's forehead. She taps her little nose, until Hadia sits up and yawns. Layla reminds her she is in charge of helping Huda with the morning routine: the brushing of hair, of teeth, the changing into clothes Layla will have laid out on their beds by then. Hadia nods. She is Mumma's little helper. She rises to every occasion.

"Mumma, is Baba leaving today?" she asks, a startled expression on her face, as if she has just remembered.

Hadia looks down at her nails. Layla allowed her to paint them for the first day of preschool a few days ago, and now they are a chipped, bright pink and deep purple. Hadia scratches a nail with another, chipping it even more, and Layla places her hand on hers to stop her.

"It will be okay," she says, her voice deep and slow to assure her daughter. "We will be fine. We will even have fun."

Hadia searches her face as if she is trying to sense if Layla is being honest or if she is only trying to comfort her. She is smart for her age, perceptive and easily affected. Layla has to be careful. Finding what she was looking for in her mother's face, Hadia nods, hops out of bed to wake Huda.

Downstairs, Layla listens for the sounds of her family's movements as she fills clear plastic bags with slices of pear or bunches of grapes and a handful of Goldfish crackers. She packs juice boxes, makes wraps of roti filled with fried okra and carefully covers them in foil, rough and silver. That is Huda jumping off of the bed onto the floor, she must be dressed, she likes putting her clothes on while standing on her bed, and Layla often admonishes her. It is so easy to lose balance. The distant rush of water on its way to the shower slows and stops. Rafiq must be stepping out. Three brown bags of lunch, all in a line, sliced pear for Huda, grapes for Hadia, almonds for Rafiq, and she pauses to look out the window, at their garden—a square of cement where the girls play jump rope, then lots of long and unkempt grass, and at the far end a lone plum tree. She had liked the plum tree when they first moved in, had warmed to the idea of owning land which contained a tree that would bear fruit. Pounding footsteps on stairs and she knows that Huda and Hadia are racing to her, and she turns just in time to see them, Hadia in the lead, Huda trailing after her, out of breath and already unhappy, a defeated look on her face.

"No running," she reminds them, but there is no point, the race is already over, they are clambering into their chairs. Hadia has won again. Layla wishes she would let her sister win once in a while. Layla pours cereal into their matching pink bowls and sets it before them. Huda complains. Hadia spills some milk on her shirt. Layla just concentrates on slicing a banana into Rafiq's cereal bowl. Every time the dull blade of the butter knife reaches her palm, she pushes softly into her skin, feels its ridges.

When they first bought the home and walked through it as a family, Rafiq pretended that they had come upon the house by complete accident. Do you think the door will be open in this house? he asked Hadia as they pulled into the driveway. They had just listened to their Nusrat Fateh Ali Khan cassette, and Layla loved the way it lightened Rafiq's mood. Hadia looked at him from her booster seat, skeptical and excited, old enough to understand his game, young enough to be fooled by it. Rafiq lifted Hadia up and onto his shoulders. Hadia adored when he did this. Her face all love and wonder. This time, some fear too. Baba—don't, what if you get in trouble? Don't become worried, he said; you trust your Baba, don't you? And she paused for a long second before she nodded and what a surprise—the door opened, and look how silent and empty the house was. No one lives here, Hadia whispered, tense but intrigued. You're exactly right, Hadia, he said. Smart girl. And she beamed. Rafiq paused in every room: kitchen, he said to Hadia, and she nodded; space where the kitchen table would be, he said to the emptiness beneath a light fixture, and Huda, almost three years old, looked at it all with boredom, a thumb in her mouth that Layla kept pulling out. He led them straight to the backyard—their old apartment only had a tiny balcony—and Layla thought to reach out and hold Hadia as he twisted the lock to open the sliding door, but he was careful, balancing her with one arm. Layla followed them closely. Hadia's arms were wrapped tight around his neck. They trudged through the grass and Rafiq spun once, and Hadia giggled, and it was possible that Layla wished, for a moment, that he were leading her with as much care through their new home as he was Hadia. But this was silly—to give her daughter love was a way to give her love. When they reached the farthest end of the backyard and turned to look at the expanse before them that would be their grassy yard, and the two-story house, Rafiq paused, looked up at Hadia, and asked, "Do you like this house?"

"Yes," Hadia said, and she leaned her chin on his head. Her hair fell just above his ears.

"Could you live here?" he asked, and Layla thought it was sweet: they had already bought it weeks earlier, had just gotten the keys that day, but he was presenting it to Hadia as if he would make it hers in that instant if she said yes. Layla hoped she would say yes.

"I guess so," Hadia said.

Rafiq lifted his shoulders and lowered them abruptly, just as he had when she was a little younger and he was pretending to be a horse or a helicopter, and Hadia started laughing her uncontrollable laughter.

"You guess so? You guess so?"

Rafiq stretched for one of the plums on the plum tree and plucked it for her, passed it into her hands.

"It's yours."

"Plum?"

"All of it."

He spun her. He nodded at the empty house. He put her down and lifted up Huda and said, "Did you hear that, Huda Jaan? This house is yours."

And Hadia just stood there, stunned, holding on to that little plum and looking up at Rafiq with big eyes and her mouth a little open. Huda looked like she did not understand but Rafiq looked happy and Hadia seemed happy so she smiled too, then put her thumb back in her mouth.

Now Rafiq has taken his seat beside the two of them at the table and is scanning the newspaper as he eats. The girls are not allowed to speak when he is reading the paper, they know this. They listen to him without even being told. They give each other looks and Layla wonders what they communicate to each other. Why is he not talking to her, if this is his last morning with them, with her? She is too nauseous to eat with them, so she stands at the counter and looks for reasons to stay in the room. Clears the surfaces, wipes them down with a sponge, looks up from time to time at the morning sunlight on the page of Rafiq's newspaper, and the light in his dark hair, the light catching the curve of the silver spoon he holds away from him.

Then he pulls back his sleeve to look at his watch, and it is his father's watch. He had worn it on their wedding day. And on the day they had flown together to America. Her heart pinches to think she has glimpsed what he did not verbalize: that this is not nothing to him either, that perhaps he is nervous for the new position or wants to take a piece of his father with him. Rafiq rises from the table with his empty bowl in hand, gathers the girls' bowls too, tells them to grab their backpacks, it is time to go.

Will he pause to embrace her, will he look back from the doorway, lift his hat or nod his head before leaving? Layla hugs the girls before she remembers the Quran, how Rafiq should walk beneath it if he is going on a journey, and she tells him this and he appears agitated, there is not much time, so Layla rushes up the stairs to the empty room next to their daughters', which they have been using as a prayer room: two prayer rugs, each with one corner folded over, and a tiny bookshelf with all their religious texts—and she grabs the Quran she likes with the blue cover and golden pages. Downstairs, Rafiq is waiting in the doorway, the girls presumably buckled into the car, and she holds the Quran up with one arm and instructs him to walk back and forth beneath it five times, as her mother taught her, as her mother had done for her on every first day of school, and on the day after her wedding, when she was taking off to fly to America, and by the fourth time Rafiq walks beneath, her stretched arm begins to ache, and by the fifth he pauses, looks up at her, and she holds the Quran up to his face and leafs through all the pages at once, its breeze causing the hair falling onto his forehead to tremble, and he leans in and kisses the cover with closed eyes.

There is a pause. Layla does not know what to say or ask for.

"Make sure all the windows are closed when you leave to pick up the girls, and check at night too. And the doors."

"I know."

"Even the garage door."

"Yes."

"*Khudahafiz,*" he says, which is good-bye, but literally it means in God's protection I leave you. In His care I trust. And it is that meaning she intends when she responds in kind.

"You will be fine," he says.

She nods. How she appreciates that he knew what she needed, and acknowledged it. He kisses her, ever so softly, on her forehead, and steps away. Layla lifts a hand in good-bye. The door closes, the house empty, the sound, after a few seconds of the car turning on, of the tires pulling away on the cement.

AT NIGHT, THE girls brush their teeth together in front of the bathroom mirror, balancing on their individual stools. Huda is always in a rush to spit out the toothpaste, but waits for Hadia to be done before she lowers her own brush, and Hadia nods her head slowly as she counts to a hundred in her head. Layla hates how night looks outside windows without curtains. She is exposed. She avoids going near them. She turns the lights off downstairs and finds she is a bit out of breath by the time she reaches upstairs. Hadia and Huda are getting into their pajamas. They are what fills her life, they really are, she thinks. What would life be like with another child? When

Rafiq called earlier, she did not tell him that she threw up twice after he drove away. Or that she lay in bed for an hour absolutely miserable before the queasiness passed. She doesn't know if it could be true—that after a year of trying she might have another child soon. But instead of the immediate excitement she had felt with her girls, the news, the possible news, made her feel even lonelier as she went about her day, picked up her daughters from school, cooked dinner, no hope of seeing Rafiq for three days, and what if she was carrying a child again, and he was so often away?

Hadia and Huda crawl into their beds and she notices for the first time that the tree outside their bedroom scrapes against the window when it is windy. She begins to read to them, but stops, tries to keep her voice even when she asks, "Do you girls want to do something fun tonight?"

"Yes, yes!" Huda says, so excited without even knowing what.

"Do you want to camp in my room?"

"Yes!" Huda stands up in her bed and jumps up and then onto the floor.

Layla follows as the two of them race into her room. They climb onto her bed. Instinctively, they know to scoot to the side that is Rafiq's; their small heads share his pillow. They look at Layla, as if waiting for instructions, waiting to see if there is a next part to this spontaneous plan. But there isn't. Layla says good night to the two of them, then moves her prayer rug into her own room, and she prays in the corner while the girls try to sleep. They shift around. She did lock the front door, and checked twice, she does not need to go down again. She will ask Rafiq to install curtains when he returns. She is a little thirsty but she can cup her hands and drink from the sink. She catches her reflection in the bathroom mirror. Her face is older now but still young. She is twenty-six. Young enough to carry another child, without complication, if she is lucky, if God wills it. Old enough to be able to do this: spend this night beside her girls who are warm and full of life. It is to be expected that the first night apart from Rafiq would be a bit difficult, that she would feel uneasy when she looked out the glass to the dark night sky and saw only her reflection, expected that she would be startled, while reading the girls to sleep, by the sound of a passing car, its lights curving up and across their walls. She climbs into bed quietly, thinking her daughters are asleep. Hadia opens her eyes.

"Awake?" Layla whispers.

Hadia nods. She looks up at the ceiling. Her nose looks so blue and small in the dark. Her tiny hands beneath her cheek, her palms together, like a photograph of a child resting.

"Mommy," she says, pausing to sigh, "I *really* love school." She says it all in English and like she is confessing, like she is attempting to make conversation, or is surprised it is this way for her when she did not expect it to be.

"*Mommy?*" Layla says. She is startled to be called that.

"Mummy," Hadia corrects herself, embarrassed.

"I'm glad to hear that," Layla says. They always speak in Urdu. She might have to make a point to enforce it as a rule now. Should she call Rafiq tomorrow, tell him this? That their daughter was speaking like an adult too.

"Did you like school?" Hadia asks. Outside, the wind whips through the trees. Layla kisses her cheek, moves Hadia's hair around gently. All praise to God, she thinks, as she looks at her, all thanks to Him, for the gift of my daughter sweet, and I having the privilege of being her mother.

"Shh," she says into her daughter's hair. "Sleep. I did like it. I liked it a whole lot. We can talk about it tomorrow." Hadia nods and closes her eyes. Layla leaves her arm over her daughter's body. It feels safe, and comforting, just to have her there.

❖

HADIA IS THIRTEEN and sitting on the top of a picnic table painted red, loosening the knot of her scarf and watching the boys from her Sunday school class play basketball during their lunch break. Amar is among them, despite being much younger. She focuses on him from time to time, to make sure he is keeping up with them, that they are not shoving him or denying him the ball. But her brother holds her attention only briefly before she returns to follow the movement of the eldest Ali boy, who weaves through the rest of the boys with an ease that looks graceful to her. From where she watches, it appears that the others are afraid of him or in awe of him—they seem reluctant to steal the ball, they cheer louder when he scores.

And he scores often. She tugs at the knot of her scarf again. It is a hot day. Abbas Ali, the eldest Ali boy, is the only one in the entire community Hadia has spent years maintaining a secret admiration for. She is not alone. The other girls have not been nearly as reticent. Already, he has a reputation in the mosque among the girls. He is kind to the youngest girls, pathetically adored by the girls his age, and even the older, teenage girls tend to comment on how incredibly good looking he will be when he grows up—sometimes to his face, because he is thirteen and so much younger than them, and that kind of compliment is not yet inappropriate. Hadia is among the adorers his age, and her mosque friends share anecdotes about him in the bathroom, magnifying his inconsequential actions: *Did you see how he asked Zainab if there was any tea left in the ladies' section?*

She finds them foolish. She has no interest in engaging with the other girls and their childish fervor, their embarrassing giggles and obvious whispering. She refuses to add to his awareness of the effect he has on girls, refuses to speak out loud her thoughts on the matter—she has not even told Huda, with whom she shares everything. To speak of it would be to lessen what she is beginning to feel.

She is ashamed by how she watches him. By the details she notices. The sweat that glistens on his neck. The way he wipes his forehead with the back of his hand. His voice commanding the other players on the court. How they listen to him, and how, when the voices drift toward her, she knows which one is his. The few seconds when he lifts his shirt to wipe his face. She looks away then, before looking back, despite herself, a heat rising to her face. He is still young, skinny, she thinks. She is still just a girl, crooked teeth and bushy eyebrows, dressed in loose clothes her mother picked for her, a shirt that falls just above her knees, jeans a size too big, to ensure any hint of her body is hidden. Not the kind of girl a boy like the eldest Ali boy would ever notice. But still. The boys stop to take a break; some head for their water bottles and others lean forward and rest their hands on their knees, breathing heavily. Amar picks up the basketball before it rolls off the court and stands beneath the hoop, begins to practice. The eldest Ali boy looks over at the picnic table. At her. She looks away.

After the bell rings, she takes her time walking into the mosque where their classes are held. The other girls go on ahead, their steps quickening from the awareness that Quran class is next and the Arabic teachers are all so strict and punctual. Hadia fiddles with her scarf, untying it and retying it again. The knot under her chin feels heavy whenever she thinks of it. In the lobby that contains cubbies for all the shoes, she removes hers slowly, loops two fingers in the straps and tucks them away. The lobby is the only section of the mosque, besides their classrooms during Sunday school, that isn't segregated. Everyone seems to slow when they are in the lobby, linger, wanting to take advantage of the brief moment when the veil between the genders is lifted. The boys who played basketball file in, sweaty and playfully shoving one another and kicking off their shoes before running to class. They do not notice her. The eldest Ali boy enters and next to him walks her brother. Amar is looking up at him in the way he would often look up at Hadia, when they were younger and her ability to make up new games mystified him. He has not looked at her that way in months, has stopped hovering in her doorway before his bedtime to tell her some trivial detail of his day.

As they approach, Hadia is suddenly more aware of herself, if only because of the eldest Ali boy's presence in the room. This is my body, she catches herself thinking for the first time as he walks toward her, her heartbeat quickening and a drum gently throbbing in her ears. These are my skinny arms, my limbs, my skin he sees. It is thrilling—the sudden realization that beneath the layers of cloth, she has a body, a beat, a drum.

49

He gives her the kind of smile that girls gather in the bathroom to talk about, hooks his arm around Amar's neck and says to her, "Your brother's not so bad, you know."

Your brother, he said. Your.

He announces to the few other boys that remain in the hallway that Amar will be on his team from now on. He pulls Amar closer to him for a moment before letting go. And it is that subtle display of affection for her younger brother that makes Hadia look at him in another way, aware of not only his eyes and how startling they are, or how he makes everyone in their Sunday school classes laugh, but also of how kind he is, how good.

Amar has a stunned look he tries to conceal; he busies himself by kicking his shoes into a cubby, smiling the whole time to himself. The eldest Ali boy walks into the corridor and heads to the Quran class that Hadia will soon be late to. Lately, Amar has had a rough time at school and difficulty keeping friends. Toward the end of last year, his grades had plummeted like never before, he had lost what little motivation he might have possessed, and his third grade teacher decided it would be best for him to repeat the year, considering he had done terribly on almost every single test. He has just begun third grade again. Amar looks at her and his smile widens before he rushes to his own class. She stands in the empty lobby, taking in the silence and the scattered shoes.

When she enters the classroom she spots the only empty seat, in the front row of the girls' section, just behind the four rows of boys' desks. The boys have the first few rows reserved, so that the order of the classroom may be maintained, so they cannot look at the backs of the girls at their desks and get distracted. Girls are not like boys, they are told, girls have control over their desires. It is up to the girls to do what they can to protect the boys from sin.

Sister Mehvish, their Arabic teacher, is the strictest of them all. She has a thick Arabic accent and a mole the size of a little grape on her upper lip.

"So gracious of you to join us, Sister Hadia," Sister Mehvish says.

"Why don't you begin our class by reciting the *surah* you had to memorize."

Everyone turns to look at her. Her face burns when she sees that the eldest Ali boy is looking too. Hadia confesses she was unable to finish memorizing the *surah*, a lie she tells to save herself from the greater embarrassment of having to recite it aloud, drawing even more attention to herself, risking the possibility of fumbling the correct pronunciation, and the look she knows she will get from the other students who, as usual, have not bothered to memorize it at all.

"Of course you didn't," Sister Mehvish says, and some of the students snicker.

The only empty seat is directly behind the eldest Ali boy's. He leans back in his chair, turns to face her when she sits, and she catches some sympathy in his eyes—but by the time she has settled and he has turned to face the teacher, she realizes it could easily have been pity. He rocks in his chair throughout the lesson, taps his pen against his blank binder paper, and she finds it hard to concentrate on the Arabic words Sister Mehvish is writing on the chalkboard. She remembers his arm around Amar, the points he scored, the moment he looked to her from the court, the vein in his neck, the skin revealed when he lifted his shirt—she feels instantly and intensely guilty for storing away that brief glimpse of his skin, especially ashamed that it has come back to her in a class for learning the holy language, holy texts. She does not recognize herself, and tugging on her loose sleeve so it covers her hand, she does not know if she likes herself. But he has a small speck of a birthmark where his hair meets his neck in the shape of a strawberry, and every so often he runs his hand through his hair, then lets his hand rest at the back of his head, so close that she would hardly have to stretch to touch him if she dared. Twice, she thinks he will turn to look at her, but he does not.

When the class is over everyone stands, no one faster than Hadia. The eldest Ali boy turns to her, nods toward Sister Mehvish, and rolls his eyes. That drum in her body again. Sister Mehvish has her back turned to the class and is erasing the words that look like scribbles from the board, creating a cloud of white dust. Hadia looks back at him. He has not looked away from her. He pulls an almost empty packet of gum out from his pocket and removes the last piece, a stick wrapped in silver foil, and extends it to her, his palm open, his eyebrows raised. Hadia reaches for it, her fingers lightly graze the surface of his palm. She wants to say thank you but does not, she can feel her face getting warmer, she fears he will notice a change in color, so she offers a small, quick smile and walks away. Her classmates have not noticed and Hadia looks up to where she imagines God is, sometimes a spot on the ceiling, other times a patch of brilliant blue in the sky, to thank Him for the moment passed unseen. She doesn't want to be the subject of the next story they share in the bathroom: *Did you see how he offered Hadia a stick of gum?*

In the corridor light, the silver wrapping of the gum gleams. She tucks it into her pocket like a secret.

THAT EVENING, SHE sits in the living room armchair and runs her finger over half of the silver gum wrapper in her hand. The other half is taped to the ceiling above her bed, the interior inside out, so the white blends with the ceiling paint, unnoticed. On it, she had drawn a small strawberry. Most days even she would not notice it there, but there it would be.

Her mother is setting the table for dinner. The smell of *kheema* and fried tomatoes sizzling fills the room. Amar is bothering Baba while Baba is trying to read the newspaper.

"Why don't you wear it every day?" Amar asks Baba, pointing to the watch on his wrist.

It had belonged to Baba's father, their dada. They asked to be shown it some nights because it was the only piece of Baba that had been there since before them, and because Baba was proud when he lifted it from the box to polish it. Dada was a mystery to them, just a photograph in Baba's office, or the few anecdotes Baba would share, and so the watch itself felt like a mystery, kept in its box unless Baba wore it.

"It still feels like my father's," Baba says to Amar. "I just inherited it, when my Baba passed away. It had been a gift to my father from his father."

"Does it always go to fathers?" Amar asks.

"You mean sons," Baba says.

Hadia knows the story. The watch had been gifted to her grandfather when he went to Cambridge to study law. Her great-grandfather had wanted his son to have a Swiss watch, like the men with whom he imagined his son would be studying.

"Hardly anyone studied in England then," Baba tells him. "He returned home a lawyer."

Baba flips the page of the newspaper, and then extends his arm to Amar so he can get a closer look. Baba says to him, "This watch will work forever. It will never stop."

Hadia smiles from her couch. She likes thinking of her ancestors as people who had done something with their lives, that her grandfather had been brave to study in England and that her father had been brave to move here, each of them doing what they could so that she and her siblings could now be brave in their lives.

"Where are you lost?" Mumma snaps at her in Urdu. "Put water on the table."

Hadia stands reluctantly to help her mother. Huda is setting the table slowly. Huda was lazy with her tasks; it was always apparent when she did not care about what she was doing. Hadia's efforts never changed; she was determined to do everything well, even the tasks she hated. Amar refused to approach what he did not care for at all. But when he did care, he put more of himself into the task than Hadia ever could. Amar begins to throw pillows into the air before catching them. Baba continues reading. He has an angry look on his face and he is moving his hand up and down his eyebrow, and she wonders what is happening in the world that is worrying him. Hadia brings down the jug and fills it with ice and

53

then water, listens to the way the cubes begin to crackle, which is her favorite part of this task. Amar is excited in a way that he is usually not, and she wonders if it is because he was included with the older boys today.

Sometimes, Amar acts so despondent that Hadia wants to hold on to his shoulders and tell him to stop. He never seems to enjoy being at home, but complains whenever he is dragged to school, to Sunday school, to mosque on weeknights. He complains until something in their father snaps and he strikes at Amar—with a look, a sharp shout, sometimes a hand—a reaction that silences his protests but alters nothing in his attitude. She is beginning to wonder if Amar acts this way on purpose, just to see how angry he can make Baba. Mumma and Baba have gone to countless appointments with his teachers, but little has changed and Hadia often overhears them talking about him on the other side of their bedroom door.

But tonight, Amar offers to help their mother. Mumma looks to him and smiles.

"You don't have to today," Mumma says, "because you were so good to ask."

It is a line *she* has never heard from her mother. That everyone in her family is occupying the same space and that none of them knows about the silver gum wrapper in Hadia's pocket, or where her mind goes, is intensely pleasing to her. She thinks of Abbas Ali. Of the color of his eyes, hazel, striking against his lightly tanned skin, a rarity in their community. Everyone is fascinated by the Ali family, their wealth and their stature, how they came from a line of esteemed scholars and politicians, their latest and loveliest fashions. But Hadia has noticed with sad curiosity how often positive things about them were discussed in a negative tone. When she first began to understand jealousy, it was the comments she had heard Mumma say to Baba about Seema Aunty that came to mind: *Did you see the purse she was holding, it is haram, that kind of excessiveness. Did you notice how highly she spoke of her children's independence, without once mentioning it is only because she is always*

at work? If she doesn't wear hijab, how will she ever expect her daugh-
ter to? Always a different lipstick shade, sunglasses atop her head, blue
jeans. Beauty is meant to be concealed, not indulged in.

And yet not one community member ever turned down an invitation to the Alis' home, nor did anyone deny themselves the pleasure
of their presence at their own parties, a presence that made them
feel both big and small at the same time. She wasn't sure what the
parents did exactly, how they had so much money—the father was
a doctor of a special kind, the mother designed clothes in India
before moving to California, and she had continued doing so in the
garage of their home until the business flourished. She owned
stores across the States. She was one of the few mothers who was
successful at work. Most mothers stayed at home. Almost all of
Hadia's and Huda's Indian clothes had been bought from her bou-
tiques. Overpriced, her mother would say, before purchasing it
anyway, because their family, and many others in the community,
always received a discount. Seema Aunty was never in the store,
which made Hadia wonder exactly what it was that she did. There
were four children in the family—three sons and one daughter,
Amira Ali, a pretty and charming seven-year-old girl, with dark
hair and rounded eyes, hazel, the exact hue of her brother's. Many
of the older community girls were kind to her, and the adults too,
because she spoke fluent Urdu and was not afraid to be witty, to
joke with them as if she were their age, and she had not yet reached
the age when that would be considered rude, when they would
begin to discourage that kind of banter. She was not told to shush
like other girls were. Hadia wondered if the girls her age were kind
to her in the hope that her older brother would one day notice them.
For this reason, Hadia was only as nice to her as she would be to any
other girl, extending no special treatment. The other boys of the
family—Kumail and Saif—were fine enough, but they were
shadows of their eldest brother, Abbas. They often walked on either
side of him. And all three of them banded together to protect
Amira, which was another reason why no one dared to treat her
unkindly. Once a boy had been throwing things in the corridors of

the mosque and something hit her. A small gash appeared at the edge of her eyebrow. Everyone still exaggerated the blood, Amira's cries, and the reaction of the eldest Ali boy who, rumor had it, pushed the boy against the wall and threatened to knock his teeth out if he ever threw anything in the hallways again. But Hadia did not like to think of him in that way—as someone with a temper. She liked to think of him walking with his little sister on his shoulders, as she sometimes saw them do, and how Amira would hold on to his neck, and how this too had endeared him to Hadia, how of course she could care for a boy who knew how to be kind to a sister, of course someone like that would be safe to love.

Amar walks up to her on tiptoe and announces, "I'm taller than you now."

He sticks his chest out and holds his hand to his forehead as if to salute her. Hadia pushes him a little so he falls back on both feet.

"No, you're not," she says. The day her younger brother would grow taller than her loomed. She knew it would be a strange, embarrassing transition and she feared it would also transform the way they thought of one another, related to one another.

"Am too," he says.

Mumma notices their quibble. She stops pouring the tomato dish into a clear bowl and wipes her hand on a towel. All right then, she says, and she forces them to stand back-to-back. Amar complies eagerly, his new confidence already beginning to annoy her. Huda stops putting the plates on the table to watch. The crinkle of a turning newspaper page cuts the air. Hadia looks to the ceiling and sends a quick, short prayer to God, *Please, do not let him grow taller than me just yet.* After placing her hand on both of their heads and shoulders, stepping close to them and then farther away, Mumma declares, "Hadia is still taller. But not for very long."

Mumma winks at Amar and he leaps into the air. Mumma catches him in her arms and tousles his hair before walking back into the kitchen. Hadia rolls her eyes and turns to busy herself with the task of filling glasses with water, but not before noticing Baba, still staring at the newspaper spread out before him on the coffee table. He is smiling to himself in a way Hadia has not seen before, gentle and grateful even, for the newfound height of his son.

✧

AMAR CANNOT STOP thinking of Amira and their unfinished conversation. He wonders if he is the only one who has returned to their exchange and if they will have another like it. He wants to call Abbas, just so he can go over to their house, glimpse her walking across the landing—but he decides against it. He cares too sincerely for Abbas to seek him out for a false reason. Instead, he shoots hoops in his front yard, returns to their questions and answers and catalogs what he now knows: she loves mornings, she stares out of her window at a single streetlight when she cannot sleep, she is brave, and because of this, beautiful.

Days pass and his mother begins to plan a *jashan* for Hadia, who will soon be on break from college. Three years ago, Hadia was accepted into a combined undergraduate and premed program, with the possibility of continuing on to med school under the condition that she work hard and distinguish herself. Recently, she had called home with the news that she had gotten the grades and test scores and faculty recommendations necessary to continue. His parents are so proud of her. He overhears his father talk about her any chance he gets to family friends who visit or to the grocery store clerk who asks a simple question out of courtesy. Even Mumma calls Sara Khala on the phone and brags and brags—but they never tell Hadia. Only say to her, good, that is good, finish soon and come home again. Amar never shows his parents his report cards. He only hopes to do well enough to graduate. Thinking of his future sometimes felt like looking down a long tunnel, and even if he squinted he could hardly picture what his life would be like when he stepped out at the other end.

Usually, he hated when his mother threw a party. How she fretted over their house, how she made them clean their rooms. He protested that no one ever ventured inside their bedrooms, but to no avail. He especially detested how it fell on him to entertain the guests, when all he wanted to do was stay in his bedroom until everyone left, or sneak off with Abbas and Kumail and take just one drag. But this time the news of the party piques his interest. Twice, he asks his mother to clarify the date. First, to mark it on his calendar, a little red x. The second time to make absolutely sure he got the day right. Fourteen days until the party. On day eleven, he gets his hair cut, knowing how terrible he looks the first few days after a new one. The last ten days take the longest to pass. When only three days remain, he gathers the courage he needs to find his mother in the kitchen.

"Which families are invited?" he asks, gripping the edge of the counter, trying to appear as nonchalant as possible, knowing how unlike him it is to do anything other than complain.

His mother is kneading dough for roti in a large silver bowl. Her cheeks are dusty with flour, her hair pulled back in a tight bun. He had assumed Amira's family would be invited. But earlier today he panicked and now he has to confirm, just to make sure his haircutting and hoping have not been a waste. Mumma takes her time answering, moves strands of her hair from her face with the back of her hand, leaving behind another streak of flour, graying her eyebrow. His pulse quickens, he is surprised at the insistence of his own heartbeat, he twists his mouth to hide his nervousness.

"Why do you ask?" She glances up at him.

He shrugs one shoulder. Mumma smiles. She resumes kneading the dough. He regrets asking immediately. She must know. She always knows everything. She begins to list the families invited, raising a dusty finger each time, but none of the last names are Amira's. She stops speaking and sprinkles more flour into the bowl, a trick for when the dough is too sticky. He turns to walk away, and fills with a disappointment or deflation he cannot precisely define.

"Oh," his mother calls after him, "I forgot one."

He turns around and she is smiling at him in her knowing way. She says the Ali family. Amar nods and walks away as calmly as he can, raises his fist in the air as soon as he is out of her sight.

On the day itself he irons his clothes for the first time in his life.

It confuses him, the knobs and the different settings. He rushes to finish before his mother is done showering. He cannot risk any more of her knowing glances, her embarrassing smile. He is ready an hour before the function begins. Another first. He asks his mother if she needs any help, just to have something to occupy his hands. She beams at him. For her, he pours cold mango lassi into plastic cups and arranges them on trays. He lounges in the living room near the entrance, though the party is outside, the men on one side of the garden, the women on the other side or in the family room. Every time the doorbell rings he looks to the door. Every time it is anyone but her family, he feels pathetic.

Hadia enters the kitchen, dressed in a baby blue *shalwar kameez* that drags to the floor. She looks nervous, knowing that the event is for her; she twists her watch on her wrist. Home is home when Hadia is in it. Amar offers her a cup of lassi and she takes it. Whenever Hadia visits, Huda and Amar remember that they are friends too, and the three of them gather in her bedroom, stay up late talking, or they take their homework to a café, just to be near her. Huda appears, puts her arm around Hadia, and tilts her head quizzically to one side as she takes Amar in.

"Someone looks good today," Huda teases him.

He fills a cup and places it on the tray. Then another.

"No better than any other day," he says.

His sisters watch him. Huda grins. He takes a sip. Then their doorbell rings, and he looks up, and Mumma opens the door, and it is her family. He tries to meet Amira's eyes without making it appear as though he's trying, but she follows her mother straight into the garden with a lowered gaze. Tables have been set up in the backyard—some for the ladies, some for the gentlemen. All afternoon he is aware of where she is. There is a gravity about her and he finds he is not the only one pulled into her orbit. A group of other girls surround her. Even the older girls lean into her; when she speaks they listen, ready to laugh. She affords whomever she is speaking to her entire attention. Once he overhears an elderly lady comment how *pyari* she looks, a word that he knows means "lovely."

She is wearing a red and orange *shalwar kameez,* a delicate red *orni* is wrapped around her neck. Her lips have been painted red. This is new. He sulks about the garden upset that they cannot be alone. A few of his friends are there too, but he engages in conversations with them as if he is only overhearing them.

"Time for a walk?" Abbas asks, their code for sneaking away for a smoke.

"Baba would be mad," he says, shaking his head, which is true, in a way, but not the reason he does not want to leave, not even for a minute. Abbas watches him a moment longer, in that same suspicious way Huda just had, and Amar wonders how he can be so transformed by his thoughts that his closest friend and sister notice instantly.

Amira stands at the farthest edge of the garden, by Mumma's mint plants. A breeze lifts her hair then lets it go. A cloud moves over the sun and the entire world is shifted. Why had he expected it to be any other way? He's upset too, that it is clear to him now that he has constructed this all in his head. That to her, he is no one, at most just a friend of her brother's.

Despite the disappointment, he cannot deny how his garden is changed just by her being there. The air, changed. The charge of his body moving through it, changed. There is even delight in knowing that Huda and Abbas noted that change within him. So she does not speak to him, she does not even lift her eyes to his, so she does not smile, it is still a pleasure, feeling this way, inhabiting this space he has lived in for years without a modicum of enchantment.

For once, he does not wish that everyone would leave as soon as possible. But as the sun begins to set they gather their coats and adjust their scarves and approach his mother to thank her for a wonderful afternoon, and one by one they go. The last moments of the day always make him uneasy, the changing color of the sky, the empty feeling of knowing another day is about to be swallowed by the dark. Even in this, he is so separate from his father, who waits for dusk to step out for his walk, either around the backyard or to the horse pasture streets away, looking up at the world as though its wonders were made to be beheld by him alone.

Her family leaves and she leaves with them. The garden is just a garden. The living room just a living room. The long haul up the staircase. The sound of the door shutting behind him. Alone again in his bedroom that is just a bedroom.

Something white on his pillow catches his eye. It is a piece of paper, folded into a tiny square. He unfolds it. It has been carefully ripped, as though it had been pressed down with a nail before being torn, and its edges are softened. He does not recognize the handwriting, but appreciates its neat, measured quality before reading it. It says: *I am afraid to lose my capacity to feel, to really feel.—A. P.S. What's it like?*

At first he is confused. Then it hits him: she is answering the question her mother had interrupted. She wants to continue their conversation.

He reads it again.

Then again.

Then one more time.

Then he sits at his desk and takes out a blank sheet of paper and a fine-tip black pen.

✧

HADIA WAKES TO a paper taped on her door: a drawing of a boy playing basketball, wearing red shoes and jumping impossibly high. Soon she realizes that posters just like it have been taped on every bare wall, on both sides of every door—even on the door of their parents' bedroom. Some posters are simple: drawings of red shoes sketched in marker, a black-and-white sketch of a boy smiling wide, the only color the red of his shoes. Some have quotes by boys in Amar's class.

> "THESE ARE THE BEST SHOES I'VE OWNED!"
> —Omar M.

> "MY PARENTS WERE SO KIND TO GET ME THESE SHOES."
> —Gabe M.

"I HAVE NOT TRIPPED ONCE WHEN WEARING THESE."
—Michael C.

Their favorite posters are the emotional appeals to Mumma and Baba, written in big, block letters:

"DON'T YOU WANT TO MAKE YOUR ONLY SON AND
YOUNGEST CHILD HAPPY FOR ONCE?"

"AFTER THIS I PROMISE TO NEVER ASK FOR ANYTHING ELSE.
LAST YEAR FOR MY BIRTHDAY I GOT A BOOK."

"ONE HUNDRED AND TWENTY DOLLARS IS NOTHING
IF IT BUYS SO MUCH HAPPINESS."

"WE HAD ENOUGH MONEY TO GET UGLY NEW
LIVING ROOM CURTAINS."

Just yesterday, Amar came home from school and announced that his best friend, Mark, had gotten new shoes. Mark was in Amar's third-grade class, and his first real friend. Amar often talked about Mark. How Mark was allowed to play video games every day. How Mark had the latest console. Mark got to eat in front of the TV. Baba told him that meant Mark was spoiled, not special. There was a rule in their house that Baba only let them bend on rare occasions: they were not allowed to go over to their friends' houses, they could only see them at school. Baba told them, "There is no such thing as friends, only family, and only family will never desert you."

Hadia disliked it when Baba said this, it was untrue and unfair, especially because Baba had friends from work and friends from mosque, who he was closer to than Mumma was to her few friends. And besides, Hadia thought, she had Danielle, who had been her friend since the first grade, and even now that they were in seventh grade and only saw each other during lunch or in PE, Danielle slowed her pace while running the mile to jog alongside Hadia, and if their classmates pointed to Hadia's head and asked her, "But aren't you dying under that thing?" it was Danielle who stood up to defend her, Danielle who shouted back at them, "Does anyone ever ask *you* if you're dying in *your* clothes?"

Hadia was the only girl in their grade who had never spent a night at a friend's house, had never spent a Saturday with one either, swinging in the park or wandering malls and trying on lip gloss and doing whatever else it was that girls did together. Instead, Hadia and Danielle shared a slam book that they decorated and filled with quizzes and journal entries written like letters to each other, and on weekends, Danielle called the house phone and Hadia would take the phone into her closet and pray to God that no one would pick up and listen in, and if Amar did, they had code names for everyone and their own version of pig latin.

Still, sometimes Hadia wondered if it was true, or possible, that someone who was not in her family could ever *really* love her. Baba's words made her think of her home like a fortress they could only leave to go to school or mosque or to the home of a family friend who spoke their language, and in this fortress she and her siblings were lucky, at least, to have each other.

Last night, before dinner, while Hadia was studying for her math test, Amar had knocked on her bedroom door and asked, "Do you think I should ask Baba to get the shoes for me?"

Amar always trusted her to know how their parents would react to things that he had done or wanted to do, as though he were not also their child who could predict them. She felt guilty about how little patience she had for her brother now. She used to appreciate his lingering in her doorway, how he would pause between his stories, thinking of what to say next, as if just speaking to her was the important thing. She did not miss their old games but did miss *wanting* to play them, wanting to run in their backyard together until she was out of breath. Amar felt it too. Sometimes the three of them would play again but Hadia would find an excuse to cut the game short, or would injure her character and die a tragic death, despite her siblings begging her to find a cure.

"How much are they?" she asked.

"A hundred and fifty dollars," he mumbled, so fast he blurred the numbers together. He watched her with a worried look on his face, as though her response would determine if he should have hope.

It was never going to happen. Mumma bought them shoes from the cheap shoe stores; they were allowed one pair a year, usually in the fall before school began, and they wore them until they became too tight or until the next school year.

"Definitely," she said, just so he would let her study in peace, but when he jumped off her desk and almost ran out the room, she did not know why she had said it.

That night at dinner Amar looked up at Baba from time to time. Mumma refilled bowls and brought the dishes out to the table, still steaming, rice and *dhaal* and *talawa gosh*, the dishes she cooked so often. She poured more for Amar before taking a seat. Amar did not even thank her. Hadia reached across the table to help herself to more rice. And then Amar asked for the shoes, and because her home was given to arguments, in the way she imagined other homes might be given to laughter, Amar continued to ask even after Baba refused him, his pleas growing more desperate as Baba's request to not be tested turned into a firm command.

"Are these the hundred and fifty dollar shoes?" Huda asked him.

Amar glared at Huda, then looked to Baba to see if he had reacted. Mumma had stopped eating but she did not look up from her plate. They knew Baba. Knew which of Baba's faces to not push further, knew that his reaction depended on how stressful his day had been. But Amar never knew when to stop. Hadia wiped her hand on her napkin so she could reach beneath the table to pat him, to warn him before it was too late.

"Baba, just this once can you—"

It was too late.

"Enough," Baba barked and banged his hand on the table and their dishes rattled. The light above them flickered. For a split second there was nothing but dark and the water in their glasses sloshed up before settling again.

"Do not ask me again," Baba yelled at him, his voice the rough and loud one, the one that made Hadia jump no matter how many times she had heard it, even when she expected it, even when it was not directed at her. In these moments she hated her father. How the fury he was capable of contorted his features and made his skin flush red. The little gems that dangled from the chandelier trembled.

"There is no sense in shoes that are over a hundred dollars. No sense," Baba said furiously.

Amar turned to Huda and spat out, "I hate you."

"What did you say?" Baba yelled.

"He said he hated me." Huda sat up in her chair.

"I heard what he said," Baba snapped at her.

Huda opened her mouth to argue but saw how Baba glared at her. Even Mumma looked at Huda angrily. And Hadia decided in that moment that she too hated them all—her brother, who made everything difficult for himself. Her mother, who turned against her own children just to stand by her husband. Huda with the smug look on her face, and how provoking Amar's anger was like a game to her. They were all cruel to each other. They could not even get through one dinner. She stared at the food on her plate and made a silent pact with herself: she would work hard, she would study, and she would find herself a new family. A new house that never got angry, a home where weeks would pass without a voice raised.

"What did you say, Amar?" Baba asked Amar again.

Amar stared at his plate. His face was blank. He pushed his plate forward. He lost his appetite so quickly. Hadia could see the way his eyes filled with tears but he bit the inside of his cheek so he would not cry.

"Amar, I asked you a question," Baba shouted. "Look at me."

He did not look up. No one in their family was as stubborn as Amar. He was even more stubborn than their father. His lip quivered and what had hardened in Hadia a moment ago suddenly softened: she did not hate him, she took back the thought, reached under the table and placed her hand on his knee, pressed on it just a little.

"You never tell your sisters you hate them, do you understand?" Baba said, pointing his finger at Amar.

Amar still did not flinch. "Did you hear me?" Baba kept shouting. Underneath the table, out of sight, Amar placed his hand, so much smaller than hers, on top of Hadia's and squeezed it.

SO WHEN SHE wakes the next morning to see pamphlets with facts and testimonials slipped under their doors, and posters taped all over the home, she is surprised. While the rest of them slept, Amar had taken a stack of Baba's good printer paper and begun his campaign. By midday, a petition circulates, five blank spaces under the line: WE, THE PEOPLE OF OUR HOUSE, BELIEVE AMAR DESERVES THE SHOES, everyone signing their name except Baba. Mumma asks Amar to come to lunch and Amar shouts from upstairs that he is protesting peacefully, and that means he will not eat, and Hadia is sent with a plate that she sets by his door. An hour later, it is found empty in the sink. And even though Baba had been so adamantly against Amar asking for the shoes last night, he remains silent during Amar's campaign, and Hadia wonders if he is curious to see how far Amar will go.

"I would like to deliver a speech," Amar announces at the head of the dinner table.

Mumma turns to Baba and touches his arm. "Let him," she says. "Let's see what he says."

Mumma smiles. She appears to be proud of him. Hadia is confused—how could she be amused by an inherently defiant act? They wait to see what Baba will say. Baba raises his eyebrows and extends his hand toward Amar, palm up, as if to say, well then, proceed. The gesture surprises Amar too. They take their seats at the dinner table and Amar waits until they are quiet and facing him before pulling a piece of binder paper from his pocket, unfolding it, coughing into his fist twice like he had seen in some movie, and beginning to read.

His hands shake. His voice trembles. He reminds everyone that Baba's signature is the only one missing from the petition. Then the rest of his speech is written in the form of a letter addressed directly to Baba, telling Baba all the things Amar will do if his wish is granted. He holds the paper high so his face is hidden, and Hadia looks from Mumma to Baba. They are both listening. There is a tenderness to their expressions. It seems very possible that Baba will grant him his wish. She has never thought to do anything like it, has never thought to continue to fight for what she wants after Baba has told her no. Hadn't she wanted a pet? Hadn't she wanted to go to the movies with Danielle, wanted to read the book Mumma said she was too young for after flipping through it and forbidding her?

"I will try more on my spelling tests," Amar says, and at this Baba leans forward and stops him.

This year, Amar has gotten no more than six correct on a twenty-word spelling test. His teacher has constantly sent letters home, concerned about his performance in various subjects, calling Mumma Baba in for extra meetings. One more hour would be cut from Amar's television time, one more toy taken away, but he has never improved.

"Let's make a deal," Baba says.

Everyone blinks at Baba. Amar lowers his paper, nods eagerly; he is more surprised than any of them.

"If you get one hundred percent on your next spelling test, I will get you the shoes."

"Done."

"Not one word misspelled."

"I can do it. I will."

"This week's test, Amar."

"Deal," Amar says, extending his hand.

Baba takes his hand and Amar shakes it solemnly, looking Baba in the eye. Then Baba claps his hands together and says let's eat, before returning to his seat, and in that moment her father seems like a gracious man, and Hadia looks up at him, and then again, in awe.

ON THE MORNING of the test they are almost late for school because Amar refuses to get out of bed. Hadia and Huda hear him whining while they brush their teeth.

"I am sick," he says. "I swear it, I can't go. I don't want to."

When Hadia peers in from the doorway, Mumma is parting the curtain and Amar is hiding under his covers.

"You have to try," Mumma says to him softly. "You have to at least try."

He peeks from the covers and relaxes a little when he sees Hadia, and Hadia tells him if he hurries she will test him one last time in the car.

"But my sore throat," he says, touching his neck, "my dizzy feeling."

Mumma pulls his covers away until he has no choice but to sit up, and she says good boy to him, good boy, using her gentlest voice as if he were still a baby, and Amar gets up slowly, still touching his throat in a last attempt to fool them.

"You're good at studying," Amar had told her the night he struck the deal. "Can you help me?"

"It's a spelling test. You just have to memorize things."

"I know that," he said, but he looked embarrassed, as if the thought had only just occurred to him. "I just know that you get one hundred percent on things."

In the few days leading up to the test, Amar came to her bedroom after school holding the list of words and waiting for her instruction. It was so simple. She hardly had to help. She glanced at him from time to time to see how often he looked at the wall, swayed in his seat, busied himself with something on the floor.

But he was dedicated. He may have shifted in his chair but he never left it. After he wrote out each word ten times he would ask her, what now? Write them ten times more, she told him. He did not doubt her, or complain, as she anticipated he might. Each night she tested him. Beautiful, she said, and watched him write it down. *Bookcase. Photograph. Analyze. Cylinder. Approximate. Consequences.* While she graded them he bit the inside of his cheek, kicked his feet back and forth. Ten right, ten wrong. When she told him that, he appeared sadder than she had ever seen, and she reassured him that he had another day to study. Hadia helped him come up with songs for the particularly difficult ones. He hummed as she tested him. The night before the actual test, she tested him again. He got them all right but one—*approximate*—the one that had given him trouble since the beginning.

"It is just one word," Hadia told him. "By morning you will have it memorized."

"You really think so?" he asked her.

"I really do," she said. She was glad she said it: it took so little of her and it put him at ease, made him happy.

But in the car he is visibly worried. Hadia tests him the whole way and he spells each word aloud. Still, he gets *approximate* wrong.

"I'm so proud of you no matter what happens," Mumma says to him. "I am so happy you studied."

Amar slams the car door and disappears behind the school gates. He becomes one of the hundreds of kids hurrying to make it before the late bell, and Hadia tries not to meet Mumma's eyes, afraid that Mumma will realize that she has not once, not ever, told Hadia she is proud of her for studying, even though it is all Hadia does.

"I'm sure I got them all right," he says to her after school that day. "Thank you. The songs played in my head when I took the test."

"What about *approximate*?" she asks.

He is silent. He twists his mouth and presses his tongue against his cheek. Then he lifts his dirty white shoe and reveals its sole. *Approximate* is written on the heel in black pen.

"I wrote it just in case. But I didn't really use it. I just checked to make sure I got it right."

Hadia's breath catches in her. It had never occurred to her to cheat.

"*Khassam* you won't tell Baba?"

"*Khassam*," she tells him.

3

BY THE TIME SHE HAS REACHED THE BOTTOM
of the stairs she has shaken the heaviness of sleep and now moves
quickly, aware of the little time they have left to eat. Fifth day of
Ramadan. Middle of the night. She flips rotis she rolled out last
night. The heat of the stove dissolves the numbness of her face, her
eyelids. One after another and they rise and she presses down with
her spatula, feels the rush of heat as they deflate. In her tired state,
the black spots appear like unique patterns. Hadia and Huda are
used to fasting but this is the first year that Amar—only ten, five
years before his *baligh* age—is trying. The first three days he kept
half *roza,* broke it when Layla coaxed him with macaroni and
sliced fruit, reminding him he was still too young. He could wait to
assume the obligation that would last his lifetime. But last night,
after she finished telling them stories about the Prophet's love for
his grandson Hussain—a rare end to their nights now—he insisted
he would fast the full day and that she should wake him for *sehri.*
She regards him as younger at ten than her daughters seemed at
nine, when they began wearing hijab and praying and fasting during Ramadan. *Were you two also that little then?* she wonders when
she sees her daughters, now thirteen and fourteen.

The rotis are put into their box and the lid sealed shut. Now she
fries an egg for Rafiq, reheats leftover spinach for the children. She
rinses a bunch of purple grapes. The month of Ramadan awakens
a primal instinct in her: she is sensitive to how much her children

eat, watches them drink a glass of water and then gulp milk and still worries for them. Some nights, when she feels particularly affectionate toward her daughters for fasting, she piles the food on trays and carries them either to the girls' beds or to a corner in her room, where they huddle and feast half awake in the night.

She does not know why Amar decided this was the year he would try to keep fasts. More perplexing is that it seems he genuinely wants to, despite fasting being the most difficult and tiring ritual for the body. First begin to pray, she had told him. First stop bothering your sisters so much. First learn to control your anger. But who was she to say no? What was the phrase—beggars cannot be choosers? If this was how he wanted to participate, she would support him. She would make it easier for all of them. She would let them stay up at night if it meant they were snacking and not waking her or Rafiq, let them sleep in during the day. She would plan the meals that broke their fast around their tastes. This was the month she allowed them takeout days in a row, endless helpings of dessert. She wondered if Amar's recent insistence might be because his friend, Abbas, Seema's boy, had just turned fifteen and begun fasting himself. Layla liked him and his younger brothers—much more than she liked Seema—partly because of how much their friendship meant to her son. But also because Abbas always made a point to say *salaam* to her and he dipped his head in that respectful way before joining Amar outside. Or maybe her son was just reacting to Ramadan, a month so holy she was sure it softened the heart of every believer.

She is startled when she hears Rafiq's footsteps. Sometimes he wakes with enough time for them to prepare *sehri* together, and they stumble about the kitchen. Other times it is just her, turning on only the lights she needs to see the space before her.

"Let's eat upstairs?" she says, and he nods his slow, half-asleep nod and brings out the trays. Layla sets glasses on one tray and pours water in some and milk in the others, ever conscious of the ticking clock, anxious there will be no time left for her children to eat before being hungry all day.

71

"We don't need to wake Amar," Rafiq says, when she counts out five plates. He lifts the heavier tray.

"But he insisted—he wants to."

"He doesn't need to yet."

"Shouldn't we encourage him?"

"On any other day, yes. Tomorrow is going to be the hottest day of the summer, the longest *roza*, and he's still going to want to play basketball."

She returns a plate to the shelf and follows with the second tray. Sometimes he surprises her with his lenience, other times it is his strict adherence that unsettles her. She could guess, but could never accurately predict, where he would stand on a matter. They set down the trays in their room and Rafiq begins to divide food onto the plates. Layla goes to wake the girls. Amar will be so angry in the morning when he realizes no one woke him. You promised you would, you promised—she would hear it all day. Promises meant more to Amar. And she had no doubt he would refuse breakfast, refuse lunch, and if he ate it would only be in secret.

She does not want another day disrupted by his bad behavior, the domino effect it has on Hadia and Huda. Yesterday there had been one of those bizarre, rare hot summer thunderstorms that forced her children to entertain themselves indoors. Before the storm passed, all three of them were in time-out—or maybe the term was "trouble" now; they were getting too old for the reprimands she knew how to implement. Some fight over the television remote and she was exhausted. The television screen black, Hadia sent to her room, Huda to hers, Layla's voice hoarse from shouting that this was not appropriate behavior, and Amar was to sit quietly in the kitchen with her and think about what he had done, how he had thrown the remote at a wall so the battery compartment came loose and the batteries fell out. Huda screamed that he had aimed it at her, while Amar insisted loudly that he had not. Layla did not know what to do, except to tell them to scatter. Maybe her hold over them was lost but Rafiq, when he was home, still had his spell that he could conjure just by looking at them, just by sitting in the same room. They listened to him and were not rude to him and for whatever reason they had decided that not only would they not listen to her, but they would be rude too, openly questioning her decisions—Hadia mumbling, of course you let Amar stay downstairs still, and Huda stomping up the stairs after her.

Amar and Layla had stood in the kitchen in silence. Amar watched the rain hit the window, anger emanating from him like steam rising from a hot mug. Upstairs, either Hadia or Huda slammed her door shut and banged things around in her room to emphasize her frustration.

Amar pointed to the glass and said, "Look, when it rains harder the drops join together more quickly."

She raised her finger to her lips to shush him, but when she turned back to the window she saw what he meant.

She waited for the rain to stop its storming and stepped out into her garden to check on her tomatoes, and the moisture from the damp grass seeped through her sandals. They were fine. Little green tomatoes just beginning to grow. Amar watched her from behind the sliding door, his face pressed against the glass so his eyebrows looked strange and flattened down. She tried not to smile. He was so alone in their home. Hadia and Huda were ready to comfort each other. Her daughters' faces were not at the window to see her and accuse her of special treatment, so she waved Amar over and he came. They walked together and he followed closely. What did he notice that she didn't? He tugged at a leaf of her basil plant as if to show her he was angry still, then let go before it snapped, the bush shaking and drops of rainwater flecking out in all directions. Her son knew how to look closely at the route of rain on glass. She had not taught him this. What could she teach him about how to be in the world other than how to behave?

Amar looked at her in a way that asked, have you forgiven me yet? And because he looked at her in that way—his initial anger replaced by shyness—she knew the power was tilted in her favor, and she could try to extend his guilt, hoping it would make him think twice next time.

"You know, Baba would be very angry if he saw what you did today."

They didn't care how she was affected. Maybe children could never imagine their mother as being anyone other than their mother.

"I already know that." He put his hands in his pockets. Then looked up at her from the corner of his eye. "Are you going to tell him?"

"No."

"Will they?" He nodded toward Huda's window. How quickly he separated himself from them.

"Maybe if you apologize they won't."

His face soured. What was it about an apology that was so difficult? It always felt like it cost something personal and precious. Only now that she was a mother was she so aware of this: the stubbornness and pride that came with being human, the desire to be loyal and generous that came too, each impulse at odds with the other.

"You have to apologize when you have wronged someone no matter what, especially if it is your sisters."

What more could she say? She felt a consistent tug to give to him, to give to all of them, sliced apples and time in the sun, a spot in the shade, but something more too, an instruction on how to be in the world. It particularly tugged at her then, watching Amar kneel and pull at another leaf until it tore. The smell of fresh basil. These were their daily battles. And every day there were fallouts, and reparations made by the time Huda asked for salt and Amar was the first to pass it to her.

By the time her girls stumble into her bedroom they have only thirty minutes left to eat. Layla tells them they have twenty, hoping they will eat quickly, then bites her tongue: her *roza* has not even begun yet and she has lied. But they never care to feed themselves as much as she cares to feed them. They sit cross-legged on the floor, eyes blinking at nothing, wincing and groaning when she switches on the light.

74

"Hurry and eat," Rafiq reminds them, and they eat so slowly she cannot believe it.

"You didn't wake me," Amar says from the doorway. There is hurt in his voice, he sounds like a little boy, he rubs his eyelids. One leg of his pajamas has gathered up at his knee.

Layla looks to Rafiq. They have not brought up a plate for him. If he is already grumpy from sleep, refusing him will only make him cry. Rafiq looks at him, and then at his watch. Then he taps at the space next to him, grabs another roti and places it folded on his plate, pours some of the fried spinach next to his egg. Yawning, Amar enters, and half asleep he leans against Rafiq as they eat from the same plate.

✧

HADIA WAKES TO the smell of biryani cooking and the news that Mumma is throwing her an early birthday party. On Wednesday, she will be nine. Mumma presents her with the dress she will wear, an American one that embarrasses Hadia when she sees it dangling from Mumma's finger. Mustard yellow and not at all fashionable: a giant swoop of a skirt that swallows her up and drags past her ankles, puffy sleeves and a lace collar. Her embarrassment only deepens when she sees Huda wearing the same only in magenta, a fact that makes Huda spin and say, look, we're like twins now. But when Mumma beams as she lines the three of them up against the wall under their old HAPPY BIRTHDAY sign, Hadia tries to push her disappointment aside and smile for Baba, who twists the camera lens back and forth before photographing them.

"You're impossible," Mumma says in the bathroom when Hadia asks if she can wear something else. "You complain if I give you Indian clothes, you complain if I get you a dress after you insist on dresses."

"I didn't mean this," she says, her voice low and head bent, speaking into the folds of the skirt. Mumma brushes her hair roughly, pulls her hair into a too-tight braid. When she finishes the braid Mumma looks up at Hadia's reflection. The expression on her face softens.

"Your ninth birthday is a very special one," Mumma says tenderly. "Are you ready to start wearing hijab? It's your choice. But you know you are nine now, and so you should choose soon."

Mumma wore a scarf whenever they left their house or whenever a man came to visit. Almost all older girls at mosque wore it. Hadia always thought it was just what would happen to her when she turned nine, never thought that she would not wear it. She considers both her options: what Mumma would think if she wore it and what Mumma would think if she didn't.

Hadia is quiet, so Mumma continues, "Remember, nine is the year your record of deeds begins to be kept. You're old enough now to know right from wrong."

"I know that," she says, louder than she intended, and she twists out from beneath Mumma's hand on her shoulder.

The doorbell rings and Mumma leaves to receive the guests. It is a midday party. Hadia tiptoes to see her reflection in the bathroom mirror. She runs her hand along the ridges of her braid, not a single hair unkempt, and considers untying and untangling it. Mumma would be angry but unable to do anything, because all the aunties and uncles would be watching, and watching her kindly, knowing it was her birthday.

Last night, Mumma had told them the first part of the story of Prophet Joseph, and it is this story she thinks of as she waits for the last possible second before having to go downstairs. It has always been one of her favorite stories, but Amar, who is five, hadn't heard it before.

"Why did the brothers throw him into the ditch?" he asked.

"Because they were jealous," Huda said.

"And is jealousy a sin?" Mumma asked.

They all nodded.

"What happens when you sin?" Mumma asked them.

She was always making good stories boring by asking them questions like that after, questions that made the stories feel less like magic and more like lessons. Amar looked at Hadia to offer an answer, but she had none.

"The angel on your left shoulder writes it down in his notebook," Huda said.

"That is true. But you also get a speck on your heart, a dark, small speck."

"A dark speck?" Amar asked.

"Yes," Mumma said, "with every sin. Jealousy is a sin. That's a speck. Lying is a sin. Another speck. Each of them like stains."

"A permanent marker stain?" Amar asked. He had recently gotten in trouble for using a permanent marker to draw on the window, a stain that had not gone away completely even after Mumma scrubbed. Now he lifted every marker before he used it and asked, is this a permanent marker?

"Yes," Mumma said, as she brushed his hair, "a permanent stain. And with every sin, the heart grows harder and darker. Until it is so heavy and black it cannot tell good from evil anymore. It cannot even tell that it wants to be good."

All three of them were silent and horrified, until Mumma said, "Of course, there is always the opportunity of asking Allah for forgiveness. One must be remorseful."

"Resourceful?" Hadia asked.

"No, remorse. Deeply regretting it. And resolving never to do it again." Mumma made her hand into a fist and shook it.

"Are the brothers remorseful?" Amar asked. They had only reached the point of Joseph's brothers throwing him into the ditch, ripping his coat and covering it with the blood of a sheep, and taking it back to their father. Hadia's favorite part of that story was when Joseph was reunited with his father, but it would probably take three nights to reach the end.

"They are very ashamed. But it is too late."

"What's ashamed?" Amar asked.

Mumma looked up at the ceiling for a moment as if she were wondering how to answer.

"When you do something you know you shouldn't have. And you are afraid to show your face."

Amar looked down, as if considering Mumma's explanation.

"Why is it too late?" Huda asked.

"Nothing can be done. Joseph is gone."

There is a knock on the bathroom door and Huda calls her name. Hadia tells her she is coming. She looks at her reflection, rubs where she imagines her heart to be, and wonders if there will be dark specks inside her heart if she does not wear a scarf after Wednesday. Last night was the first time she heard of the specks collecting like dust on the heart. And if not wearing a scarf was a speck, would a new one bloom every day she chose not to?

She weaves through the guests, lifts her cupped hand to her forehead in *adaab* to the uncles seated on the couch, accepts the gifts or envelopes from the aunties with a polite thank-you. She watches Huda, standing near the sliding door with some girls her age, telling them about the goodie bags. Huda's hair is cut short, like a boy's. There is an M&M's packet in each one, she hears her say. Huda has a whole year before she has to make any decision, and this feels unfair. She feels apart from all of them—the girls talking about M&M's and the women wearing *dupattas* or scarves on their heads discussing what she does not care about, and she looks past them all to her plum tree, its pretty purple leaves rustling, its branches swaying slightly, and no one surrounding it or standing beneath its shade. How she likes to sit there and listen to the wind pass through its branches.

Some children are playing tag and others are playing hopscotch on squares drawn with chalk on the cement. Their fingers are dusty, powdery blue and purple. The girls jumping are young, their hair is worn down and it lifts up and falls wildly as they hop from square to square. She wishes her mother had told her about the party, so she could have invited her friends, Danielle and Charlotte, but she dismisses that thought as soon as it comes, realizing she would be too embarrassed to wear this dress in front of them, too shy to explain that the dinner is biryani and that there are no games planned, just children released into the yard, and that the adults are all there because it was more a party for them to mingle and less to celebrate her turning nine. What will she have to tell Danielle and Charlotte about wearing a scarf? What are the reasons to wear it, other than that everyone she knows from mosque wears it? And a frightening thought: What if after Wednesday her friends treat her differently? Will they know that she is the same Hadia, with or without her hair showing?

Hadia reaches the plum tree at the far end of the backyard. The only thing beyond it is its own roots and the wooden fence, and she picks at the bark that she loves, picks at it until a small piece breaks off, and she looks at it jagged in her palm, turns it around. There are many trees that she appreciates but only two in this world she loves, and the plum tree is one of them. She is lucky that the other is in their front yard, the magnolia tree, visible from her bedroom window. The plums are always too high for her and she remembers when she was little her father would let her climb onto his back to pluck one. Would he speak to her after Wednesday if she chose not to wear hijab?

"Happy birthday, Hadia."

It is Abbas Ali, the eldest Ali boy. Hadia wraps her hand around the piece of bark. Its rough edges bite.

"You too," she says.

Abbas laughs a little and she feels silly, realizing her mistake. Hadia looks down at her dress. If it were a yellow crayon in a crayon box it would be the one that was never used. It would stay sharp and unbroken. That and the gray one. Even the brown would be used before this kind of yellow. Abbas walks up to the plum tree and touches it with his hand also. He is the only other person here her age. She thinks that maybe she should tell him this, and that they can be friends for the duration of the party. Abbas's hair is a little long for a boy's, it falls in his face and covers the tops of his ears. If she started to wear a scarf he would never see her hair again. Danielle and Charlotte might still, when they were in the bathroom at school or if they came to her house, but Abbas is a boy who is not related to her and so he would never.

"This is my favorite tree," she tells him.

Abbas looks up at it, and Hadia looks up too, past the branches and the leaves and the little plums straight to the bright sky. She squints.

79

"Because the leaves are kind of purple?"

"No. Just because."

Abbas nods. They stand side by side. They watch children playing freeze tag, standing still, shocked expressions on their faces, arms stretched out and waiting for someone to tap their fingers. Maybe if she started wearing a scarf she would grow up right away. Maybe she would not be able to run at a party like this one. No boy would be able to touch her to unfreeze her or tag her. And she thinks of how, sometimes, when they go to Seema Aunty's house, they all play soccer in the backyard because the Ali family has two soccer goalposts, and Abbas always invites her to play, and she does play even though she is not very good. But at least she is getting better, according to him. The last time they played was at his brother Saif's birthday, and there was a jumpy castle too, and a popcorn machine. And it is when she is looking at Abbas in his green T-shirt that she thinks, I will not be able to play soccer anymore. Not with him, anyway. And I won't get any better than scoring one goal in the last five minutes of our last game.

"Why aren't you happy if it's your party?"

Of course he is her friend. The wind blows and the branches move and make their wind and leaves sounds, and Hadia's dirty-yellow dress fills up with air and she holds it down with her hands. Even her lace collar flares up. Someone opens the door and it is one of the uncles, holding a folded white cloth, which means the men are going to gather on the lawn and pray soon.

"I didn't know I was going to have one," she confesses, and once she does, it is easy to say, "I don't know if I will like being nine. And I don't like this dress."

Abbas is quiet. He stretches for a plum, but he is too short. His fingers are inches away from the nearest branch, the plum hanging. Hadia is grateful he does not try jumping up and down to reach it, drawing attention to them and kicking up dirt. She wants to suggest climbing onto his back and reaching up. But that is forbidden. She knows that. She wonders what the size of the black mark on her heart would be if she did, and if it is worse than jealousy, worse than telling a lie. The uncle is trying to put the white sheet down but it keeps lifting in the wind.

"Why not? You look like the sun."

She smiles for the first time that day. Baba barks her name in his angry voice, then says nothing after. He begins walking across the lawn to them. She looks at Abbas and remembers why they are not friends, not really. Maybe they are "acquaintances"—the word Baba uses when he tells her, remember, boys are not your friends, they are acquaintances when you are in the classroom, and you have to keep your distance. Abbas walks away without saying anything, becomes one of the children running, lifts his baby sister in his arms. His shirt is the kind of green that would get used a lot.

"*Gee*, Baba?" She uses her almost childlike voice. The little piece of bark cuts into her palm. She drops it into the dirt when he looks like he is a little bit mad at her, she rubs her reddened palm with her thumb.

"Why aren't you playing with the other girls?" he asks.

"They aren't my friends."

The uncle silences the children, points to the house, and they begin to march inside. The older boys linger, knowing it is time to pray soon. Baba puts his hand on her head, and his hand has a weight to it, and Hadia tiptoes up to him a little to feel the pressure. She wants to say to him, remember when I climbed on your back and plucked the plums? But before she can, he reaches up, wraps his hand around one and tugs, the whole branch bending a bit before his hand returns with a small, deep-purple plum. He hands it to her.

"Thank you, Baba," she mumbles, "and for the party too."

He nods. They both turn to the men who have spread out the white cloth. Men are gathering in a row on the grass. She knows Baba will leave soon, walk up to take his place in the prayer line. As if he can hear her thoughts, he says to her, "Now you have to start praying too."

Hadia looks up at him. She senses that he is proud. When she is standing next to Baba she thinks that she is ready for it all. He places his hand back on her head and she moves the plum from hand to hand, feeling its weight.

"Baba?"

"Hm."

"Do you think I should start wearing a scarf?"

A man begins reciting the *adhaan*. She sees that Abbas Ali has found a spot in the line. Even though he does not have to. He is nine too, but won't have to start praying until he is fifteen. He will never have to wear a scarf. They are so lucky. She wonders if seeing him there makes his parents happy, and if God has an opposite of a dark spot on the heart if someone does something good, like a shimmer of gold. The wind makes small ripples in his green shirt. Baba is silent for the duration of the *adhaan*. Then the man is finished, and Hadia knows there is a small slot of time before the second call, which calls Baba to come, to pray. When Baba speaks he does so slowly, as if he is being very careful about every word.

"I think that you should. It would be good if you did. And it is *wajib* on you now, you know. It would be a sin not to. But. It is your decision."

She looks up at him, dark from the sunlight behind him. She does not squint, does not blink, reaches up to tug at the little tail of her hair that is not woven tight in a braid, the soft clump like a paintbrush, bristly at its edges.

✧

HE OPENS HIS door to his father's face and knows immediately that something terrible has happened. Rain pounds the roof, wind rattles the windows—an unexpected storm that was light drizzle just an hour ago. Hadia is still home on her break from college and the three of them are staying up late reading together. He is afraid to ask what is wrong. His father's face is pale, his expression unfamiliarly softened. He is fully dressed in a button-up shirt and pants, even though it is well past one in the morning, and he had retired hours earlier.

"The Ali boy—" his father begins, but a break in his voice stops him from continuing.

Everyone called the Ali boys the eldest Ali boy, the skinny Ali boy, the youngest Ali boy. To Amar, the Ali boys were just Abbas and Abbas's younger brothers. And their sister, Amira Ali, who was perhaps the only child in their entire community known by her full name. No one needed any other marker to distinguish her. She was already herself, even as a child. He knew he was referred to as Rafiq's boy, and when he was younger the community members would add, that naughty one.

"Which one?"

It is Hadia who asks. They both turn to look at her as if noticing her for the first time, and the look on her face makes Amar's mouth suddenly dry.

"The eldest one," his father says. "A car accident."

"Abbas?" Amar asks, and Baba nods, and next to him Amar hears Hadia make a small animal sound.

He leans against his doorframe. Then somehow he is sitting, somehow his hands are flat against the rough carpet. His father is saying, I am sorry. But he's alive? Amar thinks he asks, but his father doesn't reply and anyway, he already knows. His first absolutely stupid thought is to wonder who he will sit next to at mosque now. And just as the possibility of loss begins to open up beneath him, he thinks of Amira. Her note is hidden in the side pocket of his History notebook. He has hesitated from tucking it into his keepsake box because then his box would become not where he stored his own journals, but where he hid that one reminder of her. He has composed a dozen letters to her in the four days since receiving it, but has discarded them all. He feels a sudden urge to be beside her, and he is surprised by his thoughts—by the way they pull him in her direction.

His father says he is going to the Ali house. His voice so thin it sounds nothing like him. When someone passed away in their community, people gathered in the house of the bereaved every day until the funeral. They brought food, sat in circles, read prayers and passages from holy texts, dedicated the merits to the deceased.

"I'm coming too," Hadia says.

"Unnecessary," his father says to her. "It is late and inappropriate."

"I'm coming," she says, a determination in her voice that Amar had not expected her to ever use against their father. She looks up at the ceiling, holds tight on to her own arm.

"I want to see Amira," she insists, expressing the very thought that had become a beat in Amar's mind. Their father, worn out by the news, does not have the energy to deny her.

OUTSIDE, RAINDROPS DARKEN their clothes. His father turns to Amar as if he is about to say something, but touches his shoulder instead, just for a moment, before retracting his hand to unlock the car door. Amar does not flinch at his touch.

"You're distracted," Abbas had said to him, the last time he saw him alive, four days ago at the *jashan* Mumma had thrown for Hadia. They were standing in the food line together and it was true, Amar was distracted, and more reserved because of it. After years of not having anything to hide from Abbas, he was embarrassed to find that his first secret was about Abbas's younger sister. When Amar gave him a flimsy excuse as to why he would not join him for a smoke walk, Abbas looked at him skeptically, a look that Amar recalls so vividly now it sickens him. But Abbas shrugged, talked more to make up for Amar's silence, and instead of asking someone else to accompany him, he stayed by Amar's side.

Now there would never be another walk to the corner and back, a moment as simple as looking at him and then the sky. Abbas was young, Hadia's age. Amar is afraid he will throw up, or worse, cry, so he tries not to think of the way Abbas gave him a reason to be excited about being a member of their community. Or that time when Amar, Abbas, and Abbas's brothers, Saif and Kumail, passed a joint around for the first time, the windows open, fan on, candles and incense burning. Abbas made him feel that he had a brother, as though that bond was possible for him.

At school Amar was valued for the very qualities that were looked down upon in his house. There he was not disrespectful but funny. There it was good that he was interested in English class, in the poems and stories his teachers assigned. As far as he was aware, none of his school friends knew what it was like to come home to a house that was quiet the way his was, where everything was forbidden to them—loud music or talking back, wearing shirts with band logos printed on them. A father who yelled, a mother who looked out the window or spent the day praying and tending her garden. A family that wanted him to change who he was, to become a respectable man who obeyed his father's every word, and followed every command given by his father's God. Or what it was like to live with the knowledge that his father would disown him if he found something as harmless as a packet of cigarettes under his mattress. To not have that kind of love. To not even believe in it.

But Abbas knew these things. They would leave the mosque to walk in the parking lot, talking about what Amar could never voice to anyone else, the streetlights reflected in the murky puddles, and Amar confessing he *did* want to believe in God, in his father's God, and he was afraid to lose that desire. Abbas touching his shoulder to stop him from stepping into a deep puddle, telling him, "You know, just because you don't listen doesn't mean you don't believe."

Abbas knew when to stop fighting with his parents, and how to guard the secrets that would hurt them, and in turn cause him to be hurt by their rejection of him. He did not resent that this was the way it had to be. But Amar could not do that without feeling like a hypocrite. And now Amar pulls the seat belt away from him because it feels too tight, he bites on his knuckle, afraid to think of who he has lost. The one person in front of whom he could sin under the watch of their fathers' God without being cast aside.

His father has forgotten to turn the wipers on, and neither Hadia nor Amar reminds him. Drops of water gather on the windshield when the car slows to stop at a red light, and each drop has caught within it the color red. He turns to Hadia in the backseat. She leans her head against the car door and looks out the window. When the

85

car trembles, so does she. She refuses to meet his eyes even though she knows he is looking at her. He has always prided himself on being able to discern how Hadia is feeling by studying the look on her face, the way she carries herself, what she does not say. But tonight it is impossible to make sense of her.

Abbas's street is filled with parked cars. It seems news has reached every community member. This is a tragedy, he thinks as he steps out of the car and the door slams behind him. Tonight they have all lost a young man, barely twenty-one. This night, he knows, will be a mark that divides his life. They are soaked by the time they enter the house, which is warm from the people that will continue to visit in shifts. It is sickening to think of Abbas as a body to be buried. The first room—the family room—is full of women. Amira is not there. But Abbas's mother, Seema Aunty, is surrounded by women who are speaking to her as if she were a child, hugging her to offer their condolences, and she collapses into their embraces, each one making her cry anew. He is hit with the strange sensation that Seema Aunty has comforted him before, that he has felt safe in this very room, and he is not sure if it is from a memory or a dream. He cannot look at her. Women sit in clusters reading from the Quran. Hadia takes a seat in the corner, by herself, without reaching for one of the books. The look on her face unsettles him, a vacancy to her expression that makes him want to shake her. He turns away and follows his father into the men's section.

He tells his father he will be right back. His father nods and continues on without him. The Ali house is grand and beautiful, and Amar knows every corridor. All that playing hide-and-seek in the dark, even now he could close his eyes and find his way. The corridor to his right has a staircase that leads upstairs, one used only by the Ali family. He stands at the foot of the staircase. Behind him, he hears murmurs, no one wanting to speak loudly in a house of mourning. It is a risk to walk upstairs, an even greater risk to walk straight down the hall to her bedroom and knock on her door, and perhaps there would be nothing more shameful for the two of them than if they were caught, speaking alone in an empty bedroom.

But this is his life. This is exactly what he wants to do with it. He walks straight to the door he's known for years was hers and feels his knuckles touch it for the first time. An entire minute passes. He turns twice to look at the empty hallway behind him, afraid to hear any approaching footsteps. Then the door opens. Just enough to reveal her face, then a little more. This—that she opened the door wider upon seeing his face—feels like an accomplishment. His chest pinches when he sees the way crying has exhausted her features. He feels guilty for his quickening heartbeat, guilty for how aware he is that they are alone. She steps back from the door, giving him a space to enter, and he does.

"I couldn't be downstairs," she confesses, as though they were already friends. She speaks in a voice unlike the one he remembers. "Too many people. No one who really knew him."

He wondered, on the drive, how they would address what had happened. And now he sees it is as easy as saying "knew" instead of "know." Her eyes rimmed red are a shocking green. He takes in the little details of her bedroom—a wide bed by the window, the curtains open, the vicious downpour of rain outside. Her walls have been painted a robin's-egg blue. There is a white desk beside him and on it a framed photograph that looks like it has been set down where it does not belong. He lifts it. It is a picture of the four of them—Abbas, Saif, Kumail, and her. Abbas's smiling face is young, and Amar remembers that was the year they had all gone camping with the mosque group, and he and Abbas had taken a walk without turning on their flashlights. They thought that was courage. They stood in the center of a dark trail and listened to the sounds of the night. The pattern of the spaces between leaves that moonlight made on the path. The force of the wind through all those trees. He feels sick, almost dizzy, but tries to compose himself; he has not come to be comforted.

"It's from Kumail's birthday," she says, and he realizes he has not looked up from the photograph. Her voice is soft. She continues,

"That night we all went out to dinner. Just the four of us. Abbas Bhai had just gotten his first job, and he was eager to pay."

"That sandwich shop," he says.

Abbas had only worked there for seven months, but he bragged about his skills for years to come, made them sandwiches when they were hanging out.

"It was exciting because our parents weren't there, because we were doing something sort of grown up for once. At least that is why I was excited. I don't think they would have included me if it hadn't been Kumail's birthday."

She does not look away from his face when she speaks to him.

"That's not true," he tries.

She smiles, very slightly, as though she had not wanted to. It falls from her face quickly. She bites her lip then releases it. The door behind him is all but closed. They are so alone. Even if they spoke in hushed voices, anyone standing outside would be able to hear them. And if he knows it, so must she, but still she does not ask him to step away.

"This was the year we—"

"Broke the kitchen window?" She half smiles again.

"I was going to say all went to the camp."

She was right. That year he kicked the soccer ball so hard the kitchen window shattered. The four of them—Kumail, Abbas, Saif, Amar—stared at the space where the glass had been for a good minute, until Seema Aunty's shocked face appeared there, and even when she began yelling none of them blamed him.

"You didn't come back for weeks after that," she says.

Amar feels so shy that she remembers he cannot think of anything to say.

"I got your note," he finally speaks.

She frowns slightly and he wonders if it was a mistake to bring it up.

"Out of everyone, I was hoping you would come," she says.

She might be the bravest person he has ever met, saying what she thinks and feels without fear or hesitation.

She adds, "You were one of his closest friends. He would have wanted you here."

Abbas gone and never coming back. Her voice is so sad it makes him want to touch her, it seems wholly unbelievable that they are not allowed to touch one another, that he cannot even offer an embrace to comfort her. How could something so simple, for the sake of solace in a time like this, be a sin?

Her hair falls in her face and covers a corner of her eye. It suits her. What doesn't suit her? But her eyes are so beautiful he wants to move her hair just to look upon their full effect. He looks to the ceiling, clenches his hand into fists.

"He loved you a lot," he says, his words sounding foolish, so predictable as soon as they are spoken. But it was true. One of the reasons Amar loved and respected Abbas was because of the way he spoke about the people he loved.

"And he spoke of you often," he tries again. "More than the rest of them."

That seems to make her smile, and this time she lets it stay.

4

LAYLA HAD THOUGHT THE SEPARATION FROM HER family would be harder to bear, but when she steps from the plane into the airport for her layover, she only worries for her father, waiting for her in a hospital in Hyderabad. In this airport she is someone without anyone—without Rafiq, without her children—and it is refreshing, lonely in a way that being alone in her room is not. I am Layla, she thinks, as she drags her carry-on through the airport, studies the screen that displays the Departures and Arrivals, stops to purchase gum, and finds her gate without asking anyone. And as she watches the slowly moving planes make their way across the tarmac, she feels a strengthening in her aloneness, a comfort in knowing she can rely on herself.

It is also comforting to realize her self un-witnessed is in harmony with her self seen. That she discreetly does the minimal *wudhu* in the bathroom, seeks out a room in the airport where she can pray. That despite the fact that no one would know if she skipped her prayers and slept as she wanted to, she unfolds a napkin on the floor, sets down a small *sajdagah*, and prays. And as she lifts her cupped hands in prayer, she recalls Amar's question from months ago, do you pray for yourself and God or do you pray because you're told to? And before she dismisses the thought, she thinks now she could answer Amar with honesty: I pray for myself, and for God, who is my witness.

Three days ago, her father had a heart attack while Layla was dropping her kids off at school. She came home to an empty house and the answering machine light flashing red, a message from Sara at a moment when their father's recovery was unpredictable.

"You should go," Rafiq said on the phone, before she even finished explaining what had happened.

"The tickets," she said, thinking of how expensive they were, the reason she had not made many trips back in the past, and never on a whim. Always it was her parents who would come and stay with them for months. They gave Layla company in the daytime, and on the weekends the whole family would take trips to see the Golden Gate Bridge, or the Mystery Spot. They were planning on coming for Hadia's high school graduation at the end of this school year, and Layla called them every week to remind them to book their tickets, that Americans took graduations very seriously, and that it would mean a lot to Hadia if they came.

"It does not matter," Rafiq said, dismissing her concern. "He is your father."

She was grateful his first response was to suggest exactly what she needed and wanted to do. But who would drop off and pick up the children? School had begun just a week earlier. It was still early in September. Amar was in seventh grade now and had joined the soccer team, wanting a break from basketball, Huda was a junior, and Hadia was eighteen and in her senior year. Layla had never left the three of them in the house alone for more than a few hours, her girls never cooked the meals she made but experiments they pulled from cookbooks, and Amar fought with them often, which always angered Rafiq—and perhaps her biggest worry of all was that she could not trust Amar and Rafiq to be left in the same room alone for too long.

"Layla. We will take care of it. I will cancel my work trip next week," Rafiq said, when she asked him how they would manage.

Her tickets were booked before Rafiq returned home from work. And Layla swelled with love for him, her love born from gratitude.

When it is time to board the plane to Hyderabad she steps inside with her right foot first. As she walks down the aisle she looks at each seat number to make sure it is not her own, clutching her purse and passport in her hands, and it is Oliver Hansen she thinks she sees, Amar's teacher from years ago, tucking his bag beneath the seat before him and sitting up to buckle his belt, but of course it is not him. It surprises her: who returns in thought when one is so far from familiar life. She finds her place, recites her prayers, and soon feels the mighty force of the plane take off from the runway, pushing her back into her seat.

FOUR YEARS AGO, Amar was in the third grade for the second time, and finally flourishing. Layla was grateful for two things that year. The first was that Mark had continued to be his friend, despite the new grade gap between them. She felt for her son, who watched his classmates move on to another classroom, eat during a different lunch time, open a new set of textbooks. Still, Mark remained loyal, and Layla loved him for it. Layla became friends with Mark's mother, Michelle, an articulate woman with a closet full of bright dresses and matching shoes, and a soft-spoken demeanor that was so different from her rambunctious son's. At Christmas, Layla would gift Michelle a box of chocolates, a video game for Mark, and write their family a small card that Hadia checked over for her. Michelle waited in the kitchen when she came to pick up Mark, and while the boys finished up their games or begged for five minutes more, Layla made her tea the way she liked it, without Carnation milk and without any sugar, and the two of them spoke of the boys' antics; or Michelle, who had no daughters, asked about Hadia and Huda, and complimented Layla on having raised daughters who were sweet and polite. Even Rafiq, who was hesitant when it came to school friends, suggested inviting Mark if they were going to get pizza, or going to the movies, knowing how excited Amar would be to call and ask.

The second thing she was grateful for that year was Amar's third-grade teacher, Mr. Hansen, a young man who had just left graduate school. Amar spoke endlessly at dinner about Mr. Hansen. He recounted what Mr. Hansen had taught him, or what joke he had made even if it was not funny when repeated, or would announce to everyone if a movie came on television and Amar happened to know it was Mr. Hansen's favorite.

"Can we hear about something else, Amar?" Rafiq half joked one night.

But later, when the children got up to clear the table, Layla gently reminded him, "He's excited about school for once. Let's be grateful."

Excited about school, and responsible too; for the first time he had been the one to remind them of the parent–teacher meeting. Rafiq sighed. They always went together. They listened to the complaints in silence. Layla would nod, look around the room, and try to picture her son there, scan the little desks and wonder which one was Amar's.

"I can't skip work that day," Rafiq said.

"He's doing well this year," Layla said. "I can go alone."

The lights in the classroom were off, a purple tint, some of the curtains drawn. It was late afternoon. Amar was to wait for her on the picnic table outside and she made him promise three times he would not budge from it. He asked her to take him to get ice cream if he kept his promise, regardless of the news she received in the meeting, and because she was three minutes away from being late, she agreed. It had been years since he and Hadia and Huda had been in the same school, and still she felt the loss of that change, how comforted she would be when she said good-bye to them in the morning and watched the three of them trudge off, knowing that at least when they left her sight they would be near one another. How would she present herself, what would she say? Sometimes when in public she was so shy others assumed she did not speak English, and they would ask Rafiq or Hadia to ask her something, and she would feel deeply embarrassed, too embarrassed to respond fluently in English as she knew how to. Mr. Hansen was sitting at his desk, his head bent, hands busy shuffling papers, and she could see his light brown hair had been neatly combed, and that he had worn a tie. She knocked beneath the light switches and his head jerked up, and she asked, "Mr. Hansen?" and felt the questions she had prepared during the drive over leave her. He was so very young. Why had she come without Rafiq, who always knew what to say?

"Please, call me Oliver," he said, and he stood with his hand resting at the center of his tie. It was red with three navy blue stripes at the bottom. He didn't offer a hand to shake and she was grateful. He gestured at the open seat across from him and waited to sit until she took her place.

"So you're Amar's mother," he said, smiling, and Layla felt relief, a smile there instead of a concerned look, which she was so used to from Amar's teachers who were careful with their words, perhaps out of fear of hurting her. His jittery excitement allowed Layla's own nerves to relax.

"Layla," she said, touching her own chest, and realizing for the first time that giving a name was its own kind of intimacy.

"Your son might be my favorite of them. I know that isn't something I should say. He's in here at lunch sometimes, I give him books to read, we discuss."

"Very kind of you. He has a hard time—he, he doesn't like school very much."

Oliver nodded. Then said, "Certain kids you have to learn how to teach. Amar is like that. You have to know how to approach him. What to say that will ignite his curiosity, his wonderment. He doesn't really respond to criticism. And he doesn't try at all if he doesn't want to. But if he thinks he can do something well, or if he wants to, he does. You just have to be patient, a little delicate."

Layla wished she had brought a notebook that she could write in to help her remember what he was saying, to show Rafiq later. She glanced around the room, at the whiteboard with a chore chart corner, at Amar's name written in uppercase, beside "Paper passer," and the wall covered with sloppy paintings of faces under SELF-PORTRAITS, the rows of empty desks.

"That one is his," Oliver said, pointing to the desk in the second row. It was not as messy as some of the ones around it, with bent papers sticking out of the built-in shelves.

To be patient with him, to be delicate, to know how to approach him. To be patient, to know how to make him curious, to criticize less, to be delicate.

She asked Oliver if Amar was caught up with the other children in math, history, sciences.

"He is very good at writing. Look. Here is an assignment we did on heroes."

He passed her a sheet of paper with a photograph attached with a paper clip. She was startled to see the photograph was of her, holding an open envelope, young. She was not wearing a scarf. Rafiq had taken it when they were first married. She stared at a version of herself with dark eyeliner rimming her eyes, and dangling, golden earrings, and her ink-black wavy hair, and her fitted pink *shalwar kameez*. She remembered how she did not know Rafiq was standing in the doorway with his camera until he called her name, and when she looked up he had clicked. There was an expression of surprise on her face, her mouth a little open, barely a smile but the hint of one. That was the year his camera was always pointed at her if he brought it down from the high shelf where he kept it, a year before Hadia was born and the only photographs of her became ones where she was holding their children. She did not know what album this photo was in, or how Amar had found it, or what had possessed him to bring it to class without asking her first.

"I didn't know he had taken it," was all she could think to say, and she looked up at Oliver, watching her, his face full of pride that confused her, as though he were the one proud of Amar and not she. She was suddenly embarrassed he had seen her without her scarf, or a younger version of herself, and then wondered if the woman who entered his classroom with her face aged and hair covered disappointed him somehow.

"You can take the project with you, it may not seem like much," he said. "But if you read all of the other kids' work, you would know a lot of them wrote about imaginary superheroes, and you would

95

see how good his writing is. The details he chooses. I told him it was excellent. I gave him an A."

Layla thanked him and held the paper and photograph in her lap.

"You're the last one," he told her. "You can stay as long as you'd like."

So she asked some questions she remembered she wanted to, like what they were learning next, and if he could sense Amar's progress, if he was disruptive in class, and what Oliver meant exactly about being patient with him, if that meant that he was slower to understand or just that he needed kindness when being asked to understand something. Then she asked about Oliver. It was his first and perhaps only year teaching, this was a one-year assignment. And she told him that was too bad, that he seemed like the kind of teacher more students needed.

Layla did not read the project until she was home. She tucked it into her purse so Amar would not see that she had it. Amar asked her a hundred times to repeat everything Mr. Hansen said, then asked her if she thought Mr. Hansen liked him or not. He got a scoop of pistachio and Layla got vanilla, and Amar teased her for being so boring but she just smiled. She said she was very proud of him and Amar kicked his legs back and forth and said tell me why, exactly, and she thought no criticism, never again. They looked out the window at the cars leaving the parking lot, the storefronts on the other side of the complex with the bright red awning flapping away. When she was alone in her bedroom she pulled out his project gently, unfolded it and read Oliver's handwriting first. Green ink and all uppercase it said, "Wonderful Job, Amar. Great details, great observations." She smiled. Then began to read sentences from Amar's writing:

"Once there was a splinter in Huda's thumb. She knew what to do. She made Huda speak what she prayed for so it wouldn't hurt. She never says I am sad! Or I am angry! Or I am sleepy and you are being so loud and annoying! She likes windows. When she puts

96

seeds into the earth the earth grows. She is good at cooking and good at telling stories. Some she makes up herself so she has a good imagination but some she repeats from other people so she has a good memory too. She knows how much we need to eat like a proportion and we never run out of food and feel hungry. She cares about us eating more than her fingers. She cooked even when her thumb was burned. She gives me food first."

She stopped reading, holding back tears and unable to continue without having to bite her knuckle—was it because of his words or because of this stranger, this young man, who was kind enough to look closely at her son, and see what she had seen?

✧

THEIR DISAGREEMENT HAS escalated into a fight and Hadia has reached the threshold she knows she should not cross, should instead do as Mumma says: bite her tongue and abandon her protest. But it is Dani's sixteenth birthday so she yells, "Everyone else is allowed to go."

Baba stands from the couch so abruptly she steps back. Amar and Huda watch from the spaces between the banister. Mumma stands in the hallway but she might as well not be there at all, the way she pretends that nothing is happening.

"*You* are not everyone," he yells back. "You are *my* daughter. My daughter does not go to parties."

She refuses to show him any weakness—only wants him to know that she is angry, that he is wronging her, and if there are hot tears welling up she will not let them fall, she will blink furiously. She holds on to her wrist so tightly and pictures the marks her nails will leave when she lets go. She repeats in her mind what she wishes she could utter out loud, but maybe it is the secret of it that gives it power: I hate being your daughter.

All she asked for was permission to go to her best friend's home on Saturday night. When Baba pressed her for a reason she was careful to say it was to celebrate her birthday. She did not even use the word *party*. She had not divulged the detail about Dani's mom leaving the house, or Dani's older sister "supervising," or the other attendees.

"Baba, please." She hopes a change of tone might soften his stance. Inspire sympathy for his daughter. But Baba knows the words that will shame her, make her wonder how she could dare to even want this.

"There is no chance of my daughter going to a party where there will be dancing and boys present," he is yelling, and she can see Huda and Amar exchange frightened glances. She is focusing on the line of the staircase, blinking fast. She cannot even argue or lie about the boys that will be there, because Baba is the type to check in on the party, call Dani's mother twice, or pick her up before sunset and before anyone arrived anyway. The light overhead blurs and unblurs.

Baba points to Huda and Amar and jabs the air. "Look at the example you are setting for your brother and sister. The way you are behaving tonight. How many times have I told you, Hadia? If you are good, they will be good. If you are bad, they will follow you—more than they will ever follow my example, or Mumma's example."

"You're not being fair."

She should not have spoken: the girlish sound of her own voice makes her cry. She has made herself weak in front of him. She has lost. She turns from him and runs past Mumma, who she knows will never take her side, will only harp on the fact that she has been *batamiz* on a holy night. That she has caused him stress and pain. She runs past Huda and Amar and into her own room, where she slams the door and dissolves into a fit of quiet sobs on her bed, allows the thoughts that anger her and sadden her and frighten her to enter: that she hates Baba, hates her limited life. She only wanted to go to the party to be there for Dani, but now she will meet all the boys in the world just to spite Baba, she will shave half her head and dye the rest electric blue—but even that will not be enough because she will never escape this place unless she runs from it.

She opens her window wide and lets the cool air in. She will cry until she is tired. Until her face swells and her eyes become as red as her nose. Maybe she will not join them for the *nazr.* Why can't she continue to throw a fit like Amar, scream back at Baba until her voice is hoarse, bang the walls and furniture until something breaks. Why instead does she wait, swallow her pride and anger, and return to Baba not hopeful that he will give her what she originally asked for, but that he will not hold having asked against her.

She takes out the strand of her hair tucked behind the rest that really has been dyed an electric blue, and curls it around her finger. She dyed it with Dani last week, when Dani decided she would no longer go by Danielle and chopped off her hair so it was short like a boy's, bleached it and then dyed her bangs blue with Hadia's help in the bathroom after school. Baba had been away on a business trip, and it had been easy to convince Mumma that she had to work on a group project. She could not even enjoy her time in the bathroom with Dani. Her mind had wandered, wondering what the group project could be, what she would say they had accomplished by the end of their time together.

"Your turn?" Dani asked, when they were seated on the edge of the bathtub. Dani's hair was wrapped in foil because they had seen that done in salons and thought it might help.

"Just a little bit," Hadia said. Not that anyone would see, tucked beneath her scarf as it would be. At home she wore her hair down. But there, behind her left ear, visible only if pulled out or if her hair was lifted up, was her secret strand of electric blue. She showed only Huda. She could not trust telling Amar, who was in trouble so often he might blurt out the incriminating evidence to barter his punishment. Hadia loved to look at it before she fell asleep, loved twisting it around her finger and letting the dim light make it appear a beautiful, magnetic blue.

Dani's sweet sixteen is an event they have spent lunchtimes brainstorming plans for. It will be terrible if she cannot go. Their friendship had been through various transformations since elementary school, but each time they emerged even closer. Now Danielle

99

is changing again: throwing out her old clothes and wearing dark eyeliner, confessing to getting drunk with some of the other girls from school, but Hadia doesn't care—Dani can change into any version of herself and go by a new name and she will still be the one Hadia looks for in the lunchroom.

Hadia waits until her thoughts slow into sounds: Mumma in the kitchen preparing for the *nazr* with Huda, Amar bouncing his tennis ball against the wall, a car passing too fast. She waits until Baba is in his study to tiptoe downstairs. The night air is cold and Hadia is careful when releasing the handle of the front door behind her, so slowly it makes no click as it closes. Wind rustling the leaves. And all the stems of the flowers bent, their buds closed to brace themselves. She is wearing a thin cotton shirt and jeans. She should have worn a sweater, so she could camp out longer, but when she looks down at the goose bumps on her arms, she thinks: good, now they will know how I would rather shiver than come back inside.

It is pathetic that leaving her home without telling anyone is a thrill. She is fifteen. Standing in her own front yard should not give her that fleeting sense of freedom her friends have begun to enjoy— from attending parties she is not allowed to go to, skipping classes she does not miss. She inhales the cold air. She steps out until going any farther means crossing the indent that marks the end of the driveway and the beginning of the sidewalk. Here she stops. The indent is filled with dirt and fragments of twigs and shriveled-up weeds. Barefoot, she presses her toes against the line. She looks back at her house: her bedroom light left on, Amar's too. Bright, big moon. Sky dark with patches of lighter blue. And gray clouds, thin streaks of them. Innumerable tiny stars. How can she be upset when the world looks like this?

She sits on their driveway and then lies down, her head against the hard, rough pavement. She has lived here as long as she can remember. This is her patch of land on this big Earth. There is comfort in the feel of her entire body stretched out against the cool concrete. How furious Baba would be if he looked out a window and saw her. What would the neighborhood think of him, for having a daughter who did something like that? She smiles a little. But he won't come for her. Not after they have fought. He won't try to appease her. He will wait for the apology that is his right, simply because he is older, because he is her father, and a father is deserving of respect regardless of how she feels about his rules and the logic he uses to arrive at them.

But tomorrow, after she has apologized, she knows Baba will come straight to her room after work and he will close the door behind him. He will present to her a blended ice drink he knows she loves that costs almost five dollars each, or a book she has not yet read, or a porcelain figurine of some kind that has less to do with her and more to do with what a girl might expect to want—a girl holding her puppy, two children sitting back-to-back reading with their knees up on a bed of grass. The figurines are not inexpensive, but they are also not necessary. What good does it do to give me a gift now, she will think, when all I wanted was just for things to be another way yesterday. Still, there was always a reluctant delight in rising from her desk to claim her frozen drink or little figurine. In part, her delight came from knowing that Huda was not getting one and Amar was not getting one, nor would he. Baba loved him in ways Amar was blind to.

Baba always looked relieved when she complimented the figurine or took a sip of the drink. He would ask, "Is it the flavor you like?"

Even if it wasn't she would nod and thank him. She wanted to be firmer, or stay angry like Amar, without letting it so easily dissolve into guilt. But when she pictured her father stopping off at the store on his way home from work, wandering the aisles searching for something that he thought she might like, feeling bad for what had passed between them, though he would never be able to tell her so—she could not do anything but accept the gift, despite knowing her place in the transaction, knowing what fight she was giving up on completely.

"Drink it secretly," he'd remind her. "Don't tell Mumma I am ruining your appetite, or giving you caffeine at night."

A plane passes in the sky. After a few minutes, another one. They hum as they move, a tiny red light blinks on one side, a white one on the other. The stars take turns brightening. Her calming voice inside rises to comfort her: It's okay, it's okay, you will be all right.

Lately, in school, Hadia has felt herself losing some of her old motivation. Paying attention in class, doing well, they felt like old habits. She catches herself wondering what the point is—a question that has never occurred to her before. All anyone talked about was where they dreamed of going to college. Her friends had a reason to work hard. She would always stop before the indent in the pavement. The map of her life would never extend beyond the few places her parents dragged her to. She was fifteen already, soon she would be eighteen, she might attend a local university or community college, but either way, a proposal would come, and she would pack her bags and abandon her credits, live with her husband wherever he was, have her own children to drag from family friend's house to mosque to home again.

Still, she tries. Maybe only out of a fear of disappointing Baba, maybe a desire to make him proud. But there is also that singular pleasure of receiving her projects and tests and seeing that A+ next to her name, reading comments from her teachers in the margins. And nothing compares to the promise of stepping into a classroom knowing she will step out a different person. That she could learn something that would change the way she saw the whole world, and her place in it. There is even the private hope that if she does work as hard as she absolutely can, there is a chance she will be able to sway the outcome of her life, and maybe one day a door will be presented to her, and an opportunity to walk through it.

Behind her there is the creak of the front door opening. She hopes it is Baba. That Baba will sit next to her without getting angry at her for lying barefoot on the pavement. She does not want it to be Mumma. She has begun to expect nothing of Mumma, who would only make her apologize to Baba. But the footsteps are quick and uneven and soon Amar is standing over her, blocking the moon from sight with his upside-down face.

"Why are you such a weirdo?" he says.

"Go away," she says, but when he steps away from her she realizes she does not want to be left alone. Amar walks to the magnolia tree, and Hadia sits up to watch him stretch and climb onto a branch and tug at a blossom until a few petals fall down. He half prances as he walks back to her, takes a seat beside her, and sprinkles the petals on her. She flits her hand in front of her face and ignores him. When she lies back down he lies down too. They watch the sky. Another plane passes.

"How do they know to avoid one another? It is so dark up there."

She does not answer him. He continues, "Do they plan schedules months in advance when people buy their tickets? And what about unexpected storms?"

"Stop it," she says.

"Stop what?" He turns to look at her.

"Trying to make me talk to you normally."

She waits for a while before saying, "How did you know I was here?"

"Window."

"Did you tell anyone?"

"No."

She looks at him and narrows her eyes.

"Huda."

They turn to the stars again. She has those shuddering after-crying breaths, but they are becoming less powerful. She senses him look at her anyway. The plane has passed almost completely, and he points to it as it goes, its little blinking red light, its hum.

✧

THE EVENT IS under way. Amira will arrive, possibly soon. Amar scratches off a speck from the face of his watch, a gift from his father for his eighteenth birthday, a decent brand, but one bought in a store. He imagined his father letting the salesclerk pick it out for him after he realized on his way home from work that he had forgotten to buy him a gift. His father sits beside him, busy with his appetizer. Amar only touches the yogurt *chaat* dish to move it around in circles with the tip of his spoon. They are at the *nikkah* of someone from their community, and Amira confirmed that her family would be attending. By now he could not even note the way the hills greened in winter without wanting her there to note it with him. He is no better than those terrible clichés in books and movies and Bollywood songs, the people doodling in the margins, getting lost on their way home, staring up at the sky instead of sleeping.

He has good news he is saving to tell her in person. He had been in danger of failing high school and in all honesty had begun to entertain the idea of dropping out, doing something else for a change. He had gone as far as to research a list of successful people who had not made it to college, and was going to present it to his mother if his classes continued as bleakly as they had been. When he told Amira this, she sent him the longest e-mail he had ever received, explaining why he had to make an appointment with his counselor and stay in school. The reasons were numbered under three different headings; CONSIDER YOUR FAMILY, she wrote, CONSIDER YOUR PRESENT MOMENT, and lastly, CONSIDER YOUR FUTURE (OPPORTUNITIES, ETC.). He could not argue. She made a fair point. And besides, he did not *want* to argue. She had never articulated how she felt about him, but how thoughtfully she imagined his predicament was proof she cared.

It has been months since the death of Abbas Ali. There were times when he rose in Amar's thoughts as though he were still alive, as though he had just not seen him in a few days. Other times the remembrance of him always carried that sense of loss. He and Amira had written e-mails back and forth every few days since he knocked on her bedroom door. They had yet to speak on the phone or meet in private, and if they saw each other it was only in the moment before the partitions went up in the mosque. Last week, her letter confessed how her family was not sure if they wanted to attend the wedding of the community member. It felt too soon. Her mother was especially affected: Amira described her mother's grief like a spell, conjured up without warning in the midst of a conversation or a simple task. My eldest son, she would overhear her say sometimes, my first, at which her father would remind her, yes, but not our only. They had a family meeting to discuss it and in the end it was her father who told them that the forty days of mourning had long passed, and they had to be brave now, and being brave looked like resuming their old life, its celebrations as well as its obligations.

Amar looks up as the two Ali boys enter—still odd, to remind himself not to look for the third—and he looks back at his own father, until his father nods to him and Amar knows he is free to go greet them. He extends his fist to Kumail Ali and Saif Ali, and they pound theirs against it. Then, moved by the memory of Amira's letter describing how they had to discuss if they were ready to attend tonight, Amar hugs each of them in turn, taking them both by surprise.

After a while, he excuses himself and enters the hallway, and there she is. That first glimpse of her. She lingers by the drinks table. Tall glasses filled with juice. Orange and a kind of pink—maybe guava. When she looks at him they both smile, thinking the same thing, or so it feels. He pictures a tight rope connecting them, invisible to everyone else. She lifts a glass to her lips. He leans against the table, faces the crowd, watches people enter the hall, greet each other, and separate into the ladies' or the men's.

"Do you think we can?" she asks. She is not facing him. She takes another sip. Her bangles clink.

Every letter exchanged since that first scrap of paper left on his pillow seems to have been leading up to this moment. In his last e-mail he mentioned that maybe there was a floor in the hotel where they could meet, where no one would have any reason to go. She had not replied, and he had deleted it from his sent mail.

Now he speaks. "Ten minutes, seventeenth floor."

"You've lost your mind."

But she laughs. He looks to see if anyone has heard her. She lowers her finished glass onto the table, a pink stain of lipstick on its rim.

"You first. *Fifteen* minutes," she says, and he watches her walk into the ladies' hall.

THIS IS THE first walk they take together. The hallway on the seventeenth floor is carpeted and their footsteps make no sound. Already he has memorized the gaudy red pattern of twisting vines on the floor, and her feet encased in golden shoes, taking slow steps—maybe, he thinks, to elongate their walk. He had made a list of what he could bring up when he ran out of things to say—the main point being how his counselor told him there was definitely a chance of him graduating, so long as he did a lot of catch-up work, met regularly with his teachers, and attended mandatory tutoring sessions during some lunch hours. Amira responds with genuine relief, excitement even. He makes a note to remember to do the same for her, if she ever comes to him with good news. Every time someone opens one of the hundred doors, a panic seizes her and him too; they step away from each other as if shocked. But it is only a man holding a briefcase. Or an elderly woman in a turquoise dress, adjusting its pleats, glancing at them only once, but smiling at them as if she knows.

He is so happy he could dance, uncharacteristic of him, but maybe with her he *is* someone who dances. Maybe with her he is someone who can do anything. It is time the world knew, he thinks—a line from a poem his teacher had assigned. He marvels at how the words he read before return and ring true now. It is time the stone made an effort to flower. Celan's lines and Rilke's on his mind—how foolish he would appear if he admitted that, how she would roll her eyes and think he was trying too hard, or that he was not as cool as he seemed. But there is a part of him that does not care, that wants to take the hair that has fallen into her face and tuck it behind her ear, gently brush against the skin of her cheek, and say the line he recalls—how everything exists to conceal us.

She talks about her day. Her elaborate hand gestures. When did they become people who cared about the most insignificant details of their lives? He laughs at all the right moments. Something closed in her unlatches and she twirls, her outfit is one that fans out before falling against her legs and she gushes, "I can't believe we're doing this. What if someone catches us?"

"They won't."

"You're so sure."

He extends his hand to trace his fingers against the textured wall, the door frame, the smooth length of the door, the door frame again—because he can't touch her.

"Tell me something," she asks.

"What do you want to know?"

"Anything that counts."

So he thinks. Far behind them there is the ring of the elevator. They freeze, then look to one another and laugh. They keep walking. What can he say? He should have prepared more. There are already things he knows he cannot tell her. Partially because he does not want to set a bad example, risk influencing her negatively. He remembers how quick she was to ask for a cigarette when she stumbled upon him and Abbas half a year ago, smoking in the tall trees behind her house. Why can't I, if you can, she had said to Abbas, are our lungs so different, that different standards apply? Abbas turned to Amar as if to say, see what I have to deal with? And then he shrugged and passed her the cigarette, and said to her, I won't even mention you tried to Mumma or Baba, but only because I would rather you try with me than alone, and only if you drop it with the equality stuff for at least a week. At least a week, Amira. And she saluted him, which endeared her to Amar, and held the cigarette between her index finger and thumb, sniffed it and scrunched up her nose before taking it to her lips and smoking it, giving it back after she started coughing on her third drag. You boys are dumb, she said when she returned the cigarette to Abbas, and if it hadn't been for the fact that Amar was grinning, it might have stung. *Batamiz*, Abbas joked as she walked away, *begharat*—which meant, the one who is disrespectful to their elders, the one who is without shame. She turned on her heel and replied *khushi se*—with pride, with happiness. How much more fun it was to throw Urdu terms at one another in jest; how different it felt when the same words were spat from their parents' mouths.

So he cannot tell her, tell anyone, that he had sought out Abbas's friend Simon a few months ago. Simon was the only person who had been in the car who had survived the accident that killed Abbas. When Mumma heard there had been a survivor, she had said, "What is it about these tragic accidents, a group of people touch death and God chooses one to come back and tell us about it."

What was it that Simon could tell him, he had wondered, and in pursuit of an answer they had become sort of friends. One night, Amar followed him to a house party at the edge of town. He had smoked cigarettes with Abbas and the other boys for years; they had even, a few times, smoked weed. But that night, when a red cup of beer was handed to him, he accepted it. There was no immediate effect, the foam fizzy on his lips, but with each sip he felt like he was stepping out from his old world. Later, he took a bong hit too quickly and went outside to breathe the fresh air and massage his chest to dissolve the feeling of glass in his lungs, swaying on the heels of his feet, not knowing why he was there, accepting one drink and then intentionally going back for another and another, in a room full of people he did not know, and the only person who he did know was nothing like Abbas.

That night the bright moon hung low in the sky. As a child, Amar's belief that the moon followed him calmed him, but seeing it then, with his lungs still filled with crushed glass, he felt the panicked sensation of a hand being pressed on his neck, and he knew he could not tell anyone how far out from his world he had ventured alone, certainly not his sisters, and definitely not Amira, who he had just begun to write to, who he wanted desperately to impress. The pebbly stars took turns dimming and glowing. And though he could not remember the last time he had stood sincerely in prayer, a thought like a prayer rose in his mind and he was so surprised by its presence it struck him like a blow: that his sisters never experience the doubts he was feeling, that they never shake in their certainty of being Muslim, never think that maybe there was no hell and no heaven and therefore no point. Never wonder if everyone had gotten it wrong or maybe they had all gotten it right in their own way, which meant that no way was superior to any other. That his sisters never stray from the path outlined for them, and that if there was a heaven, they would be in line waiting to enter.

So why would he say anything that would infect Amira's thinking, now that he has started to regard her with the same kind of love he reserves for those he is closest to?

"In eighth grade I stole from grocery stores, gas stations," he says, thinking that this is what she might be looking for. An actual secret, but one that is far enough behind him that it will not change how she looks at him now.

Her eyes widen, incredulous. He imagines her sheltered life. Never really alone without a father, brother, mother nearby and watching. But his life has been sheltered too.

"You're terrible," she jokes.

He tells her he hid chocolate bars in his sleeves, but doesn't mention that he had been there with her brother, or that they would walk there with a group of other boys after Sunday school, during lunchtime while others lined up for spaghetti or sandwiches.

"Why did you do it? Just to see if you could?"

He shrugs. "I didn't even want to."

"Did you ever get caught?"

He tells her about the time the cashier at a gas station saw him on a security video, how the man ran out after him and how Amar, startled, dropped the green mint Tic Tacs and ran and ran until he couldn't breathe.

"I like how you remember the flavor," she says.

They arrive at a long mirror in the hall and stand hushed before it. She is as beautiful in the mirror as she is in real life. He looks from himself to her, at the gap between their arms. Her phone starts to ring again, her mother, no doubt wondering where she has gone. She looks at him in a way that tells him it is time for her to go back. He suggests she take the elevator first. He will take his time before doing the same. And then they move on, broken or awoken from some spell. She waves and he holds up his hand as the elevator doors close. He watches her descent, a little red dot charting her movement away, floor eleven lighting up, then eventually three, two, one. He walks the empty halls. Slight pink smudge still on his thumb from wiping the rim of her glass but no other proof. But they were those two people in that mirror, they were the ones looking back at themselves, awed by their impossible reflections.

5

PE CLASS IS LET OUT EARLY, AND INSTEAD OF RUSH-
ing to the locker room with his classmates who are eager to line up
at the snack bar, Amar drags his badminton racket on the blacktop.
Mumma is still visiting her father in India, leaving no one to slip
him spending money for a freshly baked cookie or a frozen lemonade
cup. Nana's health has been stable for two weeks now. But Mumma's
flight was canceled, and he is not sure when she will be able to come
home. Hadia says there is no need to worry. Amar has yet to figure
out how to launch a birdie into the air. Every time he tries, the birdie
thuds to the ground just as his racket whooshes past, and he looks
around to see if anyone but his partner noticed. His English teacher,
Miss Kit, taught them a new word in class this week—*melancholy*—
and he thinks of the word as he leans down to tug a protruding weed
from the blacktop, tries to whack it with the racket, and wonders if
maybe that is what he is feeling.

His shoulder is shoved and he stumbles into the brick wall. It is
Grant walking away, looking back in such a way that Amar realizes
he was shoved on purpose. He brushes dust from his shoulder. He
does not like Grant, or the way Grant looks at him: as though there
is something disgusting on Amar's face. Amar straightens his posture and raises his shoulders a little. Just in case he was shoved
because he appeared weak. He trails the racket against the wall
until he reaches the locker room. He will push Grant back if he
tries to bump him again.

Inside, the air is musty, the light gray. It smells of sweat. Light comes through the small, opaque windows at the very top of the walls, so high up that no one can see out of them. Everything echoes: footsteps of boys departing, locker doors slammed, locks snapped shut. His locker is in the farthest row, toward the end of the aisle. He likes it because not many people are around when he changes.

"Look," someone says, "terrorist in a white shirt."

Amar turns around. It is Grant speaking to Brandon. Brandon's dirty PE clothes are flung over his shoulder. Both of them are in some of his classes but he knows neither well. Brandon has broad shoulders and is taller than the rest of the boys. Amar turns to look behind him but no one else is there.

Amar is the one in white. He slams his locker door louder than he intended. The metal trembles. He busies himself with the zipper of his backpack and Grant calls out to him, "Hey, we're talking to you."

Amar pictures the rest of the locker room—empty by now—and his stomach clenches.

"Why don't you go back to your own country?" Brandon snarls.

He stands to face them.

"This *is* my country."

He wanted to sound angrier, but he is surprised by the presence of something else in his voice—discomfort or defensiveness, he can't tell. There is a slim space between Grant and the row of lockers and if he squeezes past he can make it to the door. He can ditch his last two classes and walk away from the whole stupid school until he reaches Hadia and Huda's high school, where he can wait by the gate until they are let out. He has been in fights before, not with Grant or Brandon, but with other classmates in previous years. Fights he picked or allowed to happen, knowing he would win, or that there would be no real damage done: a bloody nose, a bruised arm. But this time there are two of them. And Brandon is bigger than he is. He presses his sneaker into an old, dark gum stain. Then Mark appears. Mark had moved to another school district after his parents' divorce, but their schools had combined again in middle school. They did not really speak to each other anymore, Mark being a grade older. Still, if they passed each other in the hallway they would nod, and it was like a secret pact they kept with their younger selves. Mark nods to Grant, and Amar realizes they are friends now.

"Him?" Mark says when he sees Amar. He sounds surprised.

Amar wonders if they had planned to bother him today.

"Arabian Nights tells us he's from here," Grant explains to Mark. Brandon grins. Amar wants to tell Grant he is an idiot and that he is not even Arab. But his jaw is shut so tight his teeth hurt.

"He is," Mark says.

Mark meets his eyes for a moment but then looks away.

"That's right, you know him."

"Knew him."

There is the sound of a locker door echoing. Amar realizes he has taken a step back and hit the door with his body. Grant smiles with his head tilted back as though he has sniffed his fear.

"We should go," Mark says, looking over his shoulder.

Amar is relieved: they may no longer be friends, but at least there is something between them they could both recognize and respect.

"Is your dad a terrorist?" Brandon asks.

Amar feels silent. And sick to his stomach, like his insides have twisted into a tiny fist, and when he looks up from the gray cement floor, the gray grout, the dark gum stain, it is to look at Mark, who is avoiding looking back at him. This is not anger. This is not fear. This is not an exchange he has been in before. He feels too ashamed to even have to say, no, he is not.

"Mark, you know his dad too?"

"Yeah, man."

Once when they were ten, maybe eleven, Baba took all of them bowling. Mark's finger had been between the bowling balls when another one rolled out, and it jammed his finger enough for him to not want to bowl. Mumma wrapped ice from the soda machines in a tissue, Baba gave them a ton of quarters to go into the arcade to play games that were manageable with one throbbing hand, while Hadia and Huda took over their turns. They brought home ten sticky aliens and one glow stick.

"Is he a terrorist?" Grant asks.

"Shut the *fuck* up, man," Amar says.

Good. That was better. That sounded tougher.

Mark is the only one of these idiots who has been to his home, has eaten dinner with them, and if there is anyone who will tell them that his father is not a terrorist, but just someone who wears white shirts to work, packs brown paper lunch bags, it is Mark.

His father with his beard and his skin a little darker than Amar's. His father did have a temper, one that was undetectable until it erupted, but his anger was hardly ever directed anywhere but at Amar, and even then Amar instigated it. When the sun began to set his father took walks at a slow pace, pausing at hedges with flowers, and some evenings Amar peered down from his bedroom window and thought his father looked like a peaceful man, his hands crossed and resting behind him. Amar wants to tell them: no, my father points out the stars in the sky to us if we haven't looked up in a while, he teaches us how to look for the new moon to mark the new month, he reads books he underlines with a faint gray pencil. My father always says excuse me if he passes someone too close in the street. My father has never lost his temper at a stranger.

Mark shrugs, then says, "He sure looks like a fucking terrorist."

Amar punches him in the face. And again. So fast and so hard that Mark's head hits the locker behind him and he crumples to the floor, eyes wide and wild, one hand covering his mouth. Grant and Brandon look from Amar to Mark, as if unsure what to do. Even Amar does not know what to do. If he should run. His hand hurts so much so he holds it. Mark moves his hand and there is blood on his teeth, blood on his lip. Soon it is on his chin, on the collar of his shirt, and he holds his fingers over his mouth as if to stop it. Then there are arms around Amar and he is lifted off the floor, Brandon has picked him up and Amar begins to kick, but he can't move his

114

hands. Grant is looking at him as if he is pleased for this opportunity, so pleased, and he steps toward Amar, and then it is Amar who is receiving punch after punch after punch.

✧

IT HURTS TO touch his face in the nurse's room so he sits with his hands in his lap, careful to not rest the back of his head against the wall either, a tenderness there he is sure will become a bump. He waits with the lights turned off. He focuses in and out at the charts of what to eat, the poster of the muscles in the body and the bones, the glass containers with the cotton balls and wooden sticks. He blurs his sight and then focuses on the line of the sink, blurs and then the tick, that shift that announces another minute has passed. The nurse is being very kind to him. Her name is Mrs. Rose. She checks on him even after she has applied the bandage on his eyebrow and chin, given him a tissue to hold up to his split lip.

"What did he say?" Amar asks her after she calls his father.

"He just listened." Mrs. Rose smiles sadly at him.

When she was dabbing at his eyebrow she kept saying, "Oh, boy, oh dear. What have you boys done to each other?"

Everywhere she dabbed stung. He wanted to cry but could not. He wanted to bite his lip but that hurt too. Then, when she was done, she dropped her voice into a whisper and pointed at him and she said, "You're a strong young man. Don't listen to any hateful voice. That's what I always tell my son."

He nodded at her. And only then did he almost cry. Maybe the principal had told her his side of the story. Mark, Grant, and Brandon just said that he had lunged at Mark, and Grant and Brandon had retaliated to protect him.

"Deplorable behavior," his principal had said, after announcing all four of them were suspended equally, "absolutely unacceptable."

Grant and Brandon, who had not a single scratch on them, were sent home, and Mrs. Rose separated Mark and Amar. All four of them could not return for a whole week.

115

"If anything like this happens again," the principal warned, "you will all be expelled."

He wishes Mumma were home and that she could pick him up instead. Mumma would know what to say and would not get mad at him. But she is so far away and already so worried about them he can't even tell her what happened. What face will he greet her with when she returns? His eyebrow is split open. His forehead has a bruise so large it pains him to even touch it. His mouth tastes like blood. Mrs. Rose had said, you might be needing stitches, honey. He liked her voice; it was warm and she sweetened her sentences by calling him honey or sugar.

It has been three days since September eleventh. That morning Amar was almost ready for school, half-asleep and still eating his cereal, trying to remember if he had packed all his soccer gear for practice after school. He dabbed at the surface of his milk with his spoon, watched the little rings of cereal sink and rise up again. It was Mumma who called from India and told Baba to turn on the news immediately.

The four of them watched as the same image looped, and the newscasters repeated the same lines: Something devastating has happened. Baba took a seat on the floor. The towers and the dark plumes of smoke. Not a normal flight pattern of planes, another newscaster said. Are we going to go to school? Huda asked. They were going to be late. Baba did not reply. They watched for hours. Every time the plane appeared, a streak of dark on the screen, it felt impossible that it would happen, and then it did, and then it kept happening. The president announced it was an apparent act of terrorism. Oh God, Hadia said next to him. She pressed her fingers into her wrist the way he hated, dug her nails like she wanted to hurt herself. Please don't let them be Muslims, Hadia said. Why would you even say that? Amar wanted to say to her, but when he saw Baba's nod he knew not to. Soon they saw that all the hijackers were Saudi, that their names were the same names that belonged to people in their community, and Huda just repeated, this is horrible, how could this have happened?

That night Baba told them that they had to go to school the next day, but that Hadia and Huda could not wear their hijabs. "We don't know how people will react," he said. "We don't know where they will direct their anger if they are afraid."

Huda started to cry. Huda never cried. Hadia put her hand on Huda's shoulder.

"I refuse," Hadia said. "What have *we* done?"

"Please," Baba asked her. "Please. Listen to me."

He had never said please before. His voice, the expression on his face—he was unrecognizable. None of them spoke. Hadia and Huda went into a bedroom, closed the door. I hate them, Amar thought, picturing the terrorists they showed on TV, I hate them more than I've ever hated anyone. The next morning Baba drove them to school. They were all quiet. Huda wore one of Baba's old, faded baseball caps from a work retreat. Hadia wore her hair in a bun, clipped back so none of it fell into her face. Their eyes had the red and swollen look of having cried the night before. They looked out the window, Huda biting her bottom lip the whole drive.

But Baba did nothing to change his own appearance. His beard was always kept trimmed and neat, so he would look professional for work but still not break the religious rule of having one. But his beard could make him look like the men on TV who had ruined everything. Amar would ask him to shave it off. It would be no different than his sisters taking off their scarves.

AT HOME, HE allows Hadia to enter only after her hundredth knock. He had been lying under the covers with the blinds closed, a pillow over his face. Maybe for hours. His father drove him home and Amar said almost nothing the whole ride. He felt like a shell that had snapped shut. His father knocked immediately after he had locked himself in his room, barricaded the door with a chair in front of it, but Amar ignored him. He did not want to see his father.

But when Hadia says, "It's me, Amar. Let me in?" he goes to his door, moves the chair, unlocks it, and rushes back to his bed and puts the pillow and blanket over his face again before he replies, "Fine."

Soon he feels Hadia's weight on the bed as she takes a seat on the edge. She does not say anything. He does not want to explain, though Baba has probably already told her. There is another knock and before he can reply he hears the door open and Huda whispering, "Is he okay?"

Beneath the covers he smiles. The corner of his lip feels ripped, it stings to move his mouth. He keeps touching it with the tip of his tongue, tasting that bitter, coppery taste.

Hadia's voice is saying, "Amar? Do you want anything?"

Her voice is soft. His head is pounding. He wants more painkillers. He took four even though the directions said to take two every four hours. It was so painful he did not care. He lifts the pillow from his face and sits up.

"Oh God." Hadia flinches. She looks like she is going to cry.

"That bad?" he asks.

"No, not bad at all," Huda says quickly.

Hadia shoots her a look. The kind of look he has always been bothered by, the look of their secret language, but right now it does not annoy him and when they turn to him again they both look a little like their mother. Hadia asks what happened. He thinks of the gray light. Of Grant's smile with his head tilted back. And how he could not break free of Brandon's grip on him. How there was a moment, after kicking and kicking, when he relaxed, let it happen, how it was easier after that exhaling, after telling himself to allow anything. Grant's bruised fists and Mark's bloody mouth. And how Amar threw up after they dropped him, and kicked him, and walked out, how he was shaking as though a violent wind had passed through the room, how he kept spitting blood, tiny bubbly pools on the cement floor. How he thought he was going to cry. But he did not cry, not until Mrs. Rose pointed a finger at his chest, where it did not hurt, and said, you are a brave young man.

"Who did it?" Huda says. Her eyes burn like she is ready to fight.

"Three boys from my school. I don't know them that well."

"Why?"

Amar tells them they told him to go back to his country. He does not say that he threw the first punch. Or that Mark was among them. He especially does not say what was suggested about their father. It would make it all worse somehow. Huda leaves to get him ice. Something makes Amar feel as if they are all young again, as if they have come together to play a game.

✧

THAT SUMMER THEY meet in places enchanted, if only because there they are alone. Some afternoons on nearly empty library floors, in sections hardly frequented, paused between shelves, Amira holding a book in her hand so no one would doubt she was there to research for a project. They discover bridges where no cars they know cross, and the tunnels below them with their long shadows and walls covered in graffiti. If they are feeling particularly bold, they meet in a booth at a restaurant no community member would visit—not many vegetarian options and a too-large bar. Each place becomes their place, their secret, imbued with the tenderness and excitement of knowing this is the extent they will go to just to see one another.

On rare days, when they have hours to spend, Amar suggests a meadow near a secluded park. Their spot is past the swings and monkey bars, past rows and rows of trees; beneath a sycamore tree that looks out at a stretch of grass that eventually descends to reach a small river. They compose excuses for their families, bring food to offer one another, sweatshirts to sit on, stories they have saved and are now eager to share. Amira's mother is on a day trip to meet with vendors who sell her clothes, so no one will know Amira is not home until just after sunset, when her father will return from work. Amar thrives on the thrill of approaching their meeting spot and the magic of being by her that never dulls. The park was a long and winding bike ride for her, but she was happy when he suggested it. "I love watching you here," she had said to him once, "the way you carry yourself. The way you speak. The things you think to speak of. You're happy."

Today, she peeks her head out from behind their tree as he approaches. He does not call out her name, she would be angry if he did, so he lifts his hand to salute her, and her laughter catches on a breeze to reach him. She has set up a fleece blanket, placed rocks on the four corners to keep it from lifting, a plastic container full of blackberries and green grapes, another one of baby carrots. There is a drop of blackberry juice beneath her bottom lip. He grabs a baby carrot and sets down his own contribution: two plastic forks and a pasta salad he spent an hour making after reading three different recipes and combining what seemed like the best parts of them.

"Mumma and Baba came to me with a proposal last night," Amira says when there is a lull in their conversation. She looks down at her hands, rolls a grape between her thumb and index finger.

"I said no, of course."

She looks up at him quickly and then away. It isn't her first proposal and it won't be her last. She is young—only seventeen—but it was not unusual for a girl like Amira to have a future spouse secured by eighteen. The proposals were usually from young men older than Amar and much more accomplished—doctors or lawyers—from wealthy and well-connected families with untarnished reputations. He knew how it worked. His sisters had spent years thwarting their own proposals, Hadia excused now only because she was in medical school, and Huda because she insisted on waiting for Hadia. He lifts a nearby twig and snaps it in two, and then in four, and tries to snap it into eighths but it is too small.

Amira offers him a palmful of blackberries but he is no longer hungry. He catches a falling leaf in his hand, tucks it into his pocket. He will put it in his antique keepsake box when he goes home. Once the box was filled with basketball cards and his journals, but now it is filled with mementos of Amira, all her letters and some photographs. It is a risk to keep any record. But the box has a lock and he has hidden it deep inside his closet.

It is terrifying to be reminded that the only thing standing between this moment—where his whole body still buzzes just from having walked up to her—and that blow—her life with another person, her destiny determined so irretrievably—is her continued decision to refuse these proposals.

Every time Amira came to him with news about a suitor, he grew quiet, regardless of whether she was complaining or joking, or describing the disorder that ensued when she said no. When they first began meeting regularly, deepening the way they felt about each other, Amar promised her he would come to her doorstep when he had made himself into the kind of man her father would seek for her.

"I will do it the right way," he told her. "It will be right for you, for us, and they won't suspect we have loved each other."

She sometimes felt that they had made a mistake—rushing forward into their secret the way they had—that it would have been better not to sin, not to deceive, and that God might have looked kindly upon them if they kept Him and their parents in mind, and would have bestowed on them a good *qismat*, a happy destiny. She was betraying her parents by being loyal to him, risking their dishonor by joining him here. But he assured her it would all be made right, wanting only to have as much time with her as he could. She looked at him with an expression of such certainty, such belief, even though he was not sure he could pull it off—go through community college, transfer to a good school, force himself to study something he did not want to and did not know if he could do well at, get a promising and respectable job. But he would try, because it would be his best chance at winning her parents over, because then it would mean he had not broken his promise to her.

"I don't know how others do it," she was saying now. "I would never want to get married like that. To someone who just saw a picture of me and sent a proposal—who has already made his decision and it doesn't matter what I do or don't do, what I say or don't say, he's just going to accept it. I want it to be me because of *me*. Me because of what I have said and done and thought. I want it to be him not because of his job or good family but because of how he thinks about the world, how he moves through it. And how we feel about each other."

Amira because of how she thought. Amira because she was capable of being wildly goofy one moment and poised the next, and he could never figure out how she moved from one self to the other so effortlessly. Amira because no room was lit until she entered it. Amira because if it would not be Amira, it would be no one. She had the aura and confidence of someone who was so beloved by all who knew her that it emanated from her even when she was alone, and any stranger who came across her could not help falling under a spell she had no awareness of casting.

"Maybe it's not a flawed system—just one that will not work for me."

"Has it caused a fight?" he speaks at last.

She looks down at her hands and reaches for another grape. She bites only half and wipes away the juice on her lip with a knuckle, and he can tell she is being careful with her words. "Baba is hurt because it is his oldest friend's son, and I am not even considering it."

"Did they ask why?"

"I told them I am not ready. I am not at a place where I can decide."

She turns to him and gives him a wistful smile.

"Have you signed up for your classes yet? Do you know how many credits you need this semester to transfer quickly?" Her voice is lighter, there is a strained hopefulness to it.

He has not. He nods yes. His fourth lie that summer. But it wasn't a lie—or at least not a malicious one. And it did not count as a lie if he simply withheld information. Like the nights he still snuck out to go to parties at his friends' houses. She would be hurt if she knew. She never judged him or admonished him but she did express wanting a future in which he wouldn't, and she had begun to assume, and he allowed her to continue to believe, that since they had become more serious he did not really drink and did not smoke anymore either. In some ways that was true. In the months after Abbas died, before he and Amira acknowledged what was happening between them, he would leave the house in the middle of the night with only the intention of altering his state as quickly as he could, any way that he could, anger driving him there, God knows what pulling him back. Now, he seldom drank and weed was just a way to feel how his mind zipped through a moment or slowed to focus in on it.

There is the sound of a branch snapping and she turns. She is skittish whenever they are together, even when they know no one will come. The repercussions are always worse for a woman. He decided long ago that he did not care who he disappointed, how tarnished his reputation was, or even how it would reflect on his family. If it was between his reputation and another afternoon by her side, he would choose the afternoon. But he waited in fear of the moment it would occur to Amira that for her the stakes were different, that the community gaze would not be as forgiving.

This is the summer Abbas has been buried for over two years, but Amira's loss still strikes her and there is nothing he can say, nothing he can do but give her space to speak of it.

"I cheated in Scrabble," she had said once, "and swore I hadn't, and Abbas Bhai held me down as a joke, because Saif and Kumail were so mad I won, and he said, swear you didn't cheat? Swear? I had been careless and stupid, I had picked the q and the z and the k and the x and the j too, I think, and I said I swear I didn't I swear I didn't, and he believed me and released me. Do you think he knows now that I lied to him? That he has access to knowing things like that wherever he is?"

"I don't know," Amar had replied. "But to be honest, I'm sure he knew it as you were denying it. No one can get the q and the z and the x and the j."

She laughed. Only when she spoke of Abbas did she avoid looking at him. And only when seeking to comfort her could he look directly at her. He shares with her too. She has become the one to whom he confesses the fights with his father, the fights that make him want to leave, to forget that he ever came from this family, and she quiets his anger with a brief touch of her hand on his arm. She tries to tell him that what he feels is not all anger, that one day that anger will burn out and he will be left with what he can't see right now: a sadness, an ache. Amar dismisses this, even as he hopes it might be true.

Loving Amira was not just loving a young woman. It was loving a whole world. She was of the same world he had been born into but had only ever felt himself outside of, and sitting by her was the closest he came to feeling harmony with his own home.

Their bodies are so close, their arms almost touching. And if they do touch it is accidental, or it's a hug to comfort her or say goodbye or move the hair from her eyes—he never dares ask for more. Once it occurred to him that she was not ready, that she was not used to thinking of her body as hers, he made a point to not extend even the slightest touch that might cause her sadness or guilt later. She had had years of being told that there would be nothing more shameful than to follow the desires of the body, that any impulse was the devil's temptation. She would have to decide what she believed for herself, what she wanted for herself. He would never ask her to think about it for him, never even try to reach over and kiss her. He would wait, follow her cue.

"I want to tell you why I wanted us to come here," he says. He leans forward and brushes the hair from her eyes. She looks at him and then away every time he does. He has a sudden, sickening feeling that they will not be back here, not together.

"I've come here before, when I was very little."

He rises to his feet and asks her to walk with him. She stands and brushes off her jeans, tugs her shirt to straighten it over her hips. Weeds scrape against their legs. Today, the birds circle around the sun and the cold comes sooner than they'd like. He looks to her to commit her to memory: how she hugs her body, how she has pulled her hair back in a tight ponytail that sways as they walk down the hill. Soft dirt comes loose as they walk. They follow a small path and soon they are at the river. The water has risen. It moves forcefully around large rocks and over the surface of others.

"This is where I remember being the most happy," Amar says, pointing out at the water. He removes his shoes and socks and rolls up his jeans and steps in. It is cold. It feels wonderful. He looks back at her and she gives him a certain look, a blend of courage and tenderness, a look, he hopes, a woman wears when she is falling in love.

"I always thought we came here because it was tucked away from the traffic, far from anyone we knew. And because it was beautiful."

He shakes his head. "I don't remember why, exactly, I just know I felt so happy here. This tree," he points to a tree behind her, then gestures at the river, "this water. I only have a vague memory, but sharp enough to be sure it was this place. In high school, I went to every park near my home where there was a creek, in search of here. I didn't tell anyone in my family. I asked strangers who might know it. The librarian at my school. I looked at a map. When I finally found it, it was like stepping into an old dream."

He is silent then. She watches him. She does not ask any questions. He looks out at the cuts of water, how jagged it is, how fast it is moving, how it gushes around the rocks, how the sunlight catches to highlight every peak.

"My mother and me. I asked her to join me in the river, and she did. I remember she did."

❖

HADIA TAKES A break from packing to peek through her window: Amar, the Ali brothers, and some others. The boys have just finished playing basketball. For hours, Hadia listened to the hollow bounce of the basketball on concrete, the ring of metal, the swish of net, while she regarded her shirts, her sweaters, held them up one by one before tossing them or folding them neatly. She itched to join them, to be able to move a basketball from one hand to another, to know how to step around players and when to shoot for the basket. But that was the impulse of another life. She folded her sweater, a pale pink, and packed it into her suitcase.

She has often felt barred from hundreds of experiences—she has never strummed her fingers on the strings of a guitar, stretched her legs in dance, played a sport outside of PE class requirements, pedaled her feet fast on a bike without training wheels, on an actual street, next to moving cars—but recently the scope of her life has seemed to gasp open just a bit, and she wonders now what she will remain barred from, and what she can pry away for herself. It is quiet now except for the boys' conversation that drifts up. When she peers down, the boys are lined against the garage door, directly beneath her window. She cannot make out their full sentences, but can tell their voices apart. Abbas Ali's distinct timbre. His laugh. It is nearly the end of summer. Sun in the sky and sun caught in their stray strands of hair, Abbas Ali's dark hair transformed into an almost golden-brown crown. Amar has scraped his knee. A streak of skin on his kneecap shines a bright crimson.

Could she really leave? Earlier this morning, she had begun the task of determining how much to pack, wondering how often she would return. After years of the same meals with her family, the same boys gathering in her front yard, the same community parties and events to attend at their mosque, Amar on the other side of her bedroom wall and Huda across the hall—her window will finally look out at another view, and she will discover what life elsewhere is like, and who she is there.

When the call from the school's administration came, she walked out in a daze into the spring sunlight, until she was standing in the street, shaking a little from fear or excitement. All her life she assumed she could only leave the way others had: by marriage. As if marriage were the ticket, not to freedom exactly, but something close to it. Even Baba doubted her ability to make decisions for herself by stating: you are our responsibility until you are your husband's. Or: no, you cannot do so unless you are married, and then it is up to your husband to decide with you. Which she knew meant *for* you. Even if all she wanted was something as simple and small as cutting her hair short, standing in line with her friends at the movie theater for the midnight screenings. Then it was fall of senior year and her classmates were in a flurry to apply to colleges, and she watched the green leaves turn red and waver and thought: why not me? I can at least try. She applied to nearby schools but also one program five hours away—a special, six-year program that was both an undergraduate degree and a medical one—a long shot, near impossible to get into, but Baba had always wanted her to be a doctor, always told her she could move away only if she got married or got into medical school.

Thank you, she had said to the woman on the phone, thank you, and because the rush of emotions made her face fuzzy she gushed to her: you have changed my life. Well, the woman said, I don't think I had much to do with it, and she might have laughed. How could the woman have known that she was not just conveying the news of acceptance, but also presenting Hadia with the promise of a formerly unfathomable life? One Hadia had worked for and longed for, but never allowed herself to fully picture, never allowed herself to honestly believe that a life where she abided by her rules and hers alone, picked up a guitar if she wanted to, learned a chord to play, could be hers. She would become a *somebody*—a doctor. She would live a five-hour car journey away from this very street, this little leaf that blew right by her, the sight of the sun setting behind the tips of houses across her street.

Now the drive she and Baba will make to move her into her dorm is a week away and all she can think of is how nice the sound of a basketball thudding against concrete is, how nice that she can walk downstairs and out the front door to see the boys she has grown with since childhood, sweaty and tired and smiling with surprise at the sight of her waving at them and asking them if they want some mango lassi.

"I'm making some for myself," she explains, which is true, but Hadia knows that Abbas Ali loves mango lassi, and the boys raise their hands up so she can count cups, and Abbas Ali hollers a yes and thank you, Hadia, calling her by her name.

SHE HAD COME back inside after the call. Mumma and Baba were in the living room and she began to stutter. What has happened to you? Baba asked as she tried to tell him what the administration had said. They thought she was a good fit. Her application had impressed them. She could be a doctor, begin residency in six to seven years if all went well, *Inshallah,* it would go well. And before they registered the news, their expressions were confused and there was her fear: that it had been a lie, Baba saying she could study anywhere if she became a doctor, and now it was almost possible and he would say no to this too.

Instead he stood and wrapped his arms around her and spoke into her hair that he was proud of her. She felt her body was humming from the impact of the news and realized she had begun crying. She couldn't believe it. So she said so.

"Can't you?" Baba replied. "I did not doubt it."

Her mother too hugged her, albeit coldly, asking only how far away the program was, and Huda and Amar entered while Hadia's face was pressed into the coarse fabric of her mother's *shalwar kameez.* As if she were overhearing a conversation that was meant to be private, she heard Baba tell Huda and Amar the news, his voice animated, excited even. Huda shrieked and Amar lifted her up and over his shoulder and spun her around, and she kept saying put me down, put me down, but it was the best, the dizzying feeling, the world spinning and spinning.

The very next day, when she was called down for dinner, she saw that her family was standing in the hallway dressed in slightly nicer clothes—Mumma had put on lipstick, a very sober pink, Baba had worn his shiny shoes, Amar a button-up shirt—and they explained nothing to her as they got into the car. Huda had started wearing a scarf again and that day she had chosen an extravagant cream silk, wrapped tightly like a work of art around her face, but Hadia had not put it on again, so her hair was piled on top of her head in a messy bun, her sweater an old one for home. She would have to tell Baba that she could not see herself wearing a scarf again, and she imagined Baba would ask her, "Is it because you don't feel safe?" To which she would respond, with the sharpest honesty she had only recently found the courage for, "It is because I don't want to."

A decision that would somehow be easier to reveal because the path of her life had begun to announce and distinguish itself as separate, as having worth that her parents could understand, respect, and therefore be able to acquiesce to. That afternoon no one replied when Hadia asked where they were heading, and soon the route was familiar to her—the one they took to her favorite Thai restaurant. When they got out of the car she waited behind to walk in with Baba, and half hugged him as she thanked him.

"It was Mumma's idea," he said, nodding to Mumma, who was holding the door open and waiting for them to enter.

Huda and Baba had asked her questions about the program, the accommodation the school would provide, the breaks she would be given, Baba wondering if she knew what she wanted to specialize in yet, Amar only speaking to say that he would miss her, or asking if he could steal her room despite his being the same size as hers. But Mumma had remained thin-lipped throughout it all, and Hadia was unsure what her mother wanted from her, or if she was even happy for Hadia.

After the plates had been cleared away and the leftovers packed in boxes, Baba ordered desserts for them all, a rare treat—mango with sticky rice and fried roti and fried ice cream. Hadia returned from the restroom to find an elegantly wrapped box where her plate had been, with shiny gold wrapping paper and a plush bow.

"Aren't you going to open it?" Amar asked, when her reaction had been to just stare, to poke down an ear of the bow.

"Do you know what it is?" she asked him, and he nodded.

She looked at each face—all four of them eager and excited, even Mumma's wide smile, how Mumma dipped her head to encourage her. Hadia spoke to herself then: It does not matter what is in this box. Be so happy, so visibly grateful when you open it.

She did not tear the wrapping but tugged gently until the tape came free and folded the paper to save it. Opened the box and there, elevated on a small stand, was a watch—*the* watch—Baba's, her Dada's. Now, hers. She looked up. Baba was waiting for her reaction. Of course she had seen it before—Baba wore it on special occasions, he had let her hold it when she was a child, and she might have even slipped it over her wrist. The delicate gold rim, the perfect circle, its black hands with tiny tear-dropped ends, its most gentle tick. She had never been gifted something so simple but also ornate, so obviously valuable at first glance, unnecessary and undreamed of until the moment that it was given to her, and she knew then that she would wear it the same way she carried her last name, with pride.

"Are you sure?" she could not help but ask.

It was his most cherished possession. Baba was never sentimental, but this watch he would draw from his desk drawer, polish, and return to its box again. She had never imagined it one day being hers. Amar was smiling softly at her and tearing his tissue into small squares.

"For all you have done," Baba said, and it was clear by the look on his face that he was happy with her reaction, that she did not even have to pretend.

"But, Baba, isn't the watch for a man?" she asked him later, when they were alone in his study.

"Who says it is for a man?" Baba asked her. He straightened his papers by hitting them against the desk.

She thought for a moment.

"Men?"

Baba laughed.

"Exactly," he said.

She had worn the watch at dinner and had not taken it off since. Baba held her wrist up. It was a little big on her, but in a way that she liked, a reminder of what it signified.

"It's yours now," he said to her. "It was always going to be yours, Hadia. The only thing I did not know was when it would be the right time to give it."

IT IS COOL inside the kitchen, and the light too is cool, the sun having moved its way over the house. She brings down the blender from the cupboard and the yogurt, milk, and mango pulp from the fridge. She sets them on the counter, all in a row, by size. She likes to set out all the ingredients and pause before she begins to mix them up. And then Abbas Ali is in the hallway entrance, his hair damp, half sweaty still in his white shirt.

Her mother is upstairs napping and Baba is out of town and her sister is volunteering at Sunday school, her brother and all the other boys outside. She pours milk with a slightly shaking hand, she can feel the glugging of the milk from the flimsy plastic handle, and droplets fly from the spout to speckle her arms and shirt.

"Amar says you are leaving in a week."

She just smiles and manages a quick nod. She measures sugar into a cup. Abbas will not be going away for college. He will be going to a community college nearby until he can transfer. There is something about the boys from their community that disappoints her: they do not work as hard as they could, there is a listlessness about them, a lack of longing for another kind of life. They could be anything, go anywhere. With no one to deny them. Any word that is said against them is only to ask: where have you been, and why did you go? How lucky to have a question like that directed toward you. They are the young men of their families. They carry the family name. Everything is designed to cater to them, to their needs, to bend to their wishes. But they just gather in each other's front yards and reenact the same summer afternoons.

"I didn't congratulate you," he says. "Is it odd to say I was really proud of you when I heard?"

"No, it's nice. Thank you."

She is so shy, so spare with her words. He will think she does not want to speak with him. She begins to blend and they can't hear each other anymore anyway. The blender hums and her hands shake with it. She hopes her mother will not wake. Abbas stands in the hallway still, his head tilted, a hand in his hair, not looking at her but also not turning away. She will have to leave him too. A small departure. But still one. When she is done she begins to pour the lassi into little plastic cups. He steps into the kitchen and takes the blender from her.

"I can help," he says. "Let me."

Afraid to be in the same small tiled space with him, she steps quickly to the refrigerator, touches the side of her arm that he knocked when reaching for the blender, then busies herself by freeing tiny ice cubes from the ice tray, plops them into the cups he has filled. They work in silence. She feels heat, beneath her cheeks, spreading to her neck, a heat from the awareness that they are creating something together. How they are both aware. He is so meticulous. He pours the lassi and then bends down to examine it at eye level, as if he is in chemistry class and checking if they are all equal, and he nods to himself when he decides they are. She laughs and he looks up with a half-smile, knowing she is teasing.

"Which one will be yours?" he asks.

She points to one and he pours a little extra.

"This is my absolute favorite," he says when he is done pouring the drinks, and he places them on the plastic floral tray she hands to him.

"I know," she says, and she knows her face must certainly be red. But he is not looking, he is concentrating on balancing all the little cups of lassi, even hers, on the tray and carrying them out with great care. He watches the cups with every step, and nods to her in a way that tells her to follow him, and she follows, of course she follows.

"Will you visit?" he whispers, because they are in the hallway now and their voices can easily drift to her mother's bedroom.

She looks at the straight line of his neck as they walk, the vein that might always be there or might just be there after playing in the heat, the rise and dip of his shoulder. She likes that her sight expands when she is looking at him, likes that she is capable of feeling affection for something as small and specific as a bloom like a berry on the back of his neck.

"Every long break," she whispers back.

Then they are outside and surrounded by others. In the sunlight

Amar takes the tray from Abbas and Abbas reaches for the cup that is hers and hands it to her. Hadia looks back to the door. She presses an ice cube down until it is submerged, then tastes the sweet, sticky lassi left on her fingertip. She has done well. It is delicious.

Abbas Ali asks, "Stay for a minute?"

As though he knew what she was debating—to do what is proper or to do what she wants, a little longer with him, given that their time together is already so short. And Amar has not registered anything, he is just chugging his lassi as quickly as he can.

"Slow down and enjoy it," she calls to him.

Abbas says to her, "When have you ever known him to?"

"Never."

They laugh together. Then turn to watch Amar crush the plastic cup and drop it onto the ground, as if he were a teenager at a party. Some of the boys clap. Abbas Ali, the eldest Ali boy, the one face she has always sought out in a crowd, looks up at her with his face lowered, so that his eyebrows are raised, so that his eyes look bigger, his expression earnest, and when she looks at him, when she lifts the cup to her lips, when she nods that she will stay, he smiles to himself and looks away, past her, maybe to the magnolia tree, maybe to the street, maybe directly to the setting sun.

6

THE FAMILIAR SIGHT AT LAST IS NOT THE SILVER
of his mother's car, but his sisters walking up to where he leans
against the chain-link fence of his middle school. He recognizes
them instantly, even though they are still blurred figures approaching. His sisters look like twins, similar strides and same height,
except Hadia's dark hair sways, and Huda's black scarf frames
her face.

"What's wrong?" he asks when they are close enough to hear. He
stands straight and the fence rattles.

"Mumma can't pick us up today. Malik Uncle is coming to this
spot as soon as he's off of work." Hadia points to the ground.

"Why?"

"He didn't say."

Amar groans.

"But I have an idea," Hadia says.

It has been a while since Hadia has had an idea.

"Let's go for a walk."

"We'll get into trouble," he says.

"And you're going to be the one to tell them?" she says in Urdu.

She raises an eyebrow. She smiles mischievously. He cannot help
but smile too. Without their parents there, they can go anywhere,
do almost anything.

"Where?" he asks.

"You'll see."

He grabs his backpack and follows them down the slope. Hadia asks him to keep an eye on their route. He has a knack for directions, according to his father, and Amar prides himself in it. In a few months, Hadia will graduate and move away to college. He does not like imagining their house without her. His sisters appear excited and they laugh loudly at each other's jokes. They're speaking in their code and he feels not resentment but love for them. That they thought to include him in this afternoon, when they could have left him to wait behind his school fence. Hadia walks with her back straight. She looks both fierce and friendly. He trusts her to take them anywhere.

The trees above them are blossoming with white flowers. The sky glimpsed through the branches so blue. How can he not notice as they pass beneath them? When God first began to brainstorm the world did He think to make branches a dark brown and flowers either white or soft pink, and only like that in the spring, so that you are always startled by their bloom? Or were God's decisions scattered and sudden, beautiful by chance? He considers asking his sisters, wanting it to be as easy for him to speak with them as it is for them to speak to each other, but he stops himself, in case it is rude to imagine God in this way. Perhaps this is what Mumma means when she says not to think about God too much. Perhaps these are the kinds of questions that the *moulana* calls *shirk,* blasphemy, among the greatest of sins. He jumps up and tries to tug at a blossom but the branch is out of reach.

Recently, Amar has begun to feel as though he had been born into a world not made for him. What did it matter that his birth certificate was from a hospital in this very city, that the only house he had ever lived in was here. Where are you from? the kinder question would be. As though he could not possibly be from here. As though it were he and not they who had misunderstood. He had given up trying to explain. India, he would mumble. Even though he had not even been there for more than two weeks total, and that by now both his parents had lived here longer than they had ever lived elsewhere. Sometimes this answer would satisfy them and

135

sometimes he could see their faces twist in confusion, and they might even say, but don't people from India have darker skin?

Even at mosque, when listening to the speaker lecturing from the pulpit, he pulled little threads from the carpet and felt that none of this moved him, or was made to include him. There were moments. A feeling he got *after* praying, but never during, when the men turned to each other to shake hands, and when they settled into holding hands to recite aloud together the *dua* of brotherhood and sisterhood. Or when some of the boys said they were walking to a gas station nearby and they asked him to come. But then the moment passed. He pulled another thread. Outside, people could not pronounce his name and often asked if he had a nickname they could use, and in the mosque everyone nodded in agreement to speeches that just bored him. But if not here—where? Amar would slip away and wander the empty hallways, stop to drink from the water fountain, thinking to himself, nowhere, nowhere, nowhere.

Through the glass door one particular evening he saw the eldest Ali boy, Abbas, sitting on the front steps facing the parking lot. He went to him.

"Why are you not inside?" Amar asked.

"Pick a reason: Thought it was a nice night to enjoy the outside air. I didn't like the speaker's tone."

He was surprised to hear someone speak against the *moulana*.

"I prefer the stories to the rules about the proper way to shower when fasting," Amar said and rolled his eyes.

Abbas laughed a little. It was true. Amar loved the stories. If it were up to him that's all a mosque trip would be. No praying, no listening to Arabic recitations he didn't understand, no man telling them what the rules were and how they had already broken them.

"Won't you get in trouble?" Abbas asked him when Amar took a seat.

"I'm in trouble whether or not I sit out here."

Abbas laughed again.

"To ask for forgiveness and never permission, rule number one," Abbas said, and he lifted a finger up in emphasis.

Amar nodded, sort of understanding.

"What if you don't ask for either?" he asked.

"To never push your luck too much—that's probably a rule too."

Abbas Ali smelled faintly of cigarettes. Amar did not want to ask him why.

"You said you preferred the stories," Abbas said.

Amar nodded.

"Which ones? We might as well get something from tonight's mosque trip. In case anyone asks us what we were doing, why we were wasting time, we could say we were learning and participating in our *own* way. That could be another rule." Abbas winked at him.

It was a specific thrill, someone winking, like a secret handshake or an inside joke, but better. And not just anyone, but Abbas Ali.

Amar told him the story about the Prophet leading hundreds in *jummah* prayer. How one day when the Prophet knelt to touch his forehead to the ground in *sijda*, everyone behind him did the same, and at that moment, Hussain, the Prophet's grandson, climbed onto his grandfather's back. Instead of shaking his grandson off, the Prophet stayed kneeling. Amar imagined the sun shifting a fraction in the sky. All the men who were waiting for the cue to rise, confused about why it was taking so long. Mumma said the more hopeful believers wondered if a revelation was a cause for the delay, and the more cynical smiled to themselves, thinking they had finally caught the Prophet making a mistake, and one so public. What kind of believer was he, Amar wondered, if he liked the story so much because while everyone waited, the Prophet remained patient, forehead to the ground, and bent the rules just so his grandson could play a little longer.

"He waited until Imam Hussain decided he was ready to climb down, and as if it had never been stopped, the prayer resumed," Amar said to Abbas, copying exactly how Mumma had told them. Mumma tried to make the stories about morals but to Amar they were just about what people were willing to do for one another.

"You're my protégé," Abbas said to him after a long silence.

"What's a protégé?"

"Someone who is going to be trained to keep things relaxed around here, so boys like you and me can leave for a bit and feel fine doing it."

"Where are you going?"

"Anywhere."

"What should I learn?"

"Loopholes."

Abbas Ali winked at him again, and Amar nodded and sat up a bit straighter, so Abbas would know he was ready for the lessons.

"HERE," HADIA SAYS and stops, and the three of them stand still before a tiny street with old buildings and hand-painted signs, pots of flowers decorating the sidewalk. The place is oddly familiar. They have walked for half an hour just to get to it. Hadia explains that the street has an antique store, a barbershop, a stationery store, and an ice cream shop she wants to try.

"I don't have any money," he remembers.

"That's okay," Huda reassures him, "we do."

The ice cream parlor door makes a funny "moo" sound when they open it instead of a bell, and a mural of cows in a pasture is painted on the wall. He scans the room to make sure no one they know is inside. They look to each other as if to acknowledge this lucky fact. He remembers what it was like to pretend to be in a jungle when they were little, the bedsheets draped over the kitchen table their cave, and the three of them huddled beneath the table like a pack, alert to every noise outside that could be an animal's howl. They are a pack again now as they press their faces to the glass and pause to take in all the ice cream flavors. Huda asks for samples and Hadia squeezes his shoulder and says, "You can get anything, okay? Even a sundae."

He orders quickly and takes a seat in the red leather booth by the window, while Hadia opens up her wallet and counts dollar bill after dollar bill. She is a great leader for their pack. He will miss her. He licks his pistachio ice cream in his sugar cone, regretting that he opted for a cone and not a cup when he sees his sisters walk toward him with their mature cups and purple spoons in hand.

"So," he tells them, "the police came to our school last week, with a dog."

He has won their attention. His sisters lean in to listen. The police had come to every class to check for drugs. Hadia's eyes are wide at this, and she shakes her head and says to Huda, in middle school? And Huda says, come on, have you already forgotten? Every single backpack was lined up against the wall. Amar was terrified. Hadia asks him why he would panic. Amar says that the dog just nudged every bag with its nose but when it stopped at his it sniffed for a while and he thought, oh no, oh no, what if another kid put something in there for jokes? The police stopped the search and opened the zipper of his backpack and began to empty it of its contents. They brought out brown bag after brown bag bunched in the bottom, and with disgusted faces and white gloves they peered in each one.

"What was in them?" Huda asks.

"All of my lunches from the past month. Including a really rotten banana and a sandwich that basically looked like a bag of mold."

"Amar, that is so disgusting." Huda sits back in her seat, shakes her head.

Maybe it had been the wrong story to share with them.

"You are so embarrassing," Hadia says, but she is laughing. Then they both are. And soon he is laughing too.

Hadia pulls back her sleeve to check the time. One hour, she tells them. She is wearing Dada's watch. It is hers now. She is going to be a doctor. All their life she has made Mumma Baba so happy and she is only going to make them happier. Baba never talks about him to his friends the way Amar has overheard him speaking of Hadia, so he was not surprised when the watch went to her. It didn't even hurt to see her wear the watch. He wanted Hadia to have everything she wanted. But what did hurt was the feeling that he had always known it would never be his.

When they step outside the breeze is cool and he wants to tell

Hadia he is thankful, and Huda too, but they are eager to rush to the antique store. The lady behind the counter is old and does not look pleased to see them. It is as if she knows that they have very little money and are only curious. He wants to tell her this is his first time in an antique shop, but she resumes the paperback book in her hand after telling them not to touch anything. They disappear into the aisles. He can hear his sisters move through the store together, and he feels safe to leave their side. There are shelves of dolls with glass eyes. Board games he does not recognize. Who buys these things and what do they do with them? A typewriter black and a typewriter blue. No one is behind him so he touches a key. He presses down on the button that says *A* and jumps back when a metal rod flies up and hits the paper, and when it returns there is a tiny letter, and a little bell rings. He likes the impression the letter made on the page. He wants to put down another letter, *m*, then realizes it is not his name he is trying to spell, but hers, and he steps back abruptly. What if the shopkeeper follows the sound of the bell and kicks them out? What if his sisters come back to see him, typing her name? He is mortified, even at the possibility of it.

He leaves the typewriter to sit in a corner where there are boxes piled on the floor. One of the boxes has not been touched in a long time. It is black and old. He runs a finger across the leather surface, wiping away a thin layer of dust and making his fingertip gray. The box has a combination lock but it is open. The inside is deep and lined with soft maroon velvet. There is a zipper in the back and along the sides a bunch of tiny compartments. How much he could fill it with. Drawings. Basketball cards. Maps. Video games, if he ever got one. He snaps the lock shut and studies it. How everything about it suggests a secret.

Huda's hand on his shoulder startles him.

"We're leaving," she says, then looks at the box. "What's this?"

"I want it."

He did not know he wanted it until he said it. But now he feels like he needs it, that he would be happier if he had it in his life, filled it with his favorite things.

"You like this?" she asks, incredulous.

"Why can't I?"

"Just. I didn't expect it. The typewriter maybe, but a box?"

"With a lock."

"How much?"

He has not thought to check. He doesn't want to leave without it. He would show it to nobody. He would hide it beneath his bed or in his closet. The piece of paper taped on it has the price and instructions for the lock and he sighs.

"Fifty."

"Whoa. Well, we can't carry it out with us today anyway."

He stands up. As he follows her he looks back at it, the streak of darker leather he made.

"Don't look so moody. Your birthday is coming up in a month."

"So?"

"So. I'm just saying."

Before they step outside the elderly lady at the counter tells them about the soda she has for sale. Hadia looks at Amar and he nods. Hadia pools quarters and nickels and the coins clink onto the glass surface. The lady counts with her fingernail, painted a blood red. They are fifteen cents short but she gives it to them anyway: three sodas in glass bottles. It is so cold in his hand and satisfying to drink under a sun that promises summer is coming. They sit on the sidewalk, their legs splayed out and into the gravel street.

"Tastes better like this," Amar says, lifting the glass bottle to the sky and examining it from all sides. He is not sure if it is the bottle that makes it taste better or that they bought it for him. "Thank you," he says to them, "for everything."

"Don't be so nice," Huda jokes. "It doesn't suit you."

He has been rude to them lately, to everyone, angry all the time without really knowing why. He should try harder. He loves them. He knows that. It is easier to feel it here, after this walk, drinking soda in the sun, than it is when they are home.

"Do you remember how we got here?" Hadia asks.

"Of course," he says, and he hopes how he feels with his sisters today will last long after they've returned home.

WHEN THEY REACH their street it is packed with cars from the community. Amar looks over to Malik Uncle, who said when he picked them up that their parents had to tell them something. The look on his face suggests he did not expect the cars either. Amar turns to look at his sisters in the backseat. What Hadia sees in his face makes her immediately straighten her posture and lean forward, look out over the dash at the cars parked on their street, and before Malik Uncle has even found a spot, she has taken off her seat belt and jumped out of the moving vehicle. Amar follows her lead. He hears another door slam and he knows Huda is running with them too. He knows it is not Mumma. He knows it is not Baba. Malik Uncle said that Mumma *and* Baba had news for them. But still. Let them both be all right, he prays. Their home is filled with people he recognizes who try to hug him, but he drops his backpack by the door and maneuvers through them. His mother is in the living room, her face hidden by her hands. People surrounding her read from religious texts. Please don't let it be Baba. Please let it be anything but him. An aunty who is next to Mumma sees them and touches Mumma's shoulder. Mumma looks up. She has been crying. She holds her arms out for him, and he goes, and she begins to cry when he hugs her, her shoulders shaking, her face pressed against his neck.

"It's Nana," she says, and she shakes her head. "I was waiting for you three to come. I have been waiting for you all afternoon."

When he looks at Hadia's face he sees not only grief but also guilt, that they had stolen an afternoon for themselves, spent hours exploring under the sun, going against Mumma's and Baba's wishes, while at home Mumma waited for them to comfort her.

✦

LAYLA WATCHES HER son shiver through the sliding glass door. His hands in his pockets, his shoulders raised. How he likes to complicate what is simple—warmth easily acquired, an argument easily avoided. She smiles. He is focused on something in the dirt of her garden and presses the toe of his shoe into it, as though he is a child of seven again and not a young man of twenty. The two of them are home alone. Rafiq has taken Huda to visit the graduate school she was accepted in, a university two hours away. Huda will be a teacher. It is a good profession for her. Layla has observed her in Sunday school classrooms, how Huda knows when to be stern or gentle, how she is attuned to what each student and situation demands. Layla is not worried for her. Not as worried as she was when Hadia first left, and, watching Amar pull his notebook from his back pocket, she realizes not nearly as worried as she will be when he too goes.

One by one they will all go and she will be left with Rafiq in this house that is again too big for them, as it first was, when she walked in with Huda just a toddler in her arms and wondered how they would possibly manage to fill the rooms. Amar is in his second year of community college and has been doing well. He is motivated. He is responsible. She is grateful every day she enters the kitchen to see him studying, his books spread out on the table. She lifts the cup of tea close to her face, its steam rising. Amar scribbles in his black notebook, the edges of his pages fluttering. He is hiding something from her. She has suspected it for weeks, maybe even months.

"You'd let him get away with anything," Hadia had said recently, when they were arguing about her not answering Layla's calls. "You have no idea what he does and what he hides. You only care about what your girls do, where they go, and with who."

"No idea of what? What does he hide?" Layla had asked.

"Nothing," Hadia said. "Forget it."

Today marks sixteen years from what would have been the due date of her fourth child. It is her secret. Not in the sense that she is the only one who knows, but that she is the only one who still carries it. Rafiq assumed all sense of loss had left when the reminders had passed but Layla, even now, sometimes removes her necklaces and spare coins from the jewelry box to find the ultrasound photograph. So indistinguishable from any other that if her children were to come across it they might think it was the first image of them.

Come inside, she wants to say to Amar. It is warmer in here. The soft hum of the heater, her shawl draped over her shoulders, the cup of tea she brings to her lips. She watches him write. He is so serious. She had thought it was another whim. But it has been years and he has not been parted from his notebooks. Back when he was still in high school, he once pulled his notebook out at dinner and wrote a line before returning it to his pocket. She had tried to glance over. Hadia nudged him and sang, "Amar wants to be a poet." Stretching out the word, smiling. Rafiq had not torn his gaze from Amar. The look on Rafiq's face soured.

"My father was a painter," Layla had said to Amar.

"He painted some Sundays. It was not his job," Rafiq said. Then, after some silence, he added, "He knew better than to confuse a hobby with a respectable profession."

Amar left his plate untouched and, a moment later, his bedroom door slammed shut. She has yet to glimpse a page. She wonders if he keeps his old journals in the black box that her daughters had dragged her to an antique store to buy years ago. Such an odd birthday gift that she was convinced he would not like it, but her daughters had insisted. Layla had bought him a new net for his basketball hoop and some other, smaller, gifts, had baked him a cake and ordered pizza, but to her complete surprise when Amar ripped off the wrapping and saw the box he had gasped, unlocked the latch so carefully, and ran his hands along the deep-red velvet inside. He hugged Hadia and Huda first, as though he knew they were the ones to thank, before remembering to thank her and Rafiq. He always kept it locked. Her tea has cooled. She sips it, looking up at the framed photograph of her family, which she dislikes because the gap between Amar and Rafiq has always felt too revealing, but today it makes her think of that other child, and what it would have been like for him to have been in their lives, their family.

From Him we are and to Him we return. A phrase recited in

Arabic when hearing of someone's death. Surely there is evidence for the line present in all aspects of life, not just in the face of death. This house, this table, this teacup she sips from, who is to say one day it might not all be taken? Our children are not our own as our lives are not our own. All are a loan from God, His temporary gift. Amar looks through the glass door at her and she raises her hand to wave at him. He gives her a small smile, then tucks his notebook back in his pocket. Maybe if she shares with him what she has shared with no one else he will open up to her. A friendship will develop between them. After all, she knows her children: knows their habits and tastes, even as she is becoming increasingly aware that they can easily choose to not speak of their lives. It is they who do not know her, who make no attempt to. Amar kicks his shoes on the mat outside and closes the sliding door behind him. Without saying a word he enters and lays his head on her lap, stretches his legs on the couch. The hum of the heater quiets.

"You are hurt about something." She says it softly, touches his eyebrow from one end to the other. When he was a boy, this is how she would calm him back to sleep after a nightmare, both eyebrows at once, her thumbs reaching the edge of his face then beginning at the center again. When he got older and his nightmares worsened, he would stumble into their bedroom and in a daze would fall asleep at the foot of their bed. She would cover him with a spare blanket and whisper prayers that she blew on him, before falling back asleep herself. By morning he would be gone, the blanket folded neatly and put back in their closet.

He shakes his head, bites the side of his cheek.

"You can't lie to your mother. You can try to lie to everyone else, but a mother? A mother always knows."

He smiles.

"It's nothing, Ma. I promise you."

"Oh, Ami. There is *always* something with you."

"Maybe that makes life interesting?" He shrugs as he says it.

"Living is interesting enough. Don't make the mistake of confusing a sad state with an interesting life."

He has grown too old now for her to guess exactly what is bothering him—but the sense of knowing he is bothered has never left her. She runs her hand through his hair. He closes his eyes.

"Ma?"

"Yes?"

"Do you think I'll be able to transfer?"

"Of course. You've been working so hard."

"Do you think I'll be able to become a doctor?"

She stops moving her hand, rests it on his forehead.

"Is that what you want?" she asks.

He opens his eyes.

"You hesitated."

"No, I am only surprised it is what you want. I was just watching you writing in the garden and remembered when Hadia said you wanted to be a poet. Has Baba been talking to you?"

He shakes his head. She has let him down.

"You'd make a fine doctor, Ami."

He does not work nearly as hard as Hadia. He begins then abandons, gives up easily what he does not care for.

"Are you enjoying the classes?"

He shrugs. She bites her lip, promises herself to be more careful with her words. She will have to ask Rafiq to not pressure Amar too much. Still, she is glad he has told her he is thinking about it. Even though Hadia was their first, even though Huda their heartfelt believer, she has always felt instinctively that she and Amar had their own understanding, one she could never establish with her daughters. If her daughters banished him from their games, it was she who lifted Amar into her arms and distracted him with a walk outside, drew lines with chalk in the cement section of their garden and sang as he jumped from square to square.

Once, when her children were much younger, she had found him sniffling after her girls had shut him out of their room. He refused to tell her what was the matter until she had pried it out of him, and even then all he had said was, "They don't love me."

It was this that angered her and she led Hadia by her arm to her

146

bedroom and shut the door behind them, knelt until they were eye to eye.

"Do you think it's funny to hurt your brother?"

She tightened her grip. Hadia's eyes widened.

"Right now it is funny to you both to tease him. To leave him out. It's a big joke you forget about. Maybe he also forgets. But you are his sister. It is your duty to take care of him. If you treat him horribly, Huda will treat him horribly."

"He doesn't know the way we play. He's too little."

"Then play something else."

"That's not fair."

"One day the joke will not be funny. If you always leave him out, if you always tease him and hurt his feelings, soon you will not know how to be any other way with him, and it will affect his personality. Your relationship. For his whole life, and the rest of yours. Do you understand that, Hadia? Whose fault will that be then?"

Hadia had begun crying. Layla let go.

"Whose fault?"

"Mine."

She had wanted to have another son to give Amar a brother. She thought that a brother would make him feel less alone. That first week following her miscarriage she was certain he sensed her grieving. He would find her, sitting at the kitchen table, staring out at her garden, unwilling or unable to do the task that was before her—the simple washing of dishes, the preparing of dinner, even eating her own breakfast that Rafiq had so kindly set out for her before going to work—and Amar would wordlessly climb into her lap, rest his head on her chest, and look up at her with his big brown eyes.

"Can you keep a secret?" she asks him now.

"Depends on the secret."

His teasing smile looks unfamiliar upside down. She tsk-tsks at him. How can she tell Amar in a way that will not cause him pain?

"I was going to have a child once, after you."

"You wanted to?"

147

"I almost did."

He sits up. He faces her.

"I don't remember," he says, shaking his head.

"None of you knew. Hadia and Huda still do not know. Rafiq and I kept it a secret the first few months, hoping it would protect from *nazar*."

Amar is silent while she explains, he plays with the edge of his shirt as if trying to tear it. She is surprised to find that she is speaking in medical terminology she had not even thought she had grasped when the doctor first told her. Her voice is without any emotion, as though she has stepped aside from her own feelings so Amar can encounter the news unbiased.

"I named him Jaffer," she says, and that is when the emotion floods back into her voice, when what she is sharing becomes hers again. "I wanted you to know."

He leans against her shoulder and does not look up when she tells him how Rafiq had left them with Seema Aunty for a few nights, how he assured her that the Ali family had the most children close to their children's age, and that if they had company they would not miss Layla as much. But on the drive home from the hospital, when Layla looked to Rafiq, she felt no comfort, and in the empty house she longed for her children to be brought home to her, even though Rafiq insisted it would be best if she rested a few days without any obligations to attend to. She tells Amar about the woman in the mosque who calls for her son by that name and how hearing it sometimes shocks her. Or how, at the grocery store, if the clerk asks her how many children she has, she catches herself replying four.

"Your baba has not asked me about it once since," she says. It is the closest she has come to complaining about her husband to her son, to anyone, and when Amar does look up, his eyes are lit with anger.

❖

AFTER HEARING OF the eldest Ali boy's death, Hadia refuses to drink water for the three days leading up to his funeral. It is her only tangible act of mourning, and she keeps it in secret. She does not cry. It would have given it away: that she had loved him, in her own quiet way.

On the day of the funeral she stays in bed and waits for the call to tell her it is time. She is grateful she has been home on break. Just a week ago, Mumma had hosted a *jashan* in her honor. She would be able to go on to her university's medical school. After the reciters closed their poetry books, they all gathered in the garden for lunch and it was then that Hadia had seen Abbas Ali for the last time, leaning against the side of her house in his white shirt, laughing with Amar at a joke she couldn't hear. He had begun to wear his hair long again, the way he had when he was nine and organizing capture the flag and games of tag in their backyards. Today he will be buried. And in two days, she will have to get back in her car and drive the long five hours, keeping her grip steady on the wheel, to return to school, where she will somehow begin another semester. Life will go on normally, and this seems like the most impossible fact of all.

She is afraid to see his body, to have the news confirmed so irrefutably. The entire community is in a state of disbelief—a death so young, so sudden. Someone so well liked, by both the elders and the children, someone who occupied an unvoiced corner of every young woman's heart in the community. The fan moves slowly and Hadia tries to focus on a single blade, watching it spin and spin. She thinks of flashing lights, ambulances arriving too late, shards of glass glimmering on concrete, his sister, whose knees collapsed upon hearing the news. She knows the crossroad where people have left bouquets by the stop sign, tied balloons to the pole, left letters on the metal gates nearby, their edges flapping.

There had been four young men in the car, Abbas Ali and his friends from community college, and all were dead now except one who had been buckled in the backseat. If she had been another kind of woman, Hadia is sure she would have had the courage to seek him out, ask him what Abbas spoke of that night. The one who survived is still in the hospital. They say he is not doing well. Hadia wonders what it would be like to enter a car with close friends and be the only one to leave it.

She turns away from the fan, convinced it is making her nauseous, and there it is: that small piece of gum wrapper still taped to her ceiling from when she had stood on her bed on tiptoe as a young girl and stuck it there. She had drawn a small strawberry on the gum wrapper. Almost a decade ago. She had forgotten about it—saw it from time to time over the years and it had always struck her as silly and embarrassing, as if she were no better than the girls who wrote *Mrs.* next to the last names of their crushes. Still, she had never had the heart to take it down. The events surrounding the silver wrapper are blurred. He had given it to her, she remembers that much, as well as the soft scrape of her fingertips against his palm.

The last time she saw Abbas she had spoken to him. Each time she returns to the conversation the memory loses some of its certainty. He is already becoming a long time ago. Everyone was gathered in their backyard. People eating together, laughing together, lining up to pray together. Hadia sat in the scratchy grass, balancing her plate of food on her leg, and Huda was leaning on her because Huda was always so happy and extra affectionate the first few days Hadia came home. She could see the eldest Ali boy heaping food on his own plate, and Hadia felt surprised the community boys had managed a whole hour without once disappearing—as they always did, and as the girls were always envious they could, even if they rolled their eyes when the boys returned smelling faintly of smoke. Amar had put extra effort into his clothes and hair, and he looked strikingly like photographs of Baba at that age. She remembered thinking: maybe this is what it is like for all of us to be almost but not quite yet adults.

She was climbing the stairs for a break from everyone when she heard the eldest Ali boy call her name. She placed a hand on the banister. She turned on her heel, two steps above him, and smiled at her added height. They were eye to eye.

You're back, he might have said to her, to which she might have done the slightest of curtsies as if to respond, here I am.

"You made the lassi?" he asked.

"I helped."

What else was there for them to talk about when they were hardly allowed to? She too could bring up lists and lists of nothings, just to be talking. Hadia debated if she should continue up the stairs.

"Do you remember that day you were about to leave?" he asked.

Of course she remembered. It was the day they had made lassi together.

"That was three years ago," she said, and he raised his eyebrows in surprise.

"Do you remember what I said that day?"

She shook her head. She moved her hand to hold on to her arm. Then she let go, afraid her posture might appear weak, uninviting.

"I told you that I knew you'd make us proud," he said. "You've always been the best of us."

"You never said that," she said, shaking her head and allowing a smile to escape her.

"Didn't I? Well, I meant to."

He was smiling wide. She was too. They stood like that for a long moment and she had the sense that they were both aware of some secret. The thought she had pushed aside since she was a young girl rose up one last time—that hope or intuition that he was, in his own way, in the only way he could, courting her by being kind to her brother. Then she blinked and the moment was lost. Not knowing how to offer a response that hummed the way his did, she asked how things had been at home since her last visit.

"Same as always," he said, and he turned to the framed family photographs that trailed the wall up the stairs, and she looked too, the one of her and Huda in their horrible collared and poufy dresses, the one of them smiling with their blue braces, one of Amar climbing the magnolia tree.

"Still keeping an eye on Amar for me?" she asked, and this seemed to hum just a bit, the way she said *for me*.

"You know I don't have to answer that."

They turned when they heard someone descending the stairs. It was Amira Ali. Hadia tensed to be discovered speaking to Abbas in private, but it was Amira who looked like she had been stumbled upon, and Abbas who handled the moment gracefully.

"There you are," he said to her, as if he had been searching for her the whole time. "We're leaving soon."

Amira gestured behind her. "The bathrooms downstairs were taken."

He turned to head back outside, and Amira smiled her timid smile when she passed Hadia and followed her brother down the stairs. Just before Abbas turned the corner, he looked back and said, "Congratulations again." Or maybe it was, "I was right back then." And he held his hand up in a wave, and maybe she nodded, and maybe she stood still.

There is a knock on the door and she knows by the sound and length of pause before the second rap that it is Amar. When she opens the door to her brother, Hadia looks at him for the first time not as her younger brother, but as the young man he is becoming, the hints in his face and demeanor that allow her to picture what he will look like in ten years, twenty years. Her apprehension rises, unbridled and accompanied by a fully formed fear: she is afraid it is possible that he too could die as suddenly and as young as the eldest Ali boy. It had not occurred to her before this week that one could lose a sibling. Nor had she considered how easily the crash could have happened on one of the many nights Amar was with Abbas. Amar looks at her curiously, possibly mistaking her fear for anxiety over the event they are about to attend, and he softly says, "Ready?"

They follow their parents to the car. Everyone appears to be else-where. Amar cannot decide if he wants the top button on his shirt buttoned, so he keeps his fingers there, doing and undoing it repeatedly. Abbas treated Amar like a brother and Amar had reciprocated that tenderness tenfold. He is free to be angry and inconsolable, to invite everyone to sit with him and then to shut them out again, and when he stood in the driveway as he did last night and shot hoops over and over again in the moonlight for hours, when he kicked the basketball against the garage door and it sounded like thunder inside, his reaction was both witnessed and excused.

They drive to the funeral in silence. Hadia rests her head against the window. It surprises her, the little details she can suddenly remember about Abbas Ali, despite having spent a life only in each other's periphery. It is as though a route of her mind has been uncovered and out march the dizzying sights of him. A shirt he wore the color of leaves, the blackberries he ate from the bowl in their kitchen, the soda he once spilled at a community party, the wooden keychain of a tiger on his backpack from the days she sat behind him in Sunday school, how he asked her once why she liked her plum tree, how he slowed when playing soccer to pass the ball to her, his eyes speckled with orange and gold, telling her *Inshallah* all will be well.

Just before walking into the wake, Hadia turns to Amar and touches his shoulder as if about to speak. He looks at her, but Hadia does not know what she wants to say. Would it be easier to tell Huda? He raises an eyebrow to encourage her. She wants to tell him she loved the eldest Ali boy. She wants him to know this loss is not his alone, that when she reached out to touch his shoulder it was not just to offer solace, but to ask for comfort too.

"What is it?" Amar stops to ask her.

Hadia shakes her head and walks past him, past her parents, past the crowd of solemn faces. She catches a glimpse of the family members once inside. Uncle Ali stands to shake the hand of everyone who has come, and Amira is seated on the floor, her face hidden by her own hand. Hadia is grateful they do not make eye contact, suddenly ashamed of her audacity to think she even has a loss to grieve, when a girl has just lost her brother, a father his firstborn son.

Her mouth is dry and she walks through the halls and heads straight to the bathroom. She shuts the door behind her and turns to her own reflection. She does not cry. But she does think of how Mumma only knocked on Amar's door after the news came. How it did not even occur to her to check on her daughters. What she wanted was for someone to know. For her sadness to not go unnoticed anymore. She wanted, more than anything, to lay her head in her mother's lap the way Amar often did, and tell her she had lost the first boy she had ever loved. The one she had maintained a distant devotion for since she first realized it was possible to feel for another. She wanted Mumma to stroke her hair the way she touched Amar's after the news, over and over, as if making sure he was really there, so stunned and lucky that he was alive. All these years she imagined her life would one day merge with Abbas Ali's. Their entangling had felt inevitable to her, and for this reason, and because it would be improper, she had not broken the barrier of silence between them.

Her reflection. Her tired face. She touches her dry bottom lip and thinks of how odd it is to experience a secret loss. A loss without a name. The loss of a potential version of her life. Of what she never had, and now never will. The realization that, in her own small and sustained way, she had loved someone for years that she had only looked at in glimpses, only spoken to in passing, only thought of in secret, only ever touched when they passed a cup of lassi or a stick of gum between them.

✧

WRITTEN AT THE top of the spelling test in red ink is *100%*. Amar's teacher even wrote a little note: *Good job, Amar. Wonderful improvement!* Amar is ecstatic. He waves the paper in front of Hadia's face like it's a flag, points at the number as though the red were not enough to draw her attention to it.

"You did it," Hadia tells him the first time he shows her.

The second time she only nods. But Mumma acts like every time she sees it is the first. She tapes the test on the refrigerator door, even though they are not like other families with magnets and photographs on their refrigerator. Mumma leans in to kiss Amar's cheek. She tells him that as soon as Baba comes home, she will show him the test, and that no one is more deserving of the shoes he will get.

At night, Amar comes to Hadia's bedroom to thank her. His

pajamas are dark blue with planets and white stars. Hadia tells herself to hug him. That he *does* deserve it.

"I wouldn't have been able to do it without you," he says, and she can tell from the look in his eyes and the tone of his voice that he means it.

"It's not a big deal," she says. She had meant that helping him was not a big deal, but her voice has a sharpened edge to it she did not intend, and he flinches a bit to hear it.

Downstairs in the closet his white shoes have the word written in black ink. When she first studied his test taped on the refrigerator door, she saw that each letter was written with so much care, so unlike his usual scribbles, that at first glance Hadia confused his handwriting with hers. It occurred to her that Amar could do anything if he tried. Maybe even better than Hadia could—he had only studied two nights.

After he leaves, she opens her bottom desk drawer, where she has kept all of her important tests and papers, and all of them are A's, and none of them have been seen by anyone but her.

Amar was the one they loved the most. He was the one whose picture Mumma kept in her wallet behind her license. Him smiling with a toothless grin. Mumma ran her fingers through his hair as if it nourished her. A painting he did of a boat on the ocean was tacked above Baba's office desk when she visited him at work. Once Hadia spent an entire afternoon counting the faces in the framed pictures, and Amar had beaten them all by seven. Hadia and Huda were a two-for-one deal: if there was a framed picture of them, they were likely together. Mumma served food for Amar first, and then Baba, and she always asked Amar if he wanted seconds. She was not even aware of doing it. Hadia's daily chore was washing the dishes and Huda's was sweeping. If Amar was asked to help, the two of them would shout and cheer to mark the day. Sometimes this made Hadia so angry that if she was left in charge of the cleaning while Mumma and Baba were out, she would delegate everything to Amar. He was the only one Mumma had a nickname for. His favorite ice cream flavor was always stocked in the fridge; if Hadia helped unload the groceries and saw a pistachio and almond carton, she reminded Baba that Amar was the only one of them who ate that flavor.

"You don't love it too?" Baba would ask her distractedly, every time.

"No," she'd say quietly, thinking there was no point in correcting him at all.

Once, only once, had she confronted her mother about this, after her mother had taken his side during a fight that he was clearly to blame for.

"You love him more," she had shouted. "You love him more than all of us."

"Don't be silly."

Her mother was calm, as if she was bored by Hadia's tantrum.

"You think about him more. What he needs and what he wants."

Hadia had turned to run back into her room.

"We *worry* about him more," her mother had called after her, so gently that Hadia had wanted to believe her. "We don't have to worry about you."

She had sniffled, and locked her bedroom door, embarrassed by her outburst. She plotted to do something that would make her parents worry about her, as if their worry would prove the depth of their love. But she was afraid. They had endless patience for Amar's antics. She feared the only thing worse than wondering if they loved him more was testing their patience, proving it to be thin, and knowing for certain.

They loved Hadia because she did well. Her grades were good and her teachers said kind things about her. She was not sure if Baba would even notice her at all, if she did not work hard to distinguish herself academically. The only compliment Mumma ever gave her was that when Hadia cleaned the stove, it always sparkled.

"Even I can't clean like that," Mumma would say. And there would be actual awe in her voice, and Hadia would never know if she should feel glad for the compliment, or annoyed that it was the only thing that Mumma valued enough to note.

Amar was their son. Even the word *son* felt like something shiny and golden to her, like the actual sun that reigned over their days.

Baba would sometimes say to Hadia, "One day you'll live with your husband. You'll care for his parents. You'll forget about us."

It was meant as a joke, "you'll forget about us," or "we will no longer be responsible for you." But it was never funny.

"Amar will take care of us, right, Ami?" Mumma would squeeze his cheeks. Amar would nod.

"Why can't I?" she would say.

"Because the role of the daughter is to go off, to make her own home, to take her husband's name—daughters are never really ours," Baba would tell her.

But I want to be yours, she'd want to say. I want to be yours or just my own.

"I won't take anyone's name," she'd vow aloud, but he would have stopped listening.

Everyone important was a boy. The Prophets and the Imams had been men. The *moulana* was always a man. Jonah got to be swallowed by the whale. Joseph was given the colorful coat and the powerful dreams. Noah knew the flood was coming. Whereas Noah's wife was silly and drowned. Eve was the first to reach for the fruit. But Hadia liked to keep her examples close. It was Moses's sister who had the clever idea to put him in the basket, and the Pharaoh's wife who had the heart to pull him from the river. It was Bibi Mariam who was given the miracle of Jesus. Bibi Fatima was the only child the Prophet had and the Prophet never lamented the lack of a son. And she liked to think that there was a reason that one of the first things the Prophet ever did was forbid the people of Quraysh from burying their newborn daughters alive. But still, hundreds and hundreds of years had passed, and it was still the son they cherished, the son their pride depended on, the son who would carry their name into the next generation.

SHE HOLDS ON to the banister to guide her. Everyone but Baba is asleep. She is supposed to be asleep too—but she is thirsty, and has dared to tiptoe downstairs for a glass of water. Amar's test dominates the refrigerator door. In the blue light the ink of the *100%* appears purple. She is not sure what to name her feeling, but she knows she does not like it—the way it shrinks her heart. That there could be a limit to the happiness she could feel for Amar. Earlier that night, Baba came home and he and Amar had shaken hands like businessmen. But when Baba told him they would go that weekend to the mall, Amar became again a boy who could cheer hurray and hug his arms so tightly around Baba's legs that Baba started to laugh. Mumma had reached out and touched Baba's arm, and smiled at him when he looked at her. Baba had been generous: he said that Amar could customize his shoes, which they knew from the posters cost extra. Amar was grateful, but when he spoke to Hadia and Huda he was arrogant: his shoes would be better than anything they owned.

After Amar's test was posted on the refrigerator, she asked her mother if she could buy eyeliner and begin wearing lip gloss like the other girls at school. Maybe even wear it to Sunday school sometimes. There was a boy in her mosque that all the girls talked about, and they gathered in the bathroom and leaned toward their reflections in the mirror, their mouths little O's, to apply lip gloss with an expertly steady hand, and if he happened to walk by they always laughed loudly. Hadia did not want to laugh when the eldest Ali boy walked by for no reason and did not want to wear makeup just so he would look at her, but it would be nice to not be the only girl in her grade who was plain, who was dressed by her mother in oversized clothes. Mumma told her it was wrong to do things intentionally to attract attention.

"Don't be childish, Hadia," Mumma said when Hadia reminded her that she had gotten A's on her recent tests. "It doesn't suit you. This was a special thing for Amar. You know that."

She knocks so quietly on Baba's open office door it takes him a moment to look up from his paperwork.

"Why aren't you asleep?" he asks, and he invites her inside by folding his fingers toward him. Baba removes the glasses from his face and sets them down.

"I have to tell you something," she says.

Baba asks her to sit in the chair in front of his desk, and she sits. Baba has a paperweight on his desk that Hadia made in the fourth grade, fat and finished with glittery glaze. When the teacher first handed it back to her she was so proud of how beautiful it was. Now it looks like a blob she wishes he would throw away. But he has kept it, and Hadia thinks that maybe she has been mistaken, maybe she should count again the faces in the framed photographs, ask Mumma for what she wants in another way.

"Amar told me you helped him a lot," Baba says to her. "I'm proud of you."

It is exactly what she had wanted to hear but now that she has heard it she only wants to cry.

"What did you have to tell me?" he asks.

"Nothing, never mind," she says and shakes her head, but Baba knows she is lying.

"Tell me, Hadia." He leans forward. He uses his about-to-be-angry voice. He looks impatiently at his watch and says, "It's late."

Baba is wearing his father's watch. It is old but so nice and it makes Baba's wrist look important. The watch has passed from father to son and one day it will be Amar's. He does not even have to do anything to earn it. All he has to do is exist.

And Hadia thinks of Mumma leaning in to kiss Amar. How Mumma always says to Amar, *mera beta,* my son, but never says *meri beti,* to Hadia or Huda, as though daughters are unworthy of being called *mine.*

"Amar cheated. Look at the soles of his shoes," she blurts, and the words sound ugly as soon as they escape her mouth.

Baba sits back in his seat. She had thought he would be instantly angry—this was the worst thing Amar could do, because it was a double lie, first to the teachers and then to his parents, but Baba just looks very tired.

"Go to sleep, Hadia," he says finally, and his voice is very thin.

Earlier that evening, Amar had said to her, "You know, Hadia, I

159

always thought that you were the smartest one. I thought that because you were so smart maybe Allah didn't give Mumma Baba's other kids as much brains. But it's not so bad, not so hard to try."

Now the thought occurs to her: what if she had not even wanted him to succeed all along? What if she *liked* being the smart Hadia, the responsible Hadia, the we-are-leaving-the-house-in-your-care-while-we-go-out-okay Hadia?

She turns around in the doorway. "Baba, you will still buy him the shoes, right?"

Baba runs his hand along his eyebrow and does not look up to answer her.

"Go."

She begins to cry. She does not move. She does not know what she expected, but it was not this feeling—that she is the one who has done something very wrong.

"Will you tell him I told?" she asks, her voice so small.

He shakes his head.

"He really did study, Baba. He didn't do anything else for two days."

"Now," he barks at her, pointing out the door. "I won't tell you again."

7

LAYLA WAITS UNTIL HER CHILDREN ARE SEATED on the padded puzzle-piece mats in the children's nook before wandering the aisles. She likes how tall the shelves on either side of her are, likes the look of the dust suspended in the afternoon light. Her children seemed at peace and occupied—Huda lying on her back flipping through a book, Hadia reading aloud to Amar, and Amar half leaning on her arm, trying to look at the pictures. A pile of books are stacked by his knees from when they first arrived and ran around in a frenzy pulling far more books than they would get through in a single sitting. What exactly is she looking for, she wonders, her fingers trailing spines.

It is a Sunday. They are in a public library near their home, where Layla brings them on some weekends, especially when Rafiq is away. He left for a business trip earlier this morning and will return Thursday night. It is odd to her, how used to his absence they have all become, and odder still that she does not mind it. When she speaks to her father on the phone now she does not tell him when Rafiq is gone. Her father still worries for her in a way that he does not have to worry for Sara, who has stayed in Hyderabad, who has never driven a day in her life, who lives in the apartment complex next door and has someone to help her with the groceries and the cooking and cleaning. She realizes that her life has grown, and what she can now do with ease has expanded. Just years ago, Layla panicked at the thought of having to manage without Rafiq, but now it seems that her house is relaxed when he is gone and cautious when he is not.

Hadia is ten now but still, she cannot leave them unattended for long. Layla walks to the lobby where a librarian is typing fast on her keyboard without looking down once. She has short, black hair, coral tear-shaped earrings. Layla never gets books for herself. Maybe she should. The books she once checked out with Hadia are now in her home again, for Amar. She pauses to admire the familiar illustrations: caterpillars and bright fish, a fireplace in a darkened room, a child playing in the shade of trees.

What is surprising to Layla is that it is Hadia who picks them out for Amar. Hadia who has grand ideas of how he should move through the world. So important to her, that he reads the books that were her favorite at that age, that made her love reading. Amar should watch animal documentaries about tigers and lions and sharks. They should go as a family to the museums her school took her to. That these activities are good for Huda's and Amar's imaginations. These are Hadia's words. Her decision too that Amar not watch violent shows or movies. Amar not spend too many hours playing video games. Because she did not. All by herself, Hadia chose not to do these things, and chose to watch dolphin documentaries, brought home books she read on the stairs, or upside down on their living room couch, her hair falling down the side. Layla is amused, but also astonished, only allowing him the movie Hadia deems too scary for him if he comes to her crying. Where did they come from, her children? And how did they arrive already themselves, and unlike anyone else?

"Can I help you find something?" the librarian asks. Her earrings sway when she tilts her head to one side.

Layla nods. Her children have not followed her here, and she has been away from them for no more than five minutes. She is unsure how to ask.

"Books on children."

"Fiction? A novel, a child protagonist?"

"No, no. Maybe a book if you sense that, something might be . . .
something might be a little wrong . . ."

"Healthwise? Or, a mental illness?"

"No," she responds quickly. "No, nothing like that. At all."

"I am not sure I understand, ma'am."

She shifts from one foot to another. Looks at the cuticles of her
fingers as she tries to explain. For example, if he gets upset about
little things, upset to the point where you wonder if this is normal?
He is louder about his hurt than the girls were, they were less irrit-
able, but perhaps it is just that—that he is a boy? What kind of
stubborn behavior is normal, and what is not? If he refuses to eat,
for example. If he makes a decision and no one can shake him
from it. And this may not be important—but say he began speaking at a later age? Say, for example, he is upset and he begins crying,
he will do so until his voice is hoarse, he will kick his legs on the
wall even after it bruises him, he will cry until he is exhausted,
until he falls asleep. And it could be for the smallest reason—I
lifted the shades up too abruptly without telling him. I poured
milk when he wanted none. Or he says he did something when I
know he didn't do it, brush his teeth, for example. But he insists so
adamantly I am certain he believes himself. The woman is nodding, slowly, her earrings moving too, and Layla cannot tell if she
is concentrating or concerned. She is grateful her children are aisles
and aisles away, and that Hadia cannot overhear her and become
worried, or that this woman cannot see her son and know who she
is betraying.

Before returning to her children, she places the books at the bottom of their book bag, knowing Hadia or Huda would see the spines
and ask questions. The librarian was kind, left her post at the desk and
led her through the aisles, gestured at entire shelves but pulled certain books out, discussed them briefly. Layla nodded, thank you,
thank you, she said quickly, so that the woman would leave her to
flip through the books and then return to her children having
decided that she did not even need them. But instead, Layla found

herself pausing at sentences and sections, and every sentence seemed applicable to Amar, while also feeling impossible it could be him. She feared she was doing what Rafiq often accused her of doing: worrying herself, finding something to be wrong only because she looked for it. But still. She would keep the books hidden in her bottom drawer, read them after her children were tucked in bed and when her husband was away.

Only if she, God forbid, came across a passage that was actually concerning would she bother Rafiq with it. It might only make it worse if she brought it to his attention. She wishes Rafiq would be a little easier on Amar, prays for a deepening in his patience. He is so easily angered, offended by little things when it comes to Amar. So what if he asked Huda to paint his nails too? It was no matter that he had no interest in the trucks that Rafiq bought him; let him play in the garden kicking up leaves, let him watch the shows his sisters watched. It was true he was a little sensitive. Layla's own father had not been an angry man—he painted, showed Layla his progress every week—but he had only daughters to raise. Maybe what a son evoked in a father was different than what a daughter evoked?

It would be all right. She was only afraid that when time passed, it would not be these trips to the library he would remember, or his eagerness to learn how she made roti in the kitchen with him as her helper, but how upset he would become when Rafiq scolded him. When she sees her children again, her son is still leaning his head on her daughter's arm. Her daughter is flipping the page of a book. Her hand is angled up a little so the cover is visible, and Layla can see it really is the same book they have checked out for years. Sometimes, when Layla reads them to her children, she opens up the cover and runs her fingers down the dates stamped onto the lined paper, wonders which of these dates of return have been theirs. If she had a camera with her, she would have pulled it out. Taken a picture of the three of them unaware of her watching. How calm they are. A Sunday in their public library.

How many times has she stood, as she is standing now, and

looked at her children as she is watching them now? A way of seeing that magnifies her attention, deepens her love at the sight of them, and she notices them in a way she otherwise might not, the way the sunlight goldens the profile of their faces, the way Hadia scratches at her nose, adjusts her scarf that always looks a little big on her. Perhaps a hundred times, just in a single week. Huda memorizing a poem for her class and wanting to recite it for her, Layla smiling at the way she looked up at the ceiling as though the lines were projected there. What a little person she was and so poised. And how Huda decided, all by herself, to not wait until her ninth birthday to begin wearing a scarf, but to begin months early, on her Islamic birthday. Or Hadia reminding her that this week, eight P.M., a shark documentary was on television and they should all watch it together, maybe eat dinner earlier to make it in time. And that new favorite game of Amar's, asking her, "Guess how old I am, Mumma?"

"Ten."

"No."

"Thirty-eight?"

"No!"

"Oh, I know," she would say slowly, so he leaned in closer to hear her reply, "a hundred and fifty-six."

Lots of laughter, and then, "No. I'll give you a clue."

"What's that?"

"Five."

She smiled every time. She did not have the heart to teach him the subtlety of a clue.

"Hm," she paused, tapping all fingers on her cheek to mimic his thinking face, and he waited wide-eyed until she said, "Five?"

"Yes!" He clapped, took another bite of dinner, and then after a pause asked her to play a game, and the game was again, guess how old I am, Mumma?

A hundred times. If not more. She was stunned and stunned again by them, and her love for them. How much had been lost? Never made it into her memory, never been captured in a photograph?

Hadia closes the hard cover of her book, a snap of sound that reaches her, and she leans back a little as if she has accomplished something great and is now tired. Let this moment make it, she prays, let each of them remember it too.

"Again," she can hear her son say.

"Again?"

"Yes, I liked it."

Layla considers walking up to them and breaking the moment's spell. But she does not have to, Hadia is scanning the library, restless and waiting to be found, and when she spots Layla she relaxes and smiles before reaching for a different book and suggesting they read that one instead. Amar is reluctant; he blows the hair off of his forehead to show her he is frustrated, but then he nods, leans in, and lets his sister lead him.

❖

HE WAITS FOR Amira in the tunnel beneath the bridge, rests his head against the uncomfortable concrete slope. Here is where they come when they have no time to linger. It is the only meeting spot she can reach by foot. The tunnel is decorated with graffiti and somewhere beneath the layers is the image he and Amira's brothers once had spray-painted of their own names, laughing from the ease with which they could leave a mark.

After five days of complete silence it was a relief last night to see her name in his inbox: *The tunnel tomorrow,* she had written, *3PM. Don't reply.* Of course he is sick about it. For days he could hardly eat, woke in the morning unsure if he had even slept, wondered if she had somehow found out that he does drink, does smoke both cigarettes and weed, does not lie to her but also does not offer information she would never think to ask him for. Or maybe she had grown tired of waiting and realized he wasn't fulfilling his potential, his promises to her. He did horribly on his last chemistry exam but was too afraid to tell her. Yet another failed mark. Every semester he was scared she would discover he couldn't transfer on her hopeful schedule. The third night she left his e-mails unanswered, he had snuck from his house with Simon, who Amar had grown close to—close in the sense that neither had to speak much to have a good time, and he could count on Simon to arrive with a plan as soon as he called. They had broken onto the rooftop of a friend's father's restaurant, and sat there for hours, their legs dangling off the roof, passing a spliff back and forth and staring at the stars until the sky emptied of darkness and glowed a bare white.

It has just stopped raining. The air is thick with mist. The tunnel is dry, save for a weak stream at his feet. When will she come? What will she have to say? It is half past three already. He pulls his knees to his body, rests his head against them. If this is about drinking then I will give it up. If this is about my grades, would your father mind a different career? I will do anything. He presses his thumb to his eyebrow and follows its line to the edge of his face in an attempt to calm himself. Then at last the sound of her shoes as she descends the uneven stairs. She is not being discreet. It occurs to him that this is the first time since they have begun speaking— no, since he has become aware of her existence—that he does not want her to come. Then she is standing at the entrance and it does not matter what she has come to say to him, he hardly thinks of God and never to thank Him, but he thanks Him now.

"I don't have very long—Mumma had a doctor's appointment, and they made Kumail stay with me right until he had to leave for class; that's why I'm late."

She does not step over the stream to take a seat beside him. She is wearing a powder-blue dress he has never seen, long pleats that run from her waist to her ankles, as if she woke in another time entirely, thinking it was summer. Her hair is disheveled and tied up in a ponytail, loose strands falling over her shoulder. She breathes heavily. She must have run. But what is odd about her is not her dress or demeanor, but that her eyes are swollen and red. He knows it is raining again by the gentle ripples on the surface of the puddles outside.

"Amar," she says, and he does not turn to look at her. Each raindrop ripples out to join the ring of another. "My Mumma knows."

He swallows and closes his eyes. A car passes above them and the tunnel rumbles.

"How?"

"I don't know how."

"We made sure no one saw us."

"I know."

"It might just be a suspicion."

"She knew details."

"Let's not risk meeting for a few weeks," he says. "She will forget."

Amira is quiet. She plays with the white belt of her dress, twists it around her wrist until it tightens. He looks at her muddied shoes. If her mother sees them when she comes home she will know.

"I wanted to meet today because I thought I should tell you in person. I thought I owed it to us."

He must have known it would end, and maybe it was knowing this that made it easier for him to continue to go out at night, to keep a bottle tucked in the laundry basket in his closet if he wanted a drink before falling asleep. He could have tried harder and he did not. She speaks and speaks and sometimes she pauses between her words and sniffles; she is asking him to look at her but he does not want to look at her. Her dress falls just above her ankles, when she moves even a little it sways.

"Won't you say anything?"

How unlucky that one person has the power to determine the shape of another's life. He could laugh about it. Please, she is saying, say something, I don't have much time. But there is nothing he can think to say, and it occurs to him that it is the one who loves less who has the privilege of being able to express their feelings easily and at all.

"What did they tell you about me?"

"Is there something to tell?"

She tilts her head to one side and watches him, steps one foot behind the other, crosses her ankles. They are quiet.

"I can't do this to them anymore," she says finally.

"And what about me?"

"They are my parents."

"Have I been no one?"

"You're asking me to turn my back on everyone I love."

"I would do it for you in an instant. I wouldn't even have to think about it."

"You don't care how your actions affect others."

The little raindrops tap gently against the puddle. Is it possible he feels relief? That now it is done, now her image of him has been ruined, and he has no reason to try to be someone he is not?

"Were you waiting for them to find out so you'd have an excuse to leave me?" he finally asks.

"It's been three years since you came to my door—what has changed? You don't know how angry Mumma was. How disgusted with me."

Maybe her plan had always been to defy her parents as long as it was convenient for her. He brought her comfort and some excitement, and she experienced herself as different—the only girl from the community who dared to speak to a boy, who wrote and received letters, hid a locket beneath her clothes. Or maybe she liked feeling close to or sorry for Rafiq's boy, who everyone in the community said to stay away from, the rumors about him drinking, the gossip of him leaving every speech to wander the halls regardless of how holy the day, how sad that parents so sweet be given a boy so difficult they would say, how God tested His believers in mysterious ways.

Maybe what she loved in him was never him, but who she hoped she would inspire him to be. Maybe she always intended to withdraw as soon as her reputation, and the sterling, sparkling name of her parents, was threatened. What about *his* family name? He had been foolish. He had entered with no plan to leave, let himself be her stop on the road, on her way to a man who was dependable, decent, someone she would not have to nag to quit smoking, someone with an education, someone without anger, someone whose parents were proud of him and proud to send forth a proposal on his behalf, and good for her.

"I was wrong about you. You're just like everyone else," he says to her, surprised to find that he wants to hurt her.

"And I wish you were a little more like us."

She cups her hand over her mouth immediately. The look she sees on his face makes her cry. He bites on his cheek until it hurts.

"I didn't mean it," she says, the tone in her voice suddenly deeper, and she steps forward. "I'm so sorry. Will you look at me?"

The rumble of another car passing. She sways from one foot to another and her dress sways with her.

"I can't put them through any more pain," she says at last. "Not after Abbas. I thought I could, or that you would have become who you said you would be before they found out, and we would do this the right way. You're lucky, you know. Mumma is so upset with me, she has not looked at me in days. Everyone can find out about us and you will walk away unscathed. But it will be my parents who can no longer walk with their faces raised. For having a daughter like me."

She is so beautiful still. Even after all her crying, with her face he has known all his life. He is afraid to speak for fear his voice will betray him.

"You can hate me," she says at last.

"I could never."

She sighs. A minute passes. He is a different person by the end of it.

"Your shoes," he says, pointing. "They will give you away."

She looks at the muddied soles. Her face pinches. She steps out from the tunnel. The light outside is bright and little spots of rain darken the blue cloth of her dress. There is something familiar about her logic. Something that reminds him of Hadia, how she thinks, and it is this thought that allows him to believe that she is being sincere. To forgive her as she takes careful steps around the puddles, turns a corner, and leaves his sight.

❖

HADIA WIPES AWAY all trace of eyeliner, gets dressed in all black—it is the eighth of Moharram, and a break between rotations has allowed her to come home and attend the *majlises*. In the bathroom mirror, she regards her reflection. Since she removed her scarf she has only worn it when going to mosque, out of a deep respect for the place and its dress code, more important to her than her personal preference. Her hands and their memory—the square cloth folded until the edges were even, placed on her head just before her forehead, a safety pin poked through and clasped shut beneath her chin, and then one ear of the cloth thrown over her shoulder, her personal touch. When she looks at her reflection, tenderness for a younger Hadia overwhelms her. This was her face of years ago. It is as though she can take a pilgrimage to her younger self as easily as folding a cloth and clasping it to her neck again. There is a knock on the bathroom door and she opens it to Huda, dressed exactly like she is: all black, in a plain cotton *shalwar kameez* that they will put a black abaya over, the flowing uniform of Moharram, of mourning. Huda's face softens when she sees her.

"Mumma wants you to convince Amar to come," Huda says.

"He needs convincing?"

Amar could offer an excuse on any other day, but these days of Moharram were for commemorating the martyrdom of Imam Hussain, and one would not even want to shirk attendance. Even Amar would not think to upset Mumma and Baba in such a way. Huda gives her the look she gives when both realize that Hadia has not lived with them since she was eighteen—almost six years ago now. It occurs to Hadia that unless she is specifically informed, she will not know what it has been like at home. But things are more or less always the same: only Amar fluctuates.

"Try and talk to him. God knows he doesn't listen to us."

She opens his door when he does not answer her knocking. He is still asleep. His room is an absolute mess. A strange stuffy smell. She shakes his shoulder, gently at first, then roughly until he opens his eyes to her.

"Hadia. You're home."

His eyes are groggy.

"Get ready quick—we're leaving."

"Where?"

"What cave have you been living in? It's eighth Moharram."

"I'm not coming." He covers his head with the blanket.

"But it's your favorite day," she tries.

Each night leading up to the tenth of Moharram was dedicated to a family member or companion whose life was lost fighting alongside Imam Hussain in the Battle of Karbala. Eighth of Moharram was dedicated to Hazrat Abbas. His story was one of loyalty. Of the love between brothers.

"Leave, Hadia—I won't change my mind."

Mumma, Baba, and Huda are standing by the front door, each of them wearing the same look on their faces, the one that tells her that they have been waiting for her for days, hoping that she would be the one to reach him. She shakes her head to answer the question no one manages to ask.

THE LAST TIME she had properly spoken to Amar was months ago, near the end of summer. He had come home early from his summer class and suggested they go out, just the two of them. They drove with the music blasting, windows down, singing loudly, until they pulled into a café with patio seating. The sun shone bright in the bluest sky the way it does some California days and one marvels at the luck of living in such a place.

It was not often the two of them were alone outside of home. Here, beneath the sky, they were like old friends who had not seen each other for a long time. Hadia bought the drinks, Amar waited for them at the counter and carried them out. She smiled because Amar remembered she drank even her cold drinks with a sleeve. She was squinting, and Amar asked if she wanted to switch seats, but she liked the rays warming her cheeks and liked the way, when she did look at Amar, he was backlit, just a moving outline.

"Mumma and Baba love you a lot. You should be kinder to them," she said.

He looked to the cars that passed. The people waiting at the corner for the light to change.

"I know Mumma does."

She shook her head. "Baba loves you more than any of us, even more than Mumma."

"All he does is yell."

"If he didn't love you, you wouldn't be able to upset him so easily."

They were silent then. He leaned forward and she could see all the features of his face and she felt strange for speaking so candidly.

"But you have calmed yourself recently," she offered in Urdu, and in Urdu it sounded like a light joke, one made with good intention.

He raised an eyebrow as if to say you've noticed.

"You have. You fight with them less. You smell a bit better."

She smiled then and he did too. Hadia would comment on how terrible he smelled when it was clear he had been smoking. It was the closest she came to addressing it. For a moment she wondered if he was in love. He was smiling the way people did when a change in them was noticed, satisfied that what was felt internally could be witnessed by the world.

"I know what I want to do now," he said to her. "Transfer quick, premed, medical track."

Hadia shifted her watch a bit. It was loose and moving it around comforted her.

"But you hate the sciences."

"You don't think I can do it."

"I'm only saying that you like writing, that's what you've liked for years now."

"It wouldn't be as respectable."

She laughed. He looked hurt, having misunderstood her laughter.

"And when did that start mattering to you?" Again she spoke in Urdu, her tone intending lightness.

"So you get to be the golden child, the studious one, and I should be the one who does what I care about."

"That's not what I meant."

"Why are you trying to dissuade me?"

173

"I'm not," she said quietly, stirring her straw. "I think you can do it."

Her words felt false then and she was sure he took them as so. Amar was turning twenty soon and was about to begin his second year of community college. As far as Hadia could tell he was far from being on track. He had gone through his entire education doing the bare minimum. His high school graduation had been a kind of miracle. When he had been in danger of dropping out of high school, she had tried to convince Baba that there were other kinds of intelligence. Did I come this far, he said, did I work this hard, for you to all waste your lives? Make nothing of yourselves. She did not say to her father: but *I* am making something of myself, and *only* for you. She did not tell him that since beginning med school it had become clear to her that she had no personal interest in the subject, that she was only pursuing it for him, pushing and pushing herself and resenting how one decision made at eighteen would now determine the shape of her life.

After her conversation with Amar, she could not silence her suspicions about the sudden change in him, the way he'd pulled himself together. She had stepped into his closet looking for his keepsake box. It felt wrong, but she only wanted to know if her hunch was true. When Amar was much younger and they had first gifted him the box, he had only trusted Hadia to help him figure out how to set the combination. He had chosen his birth date and his jersey number from the jersey Abbas Ali had given him, a combination he did not realize Hadia caught the significance of, and likely thought she had forgotten. Over the years she very rarely indulged in a cruel curiosity, and allowed herself to peek in his box.

In photographs held together by a plastic band she saw the face of Amira Ali. So he loved her. She had wondered when she had caught Amar looking in Amira's direction at parties. She had once walked in on them risking a conversation in the mosque lobby. Amira had blushed immediately, offered up a flimsy excuse, and walked away, leaving Hadia free to tease Amar, but instead she gave him a grim look. Of all the girls? she wanted to say. He should be careful. But why wouldn't he love Amira Ali? She was easy to love. Something about her stood apart from the other girls. Judging by the stack of letters addressed to him (To: A, From: A), perhaps she loved him too.

What surprised her most that night, though, was not the photographs of Amira Ali, but one of her father, young and handsome and so serious. He looked exactly like Amar did now. She held it in her hand like a prize, considered knocking on her parents' bedroom and saying: look—he saved this. But what would it prove? There was another photograph she had not seen before, at a park, their mother wearing a bright yellow *shalwar kameez*. Mumma looked radiant and astonishingly young. Baba was missing from the picture. Hadia tried to recall the day but could not. Tangerines in her hand and Huda's. In the picture Amar was looking up at her. Then there was a photograph of Abbas Ali and she stopped, having not seen his face in years, and she realized she had almost forgotten its disarming effect on her. Her throat closed shut. It was taken at a camp their families had gone to years ago; Amar's arm was around him. For years she had been too shy to say his name, but alone, under the yellow light of her brother's closet, she spoke his name aloud.

Amar loved Amira Ali. And she could not help but admire how he had done something about it: he had lifted a camera and focused it on her face, he had written her letters, sat by her in a sunny place. Hadia had loved Abbas Ali and had done nothing; the love story that existed between their families was not, as she had imagined as a girl, between her and Abbas Ali, but a story that now belonged to her brother. She had been alone with Abbas in the same kitchen and had barely spoken to him. She had kept her hands dumbly at her sides.

THE NIGHT OF the eighth Moharram *majlis,* Amar comes to Hadia's bedroom. He shakes her a little to wake her.

"I'm heading out," he says to her. "I'll be back before morning."

"Where are you going?"

She sits up. Even in the moonlight, even through the fog of her sleep, she can sense that he moves strangely, unsteady on his feet.

"It's good to have you home," he whispers. "I'm leaving my window open. Cover for me in case? Don't tell, yeah?"

He leaves. After he has walked away she catches a smell she cannot quite place. At least he still tells her before he goes. A horrible thought twists a knot in her stomach: what if something happens to him, what if her parents find out she had known and did nothing? The thought wakes her. She goes to her window and looks out. He is the figure jogging across the street and getting into a car. Navy blue, four-door, a license plate she can't make out. Please God, let him come back before Mumma and Baba wake for *fajr*. The magnolia flowers glow in the moonlight, white as bones.

Once they have driven away, she steps into his bedroom on tiptoe. It might just be an invitation to a party he does not want to refuse, a young man acting like one, which would not be a problem in any other household, had their family not been their family, their faith not their faith, their father not their father. She closes Amar's bedroom door behind her. Earlier that night, in the mosque parking lot, Amira Ali had pulled Hadia aside. Amira had had the audacity to ask after Amar, and had she not seemed so genuinely blue, Hadia might have bristled at her boldness. Whatever might have existed between Amira and Amar was over. She felt for her brother but was hardly surprised. Now she lifts up his sheets. Runs her hand beneath his mattress. Lifts his pillows and shakes them. A small green case falls out and bounces off the mattress and onto the floor. He is so reckless. Baba could easily follow the same trail. It is almost as though he wants to be caught. She unscrews the lid, sniffs it: just weed. She had guessed as much. She returns the canister to his pillow. As long as Mumma Baba didn't find it and overreact, all would be well. Baba would be unable to tolerate or understand it. The longer she searches, the faster she moves: his laundry basket is heavy for just clothes and she rummages until she finds two water bottles, one clear and one honey colored. She twists the cap open and scrunches her nose from the strong scent. She considers tasting it but could never. Not on the eve of ninth Moharram, not on any other day. She is a little proud of herself: that, even in the dead of night, with no one to watch her, even while holding the alcohol in her hand, she still has no intention of acting on her curiosity. Maybe a better sister would have drained the contents into the bathroom sink but she knows it would be no solution. It is not the drink but the impulse to seek it out that is the problem. She sprays his room with freshener, wipes down the surfaces of his desk and drawers. Tired, she sits on his bed. The breeze from his open window gets caught in the curtain like a ghost's dress. She thinks of the stacks of letters and photographs she found in Amar's box months ago, and her conversation with Amira tonight, and feels deeply sad for her brother. He should have known better—there was no way her parents would think to marry her to Amar. Amar, who liked to stoke the disapproval of everyone in the community like a man fanning flames. Amar never tried to be anyone other than himself, but now she sees that perhaps, this past summer, when they were sitting on that patio squinting from the sunlight, he had been trying, for Amira Ali, to become the kind of man who could send a decent proposal. Before leaving his room she looks out the window at the empty street and trembling magnolia blossoms. The curtain fills with air before dragging back and she tries to push the uneasy thought from her mind: of how well she knows her brother, of what he is like when his desire escapes him.

ON NINTH MOHARRAM she removes all jewelry—Dada's watch, her small earrings that are shaped like little strawberries, her *akhiq* ring—and she sets them down at the edge of her desk. No adornments on *ashura*. It is still early evening. Once the stars are out, she will pray before they leave for mosque. There is a knock on her door and it is her brother.

"You're awake," she says. He has been asleep all day. She studies him as he approaches, he peers out the window, jumps onto her bed. He seems steadier on his feet.

"You see—that's exactly why I never want to become an early riser. They just look down on people who sleep in."

"It's almost six."

"It was a joke, Hadia."

She considers making a joke in return, letting the moment pass easily and undisturbed; but instead she says, "Listen, I wanted to speak to you. You're being reckless, Amar."

She knows her father. His pride, his values, his adherence to the religious rules. They are more important than love. More important than loyalty to one's child. She always sensed conditions to their parents' love and so she did nothing to threaten it. Amar sensed the same and only thought to test its limits. See how far he could push them before they left him.

"If you don't want to pray, don't pray. If you don't want to come to mosque, don't come. But please. Have some respect. They will catch you and it will break their hearts."

"There is nothing to catch."

"I found the weed and the bottles. If something is wrong, I can help."

For a moment he looks as though he has registered nothing she has said, and then, as though it took a minute for her words to reach him, his face softens. She thought he would be angry at her for trespassing, but he does not appear to be.

"No one can help me."

A break in his tone. She thinks of how they are told that God wants to help His creations, how He says: take one step toward me and I will take ten steps toward you. She is only human, but still, if her brother would only speak to her, be honest with her, she would step a hundred times toward him. He studies her for a long time.

"You think it's okay," he says, looking at her the way he would look at a friend, "but they don't."

He gives a venomous look to the closed door, where on the other side and across the hallway, their parents are setting out their rugs for *maghrib* prayer.

"I never said I think it is okay. It doesn't change how I think of you. But I can't say the same for them."

It was still the two of them against their parents. It would always be.

"But who will tell them? Not me."

"If you don't be more careful, no one will have to. Amar, is there something you're not telling me?"

"No."

He clasps his hands together. He narrows his gaze.

"We can talk about her, Ami."

She uses the name Mumma had used for him when he was younger, and she would overhear it and wish that she too had a nickname.

He stands abruptly. She steps back without meaning to.

"Don't ever," he says, so sharply she is afraid he might push her out of his way. She is suddenly still. Outside, it is now dark. He does not finish his thought, not after seeing the look on her face, how she was, for a moment, afraid of him. Amar turns to head for the door. She could let her anger keep her quiet. She could be cold to him and not speak to him for the remainder of her visit.

"Amar, wait."

He stops and turns to face her but he does not look up.

"I'm not saying don't do this. I am only saying don't go so far that you don't know how to come back home again."

She has reached him. She can see it from the way his eyebrows knit together before his face opens, unguarded, to her. She only needs him to nod or offer any reply that suggests he understands.

"Hadia," he says softly, in a tone that says she is the one who is failing to understand. "I have never felt at home here."

AMAR IS STILL sleeping. It is the day after *ashura,* three in the afternoon, and in a few days she will leave to begin her new rotation. Huda is still at mosque, meeting with her Sunday school students and cleaning up after a play she organized for them. Hadia peeks from the doorway into her mother's room and sees that she is napping.

"Hadia? It's all right. I'm not asleep. Come in," Mumma says, even though her eyes are closed.

Hadia joins her. Mumma opens her eyes and stares up at the ceiling. When Hadia saw her mother cry as a little girl, she would begin to cry instantly. Even if it was a scene in a movie that had touched her mother—it did not matter. Mumma is quiet in a way that tells Hadia not to speak. The bedcovers rustle under the movement of her head and she is aware even of the scrape of her eyelashes against the pillowcase.

"I did everything right," Mumma says.

Hadia does not ask her to clarify. She is nervous—Mumma spoke in English. Not that she could not, but that the language between them, the casual and comfortable one, when they were at home or in public, was always, unless Hadia did not know the right words, Urdu.

"I married when my parents said it was time to marry. I prayed almost every single prayer. Even the ones I missed I made sure to make up later. I never said no to my parents. Not once, not even '*uff.*' They said he lives in America. I said, whatever is your wish, whatever you say is best.

"I could have gone—like you—to more school and more school. I could have said this is *my* life. This is *my* room. *My* privacy. *My* business.

"I did not get one job. Your baba said, 'If I can support you, Layla, why don't you stay at home with the kids?' And I agreed. I would stay with you three. I wanted to. I was lucky; other mothers cannot even if they want to, but I wanted to. I was with each of you every day you were home. Never let any of you sleep over at a friend's house. Never left any of you in a park alone. Do you know what happens to children in this world? What this world is like? When you played outside I listened for cars—to make sure they did not, what's the word—screech. Some parents go together—do you know that? They go on trips or to the movies. Not us. We never. Let's go as a family, your baba and I always said. Let's go to a movie the kids will enjoy. Put you three in Sunday school. We only missed a weekend if one of you was sick. Drop and pick and drop and pick from school. Three times a week I drove you to Quran class. I waited for two hours in the car because the Arabic teacher lived far away. Every time Amar began to hate one of the Quran teachers, I found a new one, we drove even farther. We went to *ziyarat*. Every week we went to mosque. We were never a family that came only once or twice a year. There are families like that. Tell me, did I ever give you or Huda anything I did not give him?"

She stops speaking and Hadia is so still she can't exhale for fear an answer will be asked of her. Then Mumma says, in Urdu this time, "Everything. Everything we could think of doing that was good, we tried to do." And Hadia relaxes to hear it in Urdu: it doesn't change the words but it does change their effect, and Mumma covers her eyes with her hand again and whispers, "He hasn't woken up all day. When I go into his room and shake him, when he opens his eyes to mine—it's like he's not even there. It is like there is no one behind his eyes."

Mumma is not crying. So why is Hadia? After she leaves Mumma, she steps straight into Amar's bedroom. He is asleep, his curtains drawn shut. She is smarter than this. She did not study so seriously just to miss a symptom in her own brother.

"Amar," she whispers. No response. He was gone all night again, so it is not so alarming for him to still be sleeping. She tries to remember what he was wearing last night, but it had been dark. A jacket dropped by his bed. She lifts it, goes through the pockets, nothing. Sets it down again. She sits at the edge of his bed. He sleeps on his side, with his hand curled under his face like a boy. She lifts his jacket again, turns it inside out, uses her hand as sight and there, by the breast pocket, she catches a clean rip. Inside, her fingers brush against a plastic bag, and she knows that this is what she has been looking for. Four identical pills, round and white. In the hallway light she examines them. She tries to tell herself it could be anything. But he had hidden them in the seam of his jacket. Last fall, she had taken extensive notes on opiates, in a spiral notebook she kept on a shelf with her other old notebooks. For a moment she considers returning the pills but she goes to the bathroom instead, drops them into the toilet, flushes them before they begin to dissolve. A knot tightens inside her as the pills, swirling separately, converge, then disappear from her sight.

8

AT DINNER TONIGHT NO ONE IS SPEAKING. MUMMA
pushes the bowl of *saalan* toward him, asking him to take more,
but he does not want to eat. If it were not Hadia's last dinner home,
he would not be sitting with them at all. He moves the food around
his plate. Hadia can come and go as she pleases and she is sup-
ported. Welcomed home and bade farewell extravagantly: the
Quran held above her as she passes beneath it, the bag of frozen
food packed for her to defrost later, long hugs and will you please
call us more often? It should be a joke, he thinks, but it isn't—how
different it is for you if you stay in line, keep your head down, do as
you're told. It is as though to be loved at all you must be obedient.
To be respected you must tame yourself. Usually, the night before
Hadia left, he felt the same anxiety one felt as a child during the
last hours of Sunday, but tonight he feels nothing.

Hadia asks if anyone has seen her watch. No one needs to ask
which one. Amar leans forward for a bite but can feel his father
watching him.

"Now your watch is missing too?" his father says.

Amar does not look up. He is not at all hungry but he chews
slowly. His father speaks again, louder this time, each word delivered slowly and deliberately. "Has anyone seen Hadia's watch?"

No one answers. Amar stares at the shiny rim of his glass and
then he can't help himself, he looks up to meet Hadia's gaze. She
has been watching him too. Her focus on his face feels like a

betrayal. He glimpses a flash in her eyes, quick like the shade of a cloud passing over the sun, and then she looks down at her own plate, as if she were the guilty one. His father slams his hand against the table.

"That was my father's watch. That was the one thing of his I had."

No one moves. Amar experiences the moment as if from a distance, he notes how strange his father's voice is, how the hurt in it sounds coarse. Amar does not have to sit through this. He owes them nothing. He stands with his plate.

Behind him, he can hear his father's chair scoot back and he begins to yell at Amar. "You have no respect for anything, not even yourself. You will lose yourself and be forever blind to what you have lost."

"Baba," Hadia is shouting too, and Amar glances back and sees that Hadia is holding on to his father's arm to stop him from stepping any closer to Amar. "Baba, I probably misplaced it. I will check my suitcase. I will check my apartment too."

Amar scrapes his food into the trash.

"But you never misplace anything," Huda says. Amar looks up. He has the odd sense that he is not in the kitchen, but watching the scene unfold in a memory or a movie, someone else's life. Mumma presses her hand against Huda's arm as if to silence her.

"AND WHAT HAPPENS *when you sin?*"

"*You get a speck on your heart, a dark, small speck.*"

An ink-dark heart. He's lost his pills. He needs more. Simon is out of town. Before Amar steps outside in his driveway, he pulls the bottle of vodka from his laundry basket, takes three big gulps, and then, when he feels nothing within a minute, drinks it like water until it is gone. An immediate rush is more thrilling than a slowly increasing sensation.

"*A permanent stain. So heavy and black it cannot tell good from evil.*"

Cool outside and cricket sounds. Hadia is leaving in the morning. Even though she is being horrible, home is home when she is in it. He sits just past the driveway, at the edge of the sidewalk. The world trembles but only slightly. Simon said he would be back in a few days but what if he does not come?

"Of course, there is always the opportunity of asking Allah for forgiveness."

What had they been speaking about? It had something to do with wolves. Joseph and his brothers who threw him to the wolves. His coat torn and covered in sheep's blood. Or was it the boy who cried wolf, wolf, until no one came?

"Why is it too late?"

"Nothing can be done."

His head is throbbing. He rubs his chest. He sins and sins and does not hesitate before sinning again. His ink so permanent. There is a presence behind him and then it is Hadia. It is Hadia taking a seat. She leans her head against his arm and he tries to steady himself. He breathes through his nose in case she can smell it on his breath.

"Amar, I need you to listen to me. You have to be careful with pills. They are not like drinking. They are no joke. You could open a door you don't know how to close."

So she took them. A hundred fucking dollars at least. At least. He will not react at all. He will not even move. She could have found anyone's pills. Maybe even the pills for Mumma's tooth that was removed months ago.

"You would turn on me too? Spread lies about me?"

He would have more respect for her but he pulls a cigarette from his pocket and lights it. He even offers one to her. She stares back at him. Just when the drag hits he closes his eyes and tries to let the feeling calm him but it is not enough anymore and with his eyes closed he realizes how much he has had to drink, how he should be careful when he stands, and the entire world feels like it is churning in circles.

"Hadia, do you think what Mumma said about the heart has

already happened to me? So many black stains that now it is just a dark seal? Like nighttime descending and never lifting. Like nothing can be done."

She is shaking her head and his arm and is saying, "Forget your soul, Amar. I am worried about your body."

The first time he took a pill he did so because he thought it would numb his problems, soften the edges of his thoughts or at least slow them from racing: that he had lost Amira, lost Abbas, and any day now would lose his father's and mother's love for him, each loss reaching back to the one before. He had told himself it was just one night he needed help getting through.

Now the pendulum swung in extremes. The glow from the pill so warm, even his insides were coated in warmth. And Amira's face far away. Baba's disgust and disappointment in him far away. Mumma saying, but, Ami, if you love us why can't you listen, far away. Then he was returned to his body and in terror, thinking only of how badly he wanted that warmth again.

Are you listening? Hadia is asking him, her hand on his shoulder. The moon is so small he wonders why it ever awed him. Why he ever hoped his hunch was true: that it followed him home, every time he looked up and out the window of a moving car. It still says *Ali* in Arabic. And there is still the face of a man laughing at him. He lifts up his thumb and covers it. He closes one eye and it's gone.

WEEKS PASS AND his father comes home with a large box. He hauls it up the stairs, his forehead gathering beads of sweat. He does not ask Amar to help. Amar stands in the darkness of his bedroom and watches through the open door. His father drops the box with a thud when he reaches the top step and his mother emerges.

His father pushes the box into their bedroom. He does not close the door behind him. Amar listens. Hears the sound of the box being ripped open carelessly, as though his father were certain it would never need to be returned. Then the sound of Styrofoam pellets shifting and being thrown onto the floor. Amar steps into the hallway, on tiptoe; night has long set and the hall is dark.

"What's this?" he can hear his mother ask.

"A safe," his father says. Then there is silence. He imagines his father flipping through the instruction manual, the way he did whenever he opened a new appliance. There is a beep. Amar opens his mouth to silence his breathing, presses his back against the wall, until he has no shadow.

"I can see what it is. I am asking why."

"Precaution," his father says. "For safety."

Mumma does not ask safety from whom. He feels it in his stomach: the humiliation. He can't stay here. Not tonight. He is grateful Hadia is not home to see it. He moves to the staircase. A rectangle of light shines from his parents' bedroom. At the top of the stairs he looks back at his mother's pale face. She is watching his father, seated on the floor, setting up the safe, the instruction manual laid out exactly as Amar pictured.

His father has lowered his voice and Amar can only make sense of snippets of his sentences.

"Enough," he catches him saying, and then, "your wallet in here at night."

Mumma's eyes darken.

"No," she says. "No, no."

She is like a child in her defiance. His father stands and steps toward her.

"Layla, we cannot pretend anymore."

Amar steps down a stair. Mumma refuses again, louder this time. If he had not been there to witness it he would never have believed his mother could raise her voice like this against his father.

"How much has to go missing?"

"I want that safe out of my house," she says. "Nothing of mine is going in there. Not one necklace. Not one penny. Nothing."

He can sense that something has broken in her; her face is contorted in a strange expression, there is a shrillness to her voice.

Huda's door cracks open but she does not emerge. His father tries to place his hand on Mumma's arm, to calm or comfort her. But she pulls away from him, enters the hallway and stops when she sees Amar.

"Oh," she says, and wipes at the edge of her eye. Even in the darkness her face is pale and stretched tight. It is she who says she is sorry. She whispers it to him, and he feels so angry at himself, so angry that he could strike the wall the way he has before when fighting with his father. But he cannot move. Mumma crosses the space between them and wraps her arms around him. She is at the top of the stairs, and he is one below, so they are almost the same height. He does nothing. He does not lift his arms, does not even thank her. Nothing in his body feels a part of him. Behind her, his father comes to the door, sees the two of them at the stairs, and closes it. The rectangle of light narrows into a thin line.

✧

BABA CALLS WHEN Tariq is at her apartment for the first time. They have just finished dinner. She does not want to ask Tariq, who has a cough, to be quiet while she is on the phone with Baba, does not want to explain how even a casual dinner at her home could anger her father, so she silences the phone. To explain would be to point out that she is a woman and he is a man. That it is a Friday night. That they are alone.

What she first liked about Tariq when they met semesters ago was how she did not feel self-conscious in his presence. He had taken a seat next to her by chance, glanced over at her notes, and commented on how they were unreadable to him but clearly organized. He studied her face for a moment. I know you, he said then, you're the one with the sharp questions. When he asked her if she wanted to meet outside of class it was not for coffee or dinner, but to study together at the library. It was never easy with men, not easy talking to them, not easy thinking she could love them. Any interest made her nervous, mistrustful even. But she and Tariq had been friends for months before Hadia decided it was in her hands to reach for more if she wanted it, to call him over for dinner, to make plans intentionally once their excuse of studying together was gone.

Baba calls again, and again she does not answer. Tariq stands to clear the plates and Hadia tries to concentrate on the story he is telling her, but she pictures Amar the last time she saw him months ago, that tear in the seam of his jacket, his incoherent mumbling at the edge of their driveway. It could be bad news. She tells Tariq she will be right back, steps into her bedroom and closes the door behind her, takes a seat on the floor of her closet, surrounded by clothes that will muffle her voice.

"Hadia," Baba answers right away.

Something in his voice. How a voice is different if one has just woken up or is lying down—but it is not that. She sits up straight.

"When are you coming home?"

She does not have a trip planned. She has been trying to assert herself by setting the pattern of her own life, hoping her parents will grow to accept it.

"I'm not sure yet, Baba. Why?"

"Can you come soon?"

"My next break is in three weeks."

Baba is quiet for so long she wonders if he has heard her.

"I don't know what to do."

His voice quavers. She digs her nails into the carpet of her closet. He has never spoken this way, not these words and certainly not with this tone.

"What do you mean?"

"Something has happened. He's not going to his classes."

"This is normal for Amar, remember? He'll sign up again next semester."

Her delivery does not even convince her. She stares up into the dark sleeves of her hanging shirts.

"He never leaves the house. Or he goes missing for days. And then he is back, sleeping in his bedroom again. I try to wake him at midday and he does not wake up."

The four pills in his jacket pocket. She closes her eyes, leans back against the closet wall.

"Have you searched his things?"

Silence, and then, "If you can come home."

"What would I do, Baba?"

"You could talk to him. He trusts you."

After she hangs up the phone she steps into the living room. Tariq looks up at her.

"What's wrong?" he asks immediately.

She has never lost her composure in front of him before.

"I have to go home."

"Now?"

It is a five-hour drive and it is already eleven at night. Tariq's concern appears genuine. He has been so open with her. Maybe she will allow herself to become closer to him than she has been to anyone. But how can she be certain he will not look unkindly at her family?

"Do you want me to come with you?" he asks.

He is good-hearted. She is grateful. She lifts her purse and grabs her keys and shakes her head no.

THE SKY IS pale by the time she arrives. In a daze she enters her house and at this hour, even the furniture appears at peace. Sofas draped with white sheets. The plants growing in their pots by the staircase. The shoes left by the door. No one knows she has come. Even she had not known she would until after she hung up with Baba, saying to him, well, maybe you should talk to him without anger and he would trust you too, which she regretted saying—not because she did not mean it, but because instead of calling her *batamiz*, Baba had gone quiet. He had been slow to respond throughout the conversation and then he only said, yes, well, if you could come.

Once she is home she heads straight to Amar's bedroom, and he is there, fast asleep, his window wide open and cold air rushing in. All night she drove in a steady panic, not knowing what it had been like at home, not knowing if she was arriving too late. She does not know if her body is dizzy from the lack of sleep and excess caffeine or from the immense relief at the sight of her brother. She shuts his window, sits at the edge of his bed. A faint memory: the light gray, and Amar telling her that Hadia would always come for him if he called. Thank you God, she thinks, maybe I have been selfish, but You have allowed me to return before it was too late. She feels strange after the thought: it is how her mother would think to thank God, and Hadia considers her relationship to God to be slightly more sophisticated than her mother's. But if God is the one to thank, then she will thank Him, and she stands from the bed and kneels on the floor, touches her forehead to the carpet.

IN THE GARDEN Hadia leans against the plum tree and Amar sits by her, pulling grass from the ground and dropping it like confetti. This time of year the plums are still small and bitter. Every once in a while her mother's face appears at a window, but when Hadia looks again her mother is gone. Usually, being around her siblings is like returning to her original self, with no need to think of what to say or how to say it, but today she is hesitant. She is trying to get a sense of what the problem might be, or gauge the extent of it, but anytime she circles close to asking Amar directly, she retreats, afraid to anger him or lose his trust.

"I didn't mean for it to be like this," he confesses.

"Like what, Amar?"

"I can't describe it."

"Try."

"I know you don't trust me."

"I trust you."

He plucks blades of grass, then lines them up on his palm.

"I owe somebody money."

"What did you do?"

"I know you don't trust me, Hadia."

"I do, Amar. Who do you owe? For what?"

191

"Five hundred dollars."

He flips his palm and some of the blades fall to the ground. Others stick to his skin and he shakes his hand. She rests her forehead against her palm.

"That's a lot."

"Will you help me?"

He is not looking at her.

"I don't have that kind of money."

"You're a doctor."

"I'm still a student."

She tries to hide the hurt from her voice.

"I'll pay you back. I know you don't think I will, but I will."

"I know you will."

"You do?"

He looks up. His eyes are wide. He is still like a child. He has not cut his hair in months and it falls into his face. She only saw him recently and she is alarmed by how much weight he has lost. His cheeks are sunken and his cheekbones even more pronounced. Is she a fool to trust her brother because he is her brother? Against her own instincts, her own intuition, because she *wants* to believe him, because she has known him his whole life and cannot fathom a change so drastic he would be made unfamiliar to her.

"I do."

"Don't tell Baba?" he asks her.

"Don't *you* trust me?"

"I do. I knew I could ask you."

A NEEDLE, BABA had said earlier that morning, when she first spoke to him alone in the hallway while everyone slept. Baba hugged her and she braced against his embrace, realized in that moment that she did not trust him when it came to Amar. He agreed, almost too eagerly, to let her speak to him first. He could not control his anger and Amar could not control his reaction to it, and they found themselves in unpredictable territory.

"I don't understand how he could sin so severely," Baba had whispered, shaking his head.

"Baba, sinning does not even matter anymore, not in the face of this."

She was speaking with such little patience. Baba blinked at her. Hadia sensed a new space opening between them—a space in which he looked to her for answers—and realized she could say anything. Was it respect that allowed Baba to listen to her now, or desperation? Right and wrong, halal and haram—it was her father's only way of experiencing the world. She should do what she could to bridge the distance between his understanding and Amar's actions.

"Baba, what he is gambling on is not just his standing before God. This is much graver. This is about him surviving *this* life, here."

She had never seen her father so bewildered, so helpless. And she found herself not wanting to protect his weakness, as she might have hoped, but wanting to attack it, wanting him to blame himself the way she faulted him.

"You cannot approach him now as you always have," she said.

"Tell me how."

"You cannot get angry. It will only make everything worse."

Baba lowered his face and nodded.

HUDA IS READING in her bedroom when Hadia steps in. Hadia says nothing as she crawls into Huda's bed, lays her head in her sister's lap, curls her legs up close to her chest, and tucks her hand between her knees. Huda rests her hand on Hadia's shoulder and its weight is comforting. Huda's breathing somehow calms her. Hadia closes her eyes and listens to the sound of pages turning. *It might be just the two of us from now on*—the thought comes to her just like that, and the force of her grief at having thought it surprises her.

"Is this what was always going to happen?" Hadia asks.

Huda does not have to ask her to explain. She runs her hand

through Hadia's hair in the exact way she always wanted Mumma to, and what is clenched tight in Hadia breaks and somehow she is crying.

Huda speaks at last. "I think at some point it could have been different, for him, for us, but now I don't know."

"What point?"

The sound of Mumma watering the lawn drifts in through the open window and Hadia pictures Mumma covering the green hose with four fingers so the spray fans out.

"I always thought Amar stopped trying after the shoes. His attitude to Baba was different. He stopped calling him Baba. That was the year he was held back, remember? He stopped wanting to want anything at all."

It comes at once, and so vividly: the posters, the petition, the speech, the spelling test, Amar kicking his legs back and forth seated at her desk, biting the yellow pencil until the paint chipped off, the rest of the house fast asleep as Hadia held the banister, stepped into the dark downstairs and knocked against the door of Baba's office.

Huda continues, "After that I noticed his pattern: he begins to try, only to feel, at some point, helplessly unable to continue, like he decides for himself there is no point in trying."

The curtain moves back and forth. The fabric of Huda's trousers are wet from her tears. Mumma turns off the hose.

"You're going to make a good teacher," Hadia says to her, and Huda mouths a thank-you, and wipes Hadia's cheeks.

How were they to know the moments that would define them? *It will affect his personality for his whole life*, someone is saying to her, *and whose fault will it be then?*

Mine, a voice replies, and the voice is hers.

Now her brother was in danger of having nothing. And now she wanted nothing her brother could not have: not the exams her teachers handed back to her winking, not the accolades, not the watch that had been gifted to her—she was glad it had disappeared—not the career she was building or the space opening up between her and Baba that told her he finally respected her as an adult and would rely on her the way a father might a son. What had she done to her brother, so that she could survive, so that she could be the one who thrived?

SHE IS IN the living room when she hears the arguing: Amar and Baba, though she can't make out their words. She sets her mug down. She had told Baba he could not get angry. She had made it absolutely clear. They needed to proceed carefully, thoughtfully. She looks back at Mumma, who has been preparing dinner in the kitchen, and Mumma has also heard. They meet each other's gaze and it is clear neither knows if they should run upstairs and separate them. Mumma sets down the bowl, massages the back of her neck.

Then there is the sound of a loud crash: the thud of a body hitting a wall, a human noise that chills her because it sounds so animal, then glass crunching, and another crash Hadia imagines is a frame falling to the floor. Hadia thinks she will be sick. Mumma rushes past Hadia and up the stairs, and Hadia stands absolutely still, not wanting to climb the steps and look her father in the eye, not now that he has revealed himself to be a man who cannot control his anger even in the face of so fragile a moment.

When she finally does climb the stairs, Baba is standing in the hallway, a dazed look on his face. Amar's chest is heaving, he stares unfocusedly at the carpet, all the scattered glass. She was right: it had been the sound of the large frame falling to the floor. Mumma kneels to pick up the shards of glass, drops them one by one into her cupped hand.

Mumma is the only one who speaks, her voice so hoarse and unsteady it frightens Hadia. "Enough of this now. I've had enough."

IT IS ALMOST dawn when she is woken by the sound of a closet door being opened and the creak of Amar's floor.

"What are you doing?" she whispers when she opens his door

and sees him, though it is clear what he is doing: he grabs shirts and jeans, he discards some clothes on the floor and throws others into a black duffel bag. After he has finished rummaging through the drawers, from bottom to top, and left them open like a thief, he takes a step back, rests one hand on his neck, and scans his room as if checking what else to take.

"You know I can't stay here anymore." He speaks with his back to her.

She shuts the door gently behind her, intending to reach out and touch his shoulder, pick up the clothes from the floor, and return them to the drawers, but she stops herself. What surprises her is that this is a moment she recognizes. Not that she has seen this sight. But that maybe she has always feared that one day this is how he would react, that there would come a time when there were words exchanged and actions executed that neither he nor their father could recover from. And maybe there is a part of her, cruel and unforgiving, that has been waiting for Amar to realize what she has sensed all along: that there is no place for him in their home.

Amar looks wildly around the room. He is trembling. Very soon it will be time for *fajr*. Just a day ago she had returned at this hour and thanked God for the sight of him sleeping. Now she wonders if she was called home not to intervene but to say good-bye. She takes a seat on Amar's unmade bed, pulls a pillow toward her, and wraps her arms around it. Amar kneels on the floor and zips his duffel bag. He puts on the jacket with the ripped inside pocket. He grabs his backpack, steps up to his window and touches the surface of his windowsill.

When he finally turns away he takes a seat beside her. They do not speak. He seems at this moment so much taller than she.

"Tell them I went for a run if they ask."

Only Amar would think a lie like that would be believed. Her pride or fear keeps her from asking when he will return.

"At night, if they ask where I am, tell them I am staying at a friend's house for a few days. When they want to look for me tell them I've left. I've moved. I'm not coming back. I'm sorry, Hadia, but can you do this for me?"

She will come up with what to tell them herself, but even so she repeats his steps. Gone for a run, gone to a friend's house, gone to a new city. Moved, not coming back, leaving them, leaving her.

"Hadia," he says, and his hand grips the strap of his backpack so tightly it looks like he is forming a fist.

She shakes her head. She does not want to hear his explanation, does not want to be convinced he is right to do this.

"What are you waiting for? If you're really going to go."

She speaks so sharply she surprises herself. And it has worked: she has hurt him. But there is something about the determined look in his eyes that hurts her more, something that tells her he is serious, that there will be no dissuading him. Once she glimpses her fear, she follows it to its worst conclusion, and now she wonders, What if this is the last time I see my brother?

"We both know what it is you are doing," she says, kindly this time. "Do you think leaving will help you? That if you leave you can have a healthier—"

She stops. She had thought his face would harden. But he considers her words.

"I don't know," he says honestly. "But if I stay, I'll only continue to hurt them."

He watches her profile. Soon the dark outside will begin to blue.

"You should go before they wake for *fajr*," she whispers.

Amar nods. He has been waiting for her to give him permission. Her words are enough for him to know she will do what he has asked of her. He stands and lifts his duffel bag.

"You have a plan?" she asks. "A place in mind?"

"I'll be okay."

She has no more money to offer him.

"You will call me? If you ever need anything."

He nods and twists his mouth. He looks like a boy afraid, having made a decision he does not know how to execute. He stands in the doorway with his backpack hanging over one shoulder.

"If I could make myself change, Hadia, I would. If I could be like you, or Huda, if I had a choice, I would change in an instant."

"I know, Amar."

"I know it is hard for them. But it is hard for me too."

"Maybe it will be easier where you're going. Or maybe it will get easier for all of us in a few months, or years."

He smiles a little. She does too. Then they are quiet again. She can tell he is stalling, that there is something he is trying to find the words for.

"You'll take care of them?" he finally asks.

She knows what he is asking of her, to be there for their parents not only in the aftermath of his departure, but also in the distant future—and isn't this exactly what she had wanted as a girl: to be the one they depended on, for there to be no difference between daughters and sons? Now she cannot even look at him as she nods. She blinks and blinks and refuses to let herself cry. She tells herself that when he leaves, she will not go to the window as she has before. Will not want to watch him get into whichever car has come for him, knowing he hasn't asked her to leave his window open. She'll fall asleep in his bed, and Amar will continue on with the friend she doesn't know, on his way to the city he doesn't offer to name. There is no time for him to walk out beneath the Quran. And she does not know if he would even care to. But still, she steps forward, raises her finger a little and asks, "May I?"

He nods. He ducks a little so she can reach and then closes his eyes. She traces it slowly, tries to get the Arabic exactly right, wishes she knew the prayer her mother would whisper to accompany the gesture. He does not flinch. He looks peaceful, even. Please God, she begins her own prayer.

9

WEEKS AFTER THEIR MEETING IN THE TUNNEL, Amar steps from a party into the basement for a moment alone. He has not heard from Amira in almost three weeks. Every day he had awoken hopeful that she would break the silence but by night he had known. In the basement he watches a man lift and lower a credit card so fast it is like he is mincing dust, then sweeping coke into a swift and delicate line, and Amar is alarmed by the sudden presence of a thought: I'll try anything just to not feel this way anymore.

He knows then that if he does not try to win Amira back, she will be lost to him, and he too will be terrifically lost. Upstairs, the music is so loud he can feel the beat in his stomach. People are dancing in the dark, smelling of sweat, and he walks past them all until he finds Kyle, their designated driver. Can you drive me somewhere? Amar asks him, and he even says please.

"Tell me this is not about her," Kyle says. All of his friends refer to Amira as "her." They know not to say anything negative, but they have made their opinions clear too: that Amar and Amira would never work.

"Who else?" Amar says.

Kyle shakes his head. "I told you, she's not good news. Just stay here."

The song changes. People from the other room cheer. The beat thrums in his body.

"Fine," Amar says, "I'll ask Simon."

He starts to walk away. Kyle grabs his arm and holds him back.

"Simon's no good either. Come on."

They walk out into the night. Kyle has eyes like a deer and maybe this is why Amar had trusted him almost immediately. Kyle and Simon were childhood friends but lately they had begun to drift apart. Kyle thought Simon was being reckless by using and selling painkillers. Simon had even offered to supply Amar, but Amar had shaken his head. Whiskey and weed's enough for me, he had said, I don't need anything fancy.

Now he steps into Kyle's navy car and Amar gives him directions. He leans his heavy head against the window.

"Look. I've loved Simon like a brother for years. But I don't *like* him anymore. He's always been kind of an idiot. You're not an idiot, Amar. We all know that. But if a decent guy follows an idiot, what does that make him?"

"Thanks for the compliment," he mumbles, reading the names of streets until they become familiar. But something about Kyle's words strikes a nerve: it reminds him of a saying of Imam Ali that his mother taught him. About how important it was for one to choose the right friends, that it was one's friends who were the truest reflection of the self.

"It's obvious you love her. And I'm sorry your heart is breaking. Really, I am. But you can't just show up at her house at this hour. You're going to scare her. And you might not remember telling me, but you've said it to me before—that she wants someone straight-edge and religious. Look at you, man. You say it's hard enough for you to chill with your family, how are you ever going to chill if you end up with a girl like that?"

They are close to her home. He sits up in his seat and the seat belt stretches.

"I'm driving you all this way, the least you can do is listen to me," Kyle says.

"I'm listening," he snaps. "But I don't expect you to understand.

When I'm with her, it's like I can live that life. I can be that guy. It's like I *want* to. I don't want *this,* I don't care about any of this."

Amar can't expect Kyle to understand because he can't quite understand it either. All he knows is that if he were with her, he could be Muslim. He could try his best to practice, if practicing meant trying, failing, and then resolving to try again. Sometimes he suspected that it was not her he was fighting for so much as what life with her would represent and promise him: a respectable life. A daughter-in-law his parents would beam at. Sure, he could not see eye to eye with his parents now, but with Amira he could grow into that practicing believer: he could have children and take them to the Sunday school, make the weekly trip to the mosque, show his face at the community events, roll out prayer rugs, never stock their refrigerator with beer. If she were the one he would wake up next to, he would do it all. And eventually, he imagined, his father might even respect him. He felt like a dam waiting to break open and he wanted her, unfairly maybe, to keep him contained.

"Do you have any gum?" he asks.

Kyle sighs loudly, then tosses him a tin of mints. Amar drops mints into the center of his palm, pops them in his mouth, and then bites down on all four.

"Just look at yourself." Kyle grumbles. "She's going to know. It's one A.M. and your eyes are all red, for God's sake."

He flinches at the mention of God. He hates if he's high or drunk and someone begins talking about religion. And tonight is the eighth of Moharram—he had wanted to make a point to his family, had not gone with them to mosque on purpose, but now the realization that he is drunk on so important a night almost makes him panic. He pops another mint into his mouth, crushes it with his teeth. Breathes into his cupped hand and tries to sniff for any scent of whiskey. They are approaching her neighborhood and he tells Kyle to slow down.

"Holy shit," Kyle says. "She lives here?"

Amar nods sullenly. Kyle whistles.

"You didn't tell me your girl was a queen. Don't ever bring Simon here," he says darkly. Amar is too nervous to ask why not.

At the party, when he knew he was coming, Amar sent Amira a quick message to tell her he would knock on her front door if he had to. He would sleep in her backyard until morning. He would aim tiny pebbles at the rectangle of her bedroom window, like every fool in every foolish movie. She had to speak to him. She had to see him. Just once more, he begged, and then he swore to never bother her again if that is what she truly wanted.

Amar steps out of the car, but before he shuts the door, Kyle ducks his head through the window and says, "Good luck, man. I might give you a hard time, but I'm rooting for you."

It's not until he feels his face go numb in the cold air that it occurs to him how much he has had to drink. He concentrates on keeping his steps steady. He aims mint after mint at her window until a light turns on. When her face appears he sparks his lighter and waves the small flame. Amira disappears and a moment later her room is dark again. Anything to be able to tell himself he did everything. That he tried again. The sliding door downstairs opens, slowly, announced by the squeak and the reflection of the moon shifting slightly. She walks toward him on tiptoe, barefoot. He did not know his heart could even beat this hard.

"Have you absolutely lost your mind?" she hisses.

She has been crying. Even in the dark he can see her eyes are puffy and small. For the first time since the tunnel meeting, it occurs to him that maybe she has also been hurting. She looks frail. He reaches for her face and holds it between his hands. She is startled, and for a moment, silent—he has never been so bold, so abrupt. She does not step back from him.

"They were right," she says. "You're drunk."

"Amira."

"You are," and her voice is shaking. "You were never going to change."

It was true. He was drunk. He holds on to her face to steady himself.

"I only drank because we're not speaking anymore. I promise I will stop."

"Lie to everyone else, Amar, but don't lie to me. You're being selfish."

He lets go. Only his father had ever called him selfish. He doesn't care what anyone says but he does care what she says. She takes a step back. He is about to say: I won't do it again. I don't need to drink. I don't need to smoke. I don't need anything. But I can't lose this.

She looks past him to the thicket of trees where they once played hide-and-seek, where he watched her take a drag of her first cigarette. Her arms are crossed and held tight against her body. Then she looks up at him. There is a soft bruise, just beneath her eye; but maybe it is just a shadow. When he reaches out to press it carefully with his thumb, she recoils, swats his thumb away from her face like he is a fly.

"Go away, Amar. I'll be in trouble all over again."

"Everyone gives up on me. Give me one more chance."

Her feet are pale in this light. This is the very lawn he stood on year after year, pausing while playing soccer to look up, hoping for that glimpse of her.

"Have you been lying to me all these years?" she asks quietly.

He shakes his head.

"Did you really believe you could do this, become who you needed to be, send a proposal properly one day?"

He sighs. And then, "I tried harder to do that, be that, than I've tried to do anything before."

"Did you want to?"

"I wanted you."

"But that life—did you want it?"

He says nothing. She nods slowly.

"Do you believe in God?" she whispers. Her voice is so small.

They had asked each other a hundred questions. How had they missed this one. He looks from the dewy grass to her bare feet and searches his heart for an answer, his honest one.

"Not like this," he says at last. "Not my father's God."

203

He is not sure what he means, but instead of stiffening, her face softens to him.

"Now you don't have to try, to pretend."

He was never pretending about wanting to be with her. That was exactly, unequivocally, the one thing he wanted. But he cannot deny the exhalation in him—that he has spoken aloud what he so feared to be true, that he could speak the words and still continue to exist.

"Amar, maybe I've been keeping you from becoming yourself," she says, and he can tell she is being very gentle with him.

He stares at the tops of the trees, black this time of night, and feels how he had that one night years ago, as though he were venturing out from his old world into a new one, where he would be entirely alone.

"Say something?" she asks him.

"What will it be like?"

It had been their game since the note she left on his pillow: one of them would ask the other, what's it like, and the other would give a response, never specifying what "it" was. Tonight he has altered their line. What he wants to know now is how he is going to live without her. She says nothing. She reaches her hand up and touches the side of his face. She has never done this before. She has never initiated touch. The strongest wind through the tallest branches makes a sweeping sound. The longest silence is hers.

And then, after a while, after he leans his face into her warm hand, she says to him, bravely and without a hint of uncertainty, "Amar, I know this will mean nothing to you now. But I do believe that even your father's God, even He, would forgive you. To know you is to want to let you in."

"I'M SORRY, REALLY I am," Kyle keeps saying as they drive back to the party. Amar isn't sure what about his demeanor is making Kyle look over at him at every stoplight. Amar is just quiet. Mumma had begun to look at him in that way too. Like he was disappearing right before her eyes. He had been eating very little and sleeping in very late. Anytime Simon called him with a plan for the night he agreed without asking any questions. Kyle parks the car and Amar tells him he wants to stay at the party. He has nowhere else to go.

He does not love her any longer.

He only loves her.

He will leave and never return.

He will wait, by the door, until he is invited inside again.

On and on he thinks in opposite extremes, until he is not sure who he is or what he wants. Once inside, he sinks into the couch beside Simon and the guy from the basement. The dancing is over. People speak slowly and laugh easily in the dim light. He asks the guy from the basement what coke feels like.

"Like flying," he says.

Amar does not care for a thrill. He turns to Simon and flicks one finger against Simon's chest pocket, where Simon keeps the smallest bag of pills.

"What's it like?" he asks.

Simon thinks for a moment.

"Like nothing exists. Not even you."

Kyle watches him from the doorway. His eyes are gentle and big. Amar cannot look back at him, he is not quite sure why. He looks instead at the knuckle that he has been kneading with his thumb, the one that is now redder than the rest.

"How much for nothing?"

Simon throws his arm over Amar's shoulder and pulls him close for a moment before letting go.

"For you my brother, your first time, nothing will not cost you anything at all."

When he looks back at the doorway, Kyle is gone. Simon drops a round pill in his palm, white and weightless. Amar thinks that at least with this he is certain there will be no smell.

✧

LAYLA PARKS IN the empty cul-de-sac, and though she knows Amar is in the middle of his chemistry exam, she still looks around before stepping out from the car. Slowly, the Ali house comes into view. The trees surrounding their property sway so that the house with its balconies and rows of glinting windows stands like a rock in comparison. Every *jashan* and *majlis* hosted by the Alis was a production, and it was no effort for Seema—she was calm when the guests arrived, her hands soft—having hired people who did the work and catering for her. Sparkling Christmas lights wrapped around every pillar and curved banister during their *jashans,* and even the trunks of trees that led up to the driveway twinkled. Those nights it looked like stars had fallen from the sky. Now it looks like any other home. Layla pauses at the edge of the driveway. She had not anticipated feeling anything other than determination, but as she approaches the house that impulse to tuck the car away, enter and leave without being seen, unnerves her.

Seema said she would be home alone and seemed surprised when Layla wanted to meet. Their friendship was one born of circumstance and routine, and because of this, they rarely met outside of mosque or an event, and never alone. There had been a hint of worry in her voice and Layla wondered, bitterly, if she was afraid that a proposal would be sent on Amar's behalf for the girl, and Seema would have to bear the discomfort of denying her. The Ali girl received ten proposals after any event she went to. Seema would complain in the way that people would when they wanted to brag but disguised it as a burden.

"And yet Amira says she's not ready," Seema would say, lifting up her hand in frustration and shaking it. "What has gotten into the girls these days—saying they are 'not ready' as if there is something else, something more important they're waiting for, and only after that will they consider marriage."

Layla would give Seema a hollow laugh. Her daughters also received proposals. But the Ali girl was only eighteen; Layla's daughters were already twenty-three and twenty-four, and getting older every month. She dreaded the thought of their prospects dwindling as they aged. They insisted not only "not yet" but also "not him"—with no reason given. Every night she prayed God would continue to shower them with the blessing of respectable proposals and then would immediately pray for her daughters to develop some common sense. What was the use in one if they so lacked the other?

An hour ago she packed walnuts in a clear plastic bag for her son. She sliced a green apple. She filled his water bottle with cold water.

"For your test," she said as she handed him the brown bag. "For you to have energy to do well."

He was nervous. She had never seen him so driven, so concerned about his education. The sight of him with books in the crook of his arm filled her with pride. Her prayers for him had been answered. He had finally developed *ehsas*—an understanding of his actions, of the impact of them. She wanted him to do well. She wanted nothing to hinder him from becoming the man she believed he could become. As she wondered what to say to him she remembered the purple light of an old classroom, and Amar's sweet teacher who had succeeded, albeit temporarily, in encouraging him.

"Don't worry, it's just a test. As long as you do the best you can, we will be happy."

He nodded slowly, considering her words. Then that dark look of his took over and he said quietly, "It's not just a test. I *have* to do well."

Layla sighed. She had asked Rafiq to stop pressuring him and Rafiq, tired of Amar's *batamizi* and the hostility between them, had reminded Layla that he only spoke to Amar when it was absolutely necessary.

Layla held a Quran above his head as he stepped out the front door, for luck and extra confidence. She shielded the sun from her eyes and watched him leave before preparing to drive to Seema's house. He would be affected for a week, a few months, but he would recover. What was the heartache one felt in youth? Nothing but a dream. By the time he was an adult he would hardly remember it. And what was heartache when compared with public humiliation? Heartache was the quick touch of a flame. But for one's inner life to be gossiped about and judged by the entire community—it was like holding one's hand above fire until it left a scar.

She had been stunned and sickened by the contents of Amar's keepsake box. For months she knew he had been hiding something: smiling to himself whenever his phone buzzed, guarding his phone and barking about privacy if anyone came near him. It was difficult enough to see her son step so willingly toward sin; she imagined it would have been unbearable if her daughters had done the same. How had she failed to pass on to one child what was so instilled in the others? This was the question that haunted her. They had all heard the same speeches, listened to the same stories and lessons, and yet.

Layla lifts her fist and knocks. Seema appears before she can exhale. Seema smells faintly of perfume when they embrace and Layla follows her inside. Instead of the family photos that Layla has hung in her home, the Ali family has decorated their walls with ornate mirrors, purposeless tables, paintings Layla does not find beautiful. Canvases painted blocks of red, stripes of light yellow and black. Layla glimpses her reflection in a mirror as she passes and for a second it alarms her.

Biscuits have been placed on little plates in the living room. Colorful napkins stacked. Seema asks Layla if she would like tea or coffee and then disappears to prepare it. The house is very quiet. Soon she can hear the faint gurgle of the water boiling, then the whistle. Layla's heart thuds in her chest and she twists her *orni* around her finger. Their secret—Amar and Amira's—would come out eventually. If only the surface were considered, it was Amira who would be chastised. It was her innocence that would be compromised. But Layla knew that when the shock of a woman's *begharti* subsided, the root of the scandal, the reason why the parents did not just rush to make it a halal match, would be because Amar was not the kind of man worthy of marrying the Ali girl. Once they were bored with the questions of how could she, the more sinister question would rise up to sting Layla: *What had she seen in Rafiq and Layla's boy?*

Seema and Brother Ali would laugh at the proposal if it were to be sent. They would nip it in the bud before word of it even reached their daughter. They had wealth and they had beauty, they had noble lineage and the respect of the entire community. So often someone from their mosque, including Brother Ali, would report to Rafiq that they had seen Amar smoking in the parking lot, or that he had stepped away as soon as the *adhaan* began, as though the call to prayer called everyone else but repelled him. One man from the community even had the gall to tell her husband that red eyes were the sign of a man who took drugs. They thought they were doing Rafiq a favor, and Rafiq would solemnly thank them, but at night he would be unable to sleep, and Layla would have to prod him just for him to speak about it. What can I do, Layla? Rafiq would ask her helplessly. Layla would be unable to comfort him. Her own spirit had been broken by not being able to deny the rumors. She too was disheartened when her son came home with a sway to his step, smelling strongly of stale cigarette smoke and cheap body spray. If this is what reached Layla and Rafiq, she could only imagine what people whispered among themselves.

But what did it matter what *momins* of the community said when they picked apart the behavior of her son? What was a believer meant to be like when all their rituals and practices were stripped away? Amar was kind. If one of his sisters came home carrying heavy textbooks, he rose to help them before they even asked. He was generous. He had very little of his own money but still he would bring home the coffee drinks Huda or Hadia liked, or a bag of cherries for Layla come cherry season, or a candle with a floral scent. Layla gossiped sometimes, everyone did, but she had never heard her son speak ill of anyone. Once when she spoke of someone from their community, he said to her, "You don't know that, Mumma, don't say that if you don't fully know it."

Her heart had swelled. How her son was good in a way that she wasn't, in a way that could instruct her. Layla had begun to think lately that there was no real way to quantify the goodness of a person—that religion gave templates and guidelines but there were ways it missed the mark entirely. And everything a *momin* should be in his heart, Amar was.

Seema sets down the tea for her and Layla notices she has chosen a mug of coffee for herself.

"Are your boys home?" Layla asks. She dips a biscuit in her tea. The crumbs break off and float on the tea's surface.

"No. They've gone out for the afternoon. You know how kids are these days, always going out. Everywhere but their own home is a magnet to them."

Layla removes her scarf. Seema sits across from her on her plush couch, her legs tucked beneath her. She cradles her mug in her hands. Not a single hair on her head is white and Layla knows she dyes it often. Seema is one of the few women of Layla's generation who chooses not to wear a headscarf. Layla untangles her own unruly strands with her fingers.

"And Amira? Is she home?"

"She is at the library," Seema says. "The bug of going out has bitten her too. Any excuse they'll give me—Mumma, I have to go to get a book from the library. Mumma, I have to go and get a haircut. Mumma, the haircut lady was closed and so I walked to the cupcake place."

Layla sits back in her seat. She can speak without fear of being overheard. She knew when she glimpsed the contents of Amar's box that she would meet Seema in person, her words disappearing into the air once they were spoken, untraceable.

"Are you sure?" Layla asks. She traces the rim of the cup with her finger. She knows what she wants: to put an end to what has been brewing between the two. For the end to be swift. The last thing Amar needs is a young girl tempting him, distracting him from his studies, only to break his heart when a stronger proposal comes.

"What do you mean to say, Layla? Are you accusing me of not knowing where my daughter is?"

The tone of Seema's voice has sharpened, but she still smiles in a pained way. Both of them notice the shift in the air, the room suddenly hostile.

"I only mean that you should keep a closer eye on her."

Seema sets down her coffee mug, its steam still drifting up, and places her feet firmly on the ground.

"I found letters and photographs of Amira that she has been sending to my son," Layla begins, keeping her voice steady. "For months, maybe even years."

It is clear from the photographs that Amar has taken them, but she wants to conceal his part. The thought of a young girl sending photographs of herself to a young man is irrefutably inappropriate.

"You should read them—I've never known a girl to have such little *sharam*."

Seema's mouth is open and she appears completely shocked—maybe assessing if Layla is telling the truth, maybe processing what she had not predicted. *Besharam.* The word is like a slap. Modesty—the highest value a woman can embody, and the most crucial. Without it, a woman is nothing. They have drilled the importance of it into their daughters since they were little girls, as it was once emphasized to them. Guarded themselves from the gaze and touch of men until their wedding night, and warned their daughters to remain guarded. Nothing was worse for a mother than to realize her daughters had grown and abandoned regard for what she had most desperately wanted to instill.

Layla pulls a photograph from her purse. It was a risk to take it, but it was one of many. She wanted Seema to see proof. In it, Amira is smiling, her eyes dreamy, her lips glossy and one finger playfully resting at the corner of her bottom lip. Her arms are showing, her shirt is cut low, exposing her collarbone and the unmistakable line of her breast. The girl did not know what she was suggesting when she mimicked the photographs of models and actresses in magazines but it was clear to any viewer.

"We are lucky to catch this before anyone else. Now no one has to see it," Layla says as she tears the photograph very gently. Seema will have to rely on her words, scold her daughter in a general way that Amira would be unable to deny but also be unable to trace back to Amar's box.

Seema is offended. That much is clear. But more than that, she is humiliated—and she shakes her head in disbelief, maybe hoping that Layla will have no more to say. Layla knows what it is like for one moment to change your understanding of your child drastically. For a stranger to come into her home to tell of her daughter's doing—it is no easy blow.

"It is clear they have lied to us both and clear that they meet—I don't know how often. I left the letters as they were, but they gave me reason to believe there is much more to be concerned about."

Layla sips her tea. There is satisfaction in bringing down the woman who, at times, has made her feel small. Who had once made a comment about Hadia and Huda being already in their twenties and still not engaged, whose husband had in recent years been one of the men who pointed out to Rafiq the sight of Amar smoking beneath a streetlight, or asked why Amar did not participate in any of the youth events at mosque. The hypocrisy of knowing that the Ali boys also smoked. But Layla feels for Seema too, and does not want to hurt her so much as show her that neither of them were without children who would bring them pain and lower their name, or above having secrets that carry shame. To say to her—look more closely at what your daughter has done before you point a finger again at my son.

"I had no idea," Seema says. "I had noticed her gone for hours at a time and never doubted her."

"We would have heard about it if someone else had seen them. But it is only a matter of time."

Seema nods.

"I am afraid I know my son—he hardly listens to us in the small matters, he will not listen to us if we tell him to end this. It will have to come from her."

"Of course. I will speak to her."

"We do not want to push them in a way that inspires them to take this . . . friendship . . . any further. I imagine that if I went to Amar and he decided not to listen to me, he could ask her to—God knows what."

Run away. It seems an impossible implication, but these things do happen. Seema drags her hands down her face. A tired sound escapes her.

"Boys will be boys," Layla says, the line they all know. "Especially in the face of apparent temptation."

She has gone too far. Even she feels sour at having said it. But Seema only has Layla's word to rely on and what she is imagining now will likely be worse than what the box contains. She does not want Amar to be accused of anything other than falling for Amira's advances. Seema swallows, lowers her gaze; she shakes her head in disbelief at some thought she does not voice, a glazed look on her face.

"I wish I could doubt you, Layla, but instead I feel as though I've always known this was coming. When—years ago—Amar would come to see my boys, Amira would always try to join them. I would tell her it was inappropriate but—you know, it is hard to get them to realize the weight of what you are saying. I would tell her, over and over, Amira stop, Amira there is no need to follow them around, Amira what were you doing sitting with him on the couch?"

"Amira is a fine girl," Layla offers. "They are just being children. Amar is working very hard now on his studies—I do not want him to have any distraction. Especially not a distraction like this."

"Have you told anyone?"

"Only my husband. But no details—he does not know about the pictures or the content of the letters."

"Thank you," Seema says, and for a moment she looks like she will cry from relief. "I will only tell mine too."

"I ask one favor."

Seema looks at her.

"Please do not tell Amira how you found out. My son has a temper, and it has been a rough few years. He has just recently become responsible; I am afraid that if he thinks that we were the ones who told her to end it, he will react against us, and will not believe that Amira truly wants it to be over. He will try more to win her over. He can be so stubborn."

Seema looks horrified at the idea of him winning her over, of both of them abandoning all decorum and continuing their childishness until it ruined them all.

"I understand. I for one have no problem with Amira knowing just how angry we are. We have never doubted our children. We have always trusted them. Now we know."

"It will be all right. They will learn from this."

"Yes," Seema says.

There is a long silence and neither wants to find something lighter to speak of.

"If our daughters act this way," Layla says, rising to her feet and placing the unfinished cup of tea on the table, "what hope can we have for our sons?"

IT WAS WHAT Hadia had said once in passing that Layla could not shake. *You have no idea what he does and what he hides.* It returned to her as she snipped eggplants from the stem, as she chopped onions and watched them brown in hot oil. Where would her son hide what he wanted to keep secret? She remembered that birthday years ago, that box with a lock. On six different occasions she had checked if he had left it unlocked while he was out. On the seventh try, when she saw it was ajar, the spare comforters thrown over it messily, she felt only excitement and an overwhelming curiosity. It was her right to know. She was his mother.

When she looked through the journals and the photographs, the letters and the trinkets, she felt ill. Tickets to concerts he had never told them about. Neon wristbands to places she did not want to picture. For a moment, Layla glanced at Amar's journals, but she could barely make sense of his handwriting. Each deciphered sentence threatened to unravel her understanding of him and carried with it the threat of more secrets. It did not matter that she was his mother. What she could ever hope to know of him was just a glimpse—like the beam of a lighthouse skipping out, only one stretch of waves visible at a time, the rest left in the unknowable dark.

Hadia and Huda were their father's daughters. It was their father they tried to impress, his approval they sought. If he made a joke or even gestured toward a joke they would laugh. She had known this when they were little girls at dinnertime glancing at him to see if it was safe to speak, had known it from the way their eyes delighted when he let them climb onto his back. He could switch seamlessly from playmate to parent, whereas Layla was stuck in the one role, and was not given much authority even within the one.

Amar was hers. He always had been. Sometimes, she even thought that she and Amar were like friends when they walked grocery store aisles consulting each other before choosing the syrup or the chips flavor, and like friends when he tossed her fruits, saying, you can catch it, you can, and she would hesitate but if she caught it he'd cheer. And Amar asked about her day. Nearly no one did that. She could not deny that there was a part of her that could disregard the shock and the sin and confess to herself that mostly she felt hurt that there was so much he had hidden from her. She felt like she had brought it on herself—that had she not pried she would not have known, and would have less to worry about.

That night they did not eat dinner as a family and Layla was relieved. Amar took his dinner up to his bedroom, where he studied for his chemistry exam the next day. Layla waited until he was asleep before speaking with Rafiq in the amber light of their bedroom. He ran his hand along one side of his face, ruffling then smoothing his eyebrow. It was his habit when trying to think of a solution when presented with an impossible problem.

"How far have they gone?" he finally asked.

"It's unclear. They have photographs of each other in the same places but never together. His box is full of letters from her, promising herself to him, but other than how she felt during their meetings there is no indication really of what, if anything, they have done."

"Does she love him?"

"They are children."

He looked at her then.

"It makes a difference." He spoke slowly.

"What difference, what do children know about love, when they have sacrificed nothing."

He was bent forward, his elbow on his knee, his hand resting on his face in such a way that half of it was hidden from her.

"I thought you would be angrier," she said.

He shook his head.

"You surprise me."

"There is plenty to be angry with him about—but when you said you had found something, I thought you had come to me with more troubling news."

"This *is* troubling news."

"Yes."

"It would cause a scandal."

He nodded.

"The girl would be humiliated and soon after we would be—the Alis would never accept Amar," she said.

"What lack is there in our son?"

Rafiq raised his voice. He dropped his hand from his face and looked at her as though he had forgotten that he was the one who was always harsh toward Amar.

"Ask yourself. If you would feel, in good faith, able to give your daughter to someone like Amar."

Rafiq was speechless. After holding her gaze sternly for a moment he looked down at his hands.

"So what—we will never send a proposal on his behalf?" he said. A quality in his voice made her want to hold him.

"Of course not. He will continue to mature. He will make something of himself."

"He will never listen to us, Layla. If we tell him to stop this inappropriate, *apas e bahar* behavior—he will never listen."

"We won't tell him."

"So we let this continue? Knowing that they have gone as far as to meet frequently? And that poor girl—we just allow him to continue to influence her to sin? We cannot. She does not know any better. She does not know what she is doing, what this could lead to."

"*Influence?* She is the one tempting him."

Again he looked at her sternly.

"Amar does not need any tempting, Layla. Don't forget what you already know."

"We could talk to Seema," she offered.

He shook his head.

"Think about it," she pressed. "Seema would be the first to want to keep it quiet. Her daughter would be the *begharat* one, any way you look at it."

Rafiq started rubbing his eyebrow again. She reached out to touch his arm, to say to him, we are on the same side, remember?

"This could be good for Amar," he said finally. There was an unmistakable note of hope in his voice.

"How can you say that?"

"It could be, she's a good girl. I've always liked her. If it were made halal she could influence him in the right way."

"You still think she is good?"

"Our son is no saint, Layla."

"They would never consider it," she said, and then, "Right now it is good for Amar. He is happy. He sneaks away smiling when his phone buzzes. He wakes up still sleepy, after talking to her about who knows what all night. But what will happen in a week? In a month? When anyone else from the community finds out? In a year, when the girl gets proposals from someone with twice his qualifications?"

Rafiq sighed. He seemed, in that moment, suddenly very old to Layla.

"Every day this continues it is worse for him. Every day that he has hope—it will only make the fall harder."

❖

LAYLA THRUSTS THE white sheet into the air, ridding it of any dust, then lowers it onto the lush grass. Amar kneels at the corner of the sheet and tugs at the edges to straighten it. She smiles as he does so: his initiative, his consideration. The two of them leave their shoes in the grass and step into the center of the sheet to sit side by side, Amar leaning slightly on her leg.

They watch Rafiq walk toward them, the lower half of his face hidden by the basket of food he carries. Huda runs a little to match his steady stride, her tight ponytail swaying. Hadia struggles behind them. Her lips are pressed together in concentration as she juggles a plastic bag filled with paper cups, plates, plastic utensils in one hand, the plastic bag twisting and tightening its grip on her wrist, and a large bottle of lemonade in the other. Layla made it earlier in the day, fresh and frosted from the ice that melts in it.

"*Aao*," Layla says, looking up to Rafiq, come, she is squinting because of the sun, tapping twice at the empty space beside her. Something about the sweet air, the soft breeze, the cool grass that sinks beneath her weight, makes her feel bold enough to call for her husband to sit beside her, despite the presence of her children. It could be because he has granted their wish, or because neither can deny the beauty of the day, the contagious excitement of their children.

Beneath this sky, in this park tucked away from the main freeway, a side of her husband she has not often seen is brought out: this could be how he appears when he is relaxing. He comments on the cloudless sky, the birds that sing with voices that do not pester quite as much as the ones by his window.

"But, Baba," Hadia says to him, "they are the same."

The sun, still in the center of the sky, does not burn. Rafiq lies on his back and cushions his head on his interlocked hands. Layla pours lemonade into paper cups and passes them into the eager hands of her children. Days like this, days out, just the five of them, are rare. Her children are buzzing with the knowledge of its uniqueness. They might have thanked Rafiq a hundred times.

"It's a lovely way to spend a Sunday, isn't it?" she says, regretting immediately how calling attention to the loveliness of a thing diminishes its magic. Rafiq, his eyes hidden behind his dark sunglasses, nods solemnly. Amar looks up at her, radiant, she imagines, from considering himself responsible for the day. After dinner yesterday, before the plates had been cleared and the children sent to bed, he asked if they could go on a picnic and Rafiq said, why don't we do that? Layla had smiled, surprised at the spontaneity of her husband, and said she could make food they could take along. Hadia said: tangerines. Huda said: lemonade. Amar said: river. We can try, Rafiq said to them, I might know a place for us.

There is a river nearby, past the trees that surround them, past where the meadow dips beyond their sight. The sound of water moving, the gurgling, tugs at Amar and he taps her leg when he hears it. Huda points to a far-off playground and asks Rafiq if he will take them there after they've eaten. They are asking for things openly, without hesitation, pausing for a moment after they do before Rafiq's nod, out of fear that their good fortune has run out and soon routine will resume.

"It was a good idea, Amar," Layla assures him, using the kind of voice she always strives for when speaking with her children. He responds with a brighter smile, pleased with himself, looks to his sisters to see if they have noticed the praise.

They eat lunch cross-legged on the sheet, cradling the plate Layla has prepared for each of them. Layla made cashew curry chicken sandwiches, rich from the taste of peppers, crunchy from the lettuce. Hadia compliments them, and for once Huda does not complain about the taste of the chicken, masked as it is in sauce and spice. When they are finished they share tangerines and stories from Hadia's and Huda's classrooms that Amar listens to so seriously, popping the tangerine slices into his mouth and chewing slowly. He always watches them intently when they speak of school. He is only four and Layla thought to skip preschool and wait until kindergarten, not wanting an empty home just yet. He is fascinated by that unknown world. When they drop Huda and Hadia off, she looks back at him in the rearview mirror, how he stretches his neck to watch wide-eyed and openmouthed as his sisters join the crowd, their lunch boxes swinging at their sides.

After they eat, Huda asks again about the swings and Rafiq lets her climb onto his back for a piggyback ride. Hadia follows them.

"Do you want to go?" Layla nudges Amar. They watch as the three of them make their way, Huda laughing when Rafiq mimics a trotting horse. Amar shakes his head, presses his tongue against the inside of his chubby cheek.

Layla stands and brushes the crumbs off of her yellow *shalwar kameez* and scans the meadow—the playground, the sparse picnic tables, some occupied with families not unlike her own, young children and young parents.

"Come with me," she says, bending down a bit so he can reach her hand. He holds on and she pulls him up, he is still light enough for her to do so with ease. The sound of water guides them.

Before they have disappeared into the trees that will block Rafiq and the girls from her sight, she turns back to see they have reached the swings. Rafiq touches the back of one and sends her forth just as the other lands against his palm. From where she stands he appears exactly like the kind of man she would want for the father of her children, a man who knows how to lift them onto the rubber seats of the swing, knows with what gentle force to push them, knows how something as small as saying yes to a picnic would please them so uncomplicatedly. Amar lets go of her hand and walks ahead. It takes so little, just the slightest touch of his hand against their backs, and their bodies soar, their laughter reaches her, and she is shocked by a plunge inside her. Her affection for Rafiq surges and she wonders if she has ever loved him the way she loves him now.

"Mumma," Amar calls with urgency, "let's go."

He waits for her a few feet ahead, holding out his hand.

"Speak in Urdu, Ami," she reminds him. Ever since Hadia first learned English in school it has been difficult to make any of them speak in Urdu. They speak in English and so quickly that they sound like little trains zooming by. They act as though it were the superior language, the more stylish one. She has to make it a game at dinner to encourage them. It confuses her. Urdu is the language she and Rafiq speak with one another and all they ever spoke with the children, but one goes to school and the others pick it up like wildfire, as if they've forgotten their own tongue entirely. It worries her: if they so easily lose their own language, what else will be lost?

The wind lifts her yellow *orni* up like a kite and it covers her face. Amar begins to laugh and laugh. Rafiq has heard him and he turns around. Layla restrains the *orni* and waves, points to where they are walking and Rafiq nods. She catches up to Amar and grabs hold of his hand, so small in hers. He won't let her hold his hand for much longer. As they walk downhill the grass becomes a tangled mess then just dirt, Amar pulls her along, and Layla realizes she wants another child. Rafiq would not want another—he was an only child and had been against even having a third. Just one more, she had said after Huda, and after a few years Amar had been born. After the scare that was Amar's birth and the stressful first weeks of his life, it would be even harder to broach the topic of a fourth. Amar leads her down the slope and they try to steady their footing. Another child. A boy, for Amar to have a brother. A baby that would extend that feeling of a small hand in hers for a little longer.

When they first glimpse the water, Amar rushes forward and asks to be allowed in. Layla hesitates. Recently, she heard of a child, a little girl, no older than seven, playing in a river when her parents turned their backs for just a moment. The current rising and quickening without warning, the girl swept away, struggling to lift her head above the water. Layla shivers, reaches out to touch the soft hair of her son, moves it from his eyes.

"Can I, Mumma?" He uses that irresistible and manipulative voice that he, like all children, perfected so early on. She does not remember being a child capable of such powers.

The water before them is not cause for alarm. The river seems shallow, more like a creek; it moves quickly but with an unthreatening swiftness. The deepest end is likely no deeper than her knees, and she sees the soft surface of rocks, their edges worn away from time and the rush of the current. Amar can stand on them and move from one to the other without cutting his feet. She kneels and removes his shoes, and he begins to tap her shoulders excitedly, as she rolls his jeans up to his knees, tight enough that they won't fall, and she steps back and watches him turn to the creek, take it all in. How it must appear vaster to him than it does to her. He extends just one shaky leg forward, dips a toe in and pulls it back out again, testing the temperature, then he steps forward without looking back. She finds it strange that she feels a tinge of hurt that he does not turn back. The water ripples at his presence and quickly re-forms around him.

The tip of each wave looks painted gold, dashes here and there where the sunlight shimmers. She watches her son bend down to feel the water flow between his fingers and it seems impossible to her that something would break this precious space, or how she feels here, how the wind and the birds and the gurgle of water sound like music. It feels impossible that there could be days when it was not like this for them, her children's fingers sticky with tangerine juice, her husband so calm, his face so relaxed, that when he lies on their picnic sheet she wonders if he has fallen asleep. Amar cups the water in his hands and throws it up and laughs and it feels as if nothing could interrupt the bliss of the moment, bliss as bright as the sun that glimmers on the water, as light as her daughters' girlish laughter, as light.

"Mumma," Amar calls out to her, standing in the center of the creek, cupping the water in his hands and releasing it. "Come!"

Layla shakes her head but he begins to gesture with his hands to call her, little drops flying from his fingers. Her son is persistent and demanding, he knows what he wants and is devastated if he does not attain it. It alarms her: how little it takes to darken his mood.

"I can't," she replies, cupping her palms around her mouth so her voice can reach him.

"Mumma, please! Feel how cold."

"My clothes will get too wet, Ami."

"Roll them like me. Please, Mumma."

He does not appear as happy as he was a moment ago. Layla looks down at the *shalwar* that covers her legs, not wanting to reveal them. She turns around and can't see Rafiq from here. He must still be swinging the girls. She looks back at Amar calling her, unaware of what he is asking of her.

The slope protects them from view. Here it is just she and her son. She can decide how they move through the world, to each other. She can do this. Bend down and lift her *shalwar* and join him. What does it matter? She ties her *orni* at her hip so it won't get away, she rolls up her *shalwar* a little bit, then a little more, until it is just above her knees. Amar claps, throws water into the air, the splashes descend like the tails of a golden firework. Her legs are pale. The breeze is colder on bare skin than she imagined. She cannot call forth the last time the sun saw her skin. She feels like a girl. Amar notices nothing—not her nervousness, not her hesitation. Yes, Mummy, he shouts in celebration, as though they had been playing a game and she had given him the correct answer.

She steps into the water and is surprised not only by how cold it is, but also how refreshing. She looks down at her feet that appear contorted. She chooses each stone carefully and thinks: this is what it is to be alive. This is what being alive can be like. What would Rafiq say if he saw her? Mum-ma? Mum-ma? Amar is saying it like a cheer and Layla realizes she cannot control her laughter, so unrestrained and inaccessible before now. The stones are smooth beneath her feet. The current both insistent and relenting. This is a moment that lifts and becomes a memory even as it is happening, and she knows this will be the meadow she will try to return to, her son's voice the sound she will try to recall.

One day she will look back and think: It was not bad. We were so blessed. There were days like this. Sunny and beautiful, when Amar looked up at me as I reached him in the river and said, I'm so happy we did this, Mumma. Days when Rafiq's mood was as carefree as a ripple of water in a stream. There were times when I watched Hadia unpeel the skin of the tangerine with tiny thumbs and fingers with such precision and technique—the peel not tearing once—and I thought, how did she learn how to do that? I was certainly not the one to teach her. And she offered the tangerine whole to her brother, did not demand a piece in return, then peeled one for her sister before she even asked, and Huda rose to say, I'll throw the peels away, and maybe it was the same thoughtfulness that touched me that made Huda want to do something in return. Huda cupped her hands and Hadia let the peels fall like little petals into her sister's palms, and I thought, these are my children, mine, laughing together, and that is when I met Rafiq's gaze and he looked like I must have, swelling with so much pride it was apparent on his face, on mine, so apparent that we both had to look away, made shy from the force and depth of a feeling we did not expect.

Part Three

Part Three

1

THE WEDDING HAD BARELY BEGUN AND ALREADY
Layla could not locate Amar. Layla had been frustrated when Hadia
had said she wanted a mixed wedding—an unsegregated wedding
marked a family who valued entertainment over adherence—but
as she searched the hall for her son now, she felt grateful for her
daughter's insistence.

Across the hall she met Rafiq's gaze. As though the look on her
face were enough to convey her fear, Rafiq began to scan the hall.
Layla stepped out into the lobby where guests mingled, held small
plates of appetizers and sipped juice from thin glass flutes: pineapple, orange, mango. There he was. She could spot the outline of
her child in an instant. He was looking down at his plate, nodding
along to a conversation. She stepped closer. His suit sharp and his
hair combed, he was more than presentable, he was handsome,
someone she could point to with pride and say yes, that one there is
my son.

Amar was speaking to a woman. She was facing him and was
partially obscured by people walking past.

"You found him." Rafiq appeared at her side.

The people blocking her view stepped away. The woman turned
her head enough for a sliver of her profile to be glimpsed. It was her,
Amira Ali. Rafiq studied Layla as though waiting for her to react.

"Should we be worried?" he asked.

The Ali girl had wasted no time in finding her son. The sight of

227

the two of them together unearthed an old discomfort. She looked to see if Seema was nearby but she was not. Amar and the girl spoke unattended.

"No," she said, and not sure who she was reassuring she continued, "it has been years."

She smiled at Rafiq, but quickly turned back to them. Amar was not looking at her. Amira Ali was the one speaking. Even from a distance Layla could note the playful tilt in her head as she looked up at Amar, how her hair danced as she moved. Her son played with the food on his plate but did not lift his fork. Layla had not seen Amira Ali in years—she had moved across the country for college, visited infrequently. She had never come again to their home, not even after Amar left.

Amira stepped away from Amar and walked toward the main hall. Amar seemed unbothered by her departure. Layla let out a breath she did not realize she had been holding. Rafiq returned to mingling; many of the attendees were his coworkers or his oldest friends from Hyderabad.

Layla watched Amira Ali walk. Girlishness had left her: her cheeks had lost their fullness and given way to high cheekbones, an angular and attractive face. Her lips painted and lashes darkened. She was poised, her spine straight, her step steady. Her childhood charm was now confidence. She maneuvered through the crowd unaware that Layla was watching, and Layla was hit with the strange sensation of realizing she had left something behind and forgotten to turn back for it. But what was it, she wondered, as Amira Ali reached up to tuck her dark hair behind her ear, revealing that heavy, ornate jewelry of Hyderabad, the circular gold earrings with the emeralds and dangling pearls. It would be impossible now, years later, to retrace her steps, and find again what it was that had slipped her mind, what she had forgotten to turn back for.

✧

OF ALL HE had predicted, all he had feared or hoped for, Amira suggesting they meet in private had not even occurred to him. Nor had he thought he would respond so effortlessly, with no pride or hesitation keeping him from agreeing. It repulsed him: that all the work he had done to convince himself he no longer wanted her, did not even want to hear from her, could be so quickly unraveled.

The piece of chicken and samosa on his plate. He should force himself to eat but his hands trembled. He could not look at her while she spoke. But as she walked away with her posture of being seen, he had looked.

"There's a courtyard on the other side of the hotel, down a long corridor, empty this time of night," she had said.

It was the same corridor that led to the hotel bar.

"We could meet there?" she asked.

He had not known what to say. So she continued, saying maybe when the *nikkah* and speeches were done—when people sat down to eat dinner and everyone was distracted. She had formed a plan. Perhaps she had hoped he would be here just so they could execute it.

By the time she disappeared into the main hall he was in a state of disbelief. That they would meet again. That even if they did not speak to or see each other, they still felt that care and curiosity. For three years now, he had returned to their last conversations embittered at the thought of being discarded. But seeing her now, the deep green of her dress with the red accents, her golden shoes he concentrated on while she spoke—any bitterness was made insignificant by the overwhelming sight of her. And the chance to once again step toward a place that would be made theirs.

✧

AS MUMMA INSTRUCTED, Hadia sat far enough away from Tariq that two hands could rest between them. She made sure to not laugh too loudly, to not touch him, to not appear, in Mumma's words, shamelessly eager to be married. It was an absurd expectation placed on women: that they agree to marriage without appearing as though they wanted it. That they at least display innocence. Hadia never understood what was so threatening about a woman experiencing a desire and being unafraid to express it. But on the stage now, she complied with Mumma's wishes, remembering how Mumma had told her, "You chose your husband. He is not Shia. Please do us the kindness of not making it appear so obviously a love marriage." She was getting married to who she wanted. Her mother might say it like an accusation, but the fact remained true. She had won the biggest battle: the battle that would determine the rest of her life.

She and Tariq had just begun to see each other when Amar ran away. Even now, she was not sure if it had been a coincidence, that what had been previously dormant in her friendship with Tariq had suddenly bloomed and intensified. At first Hadia had hesitated. To be with him. To maybe marry him. He was not Hyderabadi and he was not Shia. He did not speak Urdu. And though he was, in many ways, familiar to her, he was also relaxed in his approach to his faith in a way that was new to Hadia. He had smoked weed in college and had tried alcohol. He did not feel guilty when they began to spend time alone together, the way she had at first. He prayed but struggled to maintain a disciplined routine.

Next to him, Hadia became more aware of her choices, of what was important for her to keep and what had just been an inherited, unexamined habit. On and on she explored and was thrilled at the exploration. Fasting was important. Cursing did not matter. She deeply respected hijab but did not wear it for herself. Her faith became a highly personal affair: what did it matter what others believed? She had friends of other faiths or no faith at all. She could be in a room where people were drinking. She would sip water and make no fuss of it. She could hold in her heart a belief in Islam as well as the unwavering belief that every human had the right to choose who they loved, and how, and that belief was in exact accordance with her faith: that it is the individual's right to choose, and the individual's duty to empathize with one another. Didn't the Quran itself contain the verse, *We have created you from many tribes, so that you may know one another.*

Her family had impressed upon her a specific belief and in a specific way—and as a young woman she had not known, when she touched her forehead to the ground, if she was praying to God because Mumma had reminded her to, or if it was her own desire. Being with Tariq allowed her to stretch herself while also remaining fundamentally herself. It was not that they made the same choices so much as he understood hers, and she his. He might not accompany her to mosque during the first ten days of *Moharram*, but he did not turn the radio on when they drove together in those days either, and for her, on *ashura*, he wore black. Theirs was a love that acknowledged the individual as separate from the whole, from the family as a unit.

Now Tariq's sisters' heels tapped against the stairs as they made their way up to the stage. His sisters hugged her first, then Tariq, and then sat on the couches beside them that were set up for the guests. The wedding would go on this way—the guests would come up in clusters, sit with them briefly, and then leave the stage. She leaned in to wipe lipstick from the chin of Isra, Tariq's youngest sister. Hadia felt at ease with them. She wanted Tariq to feel it too, she wanted him to meet Amar and think, as she did now with Isra, that this family will be mine, that any brother of my wife is a brother of mine.

✧

"ARE THE APPETIZERS no good?" Mumma asked Amar as he set the plate down to be cleared. She watched him intently and he remembered why he had sought out food in the first place: he had downed one whiskey and wanted to eat something to mask the smell. He turned his face from her before he answered.

"I'm not hungry."

"Everything is all right?"

"Yes."

"*Sachi?*" she asked in Urdu, truly? It was one word but it had the effect of implying that his first response had not been honest, and that he needed to be pressed for truth.

"Truly."

Mumma smiled.

"I would like to introduce you to some of my friends," she said.

"Friends?" he teased her. He had never known Mumma to have friends. She had women from the community who gathered by habit in the same mosque halls for the same events, who had formed something like a friendship after years of routine.

She grabbed his arm and pulled him toward the main hall. "You think you're the only one with friends?" she joked.

Amar suddenly felt sorry for his mother, sorry that maybe the only thing she had in common with these women was that they had migrated to the same place, sought the same shelter.

"Ami?" Mumma asked, her voice soft, "where should we say you have been?"

His stomach tightened. He traced his teeth with his tongue for any taste of the drink. He had arrived at the last minute. Partially so he would not be able to change his mind, and partially so they would have less time to speak of it.

"Your father and I—after—we began to tell people you had gone to India, to be with my sister."

He had made it difficult for them. They lied for him and were not asking him for an explanation.

"I can tell them that."

She held on tight to his arm and then let go.

"Only if they ask."

He nodded. He felt at the edge of discomfort, made worse by how desperately Mumma was trying to protect him from discomfort. He could lean into the feeling as it advanced toward him or he could deny it and remain present.

"You have a choice, Amar," Hadia had advised him years ago. "All of us are in this same boat, but you are the only one who chooses to thrash about, making unnecessary waves. You can be still. You can go with the flow. That way you'll save energy to swim when you need to."

She was prone to using one metaphor after another and sometimes the connections between them did not make sense. It would have been more effective if Hadia had used only one, but he never told her this. He could be still. Go where the night took him.

LAYLA DID NOT like lying. If she were to be honest with herself, there was no point: nothing hidden remained so, time had a way of unearthing the truth. She would rather not speak than speak falsely. She imagined what others might say behind her back: poor Layla and Rafiq, what a test has befallen them—saying their son has been in India when everyone knows he ran away, became an unbeliever, gave them no account of his secret life.

But he was her son. It did not matter what he had done or where he had been. Not when he was back now. A table of her friends had unwrapped the golden favor boxes and were unfolding the *ayaat* Huda had designed and printed about the love and mercy God placed between the hearts of couples.

"What a beautiful wedding this is," they said to her, and stood to greet her. The chairs had been draped with white cloth, tied together with a golden bow. She hugged them one after another, taking in the varied scents of their perfumes.

She touched Amar's arm and he stepped forward.

"This is my son, Amar."

It had been years since she had spoken the words.

"*Mashallah* he looks just like Rafiq," one said.

"Exact," another agreed, pinching her fingers together for emphasis.

Amar lowered his head and lifted his cupped hand to meet it. It was a small gesture, *adaab,* but Layla was instantly moved by how he had thought to do so without her reminding him. Her friends reached out to touch his head and they all said *gee te raho,* keep living, keep living.

"Layla, you look too young to be the mother of a young man," Khadija said.

Amar smiled at that. Layla told Amar about Khadija, who had

just recently moved from Hyderabad to live with her son and daughter-in-law.

"Do you like it here?" Amar asked in Urdu, and Layla was again touched. He had used the respectful *aap*. Why had she assumed he had forgotten?

The two of them talked, Khadija telling Amar how she had adjusted to California, the pleasant air and hills, an ocean nearby, and Amar asking her questions in a broken Urdu that was making them laugh.

"That's one thing that's a shame," Khadija said, turning then to Layla, "that the children here have forgotten their language. I fear for my grandchildren."

Layla gripped the loose fabric of her sari tight, the little beads bit into her skin. She did not want to nod and agree with Khadija, not in front of Amar and not at all.

"Nice to meet you," Amar said to her in English after a while. He stepped back into the crowd. Layla excused herself too and walked off as though called by an errand.

Khadija had raised her children in India. Her son had moved here alone. He was what her children would teasingly call "a fob"— fresh off the boat, what she liked to remind them that their own parents were once. Layla was twenty when the proposal from Rafiq came. She looked at Hadia now, twenty-seven and seated on the stage surrounded by Tariq's sisters. But she still seemed so young to Layla.

On the eve of her own wedding night, while the *mehndi* lady covered her hands with henna and drew in Rafiq's initials, the life that awaited her was a blur. She could picture just the corner of the apartment they would live in, the outline of the hills. At that point she had seen Rafiq in person twice, had received from him five letters her mother read before giving them to her, had written him back four that her mother had checked and made her rewrite before allowing the envelope to be sealed and stamped. Rafiq had sent photographs with each letter. The hills green and empty of houses. The wide gray roads and the street lamps curved at the top like drooping flowers. The promise he would purchase plane tickets for her parents to visit them. Her father would turn to her flapping the photographs around like a fan saying, "Layla *jaani*, Layla *raani*—look, it is exactly like my paintings, and how entirely appropriate that a place like a painting is where my daughter's destiny lies."

Almost thirty years ago, Layla had herself been a bride, walking to the stage where Rafiq waited, her sight obscured by rows of thick flowers she was not allowed to peek through. How was she to know then what it would be like to raise her children in an unfamiliar land, a land that held no history for her but the one they were making together. *Bismillah*, she repeated, as her sister held her to guide her to Rafiq, *I begin in the name of God.* She had never traveled out of Hyderabad before. She was like the women in the novels or the movies, the ones who stepped onto a plane or boat and watched their world shrink behind them. *The Compassionate, the Merciful.* The scent of jasmine and roses. Wondering only if her husband would be a kind man or a stern one.

✧

TARIQ ASKED HER how much longer the smiling and greeting would continue. He gestured at his jaw. Hers ached too. Never had she sustained a smile for so long—during conversations and the moments between, when the photographer asked them to look up. She scanned the wedding hall: the rows of chandeliers twinkling, casting golden light on the tables beneath them. People she had seen all her life seated at the tables, leaning into one another, laughing and talking. The guest list reflected more her parents' and Tariq's parents' circles than theirs, but neither she nor Tariq wanted to take that from them. The women had gathered on the right side of the hall and the men on the left. No partition, so everyone could move freely, especially the teenagers who wandered in hope of stealing a glance or bumping into a particular boy or girl. Hadia smiled to remember what that had been like. One by one the guests came to greet them and Amar had not come. Had still not met Tariq. Had the thought even occurred to him?

She spotted Huda and waved her over. She had not intended to lower her voice and speak quickly in Urdu, but when Huda's face was close to hers, she did. Tariq's parents spoke Urdu but he and his siblings had not learned it. Hadia had not realized how important it would be for her until she found she kept wanting to speak to him in the language she used with Mumma and Baba, the language she slipped into when afraid or when she stubbed her toe against the desk. She had begun to sense that there was a barrier between them, unnoticed on most days but still obstructing a complete intimacy, the intimacy of home, and sometimes she felt unreasonably that until she called for him in her first language and he returned her call, they would not be truly, completely, a family.

She did not want Tariq to know that her own brother had to be urged to meet him. She wanted Amar to walk up of his own volition, but if he did not come soon it would be time for the speeches. Huda gave her a look—not of sympathy or pity, but something in between—one that said that Hadia should know better than to care, than to have any expectation from Amar at all.

✧

HE WANDERED FROM the hall out into the lobby and then back into the hall again. Where he really wanted to go was the bar but he could not go back there. But what was the difference between one drink and one more? There was none. Only after a few was there an effect. One drink was like none at all, like a sip of water. He had two things on his mind and they took turns occupying his thoughts; to be free momentarily of one was to soon be assailed by the other. The first was that in an hour, maybe less, he would walk out to the courtyard to meet Amira. The second was that his father had still not spoken to him properly. When Amar looked out across the hall his father was on the other side, as though they were following separate orbits.

Just before they had left for the wedding, Amar had looked out the sliding door at his father walking in the backyard. The mist that time of day, the bluing light, his father's green sweater and white kurta rippling. It had been three years and Amar wondered, what do I feel now? He was still angry. It was an anger that had been useful to him: to step out from his home and never return to their street, not even to drive by at the darkest hour of the night. An anger he touched like a totem to gain strength: they do not understand me and make no attempt to. I can't be like them. On and on it went, each thought taking him farther to a place he could not return from.

But hours earlier, when he watched his father in the garden, he realized that the anger had dimmed, and he was surprised to find that after anger, or alongside it, was not a bitterness or resentment, but regret. *Afsoos* was the word in Urdu. There was no equivalent in English. It was a specific kind of regret—not wishing he had acted differently, but a helpless sadness at the situation as it was, a sense that it could not have been another way. He could not call his father Baba, nor could he think of him as Baba. Other women he did not know saw his father's face in his, but his own father could not see it.

Someone called his name. He turned to see it was Huda. She had come to the men's side of the hall to see him. He smiled at her.

"You look like you're enjoying your night."

She was joking. So he laughed. They walked together toward the center of the hall where there were more women. Who are you now? he wanted to ask her, but maybe she was who she always had been, and he was who he had always been, and it was foolish to think that the years had changed anything. Across the hall their father had spotted them together and he looked away as Amar looked back.

For some reason unclear to Amar now, he had decided that Huda was not kind to him as a child and that he preferred Hadia, and maybe following that decision he had been kinder to Hadia. As he walked with Huda now it did not feel like she was watching him, the way Mumma did; it just felt as though, for the moment, he had company for the night.

"You didn't meet Tariq yet."

"Whenever I look up someone is on the stage."

It seemed like a boring and exhausting structure for a wedding. But it gave him an excuse to not approach them. He was embarrassed that a stranger had taken a place in his family, that a stranger knew more about him than he knew about the stranger.

"And none of them has been her brother."

She looked up at him from the corner of her eye. He put his hand in his pocket and felt the roll of cash. Everyone was so careful with him it was both a relief and a reminder that Huda would be blunt.

The emcee tapped on the mic and introduced poets who would recite the *jashan*. The reciters took their place and Amar saw that the Ali boys were among them. They had been his friends. They looked older now and still respectable. Kumail and Saif—to see them was to feel again the loss of Abbas. They shuffled on the stage and unfolded the paper they would read from.

"Hadia's hurt you haven't met Tariq yet."

Her voice was low so that no one passing would overhear; she had her arms crossed and leaned in to tell Amar without turning her face to him.

"She said that?"

"No one should have to voice something so obvious."

The reciters began an old poem he knew by heart as soon as he heard the first line. He could not deny how happy hearing it again made him. He thought Huda would walk away, having said what she needed to, but when he turned he saw she had stayed beside him.

✧

THE ENTIRE HALL faced the stage and she knew she should look down at her hands, but she could not help but look at them, the Ali boys. They were among five men from the community reciting lines of poetry Hadia had specifically requested—a *qawali* she had loved as a child and wanted to hear a portion of today. The Ali boys had grown into the faces they would wear for their life. Gone was that awkward way about them, Kumail now with a full beard and

Saif no longer so skinny. Their features were handsome but failed to come together in a striking way, as they had in their eldest brother and younger sister. Hadia wondered if Amira was here, and if Amar had seen her. The thought made her nervous. She watched the Ali boys raise their voices to join the chorus, and Hadia realized they had surpassed the age of their eldest brother and had now begun to experience what Abbas never would.

She looked at Tariq, intently listening to the recitation. Once she had wished it would be Abbas Ali in his place. Once she had been so naïve as to think that a girlish dream could become her life. Abbas Ali scanning the mosque kids lined up in the parking lot after Sunday school, and pointing to her, the first girl picked, and his third choice, to be on his team. Abbas Ali standing from the couch if Hadia walked into the living room and telling his brothers to get up too, so that she could sit if she wanted and no one could accuse her of sitting next to a *namehram*. Only after he passed away did she look to anyone else—think of anyone else—so loyal was she, throughout elementary school, high school, college—loyal not to a spoken agreement but to a hope.

An hour—less—and she would be married to Tariq. How odd the current of one decision, even one as small as taking a seat beside him in a lecture hall. Once this choice was made, every choice after became not easier to make, but inevitable, until he asked her to marry him and she could not imagine a life in which she said anything other than yes. The poetry had reached its pinnacle and she could feel the energy of the room rising, everyone in the hall swaying, clapping along.

"Are you sure?" her mother had asked her, after she had told them about Tariq, after Baba had been so upset he had gone to his study and slammed the door with the helpless frustration of a child who knows that even his displeasure will change nothing.

"I am telling you because I am sure."

Mumma looked shocked and betrayed by the implication, but she recovered easily.

"But he is not Shia, Hadia. This decision will affect your entire life. It will determine the life of your children. And their children."

She *had* thought about it. These were the differences that kept people separate from one another. Indian, Pakistani. Shia, Sunni. When Tariq drove three and a half hours to see her during their years in residency, when she watched from her window as his silver car pulled into her apartment complex, when she unlatched her door to him after having not seen him for a long time, the thought was not, what have I kept hidden, what rules have I broken? But rather, look at what I would do for you. I would keep from my parents your presence in my life until we were ready for the next step. I would risk isolating myself, however temporarily, from them. It was what she was willing to sacrifice, what she could overlook, that proved to her the love she felt. Her mother might be upset because of a difference in faith. But wasn't the essence unchanging? Only the methods and metaphors varied. And what comforted Hadia was that she and Tariq had both held their fathers' hands as children and stepped out at dusk, excited to learn how to sight the moon that marked Eid.

And maybe it was the least important reason, but it was the day-to-day aspect of her life with Tariq that truly mattered to her. How, with him, even trips to the grocery store felt like an event, tasks as mundane as lifting up apples and pinching avocados before placing them into their basket. It was care she evoked in Tariq. It was clear in their first months of friendship and it was clear now. What better quality to evoke in another, she thought, one more durable than desire, more sustainable than excitement, one that had the possibility of growing until a sweet and gentle life was formed.

But this Nusrat Fateh Ali Khan *qawali* was the only tape Baba put on for them when they drove a long drive. It was the only tune that made him tap his fingers on the steering wheel and even Mumma nodded her head in the front seat. The prayers were all in Arabic and the poetry was all in Urdu, so Mumma would translate for them, line by line: *King of the brave, Ali. Lion of God, Ali.* Guests in the hall were clapping now. *The name that is true, the name that removes all sorrow.* Her heart opened from hearing the verses, the chorus she loved as a girl and loved still: *Ali, Ali, Ali, Ali.*

As soon as the recitation stilled, someone shouted out *naray hyderi,* and everyone who knew the call knew how to return it: *Ya Ali.* It was a call carried by her ancestors going back hundreds of years. As Hadia returned the call, she turned to see that Tariq had not, did not know to. And she feared, for the first time, if a devotion sustained over generations would end with her.

✦

THE MOMENT HE first heard the *naray* called out and maintained, one long note, he yearned to reply, and when the *naray* stilled and the crowd took a breath before answering in unison, he had responded as well, with as much gusto as all around him.

Had Huda heard him beside her? She must have. How could he make sense of how he felt hearing the recitation, how he stood through every turn and rising, as if on tiptoe. He looked around the hall. He did have something in common with them, and it was like a reflex. If there was so much he lacked in faith—the ability to fully believe and follow—why could he not also lack the desire for faith?

"Amar?" Huda asked. "Do you not want to meet Tariq?"

Her voice was cold.

"Not now, Huda," he said.

He wanted a moment to himself. He began to turn away from her. She stood in front of him and whispered through her teeth, "If not now, when? You've been gone for years. You come home at the last minute. The wedding is halfway over and still you say 'not now'?"

She was right. He could not even argue against her. But how could he explain what it was like to hear the *qawali* and remember again the dusty sunlight in their car, the black crayon marks on the plastic of his car seat, the swaying of his sister's braids. It brought back what he hardly had to think about in the apartment he now shared with friends seven hours away, where he was more at ease than he'd ever been here. Of course he missed his family. But there, he did not feel that his lifestyle was worthless. He was funny in the world he found for himself. He was good at making money fast. He could charm strangers in an instant. He was up for anything and people wanted him around. If it was four A.M. and a friend's car had been towed, he was the one they called. He went to readings at libraries and bookstores in his city and wrote his own poems in secret. He had a good rapport with the other chefs where he worked and when he got off work he could smoke a cigarette in the cool air without a worry. Meet his friends for a late drink no problem, stay at the bar until close no problem, wake up at noon no problem, sell a little weed on the side to some eager college kids and have enough to make rent. He was capable of doing it all by himself, with no one to say what a disappointment he was. He wanted to want that life and no other. He wanted to feel no loss when looking back.

Huda blinked at him and a line of worry formed between her eyebrows.

"Please, Huda. Just one minute alone."

He stepped past her on his way to the parking lot where he could smoke a cigarette, but he looked once behind him to see that Huda had not followed and he turned a sharp corner, the sound of his footsteps absorbed by the corridor's carpet.

"Welcome back," the bartender said. "Must not be a very fun wedding."

Amar tried to smile.

"The same?"

He put a twenty down.

"Double."

The bartender whistled. "That boring, eh?"

Someone at the bar made a joke about dry weddings, how they were no celebration at all, so why bother even having one, and Amar felt a dull queasiness, the kind he felt in middle school when he heard someone say something he was not meant to overhear. He reached for a napkin and tore it straight in half, and then again, until the drink appeared.

"Another?"

He had to pace himself. He lifted his palm and the bartender returned to a conversation he was having at the other end of the bar. On the TV the Warriors were playing and he imagined the living rooms across the country where the basketball game was on and a family gathered to watch and a dad opened up a beer and offered it to his son, who was twenty-one, no sneaking or shame necessary. This is how he imagined it might be for the rest of the world—simple and easy.

He had wanted to say *Ya Ali*. By the end of the recitation he had even teared up thinking of how like home it sounded, how the very name was like a beat in him and he thought: maybe it is in my blood. When he was a young boy, Nana told him about the Muhammad Ali fights that would be broadcast on TV that Nana watched even in India, how the crowd would chant *Ali, Ali,* and his grandfather poked Amar on his chest and said, "See that—even on the moon and anywhere on Earth, in any village, this is the name that will ring and ring."

Tonight he wondered if he had turned his back on something far more meaningful than he realized the night he packed his bags in a hurry, thinking only of how angry he was, how harsh and unloving his father was about what Amar had no control over: who he was.

"This is haram," his father had yelled the night he ran away.

They had been arguing in the hallway near the stairs. What use was a life lived out of fear of hellfire and nothing else? He thought: if the fires exist and I am to burn, let me burn for my own actions rather than force me to behave another way and be saved by a lie. He did not know what, exactly, his father had found: that was the year Amar spiraled from one extreme to another unthinking, proving to himself only that he could, and when he was confronted by his father he realized how tired he was of hiding. They had been arguing cruelly the way they always did, but when his father raised his hand to slice through the air for emphasis, Amar flinched.

And here is the moment that nobody knows. The nightmare he wakes from sweating in his apartment even now. His father's back had hit against the frame in the hall and Amar realized from the throbbing in his own hand that he had hit him. Amar had struck his father on the jaw, and then shoved him again, the glass of the frame crunching behind his father and then falling to the floor when he stepped away, and it was that sound, or maybe how little his father reacted, that snapped Amar from the moment, and he stepped back.

They looked at one another as though they did not recognize each other. They were silent even when his mother approached the top of the staircase, and Mumma looked at both of them but narrowed her eyes and shook her head at his father. Mumma knelt, cupped her palm and placed jagged pieces of glass into its center.

"Enough of this now," Mumma said, and her voice was shaking as each piece clinked into her palm, and she said to his father, "I've had enough."

And in that moment he knew his father would not correct her. He would not even raise his hand up to touch his jaw.

That night he packed his bags. Called Simon and said, I've got to stay with you for a few days and then I've got to get out of this town. Hadia had stood in his doorway and tried to change his mind, do you have to go? This can be made all right again. These things pass. He told her he could not stay. And it was not because he wanted a life where he was free to do as he pleased, and it was not because Amira did not love him and he could no longer try to be the kind of man she would ever love, and it was not because of the argument between him and his father, because after the sting of the words subsided he could see a future in which he forgave his father and maybe his father forgave him. They had been reckless with their words before. Like water they could return to any shape asked of them.

Amar had to make sure he left and did not return, and it was because he could not look his father in the eye after he used all his force against him. Because when the glass cracked, his father did not even raise an arm to resist him. His father who was already becoming an old man, who already worried Amar when he spotted him on his walks outside, his hair turning a stark white, walking slowly and sitting down slowly as if it hurt his knees. The last time they looked at each other, while Mumma knelt on the carpet, Amar caught a look in his father's eyes that he could only interpret as a look of loyalty, a look that tried to convey: I am with you, I am on your side, I will keep your secret.

If his father had just hit him back, cursed at him, said to Mumma, look how despicable our son is, how *batamiz*, anything—then maybe he could have gone home again. A punishment was a mercy. It marked the end of a sentence. Without one, he could not imagine recovering from his shame. Nor could he forgive himself for giving action to the hatred he had felt for his father, wanting to hurt him the way he had been hurt by him. Now he blinked around him at the people seated at the bar, tilted the glass so the last drops slid toward him, closed his eyes and heard Mumma's voice from long ago, so hazy and fragmented it was like a dream.

What does shame mean?

To be unable to show your face. To be afraid to.

Simon had come for him before dawn and as Amar stepped out from his home for the last time, he thought to himself, if I really hated this place, if I were really ready to leave, I would not look back. But he did look. For so long the sky might have lightened, the little magnolia leaves trembling like it were a normal day, the stars already dimmed, his stupid basketball hoop with its torn net and his stupid window. Looked and even thought, if Hadia's face appears in my window, I will change my mind and I will stay. Looked until Simon touched his shoulder and said, are you sure? Amar nodded because he could not speak. He felt the terror of a boy being dropped off at school for the first time as the car began to pull away, and Simon drove slowly, watched him quietly, maybe thinking that Amar would ask him to turn around, to take him back, but Amar was brave. He had thought it was bravery then. Now he thought it might have been cowardice. But whatever it was, he had not seen his father again until just hours earlier, when he had watched him step out into the blue light of their backyard and Amar had thought, even if I were to walk outside, if I were to approach him, stand by him, shoulder to shoulder, same height as we are now, we would never be near, never be close. To stand side by side in that way, to stumble through my thoughts until I had something to say, would only emphasize it—the impossibility of us.

✧

"WHAT DID YOU say to him?" Layla asked.

"Nothing."

Huda was clearly frustrated. It always surprised Layla when Huda expressed her frustrations. She depended on Huda to be respectful and even-tempered.

"Then why did he rush out?"

There were murmurs in the hall, people mingling before the speech started.

"I just told him to meet Tariq."

"Who asked you to interfere?"

Huda looked at her as if she despised her. Layla disliked the way she was speaking too, how easy it was to unleash her worry on Huda.

"Hadia asked me to."

There was a sharpened edge to Huda's voice. Layla was beginning to get a headache. Her neck hurt. She had not enjoyed the wedding since she first saw Amar speaking with Amira Ali, and could not even say why the sight had so unsettled her.

"We have to be very gentle with Amar. We have to be careful to not upset him."

"Yes, God forbid we hurt Amar's feelings. God forbid we say

anything to him, or ask him to have even an ounce of consideration for any one of us."

Huda held up her hand with her index finger against her thumb, showing how tiny. Layla pressed two fingers against her temple.

"Did he say where he was going?"

"He said he needed a moment alone."

Layla wanted to find Amar and reassure him that he could meet Tariq at his own time, but Moulana Baqir took the stage, said his *salaam,* and the hall of people responded in unison. She had to stay and listen. He had been good to them—had spoken privately with Rafiq when Amar first began to trouble them and had respected their privacy after and not pried. He often praised them on Hadia's successes. Tonight he would recite the *nikkah* on her behalf. Layla turned to Huda but she had gone. Alone, Layla suddenly felt drained. This was the night she had looked forward to for years. She had hoped Amar would come and was thrilled when he did. Now she was so tense she wanted nothing but the night to pass smoothly. Wanted the nausea of watching Amar and Amira Ali to have been for nothing—a fleeting encounter, a *salaam* out of courtesy, their brief story still sealed shut in the past. And she wanted Amar to enjoy the wedding, to feel welcome, so that by the end of the night he could stay, or leave with a plan to visit. Now that she had seen him again it was difficult to recall the three years that had just passed, a life in which she could not speak to her son or even know how he was, where he was, and even the possibility of returning to that separation felt unbearable.

Tariq was listening intently and nodding as Moulana Baqir spoke of marriage as a blessing, how people were created to look out for one another. Regardless of what she might have felt when she first learned her daughter had gone against their wishes for her, she could not help but love him now. He would be a good husband to her daughter. It was a weight lifted from her mind, that now there would be someone to care for her daughter and be responsible for her safety, someone to know if Hadia came home from work at night, someone to keep her company. These were small comforts that accumulated, and what she most wanted for her daughter was a comfortable life.

✧

HADIA THANKED MOULANA Baqir for his speech. Tariq stepped away while the two of them spoke.

"You are the first generation of our community. I am honored," Moulana Baqir said, placing a hand on his chest.

The *nikkah* was soon. Moulana Baqir left the stage and Hadia looked over at Tariq and saw he was speaking to Amar. What Amar was saying was making Tariq grin, as if they were already at ease. Maybe they would never be what she pictured and wanted for her family. But they could be something else. The two of them noticed Hadia alone and walked to her. Amar took the seat by her.

"I was just hearing about how bossy you were," Tariq said, and he winked at Amar.

"Oh?" She smiled. "Did he give you any tips?"

"There are none," Amar said, speaking directly to Tariq, in a voice that suggested he was joking.

The entire hall looked like a movie set. The stage had extravagant flower arrangements on both sides, the couch was placed atop a gorgeous Persian rug, and Hadia looked from her brother to her husband-to-be and felt that this was the beginning of the rest of her life.

"Amar was also telling me about being a chef," Tariq said.

Hadia's breath caught in her. She kept still the expression of her face, did not even look at Amar, and she nodded as if she had known it all along. She did not want Tariq to think her brother was a liar. It was like an animal instinct, to defend her pack in even the slightest of ways, despite Tariq being the man she was making into her family.

"It's true," Amar said, and he touched Hadia's knee to get her to turn to him. "It's a part-time thing, but I'm getting good."

A part-time chef: maybe this meant he was responsible where he was, maybe he was unafraid of hard work, maybe it was part-time so he could attend school as well.

"You must cook for us, then," Tariq said.

"Remember when——" she began.

"I think of it every time I cook," Amar interrupted before she could finish, as if he were excited they were grasping for the exact same memory.

"Hadia's cooking show," he explained to Tariq, caring to not leave him out.

He was in high spirits. She had been right to invite him. Amar told Tariq about the way Hadia had narrated each step, even mimicked the accent she had spoken in. It surprised her, how happy it made her to hear Amar share information that he or Huda alone had access to. She remembered those weekend mornings fondly, when Mumma and Baba slept in but she and her siblings rose early to watch the best cartoons. The three of them in their pajamas, so short they needed chairs pushed against the counter to see the countertop. She made them breakfast and garnished her sentences with phrases she picked up from cooking shows on television: "Like so," she said after each step. "Lovely," and "Voilà!" She theatrically cracked eggs into glass bowls and fished out fragments of the white eggshells when the two looked away. Amar waited patiently for his food, rested his cheek against the cold counter, looked up at her with an expression she now knew was admiration and respect, a look she never found again in anyone's eyes in quite the same way afterward. All was going well. Tariq laughed whenever Amar intended laughter. If there was an image of other "harmonious" families, this could be as close as they came and she would be happy.

"Are you enjoying your wedding?" Amar asked as soon as there was a lull.

Tariq made a sound of indifference. Then said, "Not much for us to enjoy. We sit, we smile, we talk for too long with guests."

"And you?" Hadia asked, putting her hand on Amar's knee. "How are you finding it, seeing all these familiar faces?"

She searched his dark eyes for a hint to how he was really doing. Tariq, as if sensing she wanted a moment with him, looked out across the hall and waved back at someone.

"To be honest, it is nicer to see familiar faces than I expected."

"Not too overwhelming, then?"

He thought for a moment.

"That it feels unexpectedly comforting is, in and of itself, difficult."

"Still a poet," she said, smiling and shaking her head.

The emcee took the stage and announced it was time for the *nikkah*. The two *moulanas* representing her and Tariq walked to the stage, and though she knew this was what their night was for, a hundred tiny flutters flared up in her stomach and she felt light-headed.

"Good luck," Amar whispered and he kissed the corner of her forehead, then stood.

Suddenly she did not want him to leave. She wanted to hold on to his arm, thank him for coming, make him promise to tell them more about cooking soon, about anything, but he was already stepping forward to shake Tariq's hand. Amar moved in for a hug, one arm around Tariq's back. After you ran away I began to sleep with the window open, she wanted to say to him. Even now, when it rains, I hesitate for a moment before shutting it. But there was no time. Amar stepped from the stage. She watched him become another suit in the crowd. The emcee asked everyone to please be quiet. Hadia looked down at her palms, not because she wanted to appear as shy as Mumma wanted her to, but because she suddenly felt it: this was the moment, the ten minutes that would solidify her decision, and she wanted to be absolutely present to it. She felt dizzy. Everyone shifting in their chairs. The light of the chandelier casting shapes and shadows and making her squint when she glanced up. Soon the space between her and Tariq would be closed a bit more. Photographs would be taken and she would be allowed to touch him openly, laugh loudly. Mumma Baba would no longer feel upset she was with him without being married. She would be a wife. What a strange and archaic word. She would move into her new apartment with Tariq in the Midwest, where they would both begin their new jobs. The *moulanas* began to recite verses she did not understand. An aunty handed her the Quran and whispered to her to read it. Her friends held the red cloth above her and the light changed beneath it. Hadia glanced up at Huda and at Dani, who had flown across the country to attend, and saw how their eyes were filled with tears. Married women from the community began to grate sweet *misri* into flakes that fell onto the red net. Her hands shook. Tariq looked as he did during his exams. How had she made a leap so drastic, stuck to her decision with such stubbornness, with such relentless resolve. Once she had been a girl dyeing a section of her hair blue and what a thrill it had been—to take her life in her own hands even in so small a way. She glanced out at the crowd. Mumma's lips were moving quickly; she was praying for her. Hadia calmed. Hadia should pray for something too. Mumma would always tell them to be completely silent during the *nikkah*, to put all their energy into prayer, that it was a holy time when something unseen in the universe was torn open and angels descended to bear witness to the momentous occasion. Please God, she prayed, let ours be a successful and happy marriage. Let us maintain what we have. Let us create a loving family. And let me always feel that this life is mine, experience it proudly, fully, and ever alive.

✦

TARIQ HAD A strong handshake, sharp features, and a calm presence; he seemed relaxed even onstage in front of everyone. He would be good for Hadia. Hadia was prone to anxiety, an obsessive planner; she was not one to easily change plans at the last minute or know how to relax. Tariq had gone out of his way to be nice to Amar. He was the one who waved at him when he saw him approaching, said to him: you must be Amar. Tariq asked him questions that came from a place of genuine curiosity and interest, and he did not avoid questions in an obvious way. Amar looked back now at them on the stage, Hadia with the red cloth held up like a canopy above her.

In less than twenty minutes he would sneak out to the courtyard. He scanned the hall for Amira. Did she feel as restless and nervous as he did? She was sitting at a middle table by her mother;

she had draped the *dupatta* over her head and only her bangs peeked through, out of respect for the *nikkah* recitation. Seema Aunty had aged. Everyone in the hall was completely silent for the *nikkah*. If he looked down at his hands, if he cupped them in prayer, would he want to pray? If it was Hadia and Tariq's life they were meant to pray for could he bring himself to do it? Amar recognized Moulana Baqir. For years Amar had stood in prayers led by him, sat in his speeches. It had become clear, by the time Amar was sixteen, that he would not be like the other community boys who helped bring out food and served everyone, who cleaned once the speeches were done, who sat attentive in the first row and whose hands shot in the air with questions. But Moulana Baqir had never changed in his attitude toward Amar, had continued to greet Amar with kindness, as though he *were* one of those boys.

Even the children who sat by their parents were instructed to sit still and cup their hands together, as if they were waiting to catch invisible water, and he did not want to. He looked around until he saw where his parents stood, side by side, both of them facing the stage. Mumma's hand covered her mouth the way she would hold it when she was afraid she would cry. His father held his hands together behind his back. The *nikkah* came to a close. Moulana Baqir invited them to pray. The hall was utterly hushed. He could sense everyone in the room honoring the moment. Amar looked down at his own hands, his one thumb kneading the knuckle of the other. He closed his mouth until he felt the line of his jaw tighten and teeth clench but still the thought escaped him: God, if you're there, if you're listening, let Hadia have a happy life, let hers be a fulfilling love. Let him be respectful of her, in awe of her, and tender toward her.

❖

IT WAS DONE. Her daughter was married. Layla was surprised to find herself crying. She held tight to her mouth but let her tears fall freely; soon she would force herself to stop, but for now, she welcomed the rush of emotion. Hadia was looking down at the

Quran in her lap and at once Layla saw the girl she had been, petite for her age and so bright that people at grocery stores would see something in her that Layla, being with her all the time and having no other children to compare her to, could not see. Now her first child was married and she felt grateful to God. Rafiq placed a heavy hand on her shoulder and she turned to him and his eyes were also glistening. When he nodded at her, she knew: they had arrived at this moment together.

"*Mubarak*," he said to her, and she said the same—congratulations.

Before either of them could congratulate their daughter and son-in-law, the swarm of guests approached them, and Layla and Rafiq stepped away from each other, Layla to hug woman after woman and Rafiq to shake hands with every man. Layla's body became automatic as she hugged them, her mouth moved to say thank you but her mind was quiet. Each time there was a break between people she looked up at her daughter, who had begun glowing— just like that—as though what she had been told by her mother as a girl really had been true: that the heavens opened up during the *nikkah* recitation unlike any other time in one's life, and angels descended to shower their blessings.

Then Seema Ali approached her and Layla could not help but look for Amira beside her, but Amira was not there. Amar stood at the side of the stage speaking with Huda. Layla turned to Seema and smiled.

"We are so happy for you and Brother Rafiq," Seema said.

"The next wedding we celebrate will be for your children, *Inshallah*," Layla said, and Seema smiled. It was a strange time in their lives: the children like paper boats they were releasing into the water and watching float away.

"Hadia looks *noorani* today," Seema told her. "I've always had a soft spot for your Hadia."

Layla knew this. The small pinch that occasionally announced itself in Seema's presence throbbed again. Hadia also had maintained a reverence for Seema that Layla never understood. She

253

would be on her best behavior when Seema was around. Seema had watched her children for her when Layla was in the hospital and it might have been this time that had made an impression, though her children had likely forgotten those few days. Seeing Seema now, on this day, with both Amar and Amira in the same room, opened in Layla access to that secret they shared. They held each other's gaze a moment longer as if to acknowledge this, and then smiled in a way that Layla knew they were communicating that they had moved on, that the past was in the past.

"Yes," Layla said finally, "Hadia does look beautiful."

It was her first time voicing the thought. Seema had complimented her daughter often as Hadia grew, and Layla had braced against the comments. When alone with her daughter, she reminded Hadia that it was cultivating humility and an internal beauty that truly mattered. And Hadia, a girl still, would twist from Layla's grip, and if she looked at Layla in that moment then she looked at her darkly, as though Layla had snatched her compliments from her, or worse, had denied them.

But maybe it would have been all right, maybe it would have eased the space between Layla and Hadia, if once in a while Layla had also shared how she felt about her daughter: that Hadia was beautiful and thoughtful, that she was a natural leader, that she could do anything she put her mind to, that she was smart in a way that pleased Layla but also frightened her, not knowing what life would be like for a woman like her daughter, or if she would know how to help her navigate it.

✧

IT WAS TIME for the food to be served. Her wedding, which had seemed to be going so slowly, had just sped up. Waiters lifted tops from silver dishes and suddenly the hall filled with the aroma of spices, and guests stood to flock to the food line. Huda recited the dishes she would bring her and Tariq: Hyderabadi biryani, chicken tikka masala, paneer and spinach. Then Baba took the stage and Hadia realized she had been waiting to greet him more than anyone. Mumma, surprisingly, had warmed quickly to Tariq, even asked after him on the phone and had not minded them spending time together before they were married. But Baba had avoided any discussion of him, even as the wedding approached. She felt the hopeful thud of her heart as he climbed the steps and she stepped away from Tariq to go to him, abandoning the decorum of the bride who sits still and waits for others to come to her. She knew that she had, over the years, hurt them. She consistently dashed any hope they had of finding a man to their liking for her, as her mother liked to point out, the way every other girl in the community had done for their parents.

She hoped Baba would look at her with love and pride, the same look as when she rushed inside after speaking with the admissions dean of the medical school. Even now, anything she accomplished that made her feel remotely proud was not done for her alone, but in hope that it would give her parents the thought—that is *my* daughter, Hadia. Baba took her face in his hands and he kissed her forehead.

"Are you happy?" she found she was asking him.

"Are you?" He watched her.

She nodded, as if she were a little girl still.

"Then I am happy. How could I not be? I have gained a son."

He had never expressed to her that her independent happiness was tied to his. Nor had he hinted that he would one day refer to Tariq as his son. Baba turned from Hadia and stepped forward to embrace him.

✦

ANY MINUTE NOW he would leave to find her. The hall filled with chatter. A courtyard, she had said. He had looked up at her then. Just to be certain she was suggesting what he thought she was. He had never forgotten her eyes—their shape, their dark lashes, how their color changed in the sunlight and when she cried, appeared brown when she wore brown and a vibrant emerald green when she wore green, how in the summer when her skin tanned he was even

255

more disturbed by their effect. But he had forgotten that particular disturbance: how he would need to look away to gather his thoughts again. Tonight she had looked at him with eyes as earnest as ever. And he knew it was safe to agree to meet.

Five minutes now. He looked at the face of his watch so long he thought he could hear its tick. The tables emptied around him, almost everyone stood in line for the buffet, and though he was hungry he couldn't even think of eating now. In four minutes, he would make his way. If he could smoke to calm his nerves. If he could drop by the bar for just a shot. An old man looking at him waved him over. Amar turned to see if there was someone else he could be calling, but the man smiled and pointed at him, as if to say yes, you. He rested his hands on a cane and nodded as Amar approached him, then gestured to the empty seat. Amar pretended to not notice and stayed standing, waiting for the old man to speak.

"You are Rafiq's boy. I have not seen you for years—do you remember me?"

Amar had never seen him before.

"You were this much when I visited." He indicated with his hand a foot off the floor and he said, wagging a finger, "You were a *badmash* boy—you would tease and tease your Mumma Baba and if they even looked at you like they were about to scold you, you would cry. I am an old friend of your dada's. You look like your grandfather. You stand like him too. The way you twist your wrist to look at your watch—your dada did just that. I called you over to look closely. Remarkable. Your father has a shadow of his father's features, but you are a copy. Has he ever told you that?"

Amar shook his head. Four minutes, but he took a seat. He had never met his dada, or anyone who knew him, other than his father. As a child, Amar thought of his father orphaned young and could not imagine how he had managed to move through the world alone that early. Amar listened as the old man explained how he had flown in from Arizona with his young grandson Jawad, just to attend the wedding of his oldest friend's granddaughter.

"It's a hard blow, losing a friend. You are too young to know it.

And your grandfather was very young when he died. Your father still a boy. Not only do you lose a friend, but you realize, for the first time, that you too are close to death."

Amar thought of Abbas, stepping forward to bear the brunt of Seema Aunty's anger at a window Amar had broken, even after Seema Aunty had threatened Abbas that he would have to pay for it from the little he had saved.

"What was it like for my father after my grandfather died?"

He did not know he wanted to know until he asked.

"It was difficult for him. Just him and his mother after that. Every time I visited them it seemed he had aged. Trying to be responsible. Trying to care for his mother. Very hardworking boy. But you know your father. He is a man who does not show on his face what he is going through. His father was like that. Maybe you are like that? But he would visit me many times. Always brought me sweets on Eid. Hand-delivered me his wedding invitation. Came to my house before he moved here. I felt like I was saying good-bye to a son. Then my own son, years later, moved us all to Arizona. And your father visited us anytime his work brought him there, even if he had to rent a car and drive two hours to do it. And why would he? Just because I had been friends with his father. Me—an old man to him. A rare man, your father. Not many men like that anymore."

Listening to this man praise his father, Amar felt as if a balloon were growing in his chest and he was afraid if it popped he would cry. He had been cheated out of knowing the best of his father; his father had reserved his kindness for others. Amar looked around, preparing to excuse himself, but he wanted to do something for the old man.

"Can I bring you something, some food or drink?" he asked.

The old man refused. His grandson was waiting in the food line for him.

"Anything?" Amar insisted, and he wondered for a moment if he wanted the old man to think that what he appreciated in his father had also been passed on to him. The man smiled.

"If you can bring me tea without my grandson Jawad seeing . . .

257

They keep me on strict lockdown. It is surely a sin to live if it is like this, no sugar, no rice, no—" and he began to list what he could not eat anymore, but Amar stood.

"Two spoons of sugar, please," the man said, and winked at him, "and listen—generous spoons."

Amar rushed—partly because now Amira would be waiting, and partly because he wanted to bring the tea soon, so the man could savor it before his grandson returned. The food line was moving slowly, Mumma was occupied with checking the dishes and determining which needed to be refilled. And though he hoped he was the kind of person whose intentions were pure, he caught himself looking for his father as he carried the teacup back to the old man, hoping that his father would see who he was bringing it for.

✧

HUDA SET PLATES down on the small table that had been set up for Hadia and Tariq. Tariq began to eat immediately and Hadia moved rice into the tikka sauce and blew at the fork before taking a bite. It was delicious but she had no appetite. The sound of the hundred guests talking echoed.

"I really like Amar," Tariq said between bites.

"Everyone likes Amar," she said.

Tariq stopped speaking, sensing sadness in her tone. She had kept Amar from him—both his full story and its effect on Hadia, and Tariq knew not to pry, to wait instead until she was ready to share. The sense of dread that had seized her as she watched her brother merge into the crowd was gone, but its aftertaste remained. She moved the food on her plate around with her fork. It was true. Everyone liked Amar. To know him longer was to complicate the adoration one felt for him, the desire to do something that would make life easier for him, and that ache of knowing that there was little that would. She pressed the white napkin against her lips and dabbed.

"You have a brother?" Tariq had asked her, the first time she mentioned Amar to him years ago. "You only talk about Huda."

It stung. There was something false to Hadia about the way she spoke to others about Amar, and so the more years that passed, the less she ever spoke of him. She found herself wanting to omit any hint of herself in the stories, so the undercurrent of them would be about Amar's untrustworthy nature, Amar's unhealthy tendencies, Amar's secrets. But omitting herself had the opposite effect of what she might have wanted: instead of her friends being able to comfort her, absolve her, tell her that everyone's choices in life were their own and Amar had unfortunately made tragic ones, she would hear their sympathies and feel nothing. Their words failed to reach the guilt she carried that she had hidden from everyone, even Huda.

Hadia could draw no straight lines to the past. Could not pinpoint which of the many times he had leaned in to whisper into her hair, *Don't tell Baba?* and she had whispered back, *I won't*, and say to herself: this was the moment I first failed him, this was my part in his pattern. She could not say she had kept his secrets when it would have been better for him if she had told them, or that she had given away the ones she should have guarded. She could not excuse her competitive nature nor could she fault it. She could not say it was that Baba had given her the watch and not him, because she had always wanted it, had done everything to become the child who would receive it. The only guilt she could carry without questioning it or pushing it aside, the only thing she could land on with any certainty, was the simple facts of their lives tonight: that it was she who sat beneath the chandelier light adorned in jewelry, and her brother who roamed the hall wishing he were elsewhere—or worse, wishing he could be back and feel as loved, as welcome, as at home.

2

AS AMAR APPROACHED THE COURTYARD HE FELT
that familiar rush from years ago, the fear of being caught quickening his step, the promise of seeing Amira that made his entire
body a single heartbeat. Clouds passed rapidly, hardly any stars
were out, and the moon was so bright it seemed to have been placed
just to shine a spotlight on them. Had he, even once, in the years he
had been gone and the months before when they no longer spoke,
doubted that he still loved her? Amira was seated on the cement
floor. The red of her outfit appeared burgundy, the green almost
black, the bells chimed when she moved, her lips were purple from
the dark or purple from the cold, her hair pulled up tight in a bun,
just a few stray hairs lit silver, and when she stood to greet him, the
movement of her body attracted his entire attention, and though
she waved shyly her smile was generous.

Impossible. Impossible that he had ever stopped loving her. Not
since his love for her first announced itself at that party years ago,
when she looked up from the soda she sipped through her striped
straw, and then walked to where he had been leaning against the
wall, minding his own business. She had asked the first question
and he, who did not like speaking to almost anyone, answered and
then asked his own. He was only seventeen then. He had carved
their initials into his windowsill that very night.

"I thought maybe you'd changed your mind," she said.

"I thought maybe I had too."

He did not know why he lied so totally but it made her laugh.

"How much time do we have?" she asked.

Not nearly enough. But he shrugged, and they took a seat on the cement, cross-legged and not quite facing each other. This was where the hotel staff likely came to smoke; it was tucked away from the hotel and any window.

"Let's make the most of our time then and speak honestly," she said.

She was still Amira: taking charge, forming her plans out loud, so deliberate that anyone around her would be convinced they had wanted it before she even suggested it.

"How long has it been?" he asked.

"Three years, maybe more." She did not pause before the reply.

The air between them was changed from what he remembered—there had always been tenderness, but now there was a charge too. He was aware of his body and hers alone. Of course he had felt this before, but something about the tone of her voice, the way she looked at him and then away, made him think it would not be impossible to reach out and touch her. They had been children together and were so young when they began to love each other, he knew that when he looked back. Some days, in the life he had now, it seemed unbelievable that they could have had so ardent a love without ever touching. But that is what it had been. Now her shirt was cut low and a shadow gestured to her breast. He looked down at his hands, holding on to his knees.

By now they both must have become different people. But what he felt for Amira—it was as though she had been tucked in a compartment in his heart that hadn't changed, and seeing her now he knew it never would: he could return to her at any age and feel for her the way he always had. He knew, with such certainty it shamed him, that it would not matter if he fell in love one day and married—Amira would continue to exist as a love entirely apart. If ever they could resume, even just for an afternoon, if ever she called—a sin was not a sin if it were for her. A risk was not a risk.

"What did you end up studying?" he asked.

Do you like waking up before the rest of the world?

When you were little did you think the moon followed you?

"Psychology—with an emphasis in child development."

"Done with school?"

She shook her head. She was beginning graduate school in the fall, she said she wanted to do research. She asked him what he studied. When he didn't answer right away, the peace of her face was disturbed. She was being careful like his mother, not knowing what questions to ask.

"I had to work. But I've saved a little money now, and I'm going to try to go back to school."

All of that was true. What he wanted now was to be honest with her. He had already lost; being dishonest would not win anything back for him now.

"Mumma and Baba once mentioned you were in India."

She moved the row of her bangles down her arm then up again. Their curves twinkled in the dark.

"I wasn't."

"I didn't think so," she said, and she smiled as though she was proud she had intuited it. Offering her the truth seemed to relax her. Her eyes were as big as a cat's in the dark.

"What else did you think?"

She shrugged. "I couldn't imagine you being convinced to do something you didn't want to do."

He was quiet. He had wanted to change for her.

"So," she said, tenderly now, asking the one question no one else had, "where have you been?"

Leaves circled beside them and then dispersed. The little pearls that dangled from her earrings quivered.

"I was in a bad place after us," he said. "You know me."

She winced. He listened to the scrape of leaves and wondered if it could be effortless, confessing it all to Amira.

"I couldn't go to class and if I did I couldn't focus. I fought with my father more than I spoke to anyone. I was drinking a lot and I wanted something stronger."

He paused, not knowing how to continue. For years he had hidden his habits from her but feared she had known. He had always thought that was why she had ended things: not the excuse she gave of her parents, having hardly thought of them throughout their relationship—but that she herself had grown tired of waiting for him.

"It got worse. I got into worse fights with my father. I wasn't myself. Or if I was, I wasn't anyone I recognized."

The beeping of the safe. Mumma's pale face in the hallway. Hadia asking if anyone had seen her watch. Amira looked at him with fear and care and it was thrilling to see a reaction in her. Even if it was just sympathy, the least personal of investments.

"Before I left, I started taking pills to silence this voice in my head telling me: you've sinned, you'll sin again, home for you is a place you stand outside of, looking in. Eventually it felt like I had no other choice, or I wanted that and nothing else. There was one fight with my father I couldn't take back. I moved to L.A. I wasn't sure I'd stay, but I'm still there now. It's hard to remember that first year. I worked temporary jobs. I helped move furniture. I kept what Mumma would call bad company. But about two years ago I met someone who helped me get clean. I was lucky. That voice had finally quieted, and I started to feel like I could breathe. Not breathe easy, just breathe. And now, if I do find myself walking alone, or by the ocean, looking out, and if I do think of God—I can't explain it, Amira, but it's different. It's not that I am at home where I live now. But at least there, I am not the only one standing outside."

He was surprised by what he had most wanted to share with her. He didn't mention who had helped him get clean. Realized he didn't want to say her name. Even thinking of her next to Amira made what he had felt for her in the past year shrink.

"I don't understand," was all she said, her voice small, like a squeak. "Clean?"

Maybe because he needed someone to know, or maybe to watch her face twist to prove her care for him, or to give her an image that would haunt her the way she haunted him, he rolled up his shirtsleeve and offered her his arm, and even in the darkness he could see the splatter of dots following his vein.

A dark, small speck. A permanent stain. So heavy and black it cannot tell good from evil.

"Oh, Amar," she whispered.

She touched his arm. He felt a current shoot from his arm through his entire body and he jerked back, unrolled his sleeve, and buttoned it again at the wrist. Her eyes shimmered.

"You can't tell anyone," he said, and his voice was rougher now, "not where I live and not what I did."

"We may not speak anymore but I have never, and will never, break your trust."

He wanted to believe her.

"Do you still?" she whispered.

He shook his head. "Some days it feels like that was another life entirely. Other days I am so certain I will again, it's almost as if it's my destiny, as if I am in a holding cell waiting for the sentence to be handed down to me. But I know if I did, I'd never stop."

She looked at him the way people sometimes looked at him, as though their love for him were useless, a love that pained them more than it gave them anything in return.

"I don't see the guys I met when I first moved anymore. I got a new job and I work other ones on the side. I cook at a restaurant in town that has a good reputation. I'm good at it. It's hard work, but I'm valued there."

He was not sure what she was thinking, if she was happy for him or if she was thinking what he imagined his father would, but she nodded at least.

"Promise me you never will again," she said.

"I think it's more important that I promise myself," he said, and she half smiled at that.

Every day he lived without it felt like an extra day he was lucky for, and he feared using now the way he had once feared his dreams—not at all in the sunlight but then it would be a certain hour, a darkening of the sky, and he was terrified that at night they would come for him again. She reached out her pinky like a child and like a child he took it. Again that current that lit his body.

"*Khassam?*" she asked, the Urdu word for swear it.

"*Khassam.*"

She kissed her thumb and then he kissed his. She tugged his pinky tight for a second. Then she let go. He thought she was about to say it was time to go back, but instead she asked, "Do you remember that party, the first time we really spoke?"

He remembered every question. He remembered how many birds sat on the line and how many took flight.

"My friends had dared me," she said, and even though it happened so long ago, he felt crushed, that she had not walked up to him of her own accord. "All the mosque girls thought you were something strange, always so quiet and by yourself, but I knew you from when you came over and I'd liked you for years. How you were good in a way unseen to them, to yourself, even. They didn't think I'd have the nerve but I knew they'd given me a gift—under the guise of a dare I could do what I wanted to: just talk to you."

"A lucky dare."

"Even knowing all of what we know now?"

"Especially knowing."

She smiled at him sadly.

"You know my Mumma saw us that day. In the car on the way home I was scolded in front of my brothers, my father, I was so mortified. Abbas Bhai spoke up for me then, and he told Mumma to calm down. He said to her: of course they can talk to each other. You all are the ones who make just talking such a sin—and what do you expect? We see each other all the time and can't even act human? Leave her alone, he said. Amar's a good kid. He didn't mean anything by it. Let her talk to him if she wants. So Mumma relented—she always listened to Abbas. Abbas was her moral compass when she wasn't sure what to do. But I was still so embarrassed. I thought I'd never speak to you in person again."

"Until I came to your door the night—"

"Yes. And you were the only one who comforted me even a little.

I thought of how Abbas Bhai had defended you, defended us. Hearing the knock and seeing you of all people, and realizing how reassured I felt at the sight of you, even at that horrible moment, I thought it was some kind of sign."

They fell silent. She was going to break his heart when she got up to return to the wedding. He already felt it coming his way.

"You know, Amar, our sadness might have looked different, but I was affected too. They didn't want me to come tonight, did you know that? Mumma has often mentioned you over the years. To try and explain why she had been so harsh with me, or to point out how well I was doing now and wasn't I glad that things worked out the way they had? But even if she was right, I'd still dissolve into tears. I'd hate her again like I hated her the first time she said I had brought shame to our family, and how that shame was worse than grief because I had chosen to bring it upon them."

He could not reach out to comfort her, even as it pained him to watch her bite and release her lips in the way she would when she did not want to be upset. He could only keep his hands at his sides, clenched into fists.

She continued, "Once, Mumma told me you were my 'open vein.' You were the wound that, no matter how many years passed by, how much healing had been done, if prodded would open and bleed fresh again. But I assured her tonight not to be silly, that I could come. And no one knew if you'd be here anyway."

She looked down at her bangles, spun one around. He was starting to feel at the edge of a desperate sadness. He had already lost her. Seeing her now was like losing her all over again.

"After they found out about us, Mumma and Baba took away my phone and my computer. They told me every rumor they had heard about you and I wasn't sure anymore if what they said was true or a lie. 'Do you want a husband who drinks?' they would yell at me. 'Do you want a husband who lies to you? How can a man who does not respect his parents ever respect you?'"

She paused and looked at him, as if to see if her words had hurt him. Then she smiled to herself and continued, "Once I had loved

266

you in such a way that even if it were all true it still wouldn't change anything. If they were right—that you were headed nowhere good—that's where I wanted to be too. You say that there is an entire year of your life you don't remember, and I feel the same. They took me on a long trip, Syria, Iraq, then India. I felt calm on *ziyarat*. I felt, for the first time, that all was working out like it was meant to, that we were meant to part. But every time I held the *zari* I'd think of you and pray for you. That you were happy and doing well. That you'd gone to school and that you'd stopped drinking. I had no idea that it was much worse. I already felt so terrible, I don't know what I'd have done if I had known. I stayed in India for a month. There, my life in California felt so far. I watched my cousins as they married suitable men and I noticed how there was peace between them and their parents, peace and unity that came from their listening. I wanted that peace. And I thought that maybe they would never feel for their husbands the way I felt for you, but theirs wouldn't be a false life either, just different, and easier in many ways, and that is what Mumma had wanted me to understand."

She released the hair from her bun: her nervous habit, any lull in a conversation and she would take her hair down or tie it up again.

"What had we been thinking?" she said quietly, leaning her head back and speaking to the sky, her neck stretched in the moon-light. "Approaching one another so openly, just asking to be seen. We should have never spoken to each other, if a proper way is what we wanted, we should have just waited for each other in silence."

He followed the curve of her neck until it plunged into her shirt, then looked away.

"No one saw us. I just needed more time."

"You still don't know."

"Know what?"

Again she looked at him as though the sight of him pained her, and he was suddenly afraid to know the answer.

"I didn't know how Mumma found out either. How she knew details. How she could describe a moment between us at our park and then strike me across my face." Her voice was shaking. "I didn't know until a year ago and Mumma finally told me, thinking that the vein had closed, but again I just wept."

She glanced at the door that led back to the wedding and then down at her arms that cradled her knees, still deliberating telling him. The wind lifted her hair. Amar held his breath.

"Your mother knew, Amar. She came to mine. She told her to end things between us, for both our sakes."

✧

WHERE WAS HE? Her entire experience of the wedding was being overshadowed by worry for Amar. Dinner was done and all the plates cleared, Hadia and Tariq had cut the cake and it was being served, and still he could not be located. She had not seen him since the *nikkah* and that was almost an hour ago. What was most important to her was that he be there for the family photograph so she could finally replace the framed one that hung above their fireplace.

"I'm going to go look for him," she told Huda.

People had just begun to dip their forks into their cake slices.

"Mumma," Huda said, "it's your daughter's wedding. Can't you focus on that?"

But Layla was already walking out the hall and into the lobby, where the appetizers and drinks had long been cleared away and now children from the wedding were playing. Layla stepped out of the hotel into the parking lot. She shivered. Nothing about the parking lot told her to look there. It occurred to her to look in the hall to see if she could find the Ali girl. Layla stepped back into the lobby and just when she decided she would go to Rafiq, she saw Amar walking down a long hallway and she rushed forward to meet him. The look on his face unsettled her. Something was wrong. She slowed her step. When he was almost in front of her, Amar looked up from the ground and lifted his hand, as if to stop her from coming any closer.

"Don't," he said.

"What happened? You were doing so well."

"Am I a child that needs to be monitored?" he barked at her.

She recoiled from his tone. His eyes were slightly glossy. He seemed to sway just a little. Had he been drinking? The question pierced her as she searched his face. She stepped closer to sniff for the scent of alcohol, but could only pick up the heavy stench of cigarettes. She pressed her hand against his chest and tried to calm him. He stepped back, swatted her hand away, her bangles clinking against each other. She touched her wrist, shocked at the force of his impact more than any dull pain she felt.

"Amar?"

"Hadia chooses who she is with. Hadia chooses someone who is not even Shia—and how do you react? You throw her an extravagant wedding."

He laughed an unnerving laugh, just one false note. He gestured to everything around him. The waiters clearing the cake plates averted their eyes as they walked past.

"People can hear you, Amar. You're yelling."

"Let them hear. Maybe then you will listen to what I am saying— all you care about is what people will think. What people will say."

It wasn't true. He was just like his father, letting his anger cloud his judgment. She looked helplessly around the hall. The few guests who were there looked once toward them and then at each other, then returned quickly to the main hall, whispering.

"I did exactly what Hadia is being celebrated for. No, I did what I thought was so important to you—I chose someone from the community. And I loved her, Mumma. I loved her."

His voice broke into a whisper. An instant dip in her stomach and she was sick.

"Oh, Ami."

She tried again to place her hand on his chest and again he swatted her away. Another guest looked in their direction. Layla pinched the bridge of her nose. She stood with her eyes closed. She had not prepared for this, had never thought he would find out, especially not after so much time had passed. Amar swayed on his feet.

"How could you, Mumma? You out of everyone." His voice was hoarse.

She had done the right thing: that girl was bound to break his heart.

"You were working so hard, Amar. You were so determined. I didn't want you to have a single distraction."

"You went behind my back. You ruined what I had been working for."

The dull headache had become a migraine. She pinched her nose again to keep herself from shaking.

"I didn't know," she whispered, and it was true.

Huda approached them then, holding up her sari so she could walk faster.

"What is going on here? People have begun to notice." Huda spat the words.

"Admit it. Admit that if it had been Hadia or Huda you would have reacted differently."

"It is not true. It is not why."

Layla's voice was shaking. But she found she couldn't look him in the eye.

"Look around you. Look at how true it is."

The guest book fell to the floor, the table holding it up collapsed, and with it came crashing a flower arrangement, the flowers spilling out and the water from the vase darkening the carpet. Children who had been playing in the lobby stared. One of them started to cry and an older one lifted him up. They were going to tell their parents. There is a scary man in the lobby yelling at Layla Aunty and kicking the table, they would say. Layla could not move. Huda knelt to the ground and lifted the table up and straightened the cloth on it. She picked the guest book up and unwrinkled the pages that had bent, lifted up the vase and tried to put the flowers back in, but they looked so messy Huda hid them under the table. Acting on his anger seemed to make Amar calmer. He was breathing very heavily.

"Please, Amar. People are going to come and look. I thought you needed to concentrate on your studies. You were doing so well. I thought she would be a distraction."

"You never thought I'd do well."

"*Sachi*, Ami, I swear I did."

"You wouldn't have gone to her mother if you thought I'd do well, if you really believed in me. You wouldn't have gone behind my back. You would have trusted that that could be my life."

"Come with me, Amar." Huda grabbed hold of his arm and pulled him. He pushed her off of him.

"Let go of me. You are all liars, backbiters, and you make me feel like I am the liar? You tell me that to go behind the back of the stranger is to eat his flesh? What about me?" He jabbed his finger to his chest. "I am your son. I am your son and you went behind my back. And you lied to me. And you tell me again and again that *I* am the one who has lied to you? I am the one who has betrayed you?"

Layla felt as if she had been struck across her face. She wanted to hold him until he stopped trembling and yelling or she wanted to run to the bathroom, lock the door behind her, spend the rest of the evening unseen by anyone.

"Amar," Huda hissed, "why did you come if you were going to make a scene?"

Huda gripped his arm again, tighter this time, and she shook it.

"You all betrayed me. Why did you even call me back?"

He was staring unfocusedly at the ground, as though he had begun talking to himself.

"Because we want you here," Huda said.

"You've never acted like it."

"Because Hadia wants you here."

Layla did not know she had begun crying until she moved her hand from her mouth and saw her fingers were wet. Huda held on to both of Amar's arms until he stopped trying to fight her.

"Mumma, go back inside," Huda instructed her.

"It was a mistake, Amar," Layla said, her voice very thin, and she tried to reach out to touch him. "Please. I made a mistake."

But it only made him angrier. He twisted to get out of Huda's grip.

"Maybe who I am hurts you, Mumma, but I have no choice over that. But you have intentionally hurt me."

"Go, Mumma. Go back inside." Huda was yelling at her now too. Huda let go of Amar for just a moment and pointed to the main hall. "Now."

Layla looked from Huda to Amar. She had never seen her son look so defeated and still so angry. Not against her. She turned around and walked into the hall in a daze, her hand over her mouth so tight it was as if she were keeping something from spooling out of her. Then the too-bright lights of the chandeliers. The cacophony of voices. The emcee taking the stage to announce the mirror ritual. A crowd of guests had gathered by the stage, and others sat in their seats, just waiting for a show.

✧

SHE HOPED IT meant nothing that her mother and sister were not by her side as she was led to the mirror. Hordes of people gathered around the stage. As a child, this had been her favorite wedding ritual. It seemed the most bizarre and therefore the most magical. Once she was one of the girls who watched wide-eyed from the bottom of the stage, wanting to catch a glimpse: how the bride and groom sat with a mirror between them, facing one another, under a beautiful, sheer red cloth that shimmered, their gazes lowered and only lifted to each other's reflection. It was a ritual that had come about in the days when one never even saw the face of their spouse before they were wed. It had been how her grandparents on both sides had first seen one another. By the time her parents had gotten married, it was a formality; her father had visited her mother's home twice. They had never spoken in private but had seen each other from across the room. Now that it was Hadia's turn, it was no more than a performance—she had memorized Tariq's freckle beneath his eyebrow, the spot on his beard that grew in a swirl. Each generation lost touch bit by bit. By the time it was her children's turn, would there even be a point?

"Look," someone said, and she did.

She caught sight of her own reflection first. From the angle it looked as though she were looking onto the surface of very still water. Red cloth instead of the sky. Little specks of light filtered through the fabric. Then she met Tariq's eyes, his upside-down reflection. It was Tariq, clearly and definitely, but it did not look like him. He winked at her and grinned and she smiled. The mirror was taken away, the red net removed and the room lit golden again. It was time for the photographs—one with each family until it was finally her family's turn—and then it would all be over.

✧

"HAPPY?" HUDA SAID to him in Urdu. She let go of him. The guest book had been placed back but the tablecloth was uneven; Amar tugged at it to try and straighten it. Huda made a typical Urdu joke about how quick Amar was to feel concerned about the appearance of the wedding. He shot her a dark look.

"Come outside and speak with me," she said gently.

"I don't want to speak with you."

"Then who do you want to speak with?"

He paused to think about it. He was unsteady on his feet.

"Hadia."

"Never me, *nay*?" she said.

He looked at her. He felt bad. It seemed as though an explanation was being asked of him but he had none to offer. He was depleted. He had made Mumma cry. He hadn't seen her for years, missed her all the time, and then on the one day he did see her, he had made her cry. He had kicked the stupid guest book stand. Some kid had even yelled it out loud. He was ready to go home, and that thought came with its own ache: where, exactly, was home? Huda led him gently by the arm to the parking lot, as if he were a child that had thrown a tantrum and was now being escorted out. But this was not a tantrum. He was justified in his anger. They had meddled in his life.

"You don't have to babysit me for them," he mumbled.

273

"What happened just now?"

"Whatever happened, happened long before that."

"Ah, our poet Amar," she said in Urdu, and hit his arm lovingly.

They took a seat on the sidewalk facing the parking lot. Once he would have been irritated by her teasing. Now he was grateful for the sign of intimacy.

"Couldn't you wait until after the wedding to fight, if you've already waited so long?" She was speaking very softly.

Past the parking lot, across the street, store signs blinked neon colors. A gas station, a liquor store, a store that bought and sold gold. He wanted to go back inside and find Amira, talk to her one last time.

He wanted to leave this place and never come back.

He wanted to begin this night again, wanted it to never end.

"When did you become so smart?" he asked Huda.

"I've always been."

He smiled.

"Just me that trailed behind, then?"

She touched his arm and left her hand there.

"Let's go back inside?" she said after a pause.

"Not yet."

He placed his hands in his pockets. He still had some cash, at touch it felt like forty. He pulled out his cigarettes.

"Do you mind?" he asked her. To his surprise, she shook her head.

"You deserve one, after what happened in there," she said, gesturing behind them to the hotel.

He laughed and lit his cigarette and said through the corner of his mouth, "You've loosened up. And you're the one who's earned it, the way you handled us."

"Haven't loosened up that much."

He laughed again. She was also smiling. He watched the smoke leave him and rise into the dark sky. He was careful to turn his face away from her to blow. He and Huda seemed almost like friends. Almost like they could be.

"Mumma wants to take a family photo. All of us, at the end of the wedding, just before the *ruksati*," she said.

"The part when everyone cries?"

"Yes."

"Will you cry?"

"She is my sister."

He tapped the cigarette and crushed the ash with his shoe.

"Our sister," she said.

She was being very kind to him. He felt worse for expressing his anger.

"What's happening now?"

"The mirror part."

"Which one of you liked that?"

"Hadia."

"And when will it be your turn?" He looked at her.

"Probably not for a while."

"Will you call me back for it?"

She looked down at her wrists. She had worn silver bangles that matched the stitching on her outfit. He dropped the cigarette butt and watched it burn and then dim.

"Why don't you stay. Then I won't have to call you."

He buried his face in his hands. He was not crying. He had fucked up phenomenally. He had yelled at Mumma in front of everyone. He knew that he should never have gone out to talk to Amira, but even knowing how he felt now he couldn't much regret it.

"Amar, can I ask you a question?"

He nodded.

"Is it better for you in your life now? Hadia and I wonder."

"Not better. Easier, maybe."

They watched guests with young children leave the hall and head to their cars.

"Are you ready to come back?"

"Not yet."

"But you will come?"

He looked at her. He nodded. She stood up. Straightened the

275

pleats of her sari. When she moved light reflected off of each of the gems sewn into her suit.

"The picture. Don't forget. Our family will be the last to be photographed. Then the *ruksati*."

"The hard part."

"Yes, the hard part."

Huda began to walk away. He called her name and she turned back.

"It was good speaking to you." He cupped his hands around his mouth.

"As good as Hadia?" She smiled.

"Pretty close."

He winked, but in the dark he was not sure if she saw it. Then he was alone. The stars twinkled and the neon light across the street glowed. If he had known there was a liquor store he would not have gone back to the hotel bar. The last time he went, after Amira walked away, the bartender had kindly hinted that Amar could have only one more drink before he would be cut off. It was a hotel, he explained, they had stricter rules, it had nothing to do with him. He didn't care. He paid. He held up the clear glass and looked at it like it would be his last—the golden and generous pour. He calmed just at the sight of it, at its weight when not yet sipped. Then his throat burned as if the drink could grow flames that spread to lick his insides.

"I have to tell you something," Amira had said, when they both knew they had to get up soon.

He knew what it was going to be. He felt dizzy looking at her as she swept her hair to one side. He had loved her when she was a girl hiding behind her mother's legs. When they played hide-and-seek, and he spotted her feet poking from beneath the branches, and he continued searching on purpose, not knowing why his heart thumped when he made the decision to keep looking. When she won the Quran competition at eleven, and how, when he heard her voice on the speaker reciting, he looked up and listened for once. And he had loved her when he was seventeen watching the birds on the telephone wire take flight, and she stood and stepped toward him at last, and only after that had he named it love.

She was engaged. Promised to a man she would marry once she completed grad school. He was not surprised. The paths their lives would take had been set in motion long before this blow was delivered to him.

"I wanted you to hear it from me," she said. "I wanted the chance to see how you were doing once more if I could, and tell you myself."

"Arranged?" he asked.

"Initially," she said.

It stung. So she loved him.

If there were other loves awaiting Amar, he knew they would be little loves, not: my whole life has led up to this moment with you. Every memory with you is electric. If you are there, it is you on the fence post with legs swinging, or you sipping from the striped straw, everyone else is out of focus or not there at all.

"Are you happy?" he asked.

"I am," she said, and then she twisted again the row of bangles on her wrist. "I am content. My parents are happy."

He was a dentist, a few years older. What would Amar become then to Amira? Oh, she might tell someone one day, that was my brother's friend. Or even less spoken: she would keep it a secret. One day she might push her son in the swing and look up to two kids sitting beneath a tree, too shy to scoot any closer, and she might remember herself at seventeen, defying everyone, risking everything, just to meet the boy from her community everyone warned her about.

Before she left, they stood face-to-face. She returned the jacket he had draped over her shoulders.

"I may not see you again and we may not speak again," she said, "but whatever comes, I want you to know there is a part of me that will always be who I was when I wrote that note and left it on your pillow. I never regretted that. I will always hope that you are happy, and safe, and healthy. I will pray you keep your promise. And that wherever you are, you are at home there."

277

He thought if he were to speak his voice would break.

"What's it like?" she whispered, their old game, that first question she had written him, and she looked up at him with her big eyes. He had no answer. He allowed himself to hold her in his arms and she rested her head against his chest. They stayed like that. His whole body was alive. He cast a shadow over her face when she lifted her face to his. He moved her hair from her eyes and he looked at her for one long moment, then kissed her forehead.

Now he crossed the street. The light in the liquor store window blinked OPEN, a bell sounded as he stepped in.

THE BOTTLE HE bought was the smallest one they carried, and he was proud of himself when it was the one he reached for. He knew his limits. It fit in the inside of his jacket pocket but was clunky. He needed to rest for just a minute before he could step back inside the main hall. He sat alone in the courtyard. He felt dizzy if he tried to stand. He should have eaten, he couldn't remember the last thing he had eaten or when. People were lining up to take pictures with the bride and groom when he snuck past. Soon it would be his family's turn. He would tell Mumma he was very sorry. They had been right about him. Eventually Amira would have realized it on her own too, so it did not matter how. It was inevitable. He was better off in L.A. He rested his head in his hands. And then a memory presented itself to him at so strange a time and so unvisited before, he wondered if it could even be true: he has thrown a tantrum at maybe eleven and has left his house to sit on the cement driveway beneath his basketball hoop. The sky draining of its color but not before filling first: with pink, orange, indigo, and violet clouds. When the door opens it is his father and not his sister or his mother that has come after him. And even though his father's kurta-pajama is white and easily dirtied, he takes a seat beside him on the ground and Amar still thinks of him then as Baba. He moves his basketball from one hand to the other, its rough orange surface, and he is not speaking, and Baba looks at the street and the cars passing and maybe the people in the cars wondering what is wrong with them.

"Amar," his father is trying to talk to him, "why do you think like this, these foolish thoughts, that you don't belong?"

He holds the basketball close to him, rests his chin on its curved surface. Another car passes and the person inside not looking at them. When it becomes clear that Baba is waiting for an answer, that the sky will turn black before he is satisfied with the silence, Amar shrugs. If only he could remember now what the hurt was about. Maybe that he does not want to pray and maybe that he does not want to sit still when their mother makes them listen to the *duas,* and he gets in ear-twisting trouble for making it into a joke, for trying to make eye contact with Hadia or Huda until one of them starts to laugh. Maybe just that everyone is good except for him, everyone has a lock in them that they have found a key to, and he is all shut up and closed with no key so he looks to each of them when they are listening intently to the *duas* thinking either there is no key or that he was created without one. And maybe he does not really believe in angels but maybe the ones on his shoulders look at each other and they shake their heads and shrug, saying, well, we don't know what to do with this one, even if God were to show him signs he would not listen because that is the way it is with some kids, when their hearts are just stained black.

He must have said something because Baba pokes his shoulder and says, "Don't you know—that's the thing—everyone is not just good. Everyone is *trying* to be good. And everyone feels this way sometimes, that they are not good, and not good at trying either."

"That's not true," Amar remembers saying to his father. "You are good."

✦

HADIA AND TARIQ smiled and posed as family after family lined up for the photographs. She was ready for the night to end. When the Ali family approached, Hadia saw at once that Amira Ali's face was flushed and her hair down and a little windswept. The photographer arranged each family member on the stage and Amira was directed to sit by Hadia. Amira congratulated her. Hadia thanked her and looked at her for a second longer than she might have—Amira Ali's eyes were bright green, and Hadia could not decide if her face had that raw look of having just cried.

Wonderful, the photographer said. Hadia did not look into the lens. She swept the hall for Amar and could not find him. Mumma sat alone at a far table, watching the hall empty of guests. From this distance she could not see Mumma's expression. Huda was near the stage, talking to Dani, but Hadia sensed right away that Huda was anxious, she crossed her hands in front of her as if she were guarding herself.

Hadia sometimes still returned to that conversation with Amira in the mosque parking lot years ago. It was just months before Amar was to run away, but of course Hadia had not known that at the time. She remembered being surprised when Amira had asked to speak with her. She remembered how Amira nervously looked around the ladies' hall filled with women mingling and whispered, "Privately please, ten minutes, near the basketball hoop."

By then Hadia had glimpsed the contents of her brother's box. She had not told her parents, but she had told Huda: no details, just that they had formed some sort of relationship.

"I know this is strange," Amira said when they were alone, "but I needed to speak to you. I don't know if Amar told you about us—"

Hadia shook her head no, then said, "But I had guessed."

Amira sighed. "We were so foolish."

Hadia remembered thinking that Amira was too young to look that sad, only eighteen.

"My mother found out about us," Amira said, "just three weeks ago. Amar and I have not really spoken since."

"I'm sorry," Hadia had said, and she meant it. She found, in that moment, that she felt great affection for the girl, and oddly protective of her.

"Mumma and Baba forbid it. I wake up every morning just

wanting to fall asleep. There is a part of me that knows all I want is this. All I want is to fight my parents for him."

Later, Hadia would look back on that night and tell herself that Amira Ali had sought her out on purpose, to be someone who could listen to her as a sister, but could also hold in her heart love for Amar, and look beyond the limits of propriety that their parents could not. Hadia had hugged Amira, and Amira had leaned into the hug, let herself be consoled. It occurred to Hadia that in another life, in a life where her girlhood dream or her brother's dream came true, the two of them would have become sisters.

"They say he drinks, they say he is no good, that I am better off."

She was speaking into Hadia's shoulder, her voice muffled. There was truth to what her brother was being accused of. Little by little, year after year, Hadia had given up any expectations of Amar, had tried to encounter him only as he was.

"What is it you want, Amira?" she had asked her.

They were both dressed entirely in black, flowing abayas, so her face looked even more pale and vulnerable. Amira did not answer right away. She bit her lip and looked to the mosque entrance, where people had begun to exit and head to their cars.

"I know Amar is good. I know Amar wants to be good. But I want to be with someone who is a harmonious fit. Do you think his heart is open to the life we have?"

"If that is what you want, my brother cannot be that for you. He cannot be that for any of us."

For years afterward that would be the line she returned to, asking herself why she had replied the way she had. But in that moment she had not wanted to deceive Amira, had not wanted to draw her any closer to the same chaos they were all suffering from.

"Thank you," Amira said at last. "I've been so conflicted. I think this will make it easier."

Again she held Amira and Amira let herself cry. Before Hadia turned to leave, Amira stopped her, and hesitated before saying, "I really do love him. If he wanted this life, even if it was a struggle for him to live it—I would stand by him."

Hadia did not know what to say. She told her so.

"I just wanted someone to know that. I just needed to say it to someone out loud."

✧

HE WAS WAITING for the seasickness to pass. Then he would return to the wedding, be again the brother of the bride. He had missed more than he had attended and if he did not go back now Hadia would notice. They had to stand together for the family photograph. They had to say good-bye to Hadia. And he *did* want to speak to his father. Hours earlier, when he watched his father stand in the blue light of the backyard, Amar told himself he was still angry, but in his heart he knew he was like a child who refused to allow himself the one thing he wanted: to drop the fuss and go to him. Amira had once told him he would feel something other than anger and he had not believed her. He thought his anger would never be extinguished. Now he had exhausted his anger, exhausted himself, and found that what was left—what was inexhaustible—was longing and regret, each feeling fueling the other.

Sometimes, Amar thought he could blame the distance between himself and his father on his own lack of steadfast belief in God. He could not claim to know God existed with any certainty. But there was love in his heart for the men and the women from the stories, the people of the holy book, love for the man whose name Mumma traced on his forehead, or pointed out on the moon, whose name was evoked in the *naray*; and even if Amar said to himself he did not believe, still his mouth opened to respond to the call.

What was this love, he wondered, as he twisted open and closed the cap of the bottle, and why was it still such a part of him, when all that could go had gone? First the rituals went and were replaced by guilt, and then the guilt went, and soon his belief faltered before vanishing almost entirely too—belief in hellfire and the narrow bridge one had to cross to reach heaven, as thin as a hair, as sharp as the blade of a knife. But the love for them remained, the Prophets and the Imams, the characters from the stories he heard as a child, balanced on Mumma's knee, curling her hair around his finger, and it was a love untarnished by the resentment of his father that had so afflicted everything else.

The whiskey burned when swallowed. He sank his face into his hands and hoped to feel steady soon. Every minute he remained outside was a minute that sped toward the end of his sister's wedding. He took a deep breath. Tonight had threatened all the work he had done—telling himself he did not believe and therefore did not belong. That his belonging depended on belief. If only he could tell his father: Look. I have kept this. I have held on to it. I open my mouth to criticize someone but then I close it, thinking of how the Prophet did not even tell the little girl to eat fewer dates when her mother asked him to, knowing he too shared her habit. My heart clenches at the thought of twelve brothers leading their youngest to a ditch, snatching from him his father's gift, that colorful coat. And I think and think again of that child, climbing onto his grandfather's back while he knelt in prayer, oblivious to everyone who was watching and waiting for his grandfather to set the standard for them all.

3

VASES OF ORCHIDS HAD BEEN GATHERED ONTO
one table. The staff was busy clearing clutter from the others. Final
families waited to be photographed, close family friends waited for
the *ruksati*. Layla sat alone at a far table and watched the hall blur
before her—either exhaustion or tears—the lights of the chandelier becoming geometric shapes that twinkled.

"Mumma?" Huda said, snapping the hall back into focus. Huda
took a seat by her and leaned in to look at Layla's face.

"Ma," Huda said again, her voice more loving.

"What have I done?"

Huda sighed. Huda, the daughter she counted on to speak her
mind and take a balanced stance, neither comforted Layla nor criti-
cized her.

"Was he all right?"

"Amar will always be Amar, Ma. There is nothing we can do for
him."

She had tried, hadn't she? She had tried her best. Her intentions
were good, were they not? It was hardly a comfort now. Intentions
shrank next to actions. Actions took on their own momentum.
Amar had not come back into the hall after his outburst. She had
underestimated his care for Amira Ali, then and now. She had put
too much faith in the passage of time.

When Amar was little she stayed up late after putting him to
bed, secretly read books for an answer on how to parent him. She

sat through every parent-teacher meeting mortified at how his teacher spoke slowly, assuming Layla could not understand. She tried to become the mother he needed. Preparing herself, enlarging herself, educating herself, only to have let him down the way she had. *Does she love him?* she remembered Rafiq asking, as though he believed Amira's love could change the outcome for their son. Layla had not believed—not in the girl's love, nor in her son's ability to win over Amira's family. She could say nothing when Amar accused her tonight, could do nothing but sit and wonder just how the limits to her belief in her son had so dangerously destroyed his possibilities.

Now she deserved any outcome. No longer could she say this was a test from God to prove her faith—it was that, but it was also her own actions returning to haunt her. Rafiq walked over to her. He had been managing last-minute jobs. Huda left them as soon as he approached.

"Time for our photograph soon," he told her.

Dani was on the stage now, smiling brightly, Hadia's oldest friend who Layla loved cooking for, who still came over anytime the two of them were back home for a visit.

"What's happened, Layla?" he asked, alarmed.

Again the lights became a blur of moving shapes. She blinked until it returned to normal. Rafiq took a seat by her.

"Will you find Amar?" she asked. "Will you call him back for the photo? He won't come if I go."

Rafiq sighed. There was no time for him to ask why. She had been foolish. She had asked Rafiq to not speak to Amar all night, thinking Rafiq was to blame for their troubles with Amar. Now she knew better. A saying her father had taught her when she was very young came back to her as Rafiq stood to go and bring back their son.

"Be careful who you point your blame at, Layla. And remember that anytime you point your finger to accuse someone, there are three fingers beneath it, curled to point right back at you."

✧

THERE WAS A tap on his shoulder and he looked up to see it was his father. Amar was still in the courtyard, sitting on the lone bench. His first thought was that he could get away with it, trick his father into thinking he was composed, that the edges of the world had not begun to spin. He opened his mouth to say something and then closed it. His father took a seat. The night was cold. The gray clouds that had raced across the sky when he sat by Amira were gone. His father handed him a glass of water and Amar gulped it down. He thanked him. He had not realized he had been so thirsty.

"Baba," he said, just to break the long silence. But he sounded like a child pleading—a break between the two syllables. He had not called him Baba in years. There was a day when he decided this was how he would punish his father, that he would not only with-hold affection and respect, but he would also keep from calling him father. The light of the lamp at the far end of the courtyard doubled and swayed.

His father placed a hand on his shoulder and left it there. His hand was warm and Amar could feel it through the fabric of his shirt. He did not move just in case his father's hand slipped. How did Amar get here and was this really happening? How long ago had Amira been sitting in the courtyard across from him? She wore a delicate gold necklace. She had beautiful lips. She laughed the same way she had always laughed. Some things never changed, and those things were a comfort, and a way to mark all the rest that had.

"Do you remember the story of Imam Hussain as a child, and how he climbed onto the Prophet's back during prayer?" Amar asked.

"Of course."

"Why do you think we were told that?"

Baba looked up, and then down at his feet. He shrugged.

"To show us how much he loved his grandson," Baba said.

"But what if it was meant to show us more? What if we were meant to look closer?"

There was a pause.

"I don't know, Amar. I never think about things the way you do."

"I do think about things."

He meant it as a statement but it sounded like a question.

"I know you do."

"Is it enough?"

"I pray it will be."

Baba cupped his arms in his lap then lay them open.

"I just wanted you to know that I remember that."

His father nodded. Was Amar crying? Is that why his shoulders were shaking? Is that why Baba's hand was moving up and down his back, and he was pulling Amar close to his body? And Amar knew that scent. They are driving down a long street lined with lots of trees and it is exciting to be so close to the wide window, and Baba leans across him to turn the knob of the window until the wind slaps his face and that is the scent. Now his father was saying something to him, and Amar focused on his words until he heard that he was saying it's okay, it's okay, it's okay. He was repeating it like a prayer.

How long had he wanted this without knowing it was what he wanted. It's okay, his father said, his heavy hand moving up and down his back, and Amar knew that he was crying. He nodded into Baba's arm and tried to close his eyes, but that made the spinning worse. Then he remembered there was a wedding, and the wedding was Hadia's, and that it was why he had come. I have to go back, he thought. But he must have spoken it aloud because his father shook his head.

"*I* have to go back, but you can't come back inside, Amar," Baba said.

He had fucked up. It was apparent to anyone who looked at him. He nodded.

"Will you go back now?" Amar asked.

"Not yet."

"What are you waiting for?"

Baba did not answer him.

"Why do you do that?" Amar asked.

287

"Do what?"

Amar touched his hand to his eyebrow and ran his fingers along the length of it, then back up again.

"I didn't realize I did it."

"You always have."

"I suppose I'm just thinking."

"I always thought it meant you were so angry you wouldn't speak."

Baba shook his head. He looked up at the sky again, as if he were searching for something there.

"It's okay," Amar said, repeating what had just been said to him, and he touched his hand against his father's shoulder, because even in the blue-dark it looked like Baba was the one who was now about to cry.

"Was your father a good father?" Amar asked.

He did not know why he asked it.

Baba was quiet. Then he said, "He was very strict. I was very afraid of him. He died when I was a boy, so I never knew if it would be different between us when I grew older. If he would be another way with me."

"I look like him," Amar said.

"You do."

Baba smiled a little.

"Will you leave soon?"

"In a minute."

Both of them looked at the moon in the sky. And the tiny stars. Amar shivered.

"I don't think I will make it," Amar said. "I'm sorry."

"Of course you can't come back inside, Amar—you can hardly sit up."

"No, I mean to the other place. The next place. I don't think I'll make it. I don't think you'll find me there."

He had left the path. His parents had given him a map, and directions, and he had abandoned it all. Now his heart was so ink-dark he could be lost and not know it, and not care, and never know how to find his way back.

"Listen to me." Baba held on to his arm. "You could never be more wrong, Amar. We taught you one way, but there could be others. We don't even know, even we can only hope. How many names are there for God?"

"Ninety-nine."

He knew all of this by heart. Didn't that count for something?

"And are they all the same kind of name?"

"No."

"Some contradict each other, remember? Didn't you just say to me—what if this is meant to show us more? What if we are meant to look closer?"

Amar nodded. Wind rustled the leaves. He sniffled and wiped his nose on his shirtsleeve.

"We will wait until you are allowed in," Baba said, as if to himself. "*I* will wait."

Baba pointed at the sky, and Amar looked, past the stars and past the lighter patch of the Milky Way, past the moon, and maybe God was there and maybe God wasn't, but when Baba said to him, "I don't think He created us just to leave some of us behind," Amar believed him. Amar wanted to.

Baba opened his wallet.

"Take this," he said, and he folded a bunch of notes into his hand. He did not count them. The bills were layered and layered.

"Will you have a place to sleep tonight? Is where you were near where we are now? Can you go back with ease?"

Amar wasn't sure but he nodded.

"You have enough for a taxi?" Baba asked.

He nodded again. Baba added another note and pressed it into his palm, closed Amar's fingers around it, and said, "A little more, in case it is farther. This should be enough."

Amar leaned his head against Baba's arm. Baba stopped speaking. It felt as if neither of them were breathing. Then he patted Amar's hair down, like Mumma would do for him when he was younger.

"It will be all right, *Inshallah*. But I have to go back inside now."

Amar felt as he did as a boy, when Baba dropped him off at school and before he closed the door Baba reminded him, you have to stay here the whole day. You cannot call Mumma and you cannot call your sisters. I have to go but you have to stay.

"You will be all right? You feel all right."

Amar nodded.

"It's just—it's just the drink?" Baba whispered it.

Amar nodded.

"*Khassam?*" Baba asked him.

"*Khassam.*"

They sat together. Then he blinked and Baba was gone. One night, when he was very little, before Huda began to wear her scarf, Mumma told them what it would be like in heaven: Everyone will be born again with the faces they had in their youth—mothers and daughters will look like sisters, fathers and sons will look like brothers. In heaven no one will be old. No one will be tired. There will be nothing to want. There will be rivers of water, and rivers of milk and honey. There will be homes made entirely of jewels. Emeralds and rubies and sapphires.

But just before we make it to heaven, she said, there will come the Judgment Day. Amar's heart was thumping in his chest. Mumma said, there is an angel whose entire existence is spent waiting for that moment to blow into the shell and wake every soul that has ever lived. That day, everyone will rise to fend for themselves. Everyone will forget that in life, they had a mother, a daughter, a friend, they will only worry for their own souls, if their soul will make it to the other side. We will wait so long to be called forward, it will feel like lifetimes pass before it is our turn. And then, when the long line has dwindled, and we stand to be judged, each body part will speak against us to say what we did in our life—if we had gone toward evil or stayed away from it—and the angels that sat on our shoulders will unroll their scrolls and read out our actions for God to decide our fate.

Amar had been frightened. He pictured a stampede of people. He pictured his hands speaking against him to say that he *had* shoved Huda, he pictured his tongue speaking against him to say he had told lies. But the thought of looking the same age as his parents frightened him the most. How would he recognize them? What would it be like if they all rose and no one cared for each other? Mumma continued speaking about the bridge that would be as thin as a hair and sharp as a blade, and it was Baba who noticed the look on his face.

"What's wrong?" Baba asked him.

"We won't care about each other?" he asked.

"Ami, no one will be caring about anybody," Mumma said, "not until everyone has made it to the other side, to heaven."

"How will we know what our faces in heaven will be, how will we reunite if everyone who has ever existed is there?"

He had begun to cry. He did not want this life to end. He did not care for houses made of rubies or rivers of honey, not if the sound of the shell separated him from them.

"We will find you," Baba had said, "don't worry about that. Just worry about your deeds. I could find you anywhere."

Soon the spinning would steady. He would find his way to a place where he could rest until morning. Maybe there was no God. But maybe the God of his parents was there, watching him tonight as on all nights. And if He was there, He had revealed ninety-nine names for them to understand him. There was the Avenger, the Firm, but there was also the Forgiving, the Patient. To read any *surah* in the Quran, one first had to read of God's mercy and compassion; almost every single chapter began with that line. The Prophet was the leader of the entire *ummah*, his every action an example, but when his grandson climbed his back, he had bent the rules, and what if it had been because it was more important to protect a child from pain than to be unwavering in principle? Maybe it was the exceptions we made for one another that brought God more pride than when we stood firm, maybe His heart opened when His creations opened their hearts to one another, and maybe that is why the boy was switched with the ram: so a father would not have to choose between his boy and his belief. There was another way. Amar was sure of it. He wanted them to find it together.

❖

THE PHOTOGRAPHER WAS scheduled to leave but Layla asked him to wait just a moment longer. Her husband and son were about to come back.

"Our family photo," she said to him. "It's more important than the others."

The photographer looked at Layla as if he could not decide if he was irritated by her or felt sorry for her, but he agreed, and Layla thanked him with her hand on her heart.

Her headache had worsened. She held her hand over her mouth each time she thought she was about to cry. Rafiq had disappeared at least half an hour earlier. A tightness coiled in her chest had not loosened, and she looked forward to the end of the night, when she could sit on her bed, take off her heels and jewelry and heavy sari, and just close her eyes. Rafiq approached. Amar was not with him. Still, she felt a wave of relief, stepped quickly toward him, and when they were face-to-face she reached out to touch her hand against his cheek.

"You're cold," she said. "Did you find him?"

"No."

"You looked?"

"Yes."

"Everywhere?" She looked behind him, down the corridor Rafiq had come from.

"Layla."

She began to walk past him but before she could go far he reached out and gently placed a hand on her shoulder. She glanced around. Guests passed, not noticing. He looked at her tenderly until she stilled, and then he let go. The rims of his eyes were red. There were times in their marriage when he had horrified her by the way he could yell at their children, but Layla had never felt afraid of him. What he sometimes unleashed on them he always held back

292

from her. When he spoke now, he did so softly. "We have to go back to Hadia. It's time to give her away."

They turned to look back at the main hall. A young child was asleep on her father's shoulder, her little feet bare, her mother following with her shoes hooked on curled fingers. They had their whole lives ahead of them: they moved through a world where anything was possible and did not even know it to be grateful for it. One day the possibilities of their life would narrow until there was only one outcome to a night like this. Layla stared at the family until they were on the other side of the glass door. Rafiq touched her back. She knew what he was asking of her. To give up hope of finding Amar.

"I can't do this," she said.

"You can," he said, and she looked up at him. "You have been so strong and patient for years."

He guided her back as if she had forgotten the way. Before they stepped into the main hall she spoke. "I made a terrible mistake."

It was a relief just to say it.

"What do you mean?"

"You were right—all those years ago. I should never have gone to Seema."

"Why are you thinking of this now?"

"He knows."

Rafiq stopped walking.

"If he left tonight, if he is leaving, it is because of me. They spoke—she told him. Let me go look for him. Let me apologize."

Her husband had aged in a night. He did not say anything but he looked from where Hadia stood on the stage waiting, to Layla, then back down the corridor. Amar was back there. He had found him.

"Layla, we did then what we thought was right. And now we have to do what is required of us."

He gestured to Hadia, who lifted her hand up to get their attention. The photographer was looking at them too. Rafiq was right. Layla looked over at her husband's profile as they walked. She could not read the look on his face—he hid what he felt from everyone

293

and it had the opposite effect he intended: it only made her care more. Rafiq extended his hand to help her up the stairs. Her children would all leave. But Rafiq would remain a blessing in her life, the center, the constant, the only one who truly bore the weight of this moment the way she did.

She thanked the photographer and he stood with his camera to position them. He did not ask any questions. The weakness she had felt after Rafiq returned without Amar left her when she saw a panicked look on Hadia's face.

"No," Hadia said, "absolutely not. We wait for him."

"There is no time," Layla said.

Tariq did not know what to do. He looked from Layla to Hadia, then at his lap.

"We will wait for him," Hadia said, shaking her head. Her *teekah* shifted from the center of her forehead. Huda stepped forward to fix it. Hadia moved her hand away.

"He's not coming, Hadia," Layla told her, her voice stern.

Comforting Hadia distracted Layla from her own grief. She would mourn tomorrow, alone, with no one there to witness, but tonight she would be strong for her daughter. Hadia's eyes filled at once, that sheen before crying.

"You knew about this and didn't tell me?" she asked Huda.

"He told me he was going to come back the last time we spoke," Huda said.

"Baba, will you go look for him?" Hadia asked.

"He's gone, *jaan*. Your mother is right. We have to continue."

Tariq reached for Hadia's hand and he kissed her knuckle then held it. In that instant, Layla saw Hadia give up: a vacant look came over her face. The photographer instructed Huda to stand by Rafiq. Layla took her place at the other side of Huda. She heard the photographer say smile.

"Hadia, look at me," the photographer said. "That's better."

"Perfect," the photographer said, "I got the one."

Layla knew she would never replace the photograph above the mantel.

Years ago, when she had opened Amar's box and seen photographs of him that Amira Ali must have taken, she had been surprised not only by their existence but also by how unguarded he was, how happy he looked in a way she'd never seen. Back then, Layla remembered thinking that humiliation was a deeper wound than heartache. She had wanted to protect them all from it. Now, as they stood beneath the spotlight on the stage, before the remaining guests who surely must be whispering to one another—where is their son, does he not care for them enough to stay for the family photograph?—she knew better. Knew that it did not matter what anyone thought if her own heart were not at peace. Only after her worst fears were confirmed did she realize there had been no use in letting her fears determine her decisions. She was finally free of them. She finally knew: she wanted Amar there in any state, under any circumstance, regardless of what anyone had to say about it.

Now her son was gone again. He would be the test of her life. She would have to remain graceful and patient and without despair when thinking of him. It would not be easy but it was not impossible. What was impossible was the wish, the prayer that rose in her again: Just one more moment. Just give us one more. But maybe her heart would never be satisfied; maybe it was ever-enlarging in its want for more. Because she knew that if she were granted one more moment, then another one was what she would ask for. She could live around her son for a hundred years and even then, when it was time for them to part, she would think—but it has been too brief, as brief as stepping from the shade out into the sun, and she would wish to hear again his knock at the door, look up from the *duas* she was reading to that simple sight of him leaning against the door frame, and he would ask if he could come and lie in her lap, and she would not even have to say yes, he would already know.

✧

IN HER PURSE was the small package from Amar. She needed to open it alone. It could not wait. It could contain a clue. Huda walked with her to the restroom, holding the trail of her heavy dress.

"What are you hiding from me?" Hadia asked her.

"Can you at least try to enjoy the rest of your night?"

Hadia looked at her coldly. Huda sighed. The hall was half-empty, and quieter now.

"He fought with Mumma. It was about Amira."

"What has Mumma got to do with Amira?"

"Mumma had known. She had told Seema Aunty. He spoke with Amira tonight and was devastated. That Mumma didn't believe in him, or that if it had been one of us she would have acted differently."

Hadia told Huda she needed a moment alone and stepped into the golden bathroom light. Her hands shook as she reached into her purse. Gently, so as not to tear the wrapping, she tugged at the tape. She drew her breath in so sharply it startled her. It was her watch. Her Baba's watch, her Dada's watch. Not a single scratch, the face spotless as if polished, the tick announcing each new second. She wondered if it had always been his plan to return what was not his and then disappear again. She was shaking. She leaned against the door. She turned the wrapping paper over, then again, held it up to the light, but there was no note. This, more than anything else, upset her.

Does the watch always go to fathers?

Amar asked the strangest questions, the ones none of them thought to.

You mean sons.

She had taken from him what, in another life, would have belonged to him by birth. She had worked hard to be as valuable as any son. Her betrayals to her brother were scattered throughout the years, but perhaps being given this watch was the culmination of them all. No one could see it on her wrist and deny what it meant.

Hadia opened the door and let Huda in. She held up the watch. Huda's mouth opened in shock.

"Will you tell Mumma Baba?"

She shook her head. "I'll say I found it when packing to move."

Huda nodded and said, "It will be as if he never took it."

Hadia wrapped it again and placed it back in her purse. She did not even want it anymore.

"Do you think this means he was saying good-bye?" Hadia's voice was small.

Huda did not answer. Without a note she could only guess at what he was trying to tell her: *Here, take what is yours, what has always been, what will always be—I am no contender.* Giving it back was both admitting he had taken it and attempting to apologize. Hadia had behaved in ways that she not only could not take back, but also could never admit to.

She never told Amar what it was like for her to look up at his test all those years ago, to see his handwriting that was so like hers the sight of it threatened her. Or that she had hinted about Amira and Amar's affair to Mumma. She did not even know why she had done it. Maybe to distract Mumma from Hadia's decision, still recent then, to step toward Tariq. Maybe just to disturb the golden lens through which Mumma regarded her cherished son. And she never told Amar that she and Amira had spoken years ago. Hadia had power in that moment and she had done nothing with it for her brother, had made no attempt to steer Amira back to him. *Don't tell,* he'd ask her, and what did she do but tell, and tell, and the only thing she kept from telling was her part.

All Amar had done to her was take this dumb watch. He had not even reaped the benefit of his betrayal the way that she had, and would continue to. To be the child her parents could count on. To be the one they were proud of. Any hurt he caused, any disappointment he brought—it only amplified her place in their parents' life, and their love for her.

In the hall, Baba recited the *adhaan* for the *ruksati,* though it was the brother's duty to. It was this moment she had wanted Amar to come back for. She hugged everyone from the community who had stayed to say good-bye, then her friends, she hugged her sister tight and her mother for so long. She knew there was no point in looking around but still she looked for him: just the empty stage and tables and flower vases lined up on one.

"What will I do without you?" Baba said to her, when she said good-bye to him.

She remembered watching brides cry during their *ruksati* as a child and fearing her time would come and she would not shed a tear. Now she cried like a little girl. Her shoulders shook and Baba's hug steadied her. The overwhelming feeling now, as it was almost over, was that she wanted only to love them more, to love them better.

"I'll be back," she said. "I will not leave you two."

She took Tariq's hand. Mumma held the Quran above them as they stepped out into the night. Everyone clapped behind them. The air was cool. Their decorated car was waiting. Tariq stopped walking. He pointed up at the sky. She looked and saw nothing. Just some stars. She turned to Tariq's profile.

"Keep looking," he whispered.

Then there was a hiss, and a streak of smoke in the sky, and Tariq pulled her close and kissed the top of her head, said *surprise* just as the firework boomed, and the sound drummed in her whole body and the glitter descended and disappeared.

Hadia had told Tariq about the first time she ever saw fireworks. How, even now, anytime she saw them it made her feel the way she had that night, full of wonder and excitement about all the sights life could offer her. There was another and another and another. Her heart was beating very fast. All their faces were lit up by colors: blue and red and green. Once, she had sat at the dinner table and overheard a fight between Amar and Baba. Baba's voice had shaken the beads of the chandelier. In that moment, Hadia had wished for exactly this, exactly what was being granted to her now: a new family. Her own. A new window from which to look out and think, I am home. A firework that reminded her of a rocket zipped up in coils and exploded in coils. She had seen it somewhere before: Amar was laughing in that memory. When the chandelier shook, this had been her wish. Now everything she had ever wanted had become hers. And where was her brother, and was he close enough to look up and see the rocket firework that somehow she knew he liked?

She tightened her hold on her husband's hand. She loved him. She would start her own family with him. The last of the fireworks dissolved. The sky was all smoke. Had she reached out for Amar's hand beneath the dining table that night? Had she done as much? She could not remember now.

Part Four

1

WHEN YOU WERE BORN, YOU DID NOT CRY. YOUR face turned blue, almost purple, and the relief I had felt at seeing you, at realizing you had entered the world, plummeted when the doctors and nurses huddled around your body, separating me from you. Your mother raised her head to ask if everything was all right. Her voice was pitched high but her expression oddly calm, as though she had foreseen such complications. The doctor did not reply. A nurse's sneaker squeaked against the linoleum floor. The clock ticked. Only then did I realize you had not marked your entrance into this world with the same screams as your sisters before you.

That is how you came into our lives. I held my breath. I did not move. I stood between your mother and the doctor examining you. Unable to look at either, unable to do anything but focus on my gloved hands held out helplessly in front of me. Because you could not breathe easily, I could not either.

Your mother regards it as our miracle from God, that soon your lungs were emptied and you began gasping for air, crying even. And I too thanked God, knelt in *sajda-shukr* once the nurses and doctors took you and gave us privacy. But when my forehead touched the cold floor, I wondered if it had been an omen, though I have not told Layla this, have not told anyone.

✧

NOW I AM watching the clouds quicken across the sky from my hospital window, cities away from the one I swear I was just in, pulling tight the gloves over my wrists, slipping my arms through a paper gown, going to Layla to be beside her. In that room I was a young father—I had cut the cord connecting you, my third child, to my wife. You were a boy. It was my one thought that instant before the doctor took you. I was a father to a son. It has been thirty-some years but it has felt like blinking, I am awake in one room, I close my eyes, and by the time I have opened them again I am here, I am insisting on helping myself when Hadia steps forward to peel back the foil wrapper of applesauce.

"*Bas,*" I say to her, holding up my hand, "this changes nothing."

She is not convinced. She raises her eyebrows like she does when she says—*okay,* Baba—her bad habit of stretching out the okay. But instead of saying it she bites her tongue, and though this is the respect I have wanted, it now makes me uneasy. Her beeper buzzes and she sighs, glances at it and says she will leave me in a minute, and soon after a nurse will take me for an MRI.

This is my first time seeing my daughter at work. She is professional. Her voice, when speaking to other staff members, is commanding. She wears a spotless white coat that seems big on her frame. Her stethoscope is turquoise, curled and tucked into a pocket where our last name is stitched in blue thread.

Recently, I had begun to feel a headache so blinding I could no longer ignore it, and though I told Hadia all was fine, Layla must have described enough symptoms that they alarmed her: how I became disoriented when I stood, how I waited a moment to take a step, afraid I would lose my balance. Hadia told us to drive to the hospital where she worked, so her colleague could admit me and arrange for some tests. She assured me I would be in good hands. That she trusted the staff here. That the neurologist was one of the best in the state. And that way Layla could stay with Hadia and help with our grandkids, and they could easily visit. At this, I relented.

I have been treated well. Which is a relief to me, not necessarily because of the comfort their generosity provides me, but because it has given me a sense of how Hadia treats the people around her, and how she is regarded and respected in return. You must be Hadia's father, some say when they approach with their plastic water cups and blood pressure machines, and they speak kindly of her qualities or tell me that I have done well in raising her.

"Will you bring them tonight?" I ask, when she stands to her feet.

"We'll see, Baba. Abbas has soccer practice. First let's concentrate on getting the tests done."

I sink back into the uncomfortable bed.

"But that reminds me," she says, and pulls pieces of folded paper from her pocket and hands them to me. I hold on to them, but do not look down at them; I want to save them until I am alone again. I want to ask her if I can go home after the MRI, but I know what she will tell me: how they are monitoring my blood pressure, which is too high, how they want to "get to the bottom of" the lack of balance, that it is good for me to be here until then, and that I should trust her. She is stern when she speaks with me about all this, but gentle, using a voice I have not encountered. Perhaps she is taking full advantage of this shift, and I wonder if I would not feel as uncomfortable, had I seen my own parents grow older, had I been able to care for them and find there is no shame in the matter.

"If I can't get away between patients, I'll be back with the results of the MRI," she says.

She smiles at me. I am so easily moved these days that I have to steady myself at the sight of her. You would be amazed to see her now. How she has matured, how she carries herself with confidence, how an entire streak of her hair has turned gray and how it suits her. She holds my hand for a minute and kisses its knuckle before letting go—a gesture that is intended to be loving, but I feel less love and more nervous, wondering what her fears might be. When she is gone, the sounds of the hospital return: my monitor reminding me of the beating of my own heart, the rustle of the rough blanket against my papery gown, the nurses talking together in the hallway, the sound of wheelchairs or walkers making their way across the tile.

IT IS WHEN I am alone that I think of you again. I open the card from Abbas and Tahira that I saved for this very moment. WE LOVE YOU NANA, GET WELL SOON, written in Abbas's chicken-scratch, the exact kind of handwriting I critiqued you for when you were his age. Tahira has drawn me butterflies surrounding a house on a hill. Abbas is seven, Tahira only four. They have enlarged my life in a way I could not have anticipated and cannot fully express. I have no duty toward them except loving them, and because of this I am only loved in return. I am so unwilling to hurt them in even the slightest way that I spoil them instead. Hadia does not trust me to be alone with them before dinner: the three of us giggle and deny any chocolate consumed, even as Tahira's teeth and fingers give us away. Perhaps, if we met again now, you would not recognize me: I am calmer. I rarely anger.

Perhaps you would also wonder, after years of silence and the years before in which we hardly spoke, why I now have so much I want to say. Perhaps you would even feel it is too late. That it does not matter what I have to say because it would change nothing for you, for us.

But, Amar, what if I told you that lately, I find myself driving through familiar streets, unaware of how much time has passed since I left home, until it occurs to me that these were the streets I drove to drop you off at school, or the route to our barbershop that has long since closed down. At four in the morning, if I wake alone, I walk until I am at the threshold of your old bedroom, looking out at the barely illuminated folds of the comforter on your bed, the walls so bare now—your room almost entirely stripped of any trace of you, each item packed away in boxes and put in your closet, waiting for another decade to pass before we muster the energy to try and take another look.

And it is in these moments that the fabric of my life reveals itself to be an illusion: thinking that I am fine, we all are, that we could grow around your loss like a tree that bends around a barrier or wound. That I do not need to see you again. That the reality of our life as it is now is the best that we could have done and the best we could have hoped for. Until one Sunday I am parked at your old elementary school, looking out at the empty blue picnic tables, or late when no one is looking, I crumple and toss an old test of yours in my wastebasket only to go back for it, uncrease it, fold it gently, and place it back at the very bottom of my drawer. In those moments no argument I have used to delude myself can comfort me. You may be unwilling to hear me. You may not understand, but please listen. I have told you to listen many times before, I know. But I have never asked you.

I am asking now.

THE FIRST TWO nights after you were born, you were kept in the neonatal ward. They told us you were all right, but after the brief scare of your birth they wanted to monitor you, assist you with your breathing. I would wait until your mother was asleep to walk the halls until I found myself at your floor, just one above hers, and look at you and the other tiny babies in their clear cribs. The humming of the machinery. The quiet of the night. Some of the lights had been dimmed because it would be three or four in the morning. I would stand in the same spot, at the center of the glass window, my hand closed into a fist and stuffed into my jacket pocket. Focused on the small baby that was you. Your hand rested by your face, your fingers curled, the way you would fall asleep for years to come but I did not know that then. I did not know anything. My feet would ache and I would shift my weight from one foot to the other. For hours I stood. Praying, mainly. That desperate kind of praying, the kind I have little experience with, the kind that cannot wait until I kneel in *sijda* so instead I speak directly to God: Anything if he makes it through the next few days. Anything for this.

We had named you Amar. As I stood at the glass window I

thought of your name until it became familiar to me. If I was not speaking to God I was speaking to you: *You'll be okay, Amar. We'll take you home soon.* Layla had wanted to name each of our children after holy figures—after all, she said, why wouldn't we want to give our children the best of names? But I had this funny idea that I thought then was noble. That perhaps others could name their children after the Prophet and his family, but how could I, not knowing what my children would go on to do, knowing they might sin in some way and in that way they would bring down not only themselves but a name so holy with them. Now I wonder if that was a mistake. That had I named you Ali or Mohammed or Hussain, maybe it would have been a constant and inescapable reminder for you to hold yourself to a standard they inspired.

Those nights there was a nurse on duty named Dawn. I remember how her name reminded me of a poem I encountered in college, years after the passing of my parents, that had been soothing to me. Dawn had short red hair and little freckles on her face. She had light eyelashes and was kind to me. She told me which floors had vending machines and where I could get a bagel when morning came. She made small talk, which I had never been good at, but perhaps because of the odd hour of night and the strange state of mind I was in, I was all right at talking with her.

"That one is mine," I said, touching my finger to the glass.

"Beautiful," she said. "Your first?"

She had a soft, calming voice, made softer by the fact that we were whispering to one another.

"First son. I have two girls too."

"You're a lucky man," she said. "And your son will be just fine."

There was certainty in her voice, as though it came from somewhere else, as though she had been placed there just to tell me that. I was so terrified. I could have cried when she said it.

"AND WHAT DOES an MRI reveal?" I turn my head to ask the nurse who is wheeling me down the corridor. I know in a general sense, but I want to hear what he has to say. I want to know if there is anything Hadia has kept from me. I have been hesitant to ask her questions.

"An image of your brain."

"Do you know what the doctor is looking for?"

I twist the loose plastic bracelet around my wrist and wait for his answer, holding my breath.

"No, sir. I have not spoken with the doctor. But the MRI will be painless."

I am wheeled into the bright, quiet room. I am given earplugs. Every wall here is too white. The dome and the bed in the center, which must be the machine, and the technician telling me to lie on my back. Telling me not to move.

Then I am alone. The technician is on the other side of the wall. Somewhere in this building is Hadia, comforting a patient, or looking over her notes before walking in to see another one. I realize how lucky I am, that if there is any hint of an issue she can make sense of the tests, easily ask to order others, think of what to do. The bed begins to move slowly back into the tunnel. I close my eyes. The noises are loud and erratic, even with the earplugs. I am very still. When I open my eyes again, a light is moving across the curvature of the tunnel, and I think of how unnatural it is to keep ourselves alive in this way. I want to live, I realize, but the thought that surprises me is the darker one that comes after: that I also want for there to be something wrong, and for it to be serious, and immediately I wonder if God will punish me for the thought. Then the beeping is done and I wait for a cue to move.

BEFORE YOU WERE born, I thought I knew how to be a father. Hadia was four when we brought you home. Huda only three. Making them smile was easy. Keeping them smiling, simple. Layla would tell me that they would watch for the darkening of the sky, listen for the turning of the key and creak of the door, ready to abandon their coloring books or unfinished bowls of dinner to rush to me, each one holding on to a leg that I had to drag to move, and when I managed to, they laughed and tightened their grip.

If they misbehaved I only had to glare at them. In some instances, a voice raised, a flick to their lip, the twisting of their ear. So little it took to make them obey. Once they were done crying after a punishment, they would not become cold but would wonder how to make it better. Hadia would tilt her head and speak in a voice both mature and innocent, waiting for a sign of my approval, of forgiveness. Huda would rub her head against my arm like a cat until I hugged her. And here was another thing I took for granted in those years: their ability to continue on as though nothing had happened.

You were something else. You did not let your mother sleep, did you know that? Hadia and Huda had also cried, had also woken at odd hours. But your screams came from somewhere else—not motivated by hunger or discomfort, I would think when I tried to comfort you, and that thought unsettled me. I was worn out by your screaming, or maybe it was my inability to console you, and so I would hand you to Layla. She would take you from our bedroom so I could sleep, speak to you in Urdu using a name she had begun calling you: "What is it, Ami, what's happened?"

Motherhood had been becoming on Layla. She was so young when Hadia was born. She devoted her time and attention to her daughters as if it were her choice—keeping something of herself for herself, inhabiting the role with strength and sweetness, ease and command. Hadia and Huda came to her when they needed her, busied themselves alone or with each other when they did not. But with you, motherhood became a more consuming endeavor. As you grew she became prone to anxiety and stress. While you slept she examined your bruises.

"Look," she would say, pointing to a purple mark on your thigh. "How do you think he managed to hurt himself here?"

I wonder now if she had intuited what I could not, or what I refused to: that it would not be easy for us when it came to you. Though you did not know it, you had divided the attention of our home. If Hadia and Huda were on one side, you were on the other, and Layla was turned to you. Your sisters were resilient; little denials and little losses and lectures did not alter the course of their day. You were stubborn with your sadness. You would enter it and not leave. And instead of softening, I hardened in my approach.

MOST MORNINGS, I was in charge of dropping Hadia and Huda off at school. Before I left I would look back at you, kicking your legs as you lay on your stomach to color, and wonder what you and your mother did all day with the rest of us gone. My daughters always wanted more from me. One more story, Baba. Two more minutes, Baba. They tiptoed and turned their cheeks toward me so I could kiss them. At the park they asked me to push them on swings or climbed on me like monkeys. You did not ask for any of these things. I did not know if it was indifference or a desire for independence that kept you from me.

But every few months, before you turned five, you and I had a day alone together. I would come home to find your mother had taken it upon herself to cut your hair again. The sight of you with a jagged and uneven haircut never failed to irritate me. Maybe it felt like a game to you both. Your mother lifting you up to the bathroom countertop, wrapping a towel around your neck to catch dark tufts of your hair. Layla, I would tell her, trying to control my annoyance, why do you always do this, make him look silly like this?

The following Sunday we would go together to get a haircut. When I watch Hadia and Tariq interact with their kids now, it seems strange to me that those were some of the only times we were alone. Hadia and Tariq are such different parents. In some instances they upset me greatly, letting Abbas go off into the neighborhood alone, without knowing exactly who he will be playing with. But in other ways they are getting right what we did not even think to consider. They take their children on "dates": sometimes Hadia takes Abbas and Tariq takes Tahira, and sometimes the other way around.

"We are the way we are as a family. It's special for them and nice for us to see what we can be, one-on-one," Hadia explained once, when I asked her why.

You always went with your mother everywhere. When she stood up to go to the grocery store, you rose to accompany her. If she was not present, you were Hadia's shadow. If I stood to leave for an errand, if Hadia or Huda did not offer to come, I went alone. I worried about you growing up in a house full of women, looking only to them for an example. I feared you would not know how to be, how to behave, that I was doing nothing to teach you.

"Come," I'd say, "let's go fix your hair."

The glance you gave your mother was not lost on me. The only thing worse was how she would nod to you in return, as if giving you permission to go, to trust me. I would lift you into my arms, which I never really got used to. Yes, I held my children when they were babies, but often when Layla's arms were occupied, or if she needed a break, and I would try to entertain you all the simplest way I knew how, I would take you outside and point to the sky. Look, stars. Look, moon. But when I held you and we made our way to the car, I remember you would put your head on my shoulder as if you were tired, I remember you would scratch the thread of my top button until we reached the car. And I remember wondering if my own father had ever held me, and now, when I think back, I do not think he ever did.

I risked buckling you into the front seat. I wanted you to think something special was happening. I wanted you to look out the window and feel yourself at the edge of the world as you approached it. I drove slowly. I looked out for cop cars. I looked over at you from time to time, your back straight, your hand gripping the tan seat belt, your face turned to look out the window. I tried to make conversation. Talking to anyone has always been a bit strange for me, talking to a child no less unnerving. I spoke to you as though you were already an adult. How was your week? I would ask. We would glide down the street that was my favorite in our city, one long line that curved up and down with the hills, thick trees lining both sides—the only street that ever made me feel like it was fall in California, because driving by rows and rows of trees made it apparent that the leaves were changing color. You were short with your replies. Shy, as though I were a stranger. Were we lost, even then at that early age, you three and a half years old and so quiet? I tried to not feel disappointed. I searched for things to speak of. That is a post office, I said, when we passed one, do you know what happens at a post office? You shrugged a single shoulder, as though I bored you.

At the barbershop, I would unlock the car door and you would hop out. Our barber's name was Jim. He was a nice man who recognized us, his loyal customers, and he would take one look at your mess of a haircut and say, again? He and I would laugh about it. It was like a joke between us. I would lift you into the raised seat, smaller than the rest, and Jim would wrap a black cloth around your neck that swallowed your whole body. When he approached you with scissors you would look back at me in the mirror. I never stepped away. I wondered if Jim thought that you and I were close, that I did things with you often, or if he could sense how wary we were of one another.

We would walk out holding a strawberry or watermelon lollipop. In the entire bowl, those were the flavors you gravitated to, and I took one and tucked it in my pocket to give to you later. I wanted our day to last longer and so I would ask if you wanted a scoop when we passed the ice cream shop, and your eyes would light up like Hadia's and Huda's did when I agreed to read a story to them. The door made a "moo" sound when we entered, and I lifted you up to the counter and you pressed your face against the glass to look at all the flavors, your breath leaving circles of fog. I stopped myself from reminding you that the glass had germs. Not today, I told myself. Once when I was a boy my father had taken me to the ice cream parlor in Hyderabad. No one there offered samples like they did here, when you pointed to flavor after flavor and the girl behind the counter passed you little purple spoons with a bit of the ice cream. She told me how cute you were, smiling widely, which often happened when we went anywhere with you. Sometimes, even now, I wonder if you realized that the world loved you, softened at your presence.

While I waited for you, I asked the girl for a scoop of pistachio and almond, the flavor that most reminded me of the ice cream from home. Then you would ask for the same. This happened every time. You sampled at least four flavors and then got mine, though you had not tried it. Is it silly that I felt proud that you copied me in that way? She gave you your cone and I got my cup and I tipped her generously, partly because of how kind she was to you. Shall we eat here? I asked, and you would have relaxed with me by then. When you were excited your legs swung because they did not reach the floor, and you were talkative, and moved about in your seat making wild gestures with your hands. You asked me questions, and I did my best to answer them.

"Why does forever rhyme with never?" you asked me once.

Another time you asked, "What's a tsunami?" When I answered, you asked, "Why don't we ever go to the beach?" and then, without missing a beat, as though it were the logical next question, "Why do squirrels run when I go near them?"

And I knew when you stopped asking me questions and turned to look out the window that our time had reached its final movement, and you wanted to go home to your mother. I gathered our trash and threw it away. I wet a napkin and wiped your mouth, your fingers, and rubbed roughly the stain on your shirt, so Hadia and Huda wouldn't see it and be hurt.

WHEN HADIA APPEARS again she is not alone. The doctor with her is very tall, especially when standing next to Hadia, his skin dark and eyes very bright, made brighter when he smiles, and even before he has extended his hand to shake mine, I trust him. My hand, when I lift it, feels weak, something that has been happening with alarming frequency and something I've kept from Hadia. His name is Dr. Edwards, he says, he is a neurosurgeon, and a good friend of Hadia's. When Hadia was very young, I would remind her seriously that she had no male *friends*, just colleagues and acquaintances, but as she grew older my reminder became a joke at first for her, and then, after much teasing from her, for both of us. When I glance at her seated at the edge of my bed, she is smiling mischievously, as if she has read my mind.

Nothing about Dr. Edwards's demeanor suggests that something is wrong, and so I sit back against the raised bed, fold my hands in my lap.

"Everything is okay, Baba, do not begin to worry," she says in Urdu, and she nods at Dr. Edwards.

Dr. Edwards explains what they found in the MRI. In my brain? I ask, when I hear him say tumor. Most likely benign, he responds, a meningioma, in the tissue between the skull and the brain, but it has grown enough to begin to impact the brain, mine. My mouth is dry. I look at the bracelet on my wrist and the tiny numbers that mark me as a patient and my name that marks me as a person and the blue veins beneath my skin saying I am alive. He tells me that judging by its location and size it could be removed with little effort and then taken for a biopsy. Hadia touches my leg and says that means it's no problem, Baba, saying it in Urdu as if I do not speak English, as if I do not know what benign or little effort means. I search my daughter's face. She is eerily calm. I am a lucky man, and maybe when I had opened my eyes to the light moving across the dome it was misfortune I had wished for, something grave enough to give you a reason to return.

"We will have to have a surgery to remove it, Baba, it's beginning to affect you in a way we cannot ignore. Hence the headaches. Dr. Edwards has been very kind—he scheduled you in for the end of the week."

Dr. Edwards asks me if I have any questions. I say I do not. I say thank you. I say I am glad Hadia has a good friend. And at this, I glance at my daughter, who has been calm, who has been using her doctor voice, who now looks quickly away from me and out the hospital window.

ON THE BEDSIDE table beside me, two flower arrangements: one extravagant, store-bought bouquet sent by my old coworkers, and one made for me by Layla. Her bouquet has her touch; I can spot any bouquet Layla arranges in an instant. The flowers were plucked from Hadia's garden. A giant plant leaf is fanned out in the back, framing them. Layla could have been an artist, I think now, as she lifts the page of her prayer book and continues moving her finger across the next page. It has been a recent pursuit of hers, growing and arranging flowers, and now every room in our home is adorned, and if there is a celebratory event for a family friend, we go with a bouquet.

When you were very young, maybe four, she came home with a packet of tomatoes and said she would try to plant them. Soon it became tomatoes and garlic. Then she read books that said do not plant the same vegetable in the same soil twice, and it might have been the challenging and particular methods that interested her, so she got a notebook where she drew our backyard and drew in squares to plan what would go where and in what season. On wooden Popsicle sticks she wrote what she planted and then pushed them into the dirt, and this was her favorite part, I think, when I came home to find her meticulously writing: mint, green pepper, eggplant, cauliflower, basil.

The year after Hadia's wedding, she did not walk into the garden to tend to anything at all. Hadia had moved to Chicago with Tariq. She was so busy with her work and getting accustomed to her new life and soon, her pregnancy, that she hardly visited us. Huda worked as a fourth-grade teacher at a school hours away. Her evenings were often spent preparing for the next day. They called us with their stories: Hadia's first time assisting with delivering a baby, Huda winning over a particularly difficult student. We were so proud of them both. But once the phone clicked to end their call we were so very alone. Each of you had left us in your own way. I predicted Layla would turn even more to gardening to pass the time. But instead she made tea and sat at the kitchen table with the mug before her looking out at the backyard, her hands wrapped around the mug for warmth, the steam rising. I would walk away and not long after would hear the splash of the entire mug in the sink.

Then one day, about three years ago, I came home to see little white packets I recognized to be seeds on the kitchen table in rows. I was relieved. I always feared she had been punishing herself. But this time it was just flowers. And a small stack of books in the corner: *Flowers of California. Plants of the West.* She did not explain and I did not ask. She spent months studying which flower to plant when. The first spring they bloomed was incredible, our garden so vibrant and alive. At first her bouquets were messy, the stems drooping against the glass, but soon something clicked: she deliberately chose colors that completed each other, stuck a feather in if she found a feather. I was amazed that even a jagged twig could be placed beautifully, if Layla was the one to place it.

WHEN HADIA FIRST applied to college I could not imagine allowing her to move away. We wanted her to get engaged. We wanted her to be settled and safe—with someone who would prioritize caring for her and providing for her, as I had for my family. But when she rushed inside to tell us about the program she had been accepted into, I felt all my discomfort and fear rise up. It was not the path for her I had anticipated and not the path I preferred. But how could I be the one to stand in her way? My daughter intended on navigating the world respectably, accomplishing something good, with her intelligence, her will. The night that we found out, Layla had to be convinced. She was not worried for Hadia's safety, as I was, but rather that Hadia had disregarded our wishes for her life, and from what we could see, was doing well despite it.

"If she stays home, if she accepts any of these perfectly good proposals, I will know how to guide her," Layla said to me as we lay wide awake in bed, unable to fall asleep. "If she begins her own way . . . I won't know how."

And I did not know how to answer her. I searched for a way to deal with my own discomfort quietly. The day I dropped her off at her dorm, she slept the entire car ride and I drove in the dark watching the sky slowly lighten. I stopped for coffee, something I never drink, and each hour I drove I thought, this is one hour I will have to drive back without her. This is one more hour that will separate me from my daughter. I kept looking over at her. She was wearing my father's watch and a blue button-up. *I want to be professional,* she had explained to me the night before, excited when deciding what to wear. As I drove my fears multiplied: Whether she could handle her studies. Whether she would take on too many classes at once. Whether she would have friends—oddly, I worried equally that she would not, and that she would. Whether she would know what to do when she encountered someone who pressured her to sin. But it was not until my own fears were echoed in comments from my friends that I found myself facing them and finding comfort. People would question me, how did you let your daughter move so far? Too much independence is not good for a woman. To protect her from their judgment, I would defend her, and only after I defended her aloud again and again did I realize that I believed what I told them. "Hadia will be fine. My daughter is brave and capable. She will know what to do. I trust her."

Now both my daughters work, and it is not so much that I have relented and accepted this, but that these are the very things that have become a great source of pride for me. They have shown me what to value that I did not know before them to value. When Huda calls me and says she might not be able to come visit because she is working, I am proud that she is doing something with her life that gives to others. That she teaches children, and from the stories we hear, is very good at it. Or that Hadia is regarded no differently at what she does than Tariq, and what does she do but care for human lives? She holds an intimate knowledge of what is unseen to the rest of us—what it might mean when I struggle to find balance, what it might mean if I get sharp headaches—and after asking a few questions and running tests, she can eliminate what it is not and like a hawk swoop down to claim what it is. Had they married the men we wanted for them years ago, we would have been happy, but if, God forbid, their husbands had been unable to provide, or if destiny had dealt a difficult card and their marriages had fallen apart, I would have sat here today, days before my surgery, and I would not be at peace. If I do go, I know that my daughters will be fine, as they are not only cared for but also completely capable of caring for themselves, providing for themselves, and also for Layla, and also for my grandchildren.

2

THERE IS AN OFFICIAL KNOCK AND I LOOK UP, thinking it might be Dr. Edwards coming to check in the night before the surgery, but it is Huda, my Huda, smiling at me gently and sort of sadly. I did not know I wanted so badly to see her until she was there, unflinching at the sight of me in a hospital gown, wires taped to my arm, in a way that even Layla does not muster for my sake, and even Hadia breaks from, despite this being her profession. These are the moments when Huda's presence is most appreciated. I tell her she did not have to come, that everyone has made this into a bigger fuss than it need be. Dr. Edwards himself said that the surgery will be fairly simple. It is only Hadia who insists there are other factors complicating my health and only Hadia anyone listens to anymore. You were never one for the "proper way," and so when Hadia says I must stay here, must change my diet, and Layla agrees, and even my grandson says please, Nana, eat what they tell you to, I think of you, and how you might have had it in you to side with me, if only because it meant disagreeing with the rest of them.

"Of course I came," she says as she takes a seat on the chair beside me.

Soon, Hadia appears and Layla too. Tahira rushes forward and climbs into Huda's lap. All the women of my life. Tariq is at soccer practice with Abbas, Hadia explains, and Huda tells me that Jawad had to stay in Arizona but sends his regards. I hated the clamoring of people before. Now it is silence that unsettles me. Hadia holds on to Huda's shoulders and leans into her and says to me, "Happy with your surprise?"

"I am happy," I say.

I am not afraid. For four days I have known the surgery was approaching and I have prepared for it. Tahira leans back against Huda's chest. Huda runs her hand through her hair. I am amazed at the trust between them: Tahira sees Huda only a few days each year and yet she knows somehow that this is her mother's sister, and she gives love to her that she keeps from others we see regularly. Huda is a wonderful aunt. Perhaps extraordinary—the limitless space she gives them in her heart because she has no children of her own, though we've prayed every time we pray for anything at all.

"How long is your stay?" I ask.

"Just until Sunday."

"Class is okay without you?"

She nods. Tahira lights up, remembering their game, and looks up at Huda. "Amijaan, can you give me assignment?" she asks.

This is how they play. Huda does anything Tahira asks. The same could be said for any of us. We become teachers for her or puppy dogs or patients, Tahira the doctor, asking on a scale of one to ten, how much does it hurt? Behind them, I catch a look in Layla's eyes, and I know she is wishing for more moments like this one, all of us together. I have not voiced to her, or even fully to myself, my recent and recurring wish, that all of us together again includes you.

WHEN YOU WERE almost four your mother became pregnant. Despite how much you begged for a younger brother, your mother and I had not intended on having any more children. The night you were born returned often in my nightmares. If the dream had been particularly vivid, or if we had fought badly the day before, I would not be able to help myself from stepping into your bedroom, taking a seat on the floor, placing a finger in front of your open mouth until your warm breath touched my skin. Having feared the worst,

I would naturally fear for Hadia and Huda too, and check on each of them sleeping, breathing.

I was nervous when we first learned Layla was pregnant. Her pregnancy with you had been difficult. My job required me to be away for days at a time, I would come home not knowing how sick she had been. Every time she lifted the Quran above my head for me to walk out beneath, I would look back at her, fresh-faced and chubby when carrying you in a way that she hadn't been with the girls, and I would wonder if I was shirking my duties, prioritizing work over caring for her. I feared that though she never said as much, she resented how I left week after week. But I worked for her, I told myself, I worked for Hadia and Huda, I worked for you even before I knew you.

This is good news, Layla said the night we found out, why do you look *pareshan?* I listened to her. We were lucky. Soon, we could not imagine anything else. You three were too young to inform right away, and we decided to guard the news in our hearts for a while. When my forehead touched the cool surface of the *sajdagah,* I had a new prayer on my list: for the child's birth to come and pass without complication, and for it to be a healthy boy.

Layla wore loose-fitted *shalwar kameez* around the house so the girls would not notice, and it became a pleasant secret between us as we waited for the right moment to tell them. Only you had become more tender toward her. You stopped fussing with her at dinnertime, you would climb into her lap and rest your head against her.

"He knows," Layla whispered one night, when you insisted on falling asleep in our bed. She moved your hair around your forehead the way she loved to.

"How can he?" I had said, though I believed her and was unnerved by my belief, this strange feeling I had sometimes that you had access to a kind of perception or intuition that we did not.

"I hope it's a boy," Layla confessed later when we were in the waiting room just before one of her appointments. For our first three children we had decided to let the gender be a surprise. But for our fourth we were eager to find out.

"That is also my hope," I replied.

I wanted to have a second chance at being a father to a son. It was a terrible thought; I knew it as I allowed it to enter my mind and dwell there. I grabbed a magazine from the table and flipped through the glossy pages.

"Wouldn't it be wonderful for Amar to have a brother?" she said.

When I did not reply, she continued, "He would make a great older brother. It would be good for him. Hadia and Huda have each other. He is always so lonely, *na*? Now he will have someone to grow up playing with as well."

I told her I was going to the restroom. Instead, I walked back and forth across the bridge of the hospital that connected two wings, constructed like a tunnel of glass over the parking lot. I wondered how your mother could think the way she did, how everything in her naturally considered you. Wanting to bear a child for your sake. Even in this, having you in mind. She sat there in the waiting room and wished for a boy to give you a brother. I paced the tunnel, knowing I had wished for a boy to give me a son.

And it was going to be a boy. The doctor confirmed our hopes. Your mother took hold of my hand and leaned into me as we walked out. That day, beneath the pale blue sky, I let myself hold tightly on to her hand and marveled at how delicate and small it felt in mine. Eid was approaching and we decided we would tell you all then. We would give you the gift of art sets and new outfits and then make it an exciting reveal.

Knowing I had a son coming made it easier to deal with my disappointments about us. Layla was never one to discipline you, so anytime you misbehaved it fell on me to drag you by the arm to your room for your time-out. I told myself I was going to have another chance. I even hoped that another son would ease the pressure between us. I began to imagine him. He would not be prone to outbursts. He would not be angry with me when I was angry with him. He would look up to me and respect me. He would be eager to learn. He would stand next to me in prayer, even if he was too young to understand, he would sense the respect required. He would be mine, as you were your mother's.

It was a Wednesday. Hadia and Huda were at school, your mother was at home with you. Movement toward the awareness of a loss is a strange thing. I do not understand how time seems to slow just before and days after it has become a reality. How fragments imprint themselves into memory, sharp and vivid. It was as though the phone rang on my desk and I knew it was going to be Layla as I reached for it, and before she had even begun speaking I knew why she had called, and as she spoke something solid lodged in the center of my throat that did not dissolve until hours afterward.

"Something's happened," she said in Urdu, "I need you."

She sounded disoriented.

"Don't be afraid," I said, "I am coming."

I hung up the office phone. I thanked God I was in town. Stand up, I told myself. Grab keys, coat, container of leftover lunch. Tell my boss. Call someone to pick up the girls from school. But instead I leaned back into the soft cushion of the office chair and folded my hands in my lap. It was one thirty in the afternoon. On my desk was an old desktop computer that hummed. A clear, square container held paper clips. A tape dispenser. A small calendar I had forgotten to change to the correct month. On the gray walls that formed my cubicle, I had tacked a letter from Hadia, a poem from Huda composed of the first letters of my name (Right, Awesome, Father, Interesting, Quiet), and a watercolor you painted that your mother, and not you, had given me. It was of a red boat on a blue river. I was impressed by how you knew to use different shades of blue to indicate waves, evoke movement. And there was a photograph of the three of you. You a baby in Huda's arms, Hadia with her hand resting formally on Huda's shoulder. This is it, I thought. Then, focusing on the small face that was yours, half-obscured by the blanket you were wrapped in, you are it. There would be no second son.

I did not know what to say or do to comfort your mother. I waited for her to address me or ask something of me. Ask me for water, I thought. Ask me to bring you takeout from the restaurant we like. But she said nothing. I drove you three to the Ali family's house where you would stay until I brought you back on the weekend, when I would be home to help Layla. I could not take my hands off the steering wheel, not even for a second, and my thoughts tugged me to terrible places as I drove. Now that we had suffered one loss, I wondered when the next would come for us.

"Are you all comfortable?" I asked Hadia, when I visited the three of you as soon as I was off of work.

"They're very nice to us," Hadia said. Then, looking down at her shirt and playing with the edge of her sleeve, "Is it because they know what's wrong?"

"Nothing is wrong."

She looked at me. She was too smart for me. I was, as my coworkers liked to say, in over my head. I touched her forehead and told her to go play.

"But remember—" I pointed a finger at her.

She looked back at the Ali sons playing in the garden, all three of them children, the eldest no more than seven.

"Just acquaintances." She giggled.

Back then she had a funny way of pronouncing it, the syllables jamming together at the end. "Good girl," I said, and I smiled at her.

Sister Seema told me that you either clung to Hadia or, if she was busy, chose to stay inside with her and Amira. I walked into the living room and there you were, seated on top of a sofa facing a window. You turned to acknowledge my presence before looking back outside. The look in your eyes frightened me. You were so little, but I wondered if you blamed me for your mother's absence.

"Where's Mumma?" you asked.

I sat down on the couch. I waited for you to turn to me.

"She's not here," I said.

"Can you take me to where Mumma is?"

I wanted to give you everything you wanted.

"Tomorrow," I said softly.

You nodded. You had nothing else to ask me. Once again I felt like I did not know how to interact with you. I wonder now what we could have been had I had the courage to lift you into my arms as I wanted to then, tell you that tomorrow you would see your mother but that today I was here for you, that you had lost a brother and I a son, but I had you, and you would never lose me. But instead I stood up from the couch, I thanked Sister Seema for her kindness and drove the dark roads back to our house, where your mother had still not turned on the lights. I parked in the driveway and sat there until the car cooled, until I composed myself, before stepping inside and being brave enough for your mother, and here we are.

I AM STARTLED awake. A dim light comes from the hall beneath the curtain that wraps around my bed. The medicine they give me here makes my mind fuzzy. My memories come to me sharply or not at all. I have woken uneasy. Am I afraid? The room is silent in answer. The TVs turned off all throughout the hall. The rectangular window a sheet of black. The flowers blue in their vases. WE LOVE YOU NANA faces me in gray text. My life has taken on a look I do not recognize as immediately mine.

I am not dizzy, and so, I step from my bed. My legs are chilly, I slip my feet into socks, then slippers, grab my sweater. What a decision you made over a decade ago when you first ran away. Even now, during the last stretch of my life, I cannot fathom walking willfully away. The nurses on duty are in the center of the floor. They sit behind desks and computer screens and I can hear them chatting. If I walk along the wall to the staircase to my right, I can be out unseen, and soon the door echoes shut behind me. My head does not hurt tonight. My legs move without telling me they are tired. I will step down the flight of stairs until it takes me to floor one, where I will exit out into the parking lot.

If I do not count the events of the past week, I would say I am in fairly good health. I have outlived both of my parents by decades. I thought I was just prone to headaches. I thought the weakness of my arms and legs was a symptom of aging. The railing is cold as I step down toward the bottom of the stairwell. I stop in my tracks as a nurse turns the corner and her eyes widen from surprise at the sight of me.

"What are you doing?" she asks. Her voice echoes. She glances at my gown peeking from my sweater and my silver bracelet on my wrist. "It's five A.M."

"My surgery is tomorrow." I do not know why I say it.

She does not work on my floor. I have never seen her before. I can see her trying to figure out if I am dangerous or if I am delusional, a danger to myself.

"Sir, you can't leave your room. Can you tell me what your room number is?"

"Every day of my life I've taken a walk outside. I have been in here for a week. I haven't seen the sky in days. I wanted to see it, before."

It is clear that the woman does not know what to do. I feel bad for startling her. For asking her to break code.

"I am on the fourth floor," I tell her. "Room four-oh-five."

I turn around and begin climbing the stairs. She steps next to me at my pace. She is quiet. One floor up she whispers, "Will a balcony do?"

She holds a finger to her lips and shushes. I follow her. I feel a dizziness I take for excitement. She unlocks a door and tells me it is a break room where no one will be at this hour. A couch, a coffee table, a kitchenette, and a sliding glass door. I thank her. I ask her name. Ida, she says, opening the sliding door. I step out into the cold.

"We can't stay long," she says. She looks around nervously.

She stands a little behind me. No clouds but some wisps. A clear night. A few stars. The best we can do when we are so close to the city. I think, God, if this is my last time looking at the night sky, I thank You, for having given me so many nights like this one. I cannot help it. I blink rapidly, not wanting to make her any more uncomfortable.

"When my children were very little, if I did not know how to

327

make them stop crying or make them happy, I would take them outside, show them this."

"Oh," she says softly, "that is very nice. I am sure they will remember that."

I shrug. I hoped so.

"My daughters were quick to feel better, they would begin talking to me instead. Or would ask to walk around. But my son, he would look for a long time. Until we had to go back, no need for talking."

The wisps of clouds are making their way across the far sky. Ida waits until it is appropriate to take me back. Hadia said there were no guarantees. I am not ready. There are things I need you to know. I stare at the white glow of the moon until something in me calms.

"Do you really think they will remember it?" I ask.

My voice feels as weak as my hands, and I hold them together behind my back to keep from feeling it. She reaches out to rest her hand on my arm. I do not pull away. I think of how kind strangers are to me and how maybe I have not been kind enough to other strangers to deserve it. I think of Dawn when you were sleeping in your clear crib in the hospital and how generously she reassured me you would be all right. Years later, I wander down a different hospital hallway with a different cause for the heaviness of my heart, and it is as though we live until we become other people entirely, keeping only that same need for hope, for comfort. And how miraculous it is to me that we receive in this world the very things we need from it, how tonight it is another stranger who has stepped forward to play that same part, help me get through this night until morning.

"It's a part of them," Ida says, drawing her hand away, "even if they don't know it. It will be there every time they look up."

MY FATHER DIED unexpectedly late on a Thursday night and was buried early Friday. I wore black. I did not cry—I think now because my mother was crying so much, it seemed like her energy was being drained from her. My love for my father felt small compared to my mother's. I wondered if onlookers thought I felt nothing. And of course, after that thought entered I could not cry in front of anyone, fearing I would be a hypocrite if I gave expression to my pain only after considering another's interpretation of it.

The call for prayer sounded after the funeral. It was a beautiful and soothing recitation, even on that day, or perhaps especially on that day. For as long as it was heard it was the only sound; even the birds quieted, even the shopkeepers had closed their gates. My father would often look at the animals during times of prayer and he would say—look how every creature knows what time it is. He would point up and say, for Him, even the birds and the sheep and the stray cats hush; a calm blankets everything. My father was gone. I was a kind of lonely I did not think anyone could understand. We had not been close in life. I hardly knew him. We had little in common. But every Friday for *jummah* we walked together the short distance to the mosque and I stood by him in prayer. After, I was in charge of finding our shoes. What else connected us, if not that, and the blood in our veins? That when we heard the *adhaan*, we went together, the two of us.

I walked that Friday alone. I tucked my shoes away in a corner by themselves. The men I did not know gathering like a flock about to still, finding a spot in line. Here, everyone had a place. We stood side by side. One man passed me a *sajdagah*. My father was gone. I was thirteen. Looking back, I was just a boy. And then the second call to prayer, the time to rise. I stood. No one around me knew I had buried my father that day. I lifted my hands, readying myself to focus on the prayer. I could not recall what it had been like to have had a father. I had already forgotten. Then the Arabic verses began, the murmuring of moving lips, the entire hall filling with whisper. We lifted our palms up together, we bent together, and we lowered our heads to the ground together. We were one unit composed of a hundred, all of us moving and trying to think only of God. My lips moved. I was among brothers, I was home.

*

ABOUT FIVE YEARS ago, Hadia and Tariq got jobs an hour away, in Palo Alto, and moved back. They were lucky. But Layla and I felt luckiest of all: our years of being alone, of spending entire days only occupying our room and the kitchen, were over. By then, Huda had moved to Arizona after marrying Jawad, the grandson of my father's oldest friend, who had sent the proposal after they met at Hadia's wedding.

Layla and I waited eagerly for Hadia to ask us to help her with Abbas. He was only three then. Sometimes he stayed with us for entire workdays. We were getting to know him. We had flown to Chicago when he was born, but after, we had only seen him for a few days at a time. He liked spinach. Pretending bites were airplanes did not work, but if we named each bite after a superhero, he would eat them. He always got full before the very last bite. He preferred rain to strong wind. I was Nana, and Layla was Nani. Layla made up stories that she had never told our own children, playful and funny tales about yellow chicks who were enemies and endlessly plotted pranks on each other, stories that made Abbas laugh and laugh. I laughed too, if only because Abbas's laughter was a force that caught me by surprise.

Abbas fell asleep easily with Layla and went to her when he was tired, or if he had hurt himself and begun to cry, but during his unhurt waking hours it was me he wanted, my arms he was always in. It was a mark of that age. I had slept through my children's childhood. I would not allow that to happen with him. I would hold him anytime he asked, even during the months that Hadia and Tariq were trying to break his bad habit of being held. Everything he did, I told myself to cherish the act, knowing that the age would pass, and he would stop asking me to carry him everywhere, would stop ranking the ones he loved.

"Mumma number one," he would announce, holding up a finger. Then, pressing my nose with his finger, "Nana number two."

"And what about us?" Layla would ask, and Tariq would ask.

"Baba and Nani number three," he would say.

They would feign hurt and say, "Baba and Nani the same? Can Baba and Nani be number two, too?"

"No," he refused them. "Nana number two."

I felt for Layla, and I felt for Tariq, but I could not deny it, the enlarging of my heart when I lifted him in my arms and kissed the crown of his head. That's right, I whispered to him. He did not know how to wink then but he did scrunch his nose and show his two front teeth anytime he knew it was mischievous to agree with me. Never mind number one; I had never been anyone's number two, and I vowed to do what I could to keep my rank.

THE YEAR ABBAS turned five, the news was constantly playing in the background of our home. That was the year I realized I had stopped being surprised by what people could say. It was the easiest movement, to suddenly feel hated. It was almost as though I had known it all along—so when it came, what surprised me was not the existence of hate, so much as the casual quality of it.

"Turn it off," Hadia said one night when she came to pick up Abbas and Tahira. "I want to protect them from this for as long as possible."

Tahira was napping on our couch. Abbas was drawing under the coffee table.

"He will not understand any of it," I assured her.

She seemed uncharacteristically worried. I did my best to respect her wishes as a parent. That night, I turned the television off, but the voices did not leave my mind easily. Hadia was right. He was little, but who knew what the effect would be on him? It was 2016, and that year I watched and watched the news as though watching would do something for me, would explain to me what was happening, would prepare me for something, but it only made me nervous and heavy of heart. I whispered to Layla that I was going for a walk. The sun had just begun to set. I kissed the top of Hadia's head, in case she had left by the time I returned, and I snuck out without telling Abbas, in case he tried to come along.

I did not walk in the yard but along the streets of the neighborhood we had lived in since Hadia was four and Huda was three. I still remembered the day we first stepped inside as a family. Hadia was so scared when we pretended to sneak in, she had pinched her hands into little fists. Layla and I had always planned on one day moving into a smaller home, to a more affordable area, as ours was expensive because of the good schools we now had no need for. We did not know what our children's values would be, if they would be willing to live with their parents as I would have had my parents lived, and so we talked sometimes of moving into a bungalow to make it easier for us as we aged, one close to the mosque to make our commutes shorter. But after you ran away we never spoke of it again. We both knew without ever saying it aloud that now we would never. Sometimes, still, if there was an unexpected knock on the door, my heart would quicken for just a moment, thinking, what if? But it would only be a family friend dropping by unannounced, a volunteer asking us if we were registered to vote.

As I walked that night, I waved at each of my neighbors who were out on their darkening lawns. They waved back. Had the way they thought about me changed? I did not think so. I was caught between thinking the world was changing around me and I was a changed man in it, or believing that nothing had changed, least of all my resolve to wave and smile at my neighbors. I walked and walked until the sky turned violet and I reached the field where a horse was kept behind a wooden fence wrapped with barbed wire. The horse had a shiny dark coat and a white splotch between his eyes. Some special evenings, you three would insist on accompanying me on my walk and would ask to come here. You and Hadia liked the horses a moderate amount, but Huda had a tiny figurine of a tan horse she kept on her windowsill. She spoke to the horses in the field and named them Cow or Pinocchio, and I would tease her for it, and you would laugh and laugh. Layla would send us with a plastic bag of chopped apples, and you three would take turns tossing slices into the dirt, squealing when a horse moved to eat it, the breath from its nose disturbing the dirt.

"Chopped?" I had asked Layla once, when I glanced inside the plastic bag. "What do horses care if the apple is chopped?"

She had smiled at me in a way that I cannot clearly picture now, as much as I try to, and she gave me that loving look of hers that says to me, oh Rafiq, you have never understood, and you never will.

"If the apple is chopped then the children get to feed it to the horse longer," she said, nodding to where you three waited for me at the edge of the driveway, Huda already jumping. She always thought of you three. She always thought of everything.

That evening, the horse trotted to me as soon as I approached the fence. I reached out and touched the white diamond between his eyes. The horse blinked at me and there was something gentle and almost human about him. A very dangerous anger and ignorance has been unleashed, I thought. My thoughts felt foolish and inadequate against it. I was just one man. My voice would be like shouting into the wind, only for the wind to suck it in and carry it away to nowhere. The horse kicked his hooves against the dirt and dust rose. And all of a sudden I pictured your face from years ago, when you were in seventh grade and I watched you approach me after you had been suspended, your eye swollen and your white shirt stained with blood, and that blend of absolute love and complete terror I had never felt for anyone before that moment. My breath had caught in me. I had not even known I had been capable of such a reaction. I trembled. My Abbas was five years old, he was as confident and curious as any other child, he was about to begin his first year of kindergarten, I was his second-favorite person in the world, and I was not sure what to explain to anyone in a way that would protect him. And you, wherever you were, even though I could not accurately picture your face past twenty-three, I knew the faint scar above your eyebrow, and the fainter one beneath your lip. God, I thought, it feels tonight like the forces of the world are closing in on me, the way darkness closes in to become night, slowly and then all at once, and I do not know what I can do or say so that no one will ever think to strike my Abbas's face in the future, as my own son's face had once been struck, by others, by me.

*

THE MORNING OF the surgery, I wake mid-thought, as though I had spent my sleeping hours asking questions and attempting answers in my mind. What do I owe? Who have I wronged? The surgery will take no more than four hours. Hadia wheels me into a small room and together we wait for the cue from Dr. Edwards. She tells me that as soon as I am settled with Dr. Edwards, she will join Layla and Huda in the waiting room.

"You won't be needing me in there as much as Mumma will," she says with a smile.

My children have been shielded from aging. I am impressed by them now, by their maturity, by their seriousness, by their consideration to care for me in ways I have not asked them to.

"Are you nervous?" Hadia asks.

I shake my head. The room we wait in is bare. Nothing about hospitals is designed to comfort the patient.

"Hadia," I begin, before I realize what I am trying to say. "I let my anger control me too often."

She opens her mouth to interrupt me but I raise my hand to stop her.

"Let me say it. I know I had a temper. I know it hurt you."

Hadia is still, and then, she thanks me. "Anything else you want to get off your chest?" she jokes. She takes a sip of her coffee, which battles with the disinfectant to be the strongest smell in the room. Then she reaches over and places her hand over mine. "Just focus on getting better, Baba."

She glances at her watch. When I first saw her wearing it again, years after it had gone missing, she explained its reappearance before I even asked. Still, I've wondered.

"Have you heard from Amar?"

I say it out loud. Just like that. As though only a week or two has passed, as though I failed to reach you on the phone after trying a few times and thought to ask if she has had any success. Any lightness that was in the air between us a moment ago vanishes. She does what she does now that she has become self-conscious of how

334

much her hair has grayed; she runs her hand through it as if to comb it. My heart begins thudding.

"Are you feeling all right?" she asks me in Urdu.

"Does he know I'm here?"

I didn't expect my voice to break. But it has taken years for me to draw up courage to ask. She shakes her head. Wraps both hands around her coffee, cradling it.

"Do you know where he is?"

Again she shakes her head. When she finally looks at me there is fear in her eyes—of what, I'm not sure.

"Are you in contact with him?" I ask.

She sighs. I watch her as though any action of hers will give me a clue to unpack later. Her pager beeps. It is time to wheel me into the room where Dr. Edwards is waiting, but I have not taken my eyes off her.

"No," she tells me finally, "we are not."

I feel my shoulders relax, or maybe they are sighing, or maybe they are collapsing. Maybe they are just giving up. I was not afraid before but now I am afraid. Afraid that if I wake in a few hours or do not wake, if I recover for years or just for a few more months, I will not be any closer to knowing if you are well in the world. Hadia stands. She reminds me again of the plan and procedure and I nod along. This is the easy part. This is nothing. Before she takes the handles of the wheelchair, she kneels in front of me so we are face-to-face. An entire streak of her hair is gray. We have changed. Now she knows I think of you, now she knows I wonder. I have given away the only power I had in this situation at all, the power of appearing unaffected. She seems aware of this as she studies my face, her eyes very big, copies of your mother's, ready to welcome anyone they look upon. One side of her mouth lifts into a smile so she looks like she almost pities me. She leans forward with her index finger and begins to trace a shaky *Ya Ali* on my forehead, as your mother would do for each of us, when we were vulnerable and in need of reassurance. She means to prepare me for what I am about to face, to give me a shield of protection and strength. But instead of strength I feel a wave of gratitude so overwhelming I am weakened before it, and I know that I did try my best to be a father to my children, I did, and I did fail, in some instances so completely that I do not know where my own son is, and he does not know I am here, moments away from being wheeled into my surgery, but I have also been successful, I have passed down to Hadia what I have known to be valuable, and when she pulls away her finger I open my eyes and blink at my own hands, so helpless in my lap, unable to look up at her.

3

TODAY IS THE FIRST DAY SINCE THE SURGERY I
have to myself. Layla has been relentless in her care for me during
the months of recovery: she has come along on every walk, accompanied me on every errand, interrupted any stretch of sweet silence
to ask how I am, no matter how clearly Dr. Edwards and Hadia
assure her that all is well. But she had been invited to a ladies'
jashan today and I urged her to go, and the moment she drove away,
I snuck from our home as well. The sun is setting when I turn onto
Hadia's street. Soon, I will have to explain my absence, but for now
I enjoy the freedom, the familiarity of the route, and the promise of
seeing my grandchildren and presenting Abbas with the gift I
bought him earlier today.

You would like Abbas. He looks like you. Sometimes the resem-
blance is so striking I can't take my eyes off of him. It is not just his
features that alarm me, but his mannerisms are also shockingly
yours, though he has never met you to copy you. I know your mother
realizes it too. I can tell by the way she reaches out to touch his hair.
How she glances over at him when he has fallen asleep on the
couch.

He asks about you sometimes; he is the only one who does. He
will point to photographs of you that your mother, years ago,
insisted on leaving there, untouched unless to be dusted, and ask a
question. Only if he and I are alone will I attempt an answer for

him. He asks the kind of questions you used to ask me, odd and pointless, questions I would often be too busy for, or find too silly to answer. But I've found my patience for him is boundless.

When Hadia opens the door she is surprised to find me. She glances at the box but says nothing, invites me inside, and while Abbas and Tahira gather around me I hear Hadia's voice from the hallway, telling someone on the phone, "He's here. Don't worry. I'll call you soon."

By the time she has come back I have presented the box to Abbas. I tell Tahira, who sulks in my arms, that I will be back next week with one for her as well. She makes little animal noises to tell me that my promise is not enough.

"Why, Baba?" Hadia asks from behind me, her tone concerned. "His birthday was a few weeks ago. Eid is not for months."

I ignore her. I watch Abbas open the box and lift up the red shoe, and it is astonishing, how he really does look just like you, with that same kind of sensitivity and consideration about him, because I can tell he does not know why I have gotten them and does not particularly want them, but as soon as he erases the initial perplexed look, he thanks me earnestly, ties the laces tight, and runs up and down the hall. I hear the sound of his feet hitting the tile and watch the shoes light up, alternating blue and red lights spilling onto the white tile, flashing, just as you had advertised in one of your posters. Hadia is quiet, even as Abbas breaks the rules of her home. When I look at her, her face is pale. She turns from me and gathers the tissue papers and returns them gently to the box, closes the lid.

"Mumma's worried. Go home," she says, running her hand across the cardboard surface of the box, her back to me.

"Do you like them, Mumma?" Abbas asks her when he runs back into the room.

Hadia nods at him, her lips pressed into a straight line in a look that awes me: how like Layla she has become. Abbas looks from me to Hadia, searching for an explanation as to why his mother seems upset.

Later, Hadia walks me to my car, her hands in her back pockets. I can tell she is restraining herself on purpose, not wanting to hurt me, or offend me.

"He will like them," I tell her. I want her to speak. I want her to say anything, it doesn't matter what.

"What good does it do now, Baba?" she says softly.

I drive home, thinking of Hadia, and wondering, for the first time, if it was not just you who had been affected by my refusals, but she too. One thing I never told your mother was how secretly impressed I was by the way you had organized the campaign for the shoes. I remember the little facts and drawings you included on the posters. With such determination you decided to go against my initial refusal, with such creative effort. Of course, I could not allow you to see that. But Hadia is right. It doesn't do any good now. Amar, I had thought that denying you would build character. I thought the not-having would teach you something valuable. You were always so sensitive. And your mother, out of love for you or seeking to protect you, would give you anything you wanted. I was afraid you would grow up spoiled. I especially didn't want it to be material goods that we spoiled you with. But when you stood before dinner and pulled a sheet of folded binder paper from your pocket and asked permission to deliver a speech, I allowed it. And you had done such a wonderful job constructing your argument. It was well-thought-out and persuasive, even though I knew that you had failed horribly on your persuasive essay assignment.

When we struck our deal, when you met my eyes as we shook hands to make our agreement official, I saw the focus, the dedication, what you were capable of. That night, I told myself that I would allow you the shoes even if you got ninety percent, eighty percent. I thought of how I would explain it to you: you got the shoes because you tried, because you worked harder than you had been working. Your mother was kinder to me that week. Though she never said as much, I could tell she felt more tenderness. Sometimes, I have wondered if she only gave me love when I gave you three love. That without the three of you to care for and raise, she and I would have had little between us. And that when you left, the part of her that loved me began to dwell in our loss of you instead. But I know it is unfair of me to say this. To even think it.

I wanted you to have the shoes, Amar. I want you to know that. You were so proud when you presented your test to me, and we decided we would go to the mall that weekend. You may have hugged me, I don't know. And I felt, for the first time in a long time, that I *did* know how to be a father to you. That you had shown me how capable you were of working hard, of keeping your word. That maybe what worked for Hadia and Huda would not work for you, that I could meet you where you insisted on standing, without appearing to compromise. We could find some solution, the two of us. But that night, while you slept, I heard a knock at my office door. It was Hadia. I lifted my face from my papers and invited her inside. She was hesitating with me in a way that I had not noticed before, and I pressured her, perhaps too sternly, when I should have let her keep her secret a secret.

"Amar cheated," she said. "It's on the bottom of his shoe."

To my surprise, I felt a deep disappointment, not with you, but with her. I had found comfort in knowing my children had obvious ties to one another. Even in the way you and your sisters fought, there was love. And though I did not like misbehaving or lying, I did feel an odd kind of pride in how quick you were to take the blame on behalf of your sisters. After having put your loyalty to each other to the test and finding your love for one another exceeded any punishment I might exact, I would watch you three relax, become chattier and begin joking with one another, thinking you had fooled me. But of course, I could not tell Hadia how disappointed I was. She had done what was right. What we had tried our best to teach her—to be honest, to respect the laws of the home, the classroom, and eventually, the greater world. And once she knew that I knew, I could not pretend that all was well. You had betrayed me and our agreement, you had made a fool out of me. And the more I thought about it, the angrier I became.

*

340

BEFORE GOING TO hajj, a *momin* must repay the debts owed, draft a will, and ask for forgiveness from friends and loved ones. Practically, I imagine, because the hajj is taxing and possibly dangerous, and partially because one then comes back a sinless man, and meeting those conditions might be prerequisites for cleansing one's life. The older I get, the easier it is for me to imagine that God can forgive a man for his sins when they only affect him, but maybe He wants people to mend any hurt and harm they cause their fellow brothers and sisters while in this life, while living in this realm.

Layla and I went to hajj the first year we were married. I wanted to show her that though she had left her whole life behind, I would care for her spiritual needs as well as any other. In those first months we were together, we were very careful and kind with one another and I wondered if an environment as unfamiliar and challenging as hajj would bring us together in a new and unpredictable way. I was still young. I had very little debt. I paid for my coworker's lunch as he had once paid for mine. I returned my library books. I paid rent for our small apartment in advance, so the debt would not be incurred while we were away. I called my uncle who had cared for me after my parents' passing—my mother's brother, who I had not known very well during their life, but who after their death I thought of as an older brother. I asked him if there was anything I owed him.

"You know there is nothing. Anything I did for you, you have repaid me in full."

"Is there anything I should ask forgiveness for?"

"There is nothing."

Layla and I went. The Kaaba was a cube of bricks covered by a black cloth, a simple design, and yet when I looked upon it for the first time, it was bigger than I ever imagined it, and the sea of bodies dressed in white moved around it in a thousand tiny and synchronized motions, and my breath, as they say, was taken from me. We were one with the wave of people that circled and circled the Kaaba. I touched the crack in the corner where they say the Kaaba split open for Imam Ali's mother to enter, so she could give

341

birth to him inside. I touched the black stone surrounded by people also desperate to touch it. Standing still in that rush was manageable one moment and the next my body was caught in a current of bodies, a dozen crushing in on all sides, all of us moving the inexplicable way a body of water moves, so that when I was spat from it, I emerged gasping. If separated, Layla and I would meet at our designated spot and try again to enter. For the first time, I experienced the power of spotting the face one loves in a crowd, how of all the faces that passed me, hers was the one that was capable of shocking my senses the moment I first found her. I led her to the stone, I held steady my arms around her and stood there like a dam, so she could touch the stone as well. Exhausted and in a dreamlike state, we slept and we woke, wore white, ate bread and a kind of crumbly and sharp cheese we had not tasted in either India or America, almonds and cashews. I shaved my head and we were born again— sinless as when we had begun our lives on Earth.

In the evenings now I take my daily walk, often accompanied by Layla. We are quiet together, she walks with her hands in front of her, and I with mine clasped behind me. She pays attention to the shrubbery and the flowers in people's gardens. I think of what I could do to best prepare for the next realm. I think of the debts I owe. My will. Who I have wronged. My debts, my will, my need for forgiveness.

I WAS THERE both nights my grandchildren were born. Layla and Tariq were in the room with Hadia, and I was relieved to pace the hall, never going far, ready to be called in at any moment and do what Hadia had asked me to: deliver the *adhaan* to my grandchild. I was honored. The first time I practiced the *adhaan*, nervous that I had forgotten it—an absurd fear, as I had recited it multiple times a day for years. Then the nurse came. She is ready for you, she said. That was my first child in the hospital room cradling her first child. It was a miracle if I ever witnessed one. She held the baby and I did not know if the baby was a boy or a girl and nothing mattered but that everyone was alive and here together. Hadia passed her child to me as soon as I approached her. The baby was smaller than I remembered my children being, and so light it took me a moment to realize I was the only one holding on to the child.

"His name is Abbas, Baba," she said, and I could not even see his face because my eyesight had blurred, the lights of the room caught in big gorgeous circles that shifted as I blinked. I lifted Abbas to my face, his ear was so delicate and red it reminded me of a tiny shell, and I whispered the *adhaan*, essentially saying: welcome to the world, my little one. Here, we believe in one God. Mohammed is His messenger, Ali is His friend. And I will do my best to tell you all about it.

IN SEVENTH GRADE you played soccer for your middle school and I often came home to your duffel bag of cleats and crumpled shorts and jersey in the foyer. I would open the door and yell until you came downstairs, yell while you rolled your eyes at me and picked the bag up, yell after you to not slam the doors and you would open the door and slam it again and again and again, your face blank each time you opened it, and I'd have to turn around and walk straight into the street, just to keep from acting in a way I would surely regret.

Did you know that for years, your mother never uttered a word against me unless it was in defense of you? I would return to our bedroom shaking, still angry from having dealt with you, either your *batamizi* or your usage of bad language or getting suspended after another fight at your school. I would take a seat at the edge of my bed and rest my head in my hands and try to calm myself. I let my anger get too carried away, I told myself, I should have stopped before I did what I did. Anger was my worst attribute. It was as if I left myself when it shot up in me, and by the time I was rid of it I had already done the damage. And even though I could justify why I had reacted the way I had, I always regretted my particular reaction. And Layla would be absolutely silent around me. She would not even be aware that she too had withdrawn from me.

343

The year that you tried playing soccer, the year that your duffel bag was always in the foyer and you listened to music that sounded as angry as you were, your grandfather had a heart attack. We did not know then that he would only have a few more months to live, and your mother left to visit him in India. That very week, I came home to the sound of the TV blasting through the halls and your duffel bag right where I predicted it would be. I remember I did not even yell. I swung it over my shoulder and walked into the street and shook the bag until its contents tumbled out: your water bottle, your jersey, your cleats, which I kicked until they landed feet away in different directions, your books and notebooks, their pages fluttering in the street, and I stormed back inside, yelling your name. I grabbed you by the ear and dragged you out the front door, and shoved you until you stumbled onto the driveway, and I pointed at your papers torn and flying away and your clothes and contents strewn about, and we watched the passing cars do little to avoid them.

You did not speak to me after that. I couldn't really blame you. Every time I closed my eyes I saw your belongings scattered on the road, I saw the redness of your ear when I finally released it. Would you believe me if I told you I hated myself more in those moments than I imagined you hated me? My pride bothered me. It was my own self I had to overcome: I could not even go to you, say to you that I was sorry, that I had overreacted. The twin towers fell the next morning. You still did not speak to me. I did not think of how you might be affected. You were a boy. I did not have to worry about you the way I worried about the safety of my daughters, both of them then wearing hijabs. Layla was so far away. I was so alone. I was not sure what the world outside was like, when it would regain a shape I knew, if my family would be safe inside it.

When my phone rang at work that week, I feared the worst. Maybe my father-in-law had passed away. Maybe Layla had been told she could not book her ticket home for even longer. But it was your school nurse, telling me that you had been in a fight, that you were hurt as well as suspended. My desk was decorated the same as always. Your little red boat on the blue waves still there, just the edges of it curled a bit. Each wave was distinguished from the others. I sighed into the phone. You had been in fights before. You had been suspended before. But they had never told me that you were hurt.

"Is he all right?" I asked her.

"He will be," she said, "but he might need stitches."

I was quiet for a while. The nurse, bless her, did not hang up. She told me that the scuffle had taken place in the locker room, after PE class, that a few other boys had been involved, and all of them were suspended, and while she talked I wondered how I would ever explain this to your mother, who called me every night worried after watching the news, the same footage looping and the smoke billowing in the air, asking me to reassure her that everything at home was calm. I decided I would just not tell her. I calculated the days that remained until her return and hoped it would be enough for any evidence to heal.

"Sir," the nurse asked me, dropping her tone into a serious whisper, "may I offer my honest opinion?"

"Yes, of course."

"Between you and me, it wasn't your son's fault. I think the other boys were being awful and cruel, I think they instigated it."

She did not know you as I knew you. How it likely had been your fault. You might be in her office giving her the look you give your mother, your eyes very big and dramatically sad and inspiring compassion.

Still I asked, "They were being cruel?"

"Racist, sir."

Something in me snapped, or sank, I'm not sure what it was. I told my boss I was leaving to pick you up. He's hurt, I said, stitches. Anger had always been my response to your antics. And here was another suspension, another fight. But as I drove to your school I was surprised to find that I swelled with a panicked kind of love for you. Your mother was not there beside me, ready to be the one who pulled you into her arms, ready to tell you of course it was not your fault, of course she was not mad. Layla's love and affection for you expanded so palpably, so without complexity and doubt, that what I felt for you felt small in comparison, as though there were no room for me to have my own love, my own affection, and my need to respond to you another way, to give you balance, became all the more necessary.

I went to the office and said who I was, whose father I was, I signed my shaky signature on a clipboard, and I was not ashamed, I was restless as I touched my eyebrow, looked about the office and noticed your old friend, the boy Mark, sitting there, an ice pack held to his nose, his eyes wide and afraid when they met mine. At first, I was so surprised to recognize him that I lifted my hand to wave. Mark was frozen and expressionless in response except for the ice pack that crunched as he pressed it against his face, and then I knew. The nurse said she would go back to the sick room to call you, and I told her I would wait in the car. For some reason I did not want you to know that I had seen Mark. I did not know if I should say good-bye to Mark and send my regards to his parents, whom I had gotten to know, or if I should ask him what had happened, and so I did nothing, I said nothing. I sat in my car, I tapped my fingers on the steering wheel. I turned on the car and switched on the radio, moving slowly between stations, so that the car filled with static, and then words, and then static, and then music, and then static again. At last you appeared. I may have imagined a slight limp as you approached me. You walked staring at your feet. I watched from the open window, taking inventory: a swollen left eye, a tear in your lip, blood dried on your shirt.

And I don't think I ever loved you more than when you opened the car door and I confirmed your injuries up close. You did not meet my eyes. You quickly buckled your seat belt and sank into your seat and turned to look out the window the way you would when you were a toddler and I was driving you to the barber's. I began to drive. I thought of your silence, trying to understand it. To know when and how it would be appropriate to break it. Were you embarrassed? Were you ashamed? Were you afraid I would raise my voice? After the last suspension and the school fight we had made it very clear it could never happen again. Your mother had begged you to be better. I wanted to reassure you that I was not thinking of those times, or if I was, I was not mad about the fight. I have never enjoyed meeting another's eyes, I have always preferred to look elsewhere when engaged in conversation, but on that drive I tried to look and I waited for you to look back but you did not.

We drove down the street I loved and it was autumn so the leaves were reds and yellows and slowly fluttering to the ground. What was it you wanted from me? I wondered. Did you want me to ask why it had happened? You were the kind of quiet that one has to make a decision to uphold. We had not spoken since the incident with your duffel bag. I had made a mistake. Why could I not be like your mother, who could reach over and touch your arm, why was it that before I was about to interact with you I felt a grand, growing desire to approach you in one way, generously, affectionately, but the moment I encountered you in your body I paused, stopped, my own uncertainty, my own stubbornness making it impossible for me to approach you the way that I wanted to. I turned on the radio again and tuned it to a news station and let another voice fill the air and you groaned and crumpled in your seat a little lower, as if that had been the wrong gesture and I had again disappointed you.

"You haven't left your bag in the foyer for days," I said, almost cheerfully and softly, when the car slowed to a stop at a red light, thinking of the first thing that came to me that was not connected to the swelling of your face. I wanted to acknowledge that I appreciated you remembering to put the bag away. I wanted to normalize the situation. I wanted to say something mundane so as to tell you: look, we can carry on, I am not mad, this and everything else is behind us. And you looked at me then, the stoniest look I had ever seen, and you held my gaze until I felt chills, and you said, "I really hate you."

Not in the way you usually said it, in a moment of anger and frustration and therefore easily dismissed, but calmly and evenly, and then the light turned green, and the car behind me honked, and I turned back to the road and continued driving.

WEEKS AFTER THE fight between you and the other boys, you ran after me as I approached the edge of the street. I was taking a long walk before driving an hour to pick up Layla from the airport. She was finally coming home. I was nervous. I did not know if they would bother her in arrivals, if she would be able to manage the questions without me, if they would treat her roughly. In the sunlight I studied your face as you walked beside me: your lip had healed well but there would be a scar. The swelling around your eye had gone away but there would also be a scar there that flicked through your eyebrow.

"I want to ask you something," you said.

I stopped to listen, but you kept walking, so I followed. You took a right at the road that would take us to the horses. You were taking a long time to ask me.

"Can you shave your beard?" you said. You were looking at your shoes, then at me for just a moment, then at your shoes again, as your feet picked up the pace.

"Why?" I asked. Though I was afraid I knew.

"You made Hadia and Huda take off their scarves."

My daughters had not pointed out the hypocrisy of my act, of wanting to follow my faith but wanting them to be safe more, but of course you had.

"Why can't you change for us? You make them change for you."

"Watch your tone," I said, because I could not come up with anything else to say. You kicked a pinecone and it skittered down the street. You were on a mission, you would not retreat, you wanted a persuasive answer from me.

"Baba," you said, and I was crushed. Even then, you had stopped calling me Baba. You somersaulted through your sentences to avoid calling me Baba and thought I was dumb enough to not realize.

"If you shave, you won't look like——" You paused, considered your words, then said quietly, "the bad guys."

It pained me. It was such childish wording, but you could not allow yourself to say anything else. I did not know then, as Hadia knows now, how to be a parent in the face of all this. How to turn the TV off. How to speak to Abbas and Tahira about what they did not deserve to think or hear from the kids in school, even if we could not protect them from hearing it. She reminds them again and again that what might happen in the world, and what they might overhear, cannot reach or alter what is within them, their hearts, their future. We did none of this. It is not that we thought our way was better. It was that we did not know another way.

"But I am not the bad guys," I said. We had reached the horses. You perked up a bit to see them.

"I know that," you said in your matter-of-fact voice, "but *they* don't."

One horse trotted to approach us. You stretched out your hand. I did not ask who "they" were.

"Amar. Those boys you fought, did they say anything about the bad guys?"

"No."

You pushed your tongue against your cheek. You were lying. We turned to go back. My hands were in my pockets and your hands were in your pockets.

"So will you?" you asked me.

"I can trim it," I said.

That was one of the first times I thought about it in that way— that there was a "they," people who assumed something about me, my family. There were enough troubling interactions in the years to come to know that they were there, but back then I thought of it as isolated incident after isolated incident, and not a force that tied each one, brewing with each year that passed. They stared at my wife a little too long in the park and I could not help but wonder if it was because of her hijab, or if there was a darker reason, and so I locked eyes right back, and I nodded, and I did my best to smile,

349

hello I might say to anyone we came across in passing—just in case they felt it—fear, or anger, each emotion feeding the other like a loop. I wanted to dispel even a tiny bit of it. I wanted to say, before the thought even formed: Peace be upon you. I am here. You are here. We are only passing one another in the street. Sometimes, my daughters would look down on me, if, after an upsetting interaction, they insisted we had been wronged, and they would turn on me instead, tell me that I had given in, I had been weak, I had not fought to be respected. But I did fight. I tried to leave every human I have interacted with better than or the same as when I encountered them. I have gone out of my way to apologize to a stranger I might brush against in passing, or have held the door open for a family entering the restaurant after mine. These are small things, I know. Sometimes, even I frustrated myself—why should I always have to put forth this demeanor, why could I not be bumped by the man in the café and not be the one who apologized first and always? Sometimes men bumped me and they said nothing, even as I turned my head to call after them. But on most days it was not like this. It was the way I wanted to move through the world. I had a beard, a modest one. I had my face. I had my name with the hard ending. That was my fight: to continue to do little things for people around me, so no one would find fault in my demeanor and misattribute it to my religion.

ONE EVENING I returned home from another business trip and parked my car in the driveway. My house, the magnolia tree, the patch of grass and the basketball hoop above the garage door—all of it was familiar to me and yet I felt like a stranger. The key to the front door was in my hand, but I hesitated before announcing my arrival. I had gone away for work trips for so long and so often that I feared my absence was as unnoticed as my presence, or worse. All this work done to provide for a family that could go on effortlessly without me. I walked to the wooden gate at the side of the house. If I stood on tiptoe and felt around the other side, I could unlock the hook and allow myself into the backyard. The green hose was curled in one corner and looked blue in the dark. There were fresh footsteps, and a cigarette butt in the dirt beside it. You had not thought to press it down, or flick it over the fence. By then, you were sixteen, and there was little you cared to do for our sake.

My next trip would not be for months but I wondered if I should request another sooner. I imagined that you were relieved whenever I left, because there would be no one to reprimand you or interrogate you about how your studies were going or to ask the reason for your departure. Whose home are you going to? What for? The wind blew. I shivered. It had rained hours before. The air was still misty. Little drops gathered on the waxy surface of dark leaves, reflecting light. I walked until I reached our plum tree and leaned against it. My home was framed in my view. On the second floor, the light of my bedroom was off, but Huda's adjacent to it was on, her curtains were partly drawn—lace, she wanted then, a cream lace and pale mint walls, and I had gone to the store wondering how I could have one child that wanted curtains with lace accents, and another child who had punched holes into our walls and tried to cover them with posters, had kicked his lamp so that it was permanently bent and imbalanced, had begun to smoke and did not even have the decency to step away from our premises to do so.

Your mother's face appeared in the kitchen window, she turned on the tap and began to wash something in the sink. Surely she could not see me. The window she looked out from would only show her own face, the glass a sheet of black. She turned around and then back to the window, a slight smile on her lips. She began talking, her face moving from expression to expression, and I saw it was you behind her. You were wearing that hat of yours I despised, worn backward and askew in a way that frustrated me, how even your dressing evoked attitude and arrogance. You began washing whatever it was that had been in her hands. You were good in that way. You always offered to help her. Even I did not do that then. Layla disappeared and then reappeared in the dining room area, her whole body visible through the sliding glass door, and she walked almost on tiptoe, the base of her ankle a fraction above the tile, and she turned the light above the table as bright as it could go, so that it splayed onto the concrete just outside. I am still in darkness, I thought. So far back that she would have to really be looking, would have to press her face against the glass and block out the world around her with her palms. And even then, she might miss me.

Something shifted in my sight. I glanced up to the second floor and saw Huda's light had been turned off. So the whole of upstairs was dark and I thought, well, good, they turn the lights off when I am not home, as I tell them to.

You must have said something to your mother because she leaned against the table and laughed. She looked so at ease. She lifted her hand up to cup her mouth, the way our daughters laughed timidly and yet loudly. You were good in that way too, making anyone around you laugh. I could never quite figure out how you did it. You splashed the drops of water into the sink, wiped your hands on your clean shirt. You disappeared. You reappeared. You and your mother placed plates and bowls of steaming food onto the table. All the while your lips moved, your expressions changed, whatever you spoke about engaged you both. And I thought of how I know only silence. Huda appeared and took a seat at the dinner table, her head bent over the phone in her hand. And I saw you try to read over her shoulder, the exaggerated expression on your face so I knew you only wanted to tease her with the illusion of interest, or you wanted to make Layla smile. Huda swatted you away, her hair flipping around her when she twisted her neck to glare at you after she caught you. Up close, these things bothered me, but from out here, it wasn't so bad, it was all done in play. Huda must have complained to Layla then, because Layla shrugged, that smile still on her face that I feared would fall if I entered.

My family seemed complete, save for Hadia, who was in under-grad by then and would not be back until the following weekend. The wind rustled the leaves in the trees and the neighbor's dog, a few houses down, barked. I had never thought of leaving your mother. The thought of divorce never once crossed my mind. But that night, you sat in the seat that was my seat. This is how my home must be without me in it, I thought, and it looked just fine. Warm and bright, the three of you there, talking animatedly together. Huda had put her phone away, she tied her hair up, and sat with one leg tucked beneath her. You helped spoon food onto her plate. Layla was still smiling a little. You took your hat off and hooked it on your knee. And that was when the thought first occurred to me, that I could go, I could leave, I could walk alongside the little tomatoes and mint leaves and step through the gate back into the driveway, the metal lock clicking shut behind me. Say I left that night. Would you have been able to stay, then?

AFTER ABBAS ALI passed away, I grew deeply worried for you. I had really liked that boy. He cared for you and he looked out for you and I trusted him. I was at peace anytime the two of you were together. After his death, I began to fear that the little that connected you to our faith would be severed and eventually I organized a trip for our family to do *ziyarat* in Iraq. I wanted there to be nothing I did not introduce you to that could be a tool for you and your spirituality.

When I first brought the trip up with you, you asked if you could stay back at home, but when you saw the look on my face, you quickly said you did not mean it, you would come. I could see how one might deny a night at mosque but could not fathom turning down an invitation to go to the holiest of places. Once in Iraq, my girls wore black abayas over their clothes. They looked luminous and almost unrecognizable. Even you, who respected nothing, seemed in awe. That first day in Najaf you walked wide-eyed through the streets. Men sold tea in the street from giant steaming vats, piles of sugar heaped in bowls where flies buzzed. Wheelbarrows heaped with fruit. We were patted down at checkpoints every few miles. Children ran barefoot and asked us for sticks of gum and spare change and you never mastered the art of saying no, you reached into your pocket for a bill and by the time you had pulled it out you were swarmed by other children. The markets and the hot sun and the dust and the fluttering ends of the black abayas, and soon we looked up and could see the golden dome of Imam Ali's shrine, which stood brilliantly against the blue sky.

Peace be upon you, Amir-ul-Momineen, leader of the Faithful, I whispered, and I looked to my right and to my surprise, your lips were also moving. Once inside, the ladies had to go to one side and men another. There was nothing to do there but pray, in organized groups or alone, by reading prayer books or just by speaking openly from one's heart. You were in the notebook phase that I hoped every year would leave you. I did not like it. I did not hide my dislike: I did not want you, an already sensitive man, to dwell even more in your sensitivity and become further removed from pursuing a respectable, well-paying career. But there, I did not mind it. I read from my prayer books outside while around me birds hopped from prayer mat to prayer mat, and next to me you scribbled away. In a country where we knew neither the language nor the customs and could not spend the day with Layla and the girls, you and I had no choice but to be at ease with one another, even if it was in silence.

When the rush surrounding the *zari* of Imam Ali dulled, we could easily approach his shrine. It stood proud beneath a chandelier that threw lights on the decorated mirrors of the walls, and we could hold the rounded metal of the gate, close our eyes, and pray. I rested my forehead against the metal. It was cool. I prayed for the things I always pray for, but there, in that place, so close to my Imam, whom I had spent my whole life hearing stories of and hoping to be like even in the smallest of ways, I felt even more strongly the possibility of being heard. I opened my eyes. You were still holding on to the *zari*. I had never seen you afford that attention, your eyes closed and eyebrows knit together.

"What did you pray for?" I asked later, when you took a seat beside me outside.

You sat holding on to your knees. You were eighteen then. You looked so handsome that day and so much like my father, the tips of your hair beginning to curl slightly.

"That God will forgive Abbas's sins," you said.

354

I nodded.

"He will," I said.

You looked at me. Your face was sincere and full of concern, as if you were asking me how did I know.

"God is merciful. We must not forget it. Abbas was a wonderful person."

My answer did not comfort you. You watched a bird that had landed by our feet. You reached your hand into your pocket and I predicted you would pull out a piece of that very thin bread we ate while there.

"But he sinned," you said.

You did pull the bread from your pocket. The bird cocked its head to one side and then hopped closer. You tore the bread into tiny pieces and tossed them one at a time. Like Layla, chopping up the apples for the horses. If we, just humans and entirely limited in our thinking, could think to break resources into smaller pieces so our children could feel the joy of scattering slices a little longer, then what generosity was our creator not capable of?

"Amar, God is so merciful that on Judgment Day He will forgive so many souls that even *shaitaan* will have hope for his own salvation."

"That's sweet," you said. You gestured "all done" to the bird but the bird did not go.

I lightly hit my own cheek to say *tauba*.

"Only you would find the devil sweet."

You smiled and glanced at me from the corner of your eye. I chuckled. We were getting along. Perhaps in wanting to impart fear of God and therefore adherence to His laws, I had not done enough to show you the side of God who was, above all, merciful.

"Did you have a nice time?" Layla asked when we found her at the appointed meeting spot.

"We did," you answered before I could.

You turned to watch boys in the street playing soccer. They were barefoot and most of them were children. Layla and Hadia wanted to search the markets for *akhiq* rings and Huda wanted an *akhiq* necklace.

355

"Can I join them instead?" you asked me, and gestured to the group.

They had made goalposts out of piles of bricks. One boy jumped to knock the soccer ball with his head into the goal and they cheered. You had asked me. You had cared about how your actions would affect me.

"Yes," I said. "Go."

And I squinted as you stepped, it seemed, toward the sun.

AT A WEDDING many years ago, you told me you were going to say hello to the younger Ali boys—Kumail and Saif. At this time, Abbas had recently passed away. I made small talk with the person seated next to me and eventually realized that a long time had passed and you still had not returned, and the Ali boys had taken seats by their father. I was suspicious and slightly worried, and I excused myself and went looking for you. You were not in the parking lot. You were not in the bathroom. And then, as I took a glass of mango juice from the drinks tray and scanned the hall while sipping it, the elevator door that led to the rest of the hotel opened and out stepped Amira Ali.

She was smiling to herself as if she alone had discovered the secret of the universe. She looked quite beautiful, possessing not only the beauty all women do in their youth, but also something indefinable, a poise that was not yet elegance but the promise of it. She walked quickly and it occurred to me that none of the wedding guests had any business in a place where the elevator was required to take them. Some feeling in my gut told me not to move. That soon you would appear.

And you did appear. You looked around as if you were a guilty man, but as you entered the main lobby you glanced at your reflection in the hotel mirror and your face cracked open in a wide smile, as if you were amazed at what life was about to offer you, and I was also amazed, and in that moment I knew exactly what was happening and exactly what my place in it would be.

I would tell no one. Not even Layla. You slipped into the main hall and had returned to your seat by the time I got back and you even had the audacity to say to me, "Where have you been? You're missing the wedding."

You were a terrific liar as well as a terrible one. Terrible in that no one believed you, and terrific because no one minded: you were charming and endearing even as you deceived us.

I let it happen. You were kids, it would pass, or you would change from it. For a while, you did change. In those years we hardly spoke at all but I observed the differences in your demeanor and I was even secretly grateful, I grew fond of the girl when I saw her at mosque or at events. Let their feelings grow, I thought. I was confident you could win her affection. I hoped that she would be a presence that grounded you and gave you a future to focus on. And you did choose the classes in your community college that would go toward a premed course once you transferred, and I was pleased.

"Please," Layla would tell me, "he's not made for these studies—they will waste his time and wear him out."

"I did not make him choose them," I said to her, annoyed.

"Maybe. But you have never encouraged him in any other endeavor. You have never let him think that any other path would be acceptable to you."

"That is enough."

She stepped back. I had yelled often but never at her. I tried to reach out to touch her but she turned from me.

Eventually, when Layla came to me and said what was going on between you and the Ali girl, I did not tell her what I had seen years before, and how I had always assumed it. Layla was determined it would not be good for you, for our family. She was right, if all we considered was right and wrong. But I had found myself in a strange predicament. I had laid the foundation of our family on the principles of our faith and our customs. I had set standards for what we expected of each of you, hoping that you would rise to meet them. In our family, in the culture of our home, and indeed in the texture of our religion, there was the truth and there was the lie.

357

There were sins and there was a steadfast adherence to faith. But when Layla came to me—it was I and not you who was caught. I had created neat confines to help us move through the world, only to see you, my son, disregard them all, and I was finding I did not have the heart to uphold the very standards I myself had set.

You're right, I said to Layla, because she was. Of every grievance I hold against myself, there are two I have kept against your mother that, even now, I have never forgiven. The first is that she went to Seema Ali and told her. The second is that, when you returned for Hadia's wedding, she asked me to not go to you, fearing your return was fragile and conditional and that had it not been for Hadia, you would want nothing to do with us. It was clear she blamed me for your departure. And I, also blaming myself, could not correct her or defend myself. I listened and I listened and by the time I went looking for you, it was too late.

"SUNO," LAYLA CALLS behind me as I step out to the garden, "you should take your coat with you."

I continue on, pretending not to hear her—this is the benefit now of my age, I can ignore everything I do not wish to respond to, point to my ear if I am later accused. Garden, trees, grass. Most days I move through the world automatically, on other days I am snapped from the moment and each blade of grass is its own individual blade. People pray their entire lives for things they will never receive. There are people, my friends even, who say maybe there is no soul. Maybe there is no creator. My own son once said as much to me. But I have looked up at this sky since I was a child and I have always been stirred, in the most secret depth of me that I alone cannot access, and if that is not my soul awakening to the majesty of my creator then what is it?

"You can't fool me. You are preparing to go. You are beginning to accept it."

It is Layla's voice behind me. I sigh. I turn to face her. She is holding on to my coat.

358

"Be calm, Layla."

"Rafiq, without you, I have nobody."

She looks around the garden as if nothing there pleases her. She lifts her arm and the coat sways. "I am here because you brought me here."

"Everyone goes, Layla."

She nods. She presses her lips tight against each other.

"Hadia told me why you went to her home. I find you in the kitchen or in your study mumbling to yourself. Speaking to who? Hadia says you are fine, the doctor said all tests are normal, but if something is wrong, will you tell me?"

I say nothing. She is right. I have been in a dazed state.

"Can you at least eat the food I make you, drink the water I leave you? Can you remember your medicine? I am finding the pills folded in tissues on your desk."

I reach out my hand and she hands me my coat. I slip into it.

"Thank you," she says, and she wipes at the edge of her eye with the side of her wrist and turns around and walks back inside. She closes the sliding door behind her. She takes a seat at the kitchen table and does not know I am still watching. She rests her elbow on the table and covers her mouth with her hand. Who was I thinking of when I moved here? Only myself. I was a man, I thought, without roots. I was thirteen when my father passed, sixteen when my mother followed him, I was not raised so much as funded by my uncle. I was not touched tenderly by anyone all those years until I married Layla. I had no family when I came here and no money and so I thought, nothing to lose. I was unable to get work in my field at first. I worked in a doughnut shop. I woke up at four A.M. to walk in darkness to get there before sunrise. I had a funny hat that folded and I tucked it under my arm as I walked. I practiced my English. Every ancestor of mine was buried oceans and continents away, and though I could not grasp it then, as I walked to work in the middle of the night, in making the decision to come here, I had drastically altered my destiny, and Layla's, and my children's and also my grandchildren's. I brought them here and one day I will leave them here. And what will the world be like when my Abbas and my Tahira are parents of their own children? And will they be welcome in it?

"Layla," I say when I step back into the kitchen, "I have not been myself, I know."

"Thank you," she says again.

"But I am not planning on going anywhere yet."

She sniffles. Can I tell her.

"It is becoming harder," I say, "to not think of him."

I pick up an orange from the fruit bowl and run my thumb along its grooves. I wait for her to say something.

"It is our test," she says. "It will be hard."

I nod. I am meant to remain steadfast in my faith. Remain faithful. God does not take from the human what the human heart cannot bear. I return the orange to the bowl and prepare myself to step back outside, but I look up at Layla instead.

"I do not want it to remain a test. I want to do something about it. I have to try."

4

WHEN YOUR MOTHER SHOOK ME FROM SLEEP
and told me about the small bruises that lined your arms, I was so
disoriented, I felt, at first, as though you were still a baby who had
just begun to crawl, and she was asking out of casual concern, and
not looking to me, bewildered, to answer the questions she did not
yet have the courage to ask.

Why did I choose to look closely then? I waited until it was obvious, until everything that came before aligned with such striking
clarity, it felt as if the darkness of the world was lit at once. The
money that had gone missing from my wallet. You smelling strongly
of booze. Your eyes so red, or else the dark of your eye a tiny speck.
How you would not come home for days. How Layla would say you
would be speaking to her and then, in the middle of conversation,
fall asleep. Layla insisting her gold earrings were in the house somewhere, maybe sucked up by the vacuum cleaner, and when I went to
check she told me she had not liked them that much anyway.

I stepped into your bedroom. You were sleeping so deeply. Your
hand curled and tucked beneath your chin. Anything for this, I had
prayed once, standing so still in the hospital hallway. Here you
were, years later, fast asleep and breathing. I shook you and still you
did not wake. It smelled strongly of a body unwashed, a body that
slept for hours, and something else I could not name, vinegar or the
scent of an animal. I lifted your heavy arm from beneath your
blanket and searched your skin until I found it, that black dot in the

soft inside of your elbow, and another one a bit below it, the bruise surrounding them both, and I heard your mother's voice from years ago, holding you, a baby in her arms, and pointing to the bruise on your thigh and saying, "This, how did this get here?"

I looked through your belongings until I saw the irrefutable glint of light on the tip of the needle. And every excuse I had given myself before—it was not so bad, my son might sin now but would repent later—was rendered mute.

"Well," Layla said, when I stepped out into the hallway, "what do you think is happening?"

It occurred to me for the first time that we really had no clue. I had never sipped alcohol in my life. When I first moved to America, I lived with four boys I hardly knew, and once they had handed me a can they had just opened. I waited until they were talking with one another before going to the bathroom and pouring out the contents, yellow and fizzy and smelling quite horrible, and I said to God, I am sorry, forgive me, I did not have the boldness to say no thank you. It was a story I thought I would tell you one day, and we could bond over a common response to the world. We were so very different. Now, in my own home. Now, my own son.

What was unfathomable to me was possible to you. I told Layla to sleep. I told her I would be back, not to worry. I sat in my car. I did not know what to do. I called Hadia. She did not pick up. I panicked, not knowing what my children were capable of, having been made aware suddenly that the limit of their behavior was nothing my greatest fears could even conjure. We raised them here hoping. Now it was out of our hands. They would do what they liked. Maybe it had always been out of our hands. Maybe anything we could have wanted to instill in them was, at best, a hope.

I could not face your mother. I could not bear to pray in my own home, knowing Layla would be frightened that I was driven to kneel not out of obligation, but something else, something much more desperate and unfamiliar. Layla's faith came from her own heart—she would turn often to the text, she would weep listening to *duas*, she told you three stories of Imam Ali or Abraham as if she had been the one to come up with them. Amar, I know I must have struck you as a religious man, a man of faith. And I have fasted and I have prayed and I have gone to Mecca and Karbala and I have worn black and bent my head in mourning every Moharram and I have given money to the needy and I have taught my children to stand when the *adhaan* is called. I believe, sincerely, that eating non-halal meat is a sin, backbiting is a sin, drinking is a sin, not praying is a sin, and defying one's parents is a sin.

But what I never told any of you, never even explored within myself, is that it has been a habit, my faith, a way of living I never questioned, and once you three were born it was for you all that I adhered to it as I did. I wanted you three to grow with an awareness of God, with that order and compass and comfort it provided, safe from the dangers I could not imagine and could not protect you from.

That night, I drove to the empty mosque. I had the keys from my efforts volunteering. It was dark and it was quiet and I was alone there. I could hear the beat of my own heart and it sounded like an animal inside my chest. I stepped out of my shoes. I walked until I reached the large hall with the high ceilings, where vines and verses had been painted, elaborate calligraphy I sometimes stared up at while I listened to speeches. I took a seat where we gathered to stand in prayer, where you also stood beside me on some nights. I knelt, I rested my forehead against my cold hands, the way I had in the hospital room after you were born and I only wanted to give thanks. And I thought, God, what do I do? What have I done? What is required of me as a father in this moment? My son has turned his back on You. He has learned nothing I wanted him to, he has followed nothing, he has descended in such a way that I am afraid not even You will forgive him.

Why am I telling you this? I know you think I was only angry that night that I confronted you.

THE DAY YOU were to run away I had gone to the library to do my research. Hadia had surprised me in the early morning. I was so relieved to see her I did not even scold her for driving all night. I hugged her very tight. I felt as though she was no longer just my daughter, but that she had also become my friend; I wanted to protect Layla, who would be devastated, but Hadia was wise and mature and when I hugged her I knew I could lean on her, trust her. I told her what I had found. She was silent.

"Have you known about this?" I asked.

"Not this."

She was very pale. I knew then I was not overreacting.

"What did you know about?"

She opened her mouth and then closed it, bit the bottom of her lip.

"Tell me," I said.

"I can't." She crossed her arms.

"Hadia, now is not the time to protect him."

"You'll just get mad at him. Let me try to talk to him first, when he wakes up."

I felt powerless. Everyone thought so little of me I was beginning to wonder if they were all justified and I was the delusional one to think otherwise. She made me swear I would not get mad and I promised.

"Hadia," I called after her, "I'm not angry. I'm not."

She stood in the hallway. She watched me. I deserved every unkindness they might accuse me of. But I was not mad at my son for this. I was too terrified to react in any way that was not the best way for you. I needed her to know that. Her eyebrows came together, she was either frustrated with me or felt sorry for me, I could not tell.

In the library I read article after article. I stayed away from the books. The pictures of the needles and spoons and bruised arms made me queasy. I rushed once to the bathroom and knelt on the tile floor by the toilet seat, thinking I was about to throw up, but I only breathed heavily. But this was very new behavior, I told myself. We had noticed just in time. I researched facilities that could help us. I even imagined that if you did not trust us, we could send you to live with Hadia. I could give up all hold over you, all expectations, just to keep you. I wrote a list titled PLACES, I did not want to think of it as rehab. The best ones closest to us. I called after a price. It would be a dent. One that made me sweat. Layla and I could sell the house earlier than we intended. I could keep working for a few extra years. Fine, it was all fine, it would all be well.

That night, that last night, Hadia told me she would call her attending to say she would miss Monday and Tuesday. She would tell them she was having a family emergency. The word *emergency* made me again feel as I had in the library, like the world was spinning around me and I was going to be sick. I told her my idea. She did not agree with me right away, but she did not disagree either. I could tell she could not decide if I was a part of the problem or trying to solve it.

"You didn't knock," you said, when I went to your room. I had knocked. I took a seat on your bed and watched you look for something.

You raised your eyebrows. There was something harder about you. We had often disagreed, but now there was a layer of coldness, a shield you had formed against me. It was as if you were not there, or the part of you that was there was not affected by anything I could do or say. I would be careful about this, I would not, as Hadia expected, get angry. I had spent my life getting angry at you and look at where that had gotten us.

"Mumma's making dinner," I tried, wanting to offer something neutral.

"I'm not hungry."

You had your back to me.

"Amar, can you sit next to me?"

It was the last thing you expected. You paused your search, considered my invitation. You were still there, I thought, I could still reach you, you took a seat by me. I took out my paper. My hands shook.

"We do not have to talk about it. But we can send you here, it can help you stop."

"Stop what?" you said. You glanced over the list.

I did not want to say it. I found I could not. My mouth became dry. You shook your head as if I had insulted you and you jumped from the bed.

"You went through my stuff," you said, and screamed cuss words.

"It doesn't matter," I said, holding my hand out to you, "I'm not angry. I want to help you."

You kicked your desk chair and it fell over and crashed against the wall. You had begun yelling.

"Amar, I'm not angry with you," I said it again.

You walked out into the hallway. I followed you. I stuffed my paper in my pocket. I stepped ahead, and stood in front of you, to block you from going downstairs. I reached out and put my hand on your shoulder.

"You can't control me," you shouted.

"Amar, you can't do this. It is bad for your body, for your soul. It is haram."

"I don't care about haram or halal."

You had acted that way but you had never said that before. I did not understand. One could be a bad Muslim, but one could not disregard, so totally, what was right and what was wrong.

"How can you say that? You do not care if you go to hell?"

I was yelling. I knew I was.

"I don't believe in heaven or hell. I'm not a Muslim."

There it was. Of all the things I thought might be possible when I stood in the hallway of the hospital and watched you, wrapped in a blanket, of all you might do or become, this had not even occurred to me. It was the farthest outcome from my mind. The most chilling of verses—*We will send them signs and they will still deny*—had become my own son. Amar, I know what I said next. You know what I said, and we both know what followed.

You stood there as in shock as I was. Your eyes were wide. You looked so afraid. It's okay, I had the impulse to reach out and tell you then, it's okay. It will be okay, I promise you. These things happen. You went to your room. I went to mine. Hadia looked at me like she despised me and Layla did not speak to me. It would be another forty days before she spoke to me again and even longer before she could look me in the eye. She fell asleep at the farthest edge of the bed and I lay awake blinking at the dark ceiling. I had done a terrible thing. I had disowned my child. I had been shocked by your words and out of cruelty I threw back my own, the worst I could muster. I never asked you to leave. I know that now. I remember that much.

I lay awake wondering if I should go to you. You were not Muslim. The thought pained me greatly then, and for years after, and even sometimes now, but there was no compulsion in Islam. I took comfort in the verses that expressed it. Everyone has free will. In time, I knew, we could work our way around it, I could become accustomed, even on that night I told myself there was nothing the human heart could not grow to endure, that the miracle of the human heart is that it expands in its capacity to accept, to love.

I used the wrong words, Amar. Or, I should never have spoken them at all. But I have only ever thought of you as my son, my only. I decided that in the morning, when things had cooled, I would go to you again, I would try again not to be angry. I would say to you, if you are not Muslim, fine, I accept, but I am still your father, you cannot get rid of me, you might not care if you sin and that is fine too, but I am concerned for your body. But by morning you were gone, Hadia fast asleep in your place.

HADIA HAS COME to our home to ask if we will watch the kids for her and Tariq next week. It is their nine-year anniversary. Of course, we say. As soon as we have answered, I make an excuse to leave the house, to go and check the mail. Outside, alone in the driveway, I think of how long it has been since we last saw you. The door opens and Hadia steps out. The magnolia tree is in full bloom and Hadia admires the petals, wide open as they are. I wonder what she is thinking when she says, "Mumma says you're having a hard time."

I am fine so I say nothing. I pretend to study the envelopes in my hand. Hadia takes a seat at the edge of the driveway and then looks up at me and says, "I know you hate when I do this. But join me."

She is right. It always bothered me. It would make the neighbors wonder why we were acting strange. Still, I take a seat.

"When I was younger and mad at you, I would sit out here and wish for a life where I could just step out."

"Did your wish come true?"

"Everything I ever wanted has become mine."

It is a blessed sentence but she has spoken it sadly, picks up a pebble and pinches it between her fingers.

"And are you still mad at me?" I ask her.

I look at my hands and clasp them together. Hadia does not say no but from the corner of my eye I see her shake her head. In the months since the surgery I have repaid all debts I owed. I have drafted a will and dated it.

"I remember asking you about Amar," I tell her.

She sighs.

"I wish I had some information I could give you," she says.

"You don't know where he is, then?"

She shakes her head.

"Do you think it's my fault he ran away?" I ask.

The sky is so vast and clear. I look up to no sun and still squint.

"There is no way for us to know that. I've thought about it for years and every time I do, there is a new cause to consider. Do you think it was your fault?"

I nod.

"I told him he wasn't my son."

"Baba. We said all kinds of things. Even he did. I think Amar convinced himself he did not belong, and he was waiting for any reason to go."

"I talked to him at your wedding. I was the last one who did."

She looks at me then with a look that says, please do not tell me if it will change things between us.

"I haven't even told your mother that."

"What did you say?" Hadia whispers.

"Every single day I have tried to remember that conversation. There was so much happening that night, and so little stayed here." I point to my head. "He was upset. He had been drinking heavily. I could smell it. His words were slippery."

Hadia's eyes fill. I place a hand on her shoulder. She leans into me and rests her head against my arm.

"I told him that *Inshallah*, it would be all right one day. I didn't say to him: never come home again. I didn't say that."

"I believe you."

Behind us, the leaves of the magnolia tree rustle.

"I lied," she says.

I hold my breath at once. I have known there was more. My heart leaps. I am so afraid she will speak and it will not be enough.

"A few years ago, when Abbas was about five, I came downstairs after putting Tahira down for a nap, and Abbas was on the phone. Just talking and talking. I took the phone from him. The person hung up as soon as I spoke. Who was that? I asked Abbas.

"He wouldn't tell me. No one, he said. Okay, I asked him, what did you talk to him about? Abbas didn't correct me, didn't say it was a she. About me, he said. And about Tahira.

"I knew it was Amar. How could it have been anyone else? He just asked questions, Abbas said. What kind of questions, I asked, can you try to remember for Mumma? How old Tahira is, he said, what you are like with us, what you do with us, if you are a good mummy. What did you say? I asked. He said yes, I was a nice mummy, that sometimes I took them to the park.

"He could tell I was trying not to cry. Please tell me, I said to him, you're not in trouble, I promise, just try to remember everything you can for Mumma. He eased a little. He asked a lot about Nana and Nani, he said, he wanted me to talk about them. Anything specific? I asked. No, he said, I told him what food they make and about Nana's gift drawer, what Nani likes to do and Nani's flowers. What did he say, I asked, when you told him all of this? He said, 'Keep going.'"

I do not know what to say. I turn my face away from Hadia, unable to look at her.

Hadia sits up straight and continues. "There are times, every year or so, when the phone rings from a blocked number and I answer and say hello. Hello? *Salaam?* Then I say, is it you? And the caller hangs up. After that first time, I noticed Abbas would perk up when the phone rang, and he would look at me when it did. Just a few months ago, Tariq also came upon Abbas on the phone while I was at work. When Abbas saw Tariq, he hung up immediately. Tariq asked, who was that, Abbas? And Abbas just gave Tariq that look of his when he lies and said, I don't know."

FOR YOUR SIXTH birthday your mother baked a cake and tried to make blue frosting but it turned out teal, and you said to her, I like it, it's like the ocean. I charged the video camera upstairs, and downstairs I could hear the hum of you all. We had invited a few family friends over. Blue and white balloons. Clear goodie bags filled with tiny packets of M&M's and dollar-store bracelets and tiny notebooks and pencils and those little aliens that you kids liked to throw at the ceilings, the ones that left an oily trace when pulled from the wall. Your mother made trays of biryani. Your sisters wore matching frilly dresses. Your mother's parents were visiting us from India at the time, and maybe because of this, I was thinking of my own parents, who would never see you. Who had gone before I could show them what I had made of my life, how I had succeeded in a way, a job and a house in California, three gorgeous children, a wife who made biryani and teal-frosted cake and pinned streamers and balloons to the walls.

"Baba," Huda said, standing in the doorway, "Mumma wants to light the candles now."

I stood, walked downstairs, found you all surrounding the kitchen table, where the candles had been lit, little drops of blue and white wax staining the cake and becoming solid, and you were standing right before it, surrounded by children who were struggling to find a space, pushing past one another and standing on tiptoe to see the action that was hardly exciting, hardly new.

"Baba's here!" you said, stomping on the ground, alternating one foot then the other, lifting them up a little so you looked like you were shaking from excitement.

I held the camera up, I put it to my eye and focused on you, and suddenly you were a tiny face in a tiny square bordered by darkness, and you said, "Baba's here!" to the kids around you, and I hit record, the little red dot began to blink where your shirt was, and I missed it just by an instant, you saying that. Hadia looked up at me—she too fit in the frame—and she began to sing "Happy Birthday" and it spread until all the children joined in singing it, and you beamed, and I concentrated on keeping my camera steady and focused on your face, as you looked around at everyone, smiling wide. You were missing a tooth then. Your mother's hand was on your shoulder. She was wearing the same ring she wears now. The Ali girl you would one day grow to love and be devastated by was standing in the frame too, her hand in her mouth, her big eyes turned up to the light fixture. You leaned forward when the song was done and a boy shouted, make a wish, and you paused, closed your eyes, your face in deep, sincere concentration, focused in a way it never was when we would ask you to pray with us, and you inhaled a giant breath and released it theatrically, so forcefully that spit flew from your mouth and onto the surface of the teal cake and I cringed, hoping none of the adults had caught that. And all the flames were spent. And a little smoke rose into the air, slow and meandering, and Hadia leaned forward and sniffed it, and Huda extended a finger and poked it into the cake, licked the frosting off her finger, and smiled. Your mother's face appeared in the little square then, and she held on to your cheek and pulled your face up to hers and she kissed you, and your grandfather took a spoon and fed you from your cake and you wiped the teal frosting on your mouth with the back of your hand, and I pulled the camera away from you then, zoomed out, and scanned the room. The HAPPY BIRTHDAY sign we used for every birthday for years tacked on the wall, the children

371

that had begun running from the kitchen into the living room, the pin-the-tail-on-the-donkey game taped up, a disarray of sticker tails all over the body and one on our wall, the adults talking again, and then I pulled the camera back to you, and you were still standing by your mother, still beaming, your lips and teeth now tinged blue.

Sometimes I come home and know your mother has been watching the videos. Sometimes she forgets them in the tape player. I turn the TV on to watch the news and there it is again—a moment from our life paused on the screen, how our backyard looked years ago, our children frozen in it. We don't watch them together as a family anymore, as we used to when you kids were all still under the same roof and one of you would ask us to watch them. You would always insist we only put on one that you were in, a video from after you were born. As a child, it was hard for you to imagine us having a life without you in it. Hadia would say it wasn't fair, that we never got to see videos of her as a baby, we only saw the ones with you as a kid, you as the center of attention. And that by the time you entered the videos she had already begun her ugly stage. And I would tell her not to be silly, when I should have told her she did not have an ugly stage, and I would put on a video from after you were born, and we watched your birthday, or all of us going to the zoo one day, or the three of you playing in the sprinklers outside one summer afternoon. Sometimes, I watch them again too. I press play and I think, This was the moment right after you said, Baba is here, that is why you were looking up, straight at the camera. When I watch the old tapes and look through the old photographs, it's as if I wasn't there at all. But they are mine, I remind myself, they are my memories, they are exactly how I stood and saw them.

I WAS THIRTEEN when my father died. I did not tell any of the boys in my class. I did not want anyone to pity me. I wore a black kurta-pajama to the funeral. The air smelled strongly of fresh dirt. My mother could not come to the graveyard. It was not allowed. I alone was the representative and I buried him. Every man my father had

known was there and each of them placed a heavy hand on my forehead and let it rest for a moment. At first I was confused. It felt nice.
How did everyone know to do the same? Then I remembered what
the Prophet, peace be upon Him, had said about orphans: be kind
to them, feed them, place a hand on their forehead. They were getting *sawaab*. And I was the one who had become an orphan.

The dirt was dark and very moist. It had rained. Nearby there
was a sanctuary structure where dark birds crowded the roof. I saw
my father, wrapped in the white cloth, lowered into the grave. His
face was very waxy and that bothered me. I tried to communicate
with him in my mind. I am here, Baba—you are not going alone to
the other world. We are sending you off. The *moulana* had told me
what to pray in Arabic but I forgot the verses. I spoke to my father
in Urdu instead. My father, whom I had not known very well. He
preferred *gulab jamun* to *halwa*. He insisted on paying a set price
for rickshaws and if the rickshaw driver did not match it he walked
on, looking for another. He was a man of principle. He was very
punctual. He liked watches very much. He was proud of the one he
wore every day, told me often why it had been given to him. He was
studious and competitive. He had a temper. I had been terrified of
him. Once, when I was a young boy, I had taken a magazine from
the store. When he saw I had walked out holding it he struck me on
my face so hard my ears began to ring. I did not remember if I had
taken it on purpose or if I had forgotten I was holding it, but when
I touched my hand against my burning face, I hoped I had taken it
intentionally, so that I would be deserving of the punishment and
saved from hurt that my father had assumed the worst in me.

I lifted the dark dirt. It fell between my fingers. I formed my
hand into a fist and more dirt fell, but the dirt that remained
clumped together into a ball. I dropped it into the grave. It landed
with a thud. The dirt came apart against the white cloth my father
was wrapped in. In America, years later, I volunteered for our
mosque in different ways. I dropped off and picked up *moulanas* at
the airport. We often sponsored *iftaars* during Ramadan. Another
duty of mine was performing *ghusl* on people who had passed away.

The first time I did this I was thirteen. I had never seen my father's body unclothed before. I was a child before he died but after, I was a man; I began to pray and keep my fasts, and on the day my father was to be buried the other men who did his *ghusl* had ushered me into the room and showed me the steps. In America, every time someone wanted a Muslim burial but did not have enough family members to perform the *ghusl,* I would go in and help with a handful of other men. Only men could wash men and women could wash women. Sometimes, before we stepped into the room, we would learn about the life of the body we were about to wash. Their occupation, how they died, who they had left behind. Other times, we knew them, they were members of the community, and I cataloged every memory I had with them and shared some aloud with the other men. But in the room, while we washed, when the body lay on the table before us, we were completely silent. We only spoke if it was absolutely necessary and if it related to the task at hand. The body was vulnerable and I felt for the person, who had not known, before death, it would be strangers who prepared him to rest finally in the earth. I concentrated on being very gentle as I washed the arms, the legs, each finger and each toe. Now I know I will be like those bodies that are washed without their sons present. Hadia and Huda and Layla will stay home on the day I am to be buried, or they will come to the cemetery and stand far enough away that they can only see my body lowered into the ground through the gaps of men present who surround the grave. And who will be the one to step forward first, grab a fistful of dirt, and before they have dropped it into my grave say to me, you are not going alone to the other world, we are here, I am here, sending you off.

THERE ARE SIGHTS in life I will never tire of seeing. Layla tying her hair up in a bun before beginning a task, that fluid motion of her wrist and fingers working to gather all her hair and contain it. Huda when she was three and learned how to whistle, how we asked her to entertain us and any guest who came to our home. My grandchildren calling me Nana. Tahira tugging at the edge of my kurta to get my attention. That moment I first step out and look up at the sky. Layla pointing out the leaves when the wind makes them all wave at once. Death, which awaits everyone, seems to be standing beyond a corner I can't see but feel I will turn to face any moment. Half of my life is here—my wife, my children, my grandchildren. Half has already made it to the other side—my parents, so long ago that for most of my life I did not think of death as a region to ward off, but as the place where they were waiting for me. So I am not afraid. But when I think of these inexhaustible sights something pinches in me: To never see Layla twist her hair into a tight bun. To never look up and be made a child again by the wonder of the moon. To never hear the thud of the basketball against the pavement, the squeak of sneakers, and stop what I was doing, widen the space of the blinds just enough to see you lift your arm in the pause before flight, bend your knees, your face full of such concentration that I couldn't help but wait until you shoot, score, smile to yourself wide and pure.

TAHIRA AND ABBAS are here for the weekend. Hadia and Tariq have driven up to Lake Tahoe. Layla is happy to be with them and I am thrilled she has something to focus on other than me. She has made a list of activities: a children's author is coming to the library, she has rented *The Lion King*, apples are stocked for our walk to the horses. They have gone out to Layla's flower garden, and from the window I can hear her voice and I know where Huda got her skills as a teacher, how calmly Layla explains the name of each flower, the way to cut the stem with the garden scissors, how she would think to arrange them.

Nine years married. Nine years ago the hall filled with everyone we knew, and you also came, coaxed into the suit your mother had bought you just in case, and I was at every moment thanking God for the gifts He was bestowing upon us, my daughter soon to be married, my family intact. I watched you for any sign of what we had feared when you left, but you seemed fine: your hands shook a bit and you smoked often but that was all right. Don't go to him, Layla had said, and I did not. Had I been a saint, had I done nothing to hurt you over the years, I would tell her how upset with her I still am—but I have so much guilt to bear and she has the grace to never remind me of it, so I do not.

"I want Nana to cook." Tahira teases me as dinner approaches.

She has Hadia's slightly mischievous streak. It is something she has been doing all weekend: announcing I want Nana to tell a story, I want Nana to help with my shoelaces. Had Layla not seemed so pleased at the sight of me "cooking" by stirring the ingredients she had put in the pan while Tahira was occupied, she might feel I was stealing her weekend.

Abbas brought his basketball from home and we can hear the shots he misses that hit the garage door. He is eight now, and not nearly as good as you were at that age. I finish stirring the *khorma* and think I might have liked cooking had I ever tried it properly. When Layla calls Abbas in, we eat together. The sun sets pink and I do not step out for a walk. After dinner, Abbas teaches me what his classmates have taught him about reading palms. I stretch my palm open and he tickles me with the movement of his finger.

"This is your life line," he says, and I don't know if he is making things up. "You will have a long life."

He folds my hand into a fist and studies the grooves beneath my pinky.

"It says you will have four kids," he says, then looks up at me and twists his mouth.

"That's enough," I say. "It's *maghrib* time. Do you want to pray with me?"

I never asked you to pray with me. We always told you what to do. I watch Abbas do *wudhu* after me. He does it correctly. He cups water in his little palm and washes from his elbow to his wrist, washes his face, does each step methodically and carefully.

"Did your mumma teach you?" I ask, when we dry our faces with towels.

"And Baba," he says.

"You are very good. Not a drop spilled."

He smiles. I lay out our prayer rugs. He straightens them. I recite the *adhaan*. I concentrate on looking ahead of me but I can sense his focus. He is listening. I had recited these very verses into his ear when he was a newborn. They were the first words he had ever heard. I wonder if his soul recognizes what his mind does not remember. We pray together and when it is time for us to ask for what our hearts desire, my first wish is that he remain steadfast in faith, and then, if he does not, that he never believe that God is a being with a heart like a human's, capable of being small and vindictive.

Later, I tuck Abbas in to sleep in Hadia's old bedroom, even though he is too old to be tucked in. He likes sleeping in Hadia's old bedroom. He likes going through her things and finding what she left behind from when she was his age, school projects and stuffed animals and books and porcelain figurines I once gifted her. The light by the bed is on and the room is warm and golden. I point at the window.

"When your mother was little, she and Huda and Amar made a phone out of Styrofoam cups and a string. They pushed out the screens and somehow connected the rooms from the outside."

Abbas laughs.

"I was very angry with them," I say.

"Why?" he asks.

"I don't even remember."

"Did the phone work?"

"Yes."

"Could we make one?"

"Yes."

"Was it Mummy's idea?"

"I think so."

"It sounds like Mummy's idea."

"Abbas," I begin, not knowing how I will say what I am desperate to, "am I still your number two?"

He stopped ranking us when he turned four. He smiles widely.

"Yes," he says, then lowers his voice to a whisper, "but don't tell Baba. And don't tell Nani."

He has learned how to care for others' feelings. How to have a secret.

I look around the room. Then out the window. *Bismillah*, I think, I begin in the name of God, the Compassionate, the Merciful.

"Can you keep a secret for me?" I ask.

His eyes widen with excitement.

"Can you memorize it?"

"I memorize a lot of things really fast," he says.

"You get that from your mumma."

The comment has pleased him. I search my heart and then I say, "Maybe sometimes you get a phone call from a secret friend."

He moves his body away from me a little. His back touches against his pillow. He does not say a word. He's so clever.

"Maybe you don't, maybe you do, I'm not asking you to tell me anything," I say quickly. "But I have an important message, just in case you do, to pass on from me."

At first, he does not change the expression on his face. Then he nods very solemnly.

" 'There is another way. Come back, and we will make another path.' And if he says no, and if he says nothing, will you say this: 'I used the wrong words. I acted the wrong ways. I will wait, until you are ready. I will always wait for you.' "

Abbas is quiet. He scoots close to me, his eyes very big, reaches over and touches his palm to my face. He wipes my cheeks dry.

"I memorized it," he whispers.

"Don't tell your mumma?" I ask.

"I won't," he promises.

I kiss his forehead. I stand to leave. Outside in the hallway, where

378

he cannot see me, I kneel on the floor and I touch my forehead to the ground, overwhelmed by my gratitude to God.

I SUPPOSE WHAT I need is for you to know these things. That I am sorry about the shoes. That I remember those drives we took to the barbershop. That we did not even realize how good you were at basketball. That I should have encouraged your habit of keeping a notebook. Maybe the two of us can go for ice cream alone, and I can try again to strike up a conversation with you. I'll prepare a list of the things I can talk to you about casually. And when we reach the ice cream parlor, I can pretend to peruse the cartons of ice cream flavors. I will nod at you to order first and wait to see what you ask for. I want to know if you still ask for pistachio ice cream. I want to know what kind of clothes you wear. If you still keep a notebook. What your job is. If you have a family. What they are like. I want to know if you still do that thing when you lie, if you still press your tongue against your cheek, twist your lips a little. And what that looks like on a man's face.

BECAUSE YOU WERE born as you were born. Because neither I nor your mother could hold you immediately, and the doctor advised that though all was well, it was best to take you to the neonatal ward to be observed, to monitor your body and your little lungs, because we could do nothing but agree, I could not do what all fathers must do for their newborn children: hold you up until your ear was right by my mouth and whisper to you the *adhaan*. The first sound we want our children to hear is the voice of their father, telling the child where it has come from, who its creator is, and whose care it will be in now. Telling the child, there is no God but God, and God is Great. Instead, you heard the patter of footsteps and the rolling whoosh of wheels, doors opening and closing, the ticking of a clock, voices of people who were not your father or your mother.

I was not there at the beginning for you. We were separated by a sheet of glass. And maybe this is why I fear you won't be there for me, when it comes time for my end. Because instead of holding you and delivering that message, I paced the hallway in front of the room where you slept, having already failed you in that first and crucial way.

I HAVE TRIED a hundred times to remember our final conversation. I had been stressed about so much that night—entertaining the guests, speaking with Hadia's in-laws, paying the caterers and photographers. You were missing. Layla and Huda were distraught. Layla asked me to go look for you. I didn't know what I'd find. I was mainly afraid I wouldn't find you at all. And I don't know how it is possible but I felt a force pull me as I walked through the hallways until I reached a back door and something told me to open it, and I found you there, slumped over on a bench, your suit jacket missing.

I sat by you. You did not stir right away. I don't remember exactly what we said to one another. And maybe it does not matter. You were upset. You realized what you had done—that you could not conceal how much you had drunk, and could not come back inside. I held you. You let me. You were mumbling about the story of Imam Hussain as a child, and I was touched that you had remembered it, even as I felt uncomfortable that you were drunk as you spoke of it. You said to me, Baba, what if we were meant to look closer? You called me Baba that night. I've looked closer, Amar, I have looked, and I have looked again, and I have exhausted myself looking. For his beloved grandson, out of his love for him, even the Prophet of Islam could pause the single most important requirement of faith, regardless of how many watched. What were we meant to learn from this that we had failed to?

I couldn't understand what you were saying half the time you spoke. But just the drink? I asked. Nothing more? And you swore. And believing you, I was relieved. I had to go back. I did not want to leave you. I looked up and I thought, God, help me be strong. Help me do what is required of me in this moment. On one hand my family waited for me to complete my daughter's wedding and on the other my son was letting me hold him. I had a lot of cash that I had to pay the photographers with, I gave it all to you. You tried to give it back, knowing it meant I would leave soon. And maybe you already knew then what I did not, that I would not be seeing you again after that, because just when I stood, you held my arm and though your face had matured you were still that boy who looked back at me when I sat you in the barber's chair, a look that said please, don't go. I was still your father. I would always be. I sat down again. I know I have failed you as a father in many ways. But when I look back on that night, though there is much I cannot remember, and though I was painfully aware I was in the company of a man who had been drinking, I am proud of myself for not letting that thought keep me from sitting next to my son. Once, Imam Ali had been with his companions when a drunk man had staggered by, and a companion had pointed to him and said look, there he goes, the town drunkard. But Imam Ali said two things: first, that we must imagine for one another seventy excuses before landing on a single judgment, and also, on that night, he told his companions to refrain from condemning a man, even as he staggered by showing proof of his sin, because they could not know if he would repent when alone, or fathom what existed in his heart.

You held on to my sleeve and said things I did not understand. And then all at once I did understand: you were saying good-bye. Not only in this life, but in the next, warning me that you would not make it to heaven, that our souls would not reunite there. Of all my mistakes the greatest, the most dangerous, was not emphasizing the mercy of God. Every verse of the Quran begins by reminding us of God's mercy, I tried to tell you that night, and you nodded, but how can I know what you heard or what you would remember.

Amar, here is what I tried to tell you, and if you ever come back, I will tell you again: what happens in this life is not final. There is another. And maybe there, we will get another chance. Maybe there we will get it right. I will see you again someday. I believe that. If not in this life, then in the next, the angel will blow into the shell, the soul of every being that ever lived will rise, and our sins will be accounted for, and our good deeds too. You might have made mistakes in life, but you were kind to each of God's creatures, you were considerate and you were compassionate, in ways that I did not even think to be. Alone we will all be made to cross the bridge as thin as a hair and as sharp as a knife. Alone we will be judged. Some of us will go to heaven right away, and others will have to repent, the hellfire cleansing us of our sins first. And if what we have been taught is true, I will not enter without you. I will wait by the gate until I see your face. I have waited a decade, haven't I, in this limited life? Waiting in the endless one would be no sacrifice. And *Inshallah* one day, I know I will see you approaching. You will look just as you did at twenty, that year you first left us, and I will also be as I was in my youth. We will look like brothers on that day. We will walk together, as equals.

Acknowledgments

Thank you, first and always, to my parents, Mirza Mohammed Ali and Shereen Mirza, whose way of loving, seeing, and being taught me everything: for believing in me, standing by me, and expanding your hearts each time I tested your limits. To my brothers, Mohsin, Ali-Moosa, and Mahdi, for your unwavering loyalty and confidence in this novel. Knowing you three always had my back gave me the courage to take risks and stay true to myself. Thank you, Mohsin, for your ability to understand with nuance and empathy—I know these characters, and myself, better because of it. This book is born from my love for you all: us, reenacting scenes from *The Lion King* and *Jurassic Park*, climbing to the top of the world, Mumma Baba calling us back home.

Thank you to my dada, Mirza Mohammed Kasim, my first champion and my dearest one, who throughout my childhood told me one day he would see my name in print. How I wish you could have been here to see it. To my number one amma, Meher Unnisa Begum, who once described her first voyage to the UK, looking out at the endless sea and thinking she was like a woman in a novel: for your bravery and resilience. And to my dadu, Shams Kasim, who prayed more for me and this book than I've ever prayed for anything: for tracing each *Ya Ali*, and for your steadfast belief, which captivated my imagination more than I know.

Thank you to my extended family for your love and support, but especially to my beloved mamu, Hussain Mirza, and my incomparable phuppojaan, Nishat Nusairee. For reminding me that what is essential is unchanging, thank you, Khayam Mirza, Aliza Mirza, Zainab and Laila Khan, Samana Khan, and Mirza Mohammed Kabah. Thank you, Ummul Nusairee, for being the sister I never had, and for never telling.

I am grateful to UC Riverside's Honors Program and Creative Writing Department. I will never forget the generosity of Charmaine Craig and Andrew Winer: thank you for nurturing what you saw in me and this book. Thank you to Sherin Barvarz, for your wisdom, humor, and lifelong friendship.

I am deeply indebted to the Iowa Writers' Workshop, which was home for as long as I lived there, and to my incredible teachers: Lan Samantha Chang, Ethan Canin, Marilynne Robinson, Paul Harding, and Karen Russell. Thank you, Connie Brothers, Deb West, and Jan Zenisek. Sam Chang, thank you for that first call, and for all you did after to ensure I could write this novel. I am grateful to Garth Greenwell, whose friendship warmed even the bitterest of Iowa winters and whose sharp insight shone a light on these pages. I cannot overstate my gratitude to D. Wystan Owen, whose generosity, intelligence, and close reading was an immeasurable gift and guide for me. And my fondest thanks to Hannah Rapson and Ida James: for welcoming me into your beautiful lives, and for the peace of my time with you, the porch and patio where I worked on so many of these pages.

Thank you to the Marble House Project and the MacDowell Colony for providing magical spaces in which to work and the James Michener and Copernicus Society of America for their support.

Thank you to my wonderful agent, Jin Auh, for believing in this book from the beginning and for advocating on its behalf.

I have been so moved by the enthusiasm of everyone at SJP for Hogarth. Thank you, Rose Fox, Rachel Rokicki, Molly Stern, and my brilliant and big-hearted editors: Lindsay Sagnette, for seeing all I wanted seen and for showing me what I failed to; Becky Hardie, for an eye both precise and sweeping; Parisa Ebrahimi, for knowing when I needed reassurance and when I needed to be pushed toward the finish line. My heartfelt thanks to Sarah Jessica Parker, for your faith in this family's story, for reading with love, and for bringing this book into the world with that same love.

Thank you to Charlotte Crowe, whose friendship makes this world a far more familiar and expansive place. I am so lucky to know your rare heart and radiant mind, both of which have been boundless sources of courage and inspiration for me, in fiction and in life.

And lastly, thank you to my first and most trusted reader, my brother Ali-Moosa Mirza. I would be lost if it were not for your patience and insight all these years. For never failing me, for knowing this family even when I forgot, and for always reminding me, I thank you. And I love you.

In 1917 Virginia and Leonard Woolf started The Hogarth Press armed only with a hand-press and a determination to publish the newest, most inspiring writing. They went on to publish some of the twentieth century's most significant writers.

Inspired by their example, Hogarth was relaunched in 2012 as an adventurous fiction imprint with an accent on the pleasures of storytelling and a keen awareness of the world. Our novels are published from London and New York.

In 2015 we celebrated Shakespeare's 400th year with the Hogarth Shakespeare series. Margaret Atwood, Edward St Aubyn, Tracy Chevalier, Gillian Flynn, Howard Jacobson, Jo Nesbo, Anne Tyler and Jeanette Winterson were asked to choose a play and reimagine it for a contemporary readership. The novels have been published in 24 languages around the world.

A Place for Us marks the start of our collaboration with Sarah Jessica Parker. The award-winning actor, producer and honorary chair of the American Library Association's book club was elected in 2009 by the Obama administration to the President's Committee on the Arts and the Humanities. As part of the Hogarth editorial team in New York Ms Parker selects and acquires works of literary fiction that reflect her own taste as a reader. She is directly involved in the editorial and publishing process, with her vision providing the editorial foundation for each publication.